KU-125-902

AN INNOCENT PROPOSAL

Helen Dickson

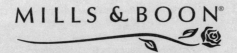

MILLS & BOON®

MILLS & BOON and MILLS & BOON with the Rose Device are registered trademarks of the publisher.

First published in Great Britain 1999
Harlequin Mills & Boon Limited,
Eton House, 18-24 Paradise Road, Richmond, Surrey TW9 1SR

© Helen Dickson 1999

ISBN 0 263 81721 0

Set in Times Roman 10 on 10¼ pt.
04-9907-104281 C1

Printed and bound in Great Britain
by Caledonian International Book Manufacturing Ltd, Glasgow

'Let us cut the preliminaries, shall we?

'I find you extremely attractive and it is obvious we were made to know each other better—that our paths were destined to cross. Should Mr Fraser find he has another engagement tomorrow night, you could accompany Mr Hacket to Dunstan House or come by yourself. You will be well received and find it extremely rewarding.'

Even though Louisa had spent all her life buried in the country, away from the sleaze and corruption of London, she would have had to be a simple, naive fool not to have known the implication of his words. Insulted, hot, angry colour flooded her cheeks again and she took a step back abruptly, gazing at him with pure loathing.

'I think you are mistaken, Lord Dunstan. I am not for sale.'

Helen Dickson was born and still lives in South Yorkshire with her husband, on a busy arable farm where she combines writing with keeping a chaotic farmhouse. An incurable romantic, she writes for pleasure, owing much of her inspiration to the beauty of the surrounding countryside. She enjoys reading and music. History has always captivated her, and she likes travel and visiting ancient buildings.

Recent titles by the same author:

THE PROPERTY OF A GENTLEMAN
AN UNPREDICTABLE BRIDE
AN ILLUSTRIOUS LORD

Chapter One

1756

It was the golden blaze of her hair and the wonderful sound of her laughter that first drew Alistair's gaze to Louisa. He was as quick as any other man to look at a beautiful woman.

She was at the centre of a group of boisterous young bucks who, if their loud and coarse laughter was anything to go by, had drunk too much wine than was good for them. Several he recognised, two of them being James Fraser and Timothy Hacket. They appeared to have an enormous capacity for enjoying themselves as they partook of an evening of music and dancing at the Spring Pleasure Gardens at Vauxhall on the Thames at Lambeth.

It was a place of informality, where extravagance and pleasure were fashionable. Vauxhall had long since been established as one of London's favourite resorts; its covered walks and dark paths leading from lamp-lit alleyways, with so many intricate twists and turns that even the most experienced could get lost, made it an ideal place for flirtation, assignation and intrigue, where ladies of the town loitered in the shade and many a stolen kiss was to be had.

Following a long and tedious debate on foreign policy in the House of Lords, and feeling replete and in a strangely mellow mood after a good meal and a glass or two of fine brandy, Alistair had left the supper box where he was dining with friends to listen to the strains of the orchestra, and to watch idly the crowds that always flocked to Vauxhall. Pavilions of entertainment shone brightly amidst illuminated trees, and he stood close to one where country dancing was being enjoyed by a good many of the younger people.

The June air was cool after the day's heat, and the gardens were a popular site for summer pleasure, a place of respectability and intrigue, where people from all walks of life could combine. Everyone was there—double-chinned, bewigged politicians, lauded writers, artists, actresses, courtesans—all resplendent in shimmering silks and satins, the women's dresses cut low to reveal smooth, bare shoulders. The gardens were illuminated with lighted lamps, beneath which the people strolled, chatting and laughing, with expectancy on their faces as they thought of the good food, good wine and pleasant music to be listened to and enjoyed.

That was when the young lady first caught Alistair's eye. With a good deal of pleasure he allowed his gaze to dwell on her, noticing that she seemed to be endowed with a boldness second to none as he witnessed the effect her intense personal charm had on those around her. It lurked in her playful eyes, in the tilt of her head, and in her soft seductive smile, which she seemed to use on any of the gentlemen who gave her the opportunity.

Thinking of her with a good deal of curiosity and interest, he hardly noticed when Lady Bricknell, having noticed his absence from their supper box, came to stand beside him, following his gaze and smiling when she detected the source of his interest. Lady Bricknell was wise in many ways, and recognised something in Alistair's expression she hadn't seen in a long time.

His gaze was warm as he looked at the young woman, and at the same time ablaze with a passionate awareness. She could see his interest and curiosity, which broadened the smile on her lips, for it was a rarity indeed to see Alistair Dunstan—self-proclaimed single man from bitter experience, who regarded all women as being dispensable and irrelevant—look at a woman as he was doing now.

'So, the young lady has taken your fancy, I see, Alistair,' she murmured. 'You always did have an eye for a pretty girl, but I think you will find that that particular young lady may be spoken for.'

With a great deal of reluctance Alistair managed to drag his gaze away from the object of his interest and smile down at Lady Bricknell. She was a strong and vibrant woman, five years older than his own thirty years. A strange friendship existed between them, having first become acquainted when she had married his good friend Lord Bricknell, a man of his own age. She was the illegitimate daughter of a countess and had been most cruelly persecuted by her family because of it all her life, until she had caught the eye of Lord Bricknell who, unable to resist such a wild and fascinating creature, a lady who lived by her wits, had married her. Her family had hoped marriage would curb her wilful ways, but it was not to be. Lord Bricknell had died five years into their marriage, leaving her an extremely wealthy woman.

'I wonder who she can be?' Alistair said, looking at the young woman once more, and seeing her give one of the gentlemen an impish glance with sparkling eyes. Her merriment was spontaneous, her laughter, which sounded like the sweetest tones of a bell, full of delight. 'I do not recall having seen her before.'

'She's certainly very pretty, popular too, it would seem, and because she shows no restraint—unlike young ladies of good family and breeding—I would say she has no silken chains to bind her to her parents, which puts her on a different plane to your own.'

'And why do you say that?'

'Owing to the fact that she is alone in the company of a group of idle, pleasure-seeking young gentlemen, with no care for etiquette or polite society. It tells me she is an ordinary girl—an actress, possibly—and from the way she is behaving I would say she is Fraser's mistress, or would very much like to be.'

'She is no ordinary young lady.'

'Not in your eyes, perhaps,' Lady Bricknell chuckled, 'but the familiarity she shows to both Mr Fraser and Mr Hacket tells me she is no innocent. I must ask them to bring her to one of my soirées some time. You must remind me.'

Alistair smiled as she moved on to speak to an acquaintance she saw in the crowd, while his bold, admiring stare seldom abandoned the young lady's perfect face and figure. The air was full of laughter and conversation, and he watched as James Fraser playfully placed a gardenia in her hair, and by way of thanks she placed a kiss upon his cheek, before being whisked into a lively dance by young Hacket, his hand firmly placed on her hand-span waist, her feet gliding effortlessly in step to his; like a butterfly her body dipped and swayed to the rhythm of the music to reveal the tips of her dainty satin shoes, the flounces and ruffles of her violet-blue gown billowing about her.

Intrigued, Alistair watched her to the point where everything else became a blur around him, as she twirled and spun, completely unselfconscious and unaware of the effect she was having on him. He saw the languor in her eyes as she gazed up at her partner, her lips parted in a smile, but then she seemed to sense Alistair's eyes on her and turned her head, calmly and irresistibly drawn to his gaze.

And then all too soon it was time for the group to leave, and on the arm of James Fraser she passed close to where Alistair stood, so close that he caught the amorous perfume of the gardenia young Fraser had placed in her hair. He saw that her eyes were filled with joyful laughter, her face aglow and her lips curving gently, her expression marked by so much pleasure that he could have had no indication of the anxiety and unhappiness that marred her life.

As their carriage travelled over the recently constructed Westminster Bridge, taking Louisa, her brother James and their friend Timothy Hacket home from Vauxhall, Timothy took hold of Louisa's hand and squeezed it affectionately.

'Have you enjoyed yourself, Louisa?' he asked, thinking how lovely she looked with her eyes still shining from the excitement of the evening, knowing that, unlike James, there were few pleasures in her life.

'Enormously,' she replied in truth, for she could not remember when she had been fêted by James so well. His suggestion that he give her a surprise birthday treat had offered her a brief respite from all the troubles that beset her life, and to forget, if just for a little while, the purpose of her visit to London.

Dreamily, Louisa found her thoughts dwelling on the gentleman who had been standing alone on the edge of the dancers, staring at her in a cool, impertinent way. She recalled the impact of his gaze across the space that had divided them, of those intense, vivid blue eyes. His look had been bold, bolder than was customary, and experiencing a feeling of feminine pleasure that she had attracted the attention of such a handsome man she had found herself looking back for a moment and smiling softly. She remembered how she had felt her limbs shiver like an aspen when his smile had broadened, before Timothy had swept her away in another dance.

She had arrived from her home in Surrey that very day. It was her twentieth birthday, but, her parents both dead, she had long since learned not to expect any form of good wishes or celebration from her brother, who was wrapped up in his own self-indulgent world of gambling and enjoyment. The purpose of her visit was to confront James, to beg him, as she had done countless times in the past, to give up his reckless, expensive way of life and return to live in Surrey, for if he did not heed their situation, then ruination would very soon be knocking on their door.

When she had broached the subject on her arrival, James was at once on the defensive and had become angry, finding her persistence to try to reform him extremely irritating. London, with its splendour and corruption, its squalor and excitement, thrilled and entertained him in a way his provincial home in Surrey had never done. His taste for pleasure and his capacity for enjoyment lifted his spirits in the restless, teeming city.

'Don't make a fuss, Louisa,' he'd admonished, frowning crossly, uncharacteristically thinking of a way he could silence her on the subject—if only temporarily. 'Today is your birthday and it's not often I have the opportunity to be nice to you, so now you are here I shall give you a birthday treat.'

With that Louisa had concurred, and she'd allowed herself to be fêted and spoiled when he and Timothy had taken her to the Vauxhall Gardens, where they had met up with a group of their acquaintances. Finding herself unexpectedly surrounded by so much beauty and gaiety, and overwhelmed by the sense of occasion and James's solicitude, it had been impossible for her not to enjoy herself, which she had done, enormously, managing to put her troubles behind her for a while. But on reaching Henrietta Street where James lived, and being told he was to go on to his club, she at once protested and they argued bitterly, at which point James stormed out of the house, an apologetic-looking Timothy following in his wake.

Her wonderful evening in ruins, and the gentleman who had admired her so openly forgotten, there was nothing for it but for Louisa to retire to bed, where she wept copious tears of bitterness and frustration, her inability to penetrate her brother's stubbornness in his determination to carry on digging them deeper and deeper into the mire plunging her into the depths of despair.

Attending Sunday morning matins the following day at St Paul's church in Covent Garden—as he often did when he was in London, which was mercifully cool after the intense heat outside—Lord Alistair Dunstan sat in the full congregation, hearing the priest in his ornate robes intone solemn, centuries-old words. It would be some time before he would be able to leave for Huntswood, his home in Sussex, his prime interest in life being his estate and his dependants. But he did his Parliamentary duty by being a regular attender at Westminster and taking his seat in the House of Lords—especially at this time with the outbreak of war, in which Great Britain and Prussia, under Frederick II, were allied against France and Austria.

The main cause of the war was the rivalry of Prussia and Austria in Germany, but from the British point of view the main interest lay in the rivalry of Britain and France, mainly in India and in Canada and at sea.

Letting his attention wander as the priest turned to the altar, Alistair's gaze rested on a young woman in a pew opposite. Remote and slender, she had a purity of profile which arrested and compelled his eyes, and into his mind came a sudden recollection—a face he had seen at Vauxhall the previous evening—of the young woman who had captured all his attention.

Her devotions as she knelt and prayed seemed absolute. Her golden hair was haloed in the light penetrating the windows, and he saw, when she lifted her head and let her gaze fall on the cross on the altar, that her expression of rapturous, holy adoration was like a medieval icon. Along with the rest of the congregation he knelt, automatically saying the familiar words of the prayer, but his gaze kept straying to the young woman across from him, on the gracefulness of her head, now bent in utter submission, her lips moving in silent prayer.

As if aware of his eyes on her, suddenly she raised her head and shot a glance at him, her eyes hot and amber, and intensely secretive in the atmosphere of reverence, a flickering of recognition stirring in their depths. The sheer desperation of that glance, the nakedness of it, and the intimacy, made Alistair feel that they were the only two people inside the church.

Then the service was over and he stood, momentarily distracted by the people moving all around him. The priest, recognising him, paused to exchange a few words, and when he looked again for the young woman she had disappeared outside into the blazing sunlight. He, too, left and he could still feel the imprint of the woman's secretive glance. He had been made uneasy by it. There was something different about her, something that reached out and touched him in half-forgotten obscure places.

Two months later, breathing in the sharp mysteries of the night, Louisa hurried through the dark London streets, knowing her parents would turn in their graves if they knew the dangers their only daughter was placing herself in. But her brother James's carriage was unavailable, as he'd taken it himself, and she'd shelved the idea of ordering a hackney or a chair to take her the short distance from the small house he rented in Henrietta Street to Lady Bricknell's magnificent residence on the Strand, deciding to walk instead.

One of London's most popular socialites, Lady Bricknell was throwing one of her notorious parties, to which, according to Alice, the only servant James could afford to employ, James and his good friend Timothy Hacket had been invited.

Louisa reminded herself that the streets held all kinds of dangers and terrors, where young women alone were easy prey for all kinds of villains with evil intent, especially after dark when no one was safe, but such was her anxiety to find her brother that she would

have braved Hades itself—the underworld abode of dead souls—
that night.

With her heart thumping in her breast, she drew her cloak about
her and averted her eyes from the shadows which stirred and
shifted down dark alleyways. She heard a cry—human or animal
she knew not which, but it was probably a cat foraging for food.
Thankfully several people were abroad along the Strand and no
murderer or rapist leapt out at her. The only light came from the
lamps hanging above the front gates of the larger houses, and glass
globes half filled with whale oil, which were fixed to posts at
regular intervals or suspended from poles sticking out from the
walls on either side of the street, but most of them were so black
with dirt that they cast a mean light. It was with immense relief
that at last she saw the lights of Bricknell House ahead.

Hearing the sounds of music and laughter coming from within,
Louisa paused at the bottom of the steps, reluctant to enter what
she considered to be a house of ill repute, despite the distinction
of its owner, who was rumoured to be a beautiful, very merry
widow, whose husband had left her immensely rich, enabling her
to pursue a passion for high living. Her parties were infamous,
where gentlemen of breeding and rank, having ingratiated themselves with her to procure an invite, were entertained, and where
no respectable lady would be seen dead.

The women who attended these parties were common actresses
and courtesans—ladies of pleasure—and the moment Louisa
stepped through the door at the top of the steps everyone would
assume she was one of them. As a well-bred innocent from the
country, how far removed that was from the truth, but for James's
sake she must be careful to give no one reason to suspect she was
anything else.

Drawing a long, steadying breath, she nervously climbed the
steps towards the double doors, knowing she had a part to play if
she was to be admitted in order to see James, and that to avoid
him any embarrassment she must not let it be known that she was
his sister, come to persuade him to return home like a naughty
boy—before he lost everything they owned at the gaming tables.

Assuming an air of confidence and superiority when a young
footman apprehended her in the doorway, politely requesting her

name so that she might be announced, she laughed forcibly, removing her cloak and handing it to him. Shaking loose her wonderful mane of strawberry-blonde hair which had become flattened beneath the hood, and in a casual manner that surprised even herself, she leaned towards him.

'I am expected,' she said, a quiet, conspiratorial smile playing on her lips as she gave him a provocative glance from under her thick black eyelashes which made him immediately her willing accomplice. 'It is my wish to surprise a certain gentleman, you understand?'

The footman understood perfectly and nodded, thinking her a pretty wench. Her attire was somewhat plain in comparison to the flamboyant painted doxies who usually attended Lady Bricknell's parties, but she did look quite stunning in a gown the colour of a newly opened, moist magnolia, which set off her creamy skin to perfection.

Louisa suddenly found herself in a glittering house full of colourful peacocks, and she was startled when the proudest, most arrogant peacock of them all suddenly appeared by her side, having followed her up from the street and seen her hesitate in the doorway. Wearing a short wig of exquisite whiteness, he was tall, dressed in a violet-coloured frock suit of heavily embroidered silk; a fine lacy jabot spilled from his throat in a frothy cascade and lace ruffles dripped over his wrists and over well-shaped hands, caressing his elegant, bejewelled fingers. He was attractive, with sultry features and dangerously hooded eyes, and he exuded all the confidence of a conceited charmer.

'Now, who can you be?' he enquired with unconcealed curiosity, his voice as smooth and seductive as the softest silk, his eyes absorbing every detail of her face and figure. 'I cannot say that I've seen you at any of the soirées I have attended before. However, I cannot leave such a lovely lady floundering in the doorway. Please allow me to escort you inside. Come, take my arm. I am eager to see the effect your appearance will have on the other ladies present. I have no doubt you will ruffle a few feathers and cause quite a stir.'

Unable to resist such charming flattery, especially when it was spoken by a man whose eyes twinkled with such wicked mischief,

Louisa responded with a smile and laid her hand on his arm, which was offered in such a way that it was a masterpiece of gracious arrogance.

'Is it because of my looks and because I am a stranger that I will cause a stir—or because I am with you, sir?' she murmured with an impudent smile and a delicate, knowing lift to her brows.

He laughed outright, showing teeth as white and strong as those of a wild animal. 'You read me too well, dear lady—my reputation has gone before me,' he said, his heavy lids drooping over his eyes suggesting at intimacy, and a salacious, lazy smile curling his full lips. 'It is not merely a stir I would like to cause with you, but an outright scandal.'

'I suspect a scandal would not concern you, sir—only the making of one,' Louisa replied coolly, forming her own judgement of him and sensing he was of an unpredictable, dangerous nature, of which her instinct told her to beware.

Seeing the smile fade from her lips and a wariness enter her eyes, her companion chuckled under his breath as they moved into the room. The spontaneous smile he bestowed on the women he passed had the desired effect, for their lips twitched and melted into smiles, which they hid behind fluttering fans that spoke a language all of their own.

'Come, now, do not pretend to be shocked,' he murmured. 'I am sure—looking as you do—that you must be quite used to such flattery. You mustn't mind my flirting with you. Most women who attend these parties expect it and are mortally offended if they find themselves ignored.'

'Really? You astonish me,' Louisa replied, with a delicate lift to her eyebrows.

'And don't worry. I haven't been invited either, but I do not think Lady Bricknell will have either of us thrown out. She is far too obliging to do that,' he confided. Earlier he had been undecided whether to go to a regular gambling haunt of his on the south side of the river or pay a visit to Bricknell House, knowing Lady Bricknell was holding one of her famous parties. Casting an appreciative, predatory eye over the young woman by his side, he was glad he had chosen the latter.

'I'm glad to hear it,' said Louisa.

'Tell me, who is it you are looking for? I overheard you telling the footman that you were here to surprise a certain gentleman. Who is the fortunate fellow?'

'James Fraser.'

At the mention of the name his eyes opened wide with surprise. 'Good Lord! I had no idea James could spare time away from the tables to become amorously involved with anyone.'

Louisa winced, although she tried not to show how deeply wounding his words were to her, reminding her so brutally of her brother's shortcomings. 'Are you a friend of his?' she asked, trusting this was not the case, as she suddenly found she had small liking for this particular gentleman, despite his geniality, and hoped that James was more selective in his friends.

'Shall we say I am an acquaintance?' he answered, drawing her into the crowded room.

Louisa stared around in fascination, feeling as if she had suddenly stepped into a dangerous, unrecognisable world, never having seen anything quite so bizarre as what she now saw. At any other time she would have been impressed by the sumptuous surroundings, had her whole being not been concentrated on finding her brother.

Quietly and firmly she excused herself to her companion and moved away, not wishing to draw undue attention to herself—which was no easy matter for she was exquisitely attractive, a figure of elegance, one who instinctively drew a second, lingering glance. There was not a thing she could do about it, for it was innate in her—like drawing breath. She was unaware that in her plain gown, with no ornamentation other than a fine lace edging around the modestly cut neckline, she was scintillating, and was far more alluring than if she had been adorned from head to toe in jewels.

Unaware of the continued attention of her escort as his eyes followed her with a determined, interested gleam, she mingled with the crowd of people, taking a proffered glass of champagne from a silver tray being carried among the guests by a splendidly attired footman. She had no liking for liquor of any kind and did not intend to drink it, but knew she would be less likely to draw attention to herself with a glass in her hand and looking as though she was enjoying herself.

As she moved among the people gathered in groups, some standing, others lounging indolently on gilt sofas and chairs, and with every face flushed to all shades of crimson, she tried not to appear shocked at finding herself in such a place, deliberately not looking too closely at what was going on. But while the moralist in her disapproved of this kind of behaviour her rebellious Bohemian instinct secretly admired it.

The room was hot, crowded and noisy. The men were dressed in elegant frock coats, and some wore powdered wigs, and their cravats were becoming limp and their clothes soiled with food and drink.

But the men were outshone by the ladies, who were painted and powdered saucy creatures—a languid bevy of scented, fan-waving beauties of the *demi-monde*—with not very respectable origins, but holding great fascination. They hung onto the gentlemen's arms, and were devoured by them with hungry eyes as they flaunted and flirted with them outrageously. They were dressed in gaudy, disgracefully low-cut gowns, and were drunk on champagne and behaving in a manner which Louisa could not pretend to, making her blush and look away. No doubt they would become more loud and vulgar as the night wore on, she thought.

Managing to avoid the groping hands of some of the gentlemen who reached out as she passed, and ignoring their lewd suggestions and exaggerated winks, she was beginning to wish she had not come. But then she remembered the purpose of her being there, of Bierlow Hall, her wonderful home in Surrey, impoverished though it was, and that James, being a man of expensive tastes, in his reckless desperation to improve their lot, was in danger of gambling it all away. She had come to London two months ago to beg him to abandon his dissolute way of life and return with her to Bierlow. He had done so, but he had not stayed much longer than four weeks before he had become bored and returned to London.

Louisa's resolve to find him before it was too late sent her towards a room where several card tables had been set up, knowing she would find her brother there.

Here the noise was curiously muted so as not to distract the players. Small tables for dice, whist, French hazard and other games that took the guests' fancy had been set up. Louisa's eyes scanned the groups of people clustered around them, where several games were in progress. The players were obscured from view but on seeing the tall figure of Timothy Hacket standing in a small group she moved towards him.

Timothy turned when he felt her press herself against him, his face registering shocked surprise when he recognised her. He immediately took her arm and drew her away, but not before she had seen her brother sitting at the table, his body taut, and a wild, concentrated gleam in his eyes which only gamblers had when, intent on winning, they saw nothing except the cards in front of them.

'Good Lord, Louisa! What are you doing here? I thought James had left you at Bierlow?'

'He did, but after he left for London four weeks ago... I discovered just the other day that the only valuables remaining in the house had disappeared, and I knew James must have taken them, and exactly what he intended doing with them—that he would sell them in order to pay for his gambling. I had to come.'

'He will be outraged if he sees you—here of all places. It is hardly the kind of establishment where he would care to see his sister.'

'I do not care, Timothy. I am well aware that if I had a place in society I would be disgraced for all time—but with so much at stake the ethics of the matter do not concern me. Our situation is desperate, you know that. James must be made to stop before it is too late and we have nothing left to sell or gamble but the estate— such as it is.'

'I know that, but he is determined. He will not be stopped.'

'Have you tried?'

'Yes, but you know what James is like when he has his head set. He will not listen.'

'Then I shall speak to him. He must listen to me,' Louisa said in desperation, making a move towards the table.

'Wait, Louisa,' Timothy said, putting a restraining hand gently on her arm. 'Leave him. It may surprise you to know that James is winning. He will not thank you for interfering.'

'Winning?' Louisa exclaimed in surprise, staring up at her brother's long-time friend. 'By how much?'

'Fifteen thousand guineas.'

Louisa gasped, astonishment mingled with relief flooding over her, unable to believe what she was hearing, her mind already racing as she calculated what could be done at Bierlow Hall with such an enormous amount of money.

'Then before he begins to lose, please tell him to stop now.'

Timothy sighed. 'I will try, but I know he will refuse. I've seen him in this mood before when he thinks everything is going his way—and I have to tell you that the liquor he has consumed has increased his habitual readiness to take risks to a point of madness.'

About to move away, Timothy looked sideways sharply when a man moving close to Louisa caught his attention. She acknowledged the man with a faint smile and a nod, which gave him the feeling that they had already met. It was Sir Charles Meredith, a notorious rake and debauchee of the worst possible kind, and Timothy did not like the way he clung to Louisa's side, watching her, speculative and predatory.

But Louisa had already forgotten Sir Charles Meredith, and she felt her heart lurch to a sickening degree as she watched the group part to let Timothy through, seeing once more her brother's flushed, handsome countenance and his sleek, ash-blond hair falling untidily over his brow. There was a glazed set to his features and a grimness in his eyes.

Through the gap James looked blindly in her direction, his eyes registering surprise when they focused on her presence and her worried amber eyes. Anger flared in his own and his full lower lip curled with disapproval, but he refused to allow himself to become sidetracked from the game in hand by an angry sister, who should have known better than to follow him to London. He brushed Timothy aside when he bent and whispered in his ear, refusing to listen, uttering disappointment when his partner rose from the table, having lost the game and reluctant to play on.

Louisa was swamped with relief, sure that he would finish now and come away. But another man came and sat opposite James, cutting one of two packs of cards on the table with slender, flexible fingers as they prepared to begin a game of piquet. It was a game for two people which offered excellent scope for both intelligence and judgement, something which James would have risen to had his head not been fogged with the fumes of alcohol.

Louisa's eye was caught by a woman coming to stand behind James's opponent, a bold woman with a handsome face, stunning in a purple and mauve gown cut so low as to leave little to the imagination. Her hair was red, too red to be real, and in response to her whispered question Timothy told her it was none other than their hostess, Lady Bricknell. The flamboyance in her attire and jewels showed that she had been left well provided for by her departed husband.

Curious now she was seeing the notorious Lady Bricknell in the flesh, and recollecting the reputation she had acquired over the years, Louisa found herself staring at her; despite having a taste for the theatrical which verged on the vulgar, Lady Bricknell was a desirable asset to London's social scene—a woman who lived for pleasure, and a woman of taste and wit who was prized as much for her company as her beauty and flaming red hair.

Seeing that both men were so intent on the game and each other that they barely glanced at the small crowd gathered around the table, with a charming smile on her crimson painted lips, Lady Bricknell moved away to pay attention to her other guests, but Louisa sensed by the way she gently squeezed the gentleman's shoulder with bejewelled fingers, before drifting away, that their relationship went way beyond that of mere acquaintance.

The game followed the classic pattern with James winning a little, then losing more and more, until he ceased to win anything at all as his partner, who, unlike James, was completely unaffected by alcohol, raised the stakes higher and higher. With a mixture of languor and self-assurance, his eyes on the cards did not stir.

Louisa watched with the sickening knowledge that because of James's reckless stupidity they were about to lose everything they owned.

'Dear Lord,' said Timothy quietly, careful not to let Sir Charles, who had not relinquished his stance beside Louisa, overhear—

although, like every other spectator, Sir Charles's attention had become taken up with the game. ''Tis sinful the way James loses money.'

'Sinful? This whole house reeks of sin, Timothy, and it is sinful of James to gamble away what little we have left. No doubt he will blame me for changing his luck,' she whispered to Timothy, who was looking on with deep concern.

'If he loses it cannot be blamed on you. Not when he is playing Lord Dunstan.'

Louisa glanced at him. 'Lord Dunstan? Who is he? I cannot say that I have ever heard of him.'

'Perhaps that's because he doesn't often come into society. He is extremely skilful at cards and a great number of people have lost whole fortunes to him. His personality is so strong that with a lift of one of his arrogant eyebrows, or a flare of a nostril, it is not unknown for his opponent to tremble with fear and drop his cards. He is hard and ruthless and enjoys winning at any form of gambling—and cares little for those who suffer as a consequence.'

'Why is he so unpleasant?'

'It isn't that he's unpleasant. In fact, he can be quite charming, especially to the ladies, who fair drool over him—and it's not difficult to see why with his looks. It's the way he rides roughshod over everything and everybody that puts people's backs up.'

'He sounds positively horrid,' said Louisa.

'Lord Dunstan can afford to be anything he wants to be. He is immensely rich and extremely important. His estate in Sussex is fabulous and his stable envied by all.'

Louisa sighed. 'Poor James. He doesn't stand a chance of winning against such a man.'

She looked at the aforesaid gentleman properly for the first time, recognising authority when she met it. Then she frowned, for there was a faint glimmer of familiarity to his features, but she could not for the life of her think where she could have seen him before. Excitement that was due as much to his appearance than anything else swept over her. Although he was seated, she could tell he was extremely tall, with powerful shoulders and long muscular legs. Unlike the other gentlemen, who were dressed like peacocks in a multitude of the customary bright colours, he was clad in jet-black, with the exception of his snowy white shirt and cravat, which gleamed in stark contrast to his black suit and silk waistcoat.

He wore no wig, and his own hair was thick and deep brown, with, Louisa suspected, a tendency to curl. It was smoothly brushed back from his wide brow and fastened at the nape of his neck. There was a strong, arrogant set to his jaw and his face was as hard and forbidding as a granite sculpture, his fingers handling the cards with expert ease long and slender. In fact, everything about him exuded brute strength and arrogant handsomeness.

He was the kind of man who was capable of silencing a room full of people just by appearing in the doorway—whose attitude was that of a man who knew his own worth.

She didn't realise she was staring at him until his instinct made him look up, as if sensing her gaze, and Louisa felt her breath catch in her throat when his eyes locked onto hers, compelling and piercing, and the most startling shade of blue. In fact, they stirred some vague memory and it bothered her, for she was convinced she had seen eyes that colour once before, but where? His dark brows lifted a fraction in bland enquiry at her gaze and he appeared to look her over in a hard, contemplative way, smiling ever so slightly in an appraising manner when he seemed to like what he saw, bringing a crimson flush to her cheeks.

Suddenly his gaze was arrested by the sight of her companion, Sir Charles Meredith, and Louisa saw a tightening to his features as his eyes narrowed and swept over the other man like a whiplash. The look that passed between them crackled with hidden fire, and for just a moment she saw something savage and raw stir in the depths of Lord Dunstan's eyes, before they became icy with contempt.

Looking up at Sir Charles, she saw his lips curl with something akin to sly amusement mingled with hatred, and he nodded ever so slightly in acknowledgement, which Lord Dunstan did not deign to return. Undeterred, Sir Charles casually took out an elegant ornamented silver snuff box and took snuff, delicately touching his nostrils with a lace handkerchief before smiling down at Louisa's upturned face and charmingly excusing himself before moving away.

Louisa was puzzled by the incident, curious as to what had

induced this unconcealed dislike between the two gentlemen, but she was more puzzled by the fact that she remembered Lord Dunstan's face but could not quite place it. Her mind raced through the places she had been where she might have seen him, but in the end she gave up, which was odd, because it would not be easy to forget the startling directness of those vivid blue eyes.

For the next half-hour Louisa watched every move of the game with a sinking heart, the tension becoming unbearable as James lost more and more of his winnings to Lord Dunstan, who presided over the game like a predatory hawk. Her anger was growing by the second but she tried not to show it, attempting to maintain a façade of disinterest and indifference. She tried to look as relaxed as the other women and to pretend to be one of them, pinning an artificial smile to her face when a florid-faced gentleman next to her complimented her on her beauty, and moving closer to Timothy with an intimacy which told the gentleman she was not available.

Fixing her attention once more on the game, she saw that Lord Dunstan was experienced, and that the more James lost, the more Lord Dunstan incited him to go on playing, to bid higher and higher. He must have been able to see James was drunk and not in possession of his right senses. He would have had to be blind not to, but he lounged indifferently across from him, his expression bland as he coolly regarded her brother, whose flushed face and nervousness clearly betrayed his emotions.

When James had lost his former winnings, pushing a pile of banknotes into the centre of the table, Lord Dunstan raised the stake yet again by one thousand guineas, and Louisa could not believe it when James, in an agitated state, accepted the bet, knowing all he had left to stake were the deeds of Bierlow Hall.

No longer able to stand by and watch his friend lose every penny to his name, Timothy stepped forward.

'Don't be a fool, James,' he told him. 'You cannot cover the bet if you lose. After losing what you have won tonight, you no longer have one thousand guineas to your name.'

Impatient at being interrupted, James shot him a look which told him not to interfere as he put his signature to a chit and placed it with Lord Dunstan's money in the centre of the table. 'There you are mistaken. I can afford it. I will take the bet, and I aim to win it back on the next hand.'

Lord Dunstan seemed irritated by the interruption, noticing James's slight hesitation. 'Do you continue?' he asked curtly.

'I continue,' James replied firmly.

Louisa flinched, trying not to look at Lord Dunstan's glacial expression, making up her mind there and then that the man was despicable, but her anger was also directed at James. How could he go on playing, gambling away everything they owned? Their father would be horrified—although if he had not invested his money so badly when he had been alive, she and James would not be in the position they were in now. Their father had been too interested in his horses and his dogs, paying little interest to what was happening in the financial world until it was too late to do anything about it.

At twenty years old Louisa was younger than James by two years, but she had always been the sensible, practical one, while James was somewhat reckless and foolhardy and liked to live life to the full and in comfort. She had tried to guide and protect him since the death of their father four years ago, and would have dearly liked him to buy a commission in their father's old regiment, but they could not afford it. However, with Britain now at war with France, at least she could take comfort in his not being killed on some far-off battlefield.

But James was not entirely selfish, believing that once he had established himself a fortune he would bring Louisa to London, where he would set about finding her a suitable husband.

Louisa turned and left the table just as the last hand was being played, no longer able to watch James lose all the money he had won earlier. No doubt four thousand guineas was a modest sum to Lord Dunstan, whereas to herself and James it was a fortune. Not until the game was over did she turn back to see Lord Dunstan rise from the table.

'Thank you. That was an excellent game,' he said as James quickly signed an IOU for the four thousand guineas he owed. James handed it to him and watched Lord Dunstan pocket it before slumping in his chair with the knowledge that he would have to face the enormity of his loss and his sister.

For the first time a thin smile curled Lord Dunstan's lips, his eyes showing contempt for his victim, utterly unconcerned for the pain he knew he must be feeling, and knowing that in situations such as this it was not uncommon for a man who had staked his entire fortune on a game of cards to go out and shoot himself.

'Rotten luck,' Lord Dunstan said calmly, his voice of a rich, deep timbre, 'but that's how it goes. I think refreshment would be in order now, don't you? Come, Fraser, what do you say?'

Trying to maintain some semblance of dignity, James rose. 'Yes, of course. Please—excuse me a moment,' he said, moving to where Louisa was standing with Timothy, feeling so utterly wretched and miserable that he had forgotten his earlier outrage her presence had caused him, and that normally he would have chastised her most severely for daring to set foot inside such an establishment as this and ordered her home at once.

Lord Dunstan followed him.

'If you wish to try to recoup your losses and exact your revenge, I will give you the opportunity of doing so. Please accept my invitation to Dunstan House on Thursday night. You and Mr Hacket will be more than welcome,' he said, his gaze including Timothy, 'and might I suggest you bring your lady friend? The company will be mixed,' he added, his eyes flicking over Louisa without the slightest acknowledgement, which set her blood boiling. She was insulted that he thought her of so little consequence that he had no interest in being properly introduced, which courtesy and good manners demanded when one addressed even the meanest of women. The man was truly a monster.

'Yes, of course. Thank you,' said James, unaware of the murderous look his sister was giving him.

'Oh, but you can't,' Louisa burst out suddenly, causing James to turn and gape at her in angry surprise, and with a presence of mind she didn't know she possessed she smiled brightly at all three, using all her feminine wiles as she leaned towards James, coquettish and enticing, and spoke in a flirtatious tone while focusing the full force of her dazzling amber gaze and bewitching smile on her brother with merry defiance. 'You are already promised to me that evening, James. You promised to take me to the pleasure gardens across the river, if you remember.'

'I did no such thing,' James said indignantly, giving her an angry, censorious look which she ignored, determined to keep him away from Lord Dunstan and his card games at all costs.

'Yes, you did,' she argued gently. Normally she would not have dared to be so bold or so outspoken, but anger gave her the courage to refuse to feel intimidated by this arrogant, despicable man. Linking her arm possessively through James's, she gazed up at him languidly from under her thick lashes. 'I shall be mortified if you disappoint me and break your word. I am so looking forward to it, as well you know. After neglecting me so abominably all evening, I will not allow you to push me aside yet again for a game of cards which, I observed, you do not seem to possess a talent for and which I consider in such cases is best left alone.'

James was clearly furious, finding his sister making up to him as though she were his doxy quite shocking. He was at a loss to know what to say or how to deal with the situation, and before he could say anything Lord Dunstan had fixed his gaze on Louisa, trying hard to decide if she was genuine in her claim that Fraser had promised to take her to the pleasure gardens or a gifted diplomat.

'One can visit the pleasure gardens any evening, Miss—?'

'Divine,' Louisa said hurriedly, drenching him in her most charming smile, without thinking of the consequences of her fabrication or the connotations of the name she had chosen at random.

'Miss Divine,' he went on, with a slight lift to his sleek eyebrows, his hard face wiped clean of all expression, except for a faint smile in which Louisa caught a glimpse of dazzling white teeth, 'whereas invitations to Dunstan House are seldom given and, if they are, are not issued lightly.' He fixed his gaze once more on James. 'The invitation stands if you should change your mind.'

He seemed to study Louisa for a moment, his blue eyes levelled on hers, penetrating and disturbing, before inclining his head in the faintest mockery of a bow and moving away. He'd realised the moment he had set eyes on her standing between young Hacket and Charles Meredith that she was the woman he had seen at Vauxhall Gardens and again at St. Paul's Church two months ago—the woman who had left an indelible trace on him. Clearly she was Fraser's mistress, and familiar with his own most hated enemy and neighbour, Sir Charles Meredith, but that did not prevent him being curious and wondering about her, wondering how a woman who prayed in church so fervently could live the life she did.

His lips curled in a smile, his mind already working on ways he could get to know her better, undeterred that she might belong to Fraser. His sharp eyes had noticed that Charles Meredith also had designs on her—the signs he recognised from bitter, past experience—and the idea of scoring off him appealed greatly to his sardonic sense of humour, knowing how immensely satisfying it would be to steal her from under Meredith's nose, to avenge himself for all the villainous acts the man had inflicted on him in the past.

But, on reflection, all such dealings were abhorrent to him. Alistair had many faults, but it was not in his nature to inflict injury or insult on any man who was guilty of wrongdoings against himself, and he wanted nothing more to do with Sir Charles Meredith.

Chapter Two

When Lord Dunstan had moved on, James turned on Louisa, furious with her.

'What in God's name do you think you're playing at, Louisa? How dare you humiliate me in this manner? What are you doing here?'

'Do I really have to tell you?' she answered accusingly. Aware that people were beginning to glance their way, becoming curious as to her identity for she was a stranger to them all, she had no intention of airing their grievances in public. 'Take me home, James. I do not wish to remain in this place a moment longer.'

James did not need to be asked twice. Timothy chose to stay, hoping to spend the rest of the evening in the company of a wench he had been wooing assiduously for weeks. Besides, he thought that James would be better left alone to be admonished in private by his sister.

Timothy had always admired Louisa—although they had been friends for too long for there ever to be anything of a more intimate nature between them—and he had frequently reproached James for neglecting her for the amusements in London. James had been his closest friend since their school days, and he had often thought it a pity James had not been blessed with his sister's common sense.

James had felt the lure of the amusements in London soon after his father's death—his mother having died a year earlier. The green baize tables had attracted him with the promises of pleasure and reward more certainly than anything Bierlow had to offer, and the heady temptation to gamble and to go on gambling was something he could not resist.

Not until they were in the carriage taking them home did either Louisa or James speak, James being the first to do so, still enraged by his sister's behaviour and his own foolishness. He cursed himself severely, knowing he should have taken Timothy's advice and left the table when he was in front. The seriousness of the situation had not hit him yet, but when it did it would be with the force of a hammer blow.

'How dare you come to London without my permission, Louisa?' he exploded. 'Your behaviour is totally out of character. You had no business turning up at Bricknell House like that—an establishment totally unfitting for a sister of mine. And as if that weren't bad enough, you have to appear on the arm of Charles Meredith of all people. He's one of the most notorious rakes in London, a rampaging womaniser who sows the wildest of oats. His father may have left him a fortune when he died, but the manner in which he squanders it at the gaming tables will very soon lead him down the same path as myself.'

'*That*, James, is rather like the pot calling the kettle black,' accused Louisa harshly. 'You both share a penchant for wild extravagance and high living.'

'Perhaps. But that is where the similarity to myself ends. He is a worthless libertine and no one with any sense will have anything to do with him.'

'How was I to know that? Although I have to say,' she admitted when she recalled his predatory manner and the glib way he had spoken to her, 'I did not care for him in the slightest. But I confess it was gratifying to gain a man's interest and admiration—even if the gentleman paying me the compliments did happen to be a notorious rake. He did try flirting with me—quite shamelessly, in fact—and it makes me realise just how dull and dreary my life is at times, in comparison to all the ladies I have seen this evening.'

Louisa knew that James was displeased by her reply but chose to ignore it, in no mood to listen to her complaints. 'What is this business of pretending to be Miss Divine?'

'I came to London when I discovered you had taken certain

items of value from Bierlow, which I knew you intended selling in order to pay for your gambling. And do not try to deny it because I know you too well. And as for turning up at Lady Bricknell's and calling myself Miss Divine, I had no choice...although I do regret my ridiculous choice of name. I suspect it might have had something to do with having just set eyes on the glorious and extremely colourful Lady Bricknell, who certainly lives up to how people describe her,' she said. 'I had no wish to embarrass you by announcing I was your sister.'

'How very thoughtful of you,' he replied drily. 'How did you know where to find me?'

'Alice told me. I came as soon as I could with the vain hope that I might be in time to prevent a major disaster from occurring at the tables. Unfortunately I came too late,' she sighed. 'Perhaps if you hadn't drunk so much in the first place you might have retained a little of what you had won.'

'If Lord Dunstan hadn't been there—blast him—I would have won more. Hell and damnation! Just when things were going well for me. It had nothing to do with the drink—it's just that his skill at cards is not to be matched by anyone I know.'

'Then why did you allow yourself to be drawn in by him?'

'Must you always disapprove of everything I do, Louisa?' James remarked crossly.

'Of course I disapprove. I cannot condone your private life or your behaviour. Oh, James, how could you?' she accused him bitterly. 'How could you gamble away everything we own?'

'It is not as bad as you think,' he replied lamely.

'How can you say that?' Louisa admonished harshly. 'Don't be stupid. Of course it is. Things are bad, very bad. In fact they could not be worse. We are in a hole and I cannot see any way out—unless we throw ourselves on Lord Dunstan's mercy and persuade him to tear up your IOU.'

James was clearly shocked by her suggestion, which no gentleman would even consider. 'That is quite out of the question, and, besides, Lord Dunstan would refuse. But if I don't honour the debt I will be thrown out of my club and into the debtors' prison. I couldn't bear that, Louisa. The shame would be unbearable.'

'Better that than we lose everything. You do realise we will have to sell Bierlow Hall, don't you, James?' she said despairingly, the mere thought that their home, which had been in their family for two hundred years, would be gone for ever bringing tears to her eyes. 'There is no other way we can obtain four thousand guineas that I can see, and I doubt that will be enough to cover the whole debt or that the bank will grant us a loan.'

As if ashamed of his recklessness and the hurt he had caused his sister, James's expression became contrite. 'Forgive me, Louisa. I do realise that we're in the deuce of a mess.'

'How long before the debt must be paid?'

'A week.'

'As soon as that?' she whispered. 'You will not accept Lord Dunstan's invitation to go to his house, will you, James? Nothing can be achieved by it.'

James frowned, impatient at her naivety, still determined to try and recoup his losses in the only way he knew how. 'You are a simpleton, Louisa. Don't you know anything? You have spent so much of your time in the country with your head in the clouds that you have no conception of life in fashionable London. Lord Dunstan is one of the most important men in town. He rarely entertains, and no one in their right mind turns down an invitation to dine at Dunstan House.'

Louisa's face turned pale. 'That may be, but what is the point in going when you have nothing to gamble with? You have nothing left to cover your bet if you should lose. James, we can't let Bierlow go.'

'If it comes down to it we'll have to,' he replied, not sharing Louisa's fondness of the family home. Anger at himself coiled within him, which he turned momentarily towards his sister. 'Bierlow is the only thing left that would be worth money in the sums I need. You would have to come up to London and live with me.'

'No, James,' Louisa replied sharply, his airy tone whipping up her anger, unleashed irritation flooding through her. James had always been selfish—selfish and unthinking in his impulsiveness, in his assumption that what he did was all that mattered, forcing her to adjust her life to his. 'I couldn't.'

'You'll have to. There's nothing else for it.'

Louisa fell silent. James was becoming irritable and soon he would become more angry. How well she knew his moods, she thought miserably. An inexplicable weariness and pain lay heavy on her heart, the deepest, cruellest pain she would ever know. Despite James's willingness to sell Bierlow Hall, it would tear her apart if she had to leave her beloved home. She would fight tooth and nail to hold onto it. Ever since their father had died, leaving them in dire straits, she had come up against so many obstacles, just managing to surmount them, and almost wearing herself out into the bargain, but this seemed to be just one obstacle too many.

No greater crisis had ever confronted her.

With his head pounding with a frightful hangover, after having spent most of the night trying to obliterate what he had done in a bottle of brandy, James Fraser rose the following morning from the bed in which he had fallen into a dissolute, drunken slumber in the certain knowledge that ruination was staring him in the face, unable to see how he could survive it. He surveyed bleakly what the remainder of his life would be like and it was not pleasant. It was not only himself who would suffer as a consequence of his recklessness at the card tables, but his sister also, and in that he could not defend himself.

When he entered the breakfast room Louisa was there already, looking unnaturally calm, her face pale through worry and lack of sleep. There was only a slight resemblance between brother and sister. Both were fair, but there the resemblance ended. Louisa was like a piece of thistledown with a finely structured face, whereas James was six feet and stockily built, with a strong square chin and grey-blue eyes.

Louisa was shocked by her brother's appearance. Last night had aged him ten years. He looked thoroughly broken, his handsome face creased with deep lines of anxiety, his clothes and hair dishevelled.

'Dear God, Louisa! How could I have done it? We are in the devil of a fix. We are ruined. Quite ruined.' He threw himself down in a chair, staring with a stricken look out of bloodshot eyes at his sister. 'What's to be done? How are we to be saved?' he cried, looking at Louisa as if she knew the answer.

The appeal in his voice went straight to her heart. Without thinking of how they could save themselves, she went to her brother and put her arms round him. Her eyes were soft and tender and she spoke impulsively, lowering her cheek to his.

'We'll think of a way, James. Something will come up, you'll see.' she said, but she knew in that moment that there was not even the suspicion of a hope that something would happen to save them.

Later Louisa left the house to walk the short distance to Fleet Street to pay a visit to Mr Brewster's second-hand bookshop, in the hope of obtaining for a few pence a book by William Collins of sentimental lyric poetry, a style that Mr Collins and others had first made fashionable in the 1740s. She was also glad of the opportunity to be out in the fresh air and to be alone for a while so that she might think.

She wanted nothing more than to return home to Bierlow and forget she had ever come up to London. But she couldn't leave now. She did not trust her brother not to make matters worse—if they could be worse—and she was dreadfully afraid that he would become suicidal. Their situation was quite desperate, and, not possessing a plethora of relations they could turn to in order to bail them out, she knew that it would require all their brains and ingenuity if they were to survive.

After the death of their parents, James had selfishly taken himself off to London, preferring to live there rather than bury himself in the country, where he bemoaned the fact that there was nothing to do other than fish and hunt—which he could no longer do anyway, having sold all but three of his father's horses. Two of these he had taken to London to pull his carriage and the other, an ageing mare, Louisa kept for domestic purposes.

She had soon learned that where James was concerned her own wishes were not to be consulted, and she had been forced by circumstances to live in genteel poverty, to be the keeper of Bierlow Hall and to put all her youthful energies and her loneliness into their home, where she was responsible for all the household matters and the staff—of which only two old retainers and a housemaid remained, the only three they could afford.

Mrs Marsh had taken over the duty of cook as well as housekeeper. Her husband, whose health was ailing, managed the stabling of the one horse and the kitchen garden and did odd repair jobs about the house, anything else being too much for him.

Over the years, as the money had dwindled, the old house had fallen into a sorry state of neglect. The curtains were faded and chairs and carpets threadbare. Windows were broken and the roof needed mending, and the garden was overgrown with a wild tangle of weeds. Life was a constant struggle and Louisa fought a never-ending battle with tradesmen and shopkeepers alike, stripping the house of several valuables which were not of sentimental worth and pieces of furniture to pay them.

All this had caused something to harden inside Louisa, to die, even. The lessons since her parents' demise had been hard and she had learned them well, knowing she could expect little support from James as he went on his merry way unhindered. She had learned to deal with relentless adversity, to hide her disappointment in her brother and her fear for the future, and to hold her head high. And because of the time she spent alone at Bierlow Hall, making decisions and being responsible for others, she had acquired an independence of attitude and spirit.

But, despite James's neglect of duty, Louisa understood him and loved him well, and would forgive him almost anything. Whenever he came down to Bierlow Hall to placate her, he would leave her a little money he had won at the tables, promising her that the day would soon come when he would make his fortune and bring her to London and find her a husband who would be worthy of her, before rushing off back to town.

Louisa would listen calmly, knowing this would never happen, and was resigned to remain at Bierlow Hall in semi-isolation for ever. The only luxury she permitted herself was her books, for it was only in these that she could find solace and escape from the daily concern of money.

Fleet Street, with its bookshops, printing establishments and coffee-houses, was a popular area for writers and poets. As always, it was crowded with journalists and salesmen, with newsboys running up and down carrying the latest broadsheets. Louisa kept close to the wall, for often it was difficult to walk in the streets, congested with draymen, hackneys and other hazards, without fear of injury.

She had come here once before when she had been in London and she remembered how she had loved the bustle of the busy street. Finding herself in front of Mr Brewster's shop, the familiar sign above the door framed in iron and hanging out on a long bracket, vying with all the others along the street—and it was not unheard of for any one of them to fall down, to the danger of pedestrians—she entered the shop, where the smell of ink, paper and leather-bound books assailing her nostrils was surprisingly pleasant.

Like many other establishments, Mr Brewster's shop stocked items other than books; book-selling alone was rarely sufficient to make a prosperous living. His shop was much frequented by scholars, who were able to afford the wide range of cheap, second-hand books he had on sale.

Several gentlemen in flamboyant wigs and brightly coloured frock coats were examining the books lining the shelves and paid her scant attention. Journals and pamphlets were stacked in piles on the floor, while books ranging from classics, educational, drama, romance, prose and many more filled the shelves.

Mr Brewster was unpacking some pamphlets and looked up when she entered, smiling brightly. She told him which book she wanted by William Collins and he frowned, evidently thinking hard as he rubbed his whiskery chin with ink-stained fingers.

'Let me see—I should have a copy somewhere. You browse, my dear, while I have a look in the back.'

Louisa did as he told her as he disappeared into the back of the shop, happy to wander among the narrow aisles crammed with books on dusty shelves. She examined books by Fielding and Defoe with avid interest, having read all of them, then took *Clarissa,* a book written by Samuel Richardson that was a particular favourite of hers, from the shelf. She had read it several times and agonised over poor Clarissa Harlowe's fate on finding herself in the clutches of her abominable persecutor, Lovelace.

So lost was she in the print as she flicked through the well-thumbed pages that she was not aware that someone had come to stand beside her until he spoke.

'Why, Miss Divine. This is a surprise.'

Louisa looked up, amazed to find herself looking into a pair of familiar, vivid blue eyes. So abrupt was his appearance, and so unexpected, that her heart lurched, disbelief mingled with surprise holding her immobilised for a split second. Her first instinct was to turn on her heels and run, but her feet were firmly rooted to the spot, and, besides, he blocked her one way of escape. Immediately there was a resurgence in her of that frightening awareness of his vitality and magnetism that had affected her at Bricknell House when their eyes had met for the first time. He seemed to have set the whole atmosphere inside Mr Brewster's bookshop vibrating.

'L-Lord Dunstan! Do forgive me—you startled me,' she stammered, her cheeks overspread with a deep flush, unable to prevent a picture of him and the unpleasantness of the previous evening from flashing through her mind. She felt overwhelmed by his close presence and he seemed to invade every part of her, but somehow she kept her head. She observed that he was as immaculately dressed as he had been at Lady Bricknell's party, and she could not help noticing how black became him and how his pristine white cravat had been tied with a master's hand.

'I apologise. I did not mean to,' he said, having recognised her instantly, even though she did not remotely resemble the young woman he had encountered at Lady Bricknell's the previous evening.

He looked at her intently, startled once more by her beauty, finding himself looking into two warm and wonderfully expressive amber eyes flecked with yellow, opened wide in her heart-shaped, strikingly lovely face, her skin creamy, flawless and glowing with health, with an aureole of strawberry-blonde hair falling in a luxurious, shining tumble over her shoulders. Ever since he had first seen her he had wanted her, and meant to have her, her face never drifting from his mind's eye.

'Mr Fraser is suffering no ill effects after last night, I hope?' he enquired in a bored, matter-of-fact way, as if it were of no consequence that James had lost his entire fortune to him.

Anger seared through Louisa like a hot knife at the lightness with which he spoke, but her pride forbade her to tell him of the devastation his game of cards with James had brought them. With a superhuman effort she managed to smile sweetly up at him.

'It is not the first time James has lost at cards, Lord Dunstan, and I am quite certain it will not be the last.'

'You have known each other long, Miss Divine—you and Mr Fraser?'

Louisa cringed when he addressed her as Miss Divine, thinking it a silly name and quite ridiculous, but a peculiar instinct born and bred in her told her not to let him know she was James's sister. Let him continue to think she was his paramour; it was of no concern to her.

'Yes—quite some time,' she answered.

'And Sir Charles Meredith? It would appear you have an admirer in that gentleman. Do you know him well?'

'Why, no. In fact I do not know him at all. We had not met before last night,' Louisa told him. She saw that he was watching her closely, giving her the distinct impression that he was more concerned with how well she knew Sir Charles than how close she was to James, and making her wonder once again what could have happened to cause so much dislike between himself and Sir Charles Meredith. But she pushed the matter away, telling herself that no matter how unpleasant the situation might be that existed between the two men, it was their business and had absolutely nothing to do with her. She had troubles enough of her own without bothering her head about that.

Alistair nodded slightly. 'I see. Then if, as you say, he is a stranger to you, take my advice and be very careful before becoming better acquainted with him. Do not allow yourself to be taken in by him. Oh, he can be charming and persuasive, I grant you, but he is not what he seems.'

Louisa gave him a cool stare. 'Thank you, Lord Dunstan,' she said curtly, 'but your opinion does not interest me. I choose my own friends.'

Alistair's answer to this was a faintly sardonic smile. 'Of course. Tell me, are you here alone today?'

'Yes. I enjoy browsing among the bookshelves. Besides, James is not a reader.'

'And you are?'

'Yes, very much so. Are you here to purchase a book yourself, Lord Dunstan?'

'No. I am here to see an acquaintance of mine on the *Morning Chronicle*. We are to meet in the Mitre tavern further along. I happened to be passing when I saw you enter the shop. I was curious. I thought I recognised you. I do recall seeing you once before, albeit some time ago,' he said with a crooked grin, full of charm. 'Or perhaps I should say twice?'

Louisa looked at him sharply, having recognised his features at first glance the previous evening. But she was still unable to remember where.

'Let me enlighten you. The first time was at Vauxhall Gardens—some two months ago, as I recall—when you were in the company of Mr Fraser and Mr Hacket. You seemed to be enjoying yourself, as I remember.'

Instantly Louisa recalled the occasion in Vauxhall Gardens, when James had insisted upon taking her there to celebrate her birthday, and she flushed, feeling defenceless suddenly when her memory of that night came flooding back. At last she recalled where she had seen Lord Dunstan before, remembering how he had stood and watched her for some considerable time while she had danced with Timothy and James. The fact that he had observed her so clearly—and recalling how she had unashamedly returned his bold stare, and the pleasure she had derived from it—swamped her with mortification and embarrassment.

Quickly she composed her features, giving Lord Dunstan no indication of how much her recollection of that occasion affected her, but he was not deceived, being well schooled in the way women's minds worked, and he was secretly amused by it.

'Isn't that what one's supposed to do when visiting the pleasure gardens, Lord Dunstan?' Louisa replied a little breathlessly. 'It was my birthday, and James took me there as a special treat. But I must say that I am flattered to think you even remember seeing me there amongst all the other ladies present.'

'I never forget a beautiful face, Miss Divine, especially not when it happens to be as lovely as yours,' he complimented, enjoying the slight unease this seemed to cause her. 'The second time I saw you was the morning after at St Paul's Church in Covent Garden,' he went on. 'I remember how intent you were on your devotions, how concentrated.'

Louisa also recalled seeing him in St Paul's Church, which was close to Henrietta Street. Feeling the need of prayer that day, after a bitter and heated exchange with James the previous evening on their return from Vauxhall Gardens, when he had stormed out of the house to visit his club, she had attended the service, finding the small church an oasis of peace.

'Isn't everyone when they go to church, Lord Dunstan?' she answered, thinking how quickly she had forgotten him because of what had followed with James. 'Otherwise what is the point in going at all? Although it is clear to me you were not as intent on your own devotions if you allowed your attention to stray to me.'

'However, I am flattered to learn that I made such a distinct impression on you, causing you to remember me after two whole months—which is more than can be said of myself. I confess that when I saw you yesterday your face did seem a trifle familiar, but I could not recall where I might have seen you.'

'Which tells me you were not as impressed by me as I was by you.' He chuckled, unoffended.

'Most of the ladies I meet are more than eager to be amiable to me because of who I am, but you have the unique distinction of being the only woman I have ever met who is honest enough to tell me to my face that, having met me, she does not remember me.'

'Really? And you are not put out?' Louisa asked drily, thinking that what he said must be true; that if he was as wealthy as Timothy had said he was—and with his kind of looks—he must have women falling at his feet like dominoes in a row, all rendered quite helpless when confronted by his charm and allure.

'Not in the slightest. In fact I find it a refreshing change. Tell me, do you often worship at St Paul's Church?'

'No. Only on the odd occasion when I happen to be in London—when I find the need to atone for my sins,' she said softly, her eyes teasing, a faint smile playing at the corners of her lips. 'Which was, perhaps, your own reason for being there, Lord Dunstan?'

He smiled mischievously. 'What else? And are you a frequent visitor to Brewster's bookshop?'

'No,' she answered, suddenly beginning to feel slightly uneasy. She did not like the way he had followed her inside Mr Brewster's bookshop, nor did she like his easy manner and the steady, unsettling gaze of his penetrating blue eyes. He was the most lethally attractive man she had ever met, and she would have to take care not to be drawn in by him. Swiftly she raised her defences. 'I do not pretend to be knowledgeable about books, but I do enjoy reading. You seem surprised, Lord Dunstan?'

His handsome mouth curved into a slight smile. 'I can imagine you in many places, but a bookshop is not one of them—unless, of course, you are on the stage and looking for some material to do with a play,' he said, sounding casual, his eyes filled with idle speculation as he studied her closely.

'No,' Louisa answered calmly, knowing he was fishing for information about her, but preferring to keep him guessing. The less he knew about her, the better she would feel.

He frowned. 'You are a complete contradiction in terms of appearance.'

'A contradiction?'

'Yes,' he answered. 'Let me see the book that has caught your attention.' Reaching out, he took the book she had been flicking through from her hands. Reading the title on the spine, he raised his eyebrows in surprise. '*Clarissa*! It would not be my choice of good reading, but I can quite see why it appeals to the ladies.'

'No matter what your opinion, Lord Dunstan, the book has met with considerable success and is a fine work,' said Louisa quickly, in defence of her favourite book. 'I cannot understand why you should pour scorn on it.'

He smiled. 'Clarissa is a nervous young woman of excessive sentiment and sensibility. I confess to having read the book but she did not endear herself to me in the slightest.'

'And how do you define sentiment and sensibility, Lord Dunstan?'

'As expressions of intense human feelings—of which the heroine in question is in possession to excess. The two words are often confused. Sentiment is ruled by the human heart—which is the centre of all emotion—whereas sensibility is the key to bodily sensations—touch and such things,' he said softly, his eyes filling with amusement when she flushed and lowered her gaze at his definition and the hidden connotation of the words. He smiled, knowing exactly the effect he was having on her. 'Clearly you enjoyed the book?'

'Yes,' she replied, wishing she had not asked him to define the two words because she knew she was blushing at the intimacy of his tone. There was altogether something too explicit and intense in his eyes. However, she refused to be deflected. 'So much so that I have read it several times. I confess I was much moved and felt a great deal of sympathy for Clarissa—being pursued and persecuted so cruelly by the abominable Lovelace.'

'Ah, but she did throw herself on his mercy.'

'She accepted Lovelace's offer of help because she was quite desperate to save herself from a dreadful marriage, only to find herself in a worse situation than she was before.'

'And you have an affinity to Clarissa, have you, Miss Divine?'

Louisa smiled with a faint trace of cynicism. 'Oh, I believe there is a Clarissa in most women, Lord Dunstan—just as there is a Lovelace in most men.'

'Perhaps you are right, but we do not all have to resort to kidnap to engage the affections of the ladies we desire. You speak from experience, I think, Miss Divine?' he said slowly, meaningfully, in a voice low with seduction that made Louisa think improper things; it was a voice few women would be able to resist, especially not if the man speaking happened to look like Lord Dunstan—over six feet tall and built like a Greek athlete of old.

She looked at him, suddenly beginning to feel out of her depth, unable to answer his question, and feeling a wave of hot colour burn her cheeks under his close scrutiny. She was relieved when Mr Brewster chose that moment to come shuffling along the aisle towards her.

'I must apologise, my dear young lady, for taking so long. I thought I had a copy of Mr Collins' poems but I was mistaken.'

'That's all right, Mr Brewster.' Louisa smiled. 'Thank you for taking the trouble to look.'

When he had moved away, Louisa looked up to see Lord Dunstan eyeing her with some amusement and a hint of mockery, his eyelids drooped down over his glorious blue eyes giving him a lazy, sleepy look.

'William Collins! A book of sentimental lyric poetry that is fashionable and much sought after in some circles, I believe.' His smile widened. 'I salute your taste, Miss Divine—a veritable catalogue of sensation. Perhaps Mr Brewster might order it for you if you are so desirous to obtain it.'

'I am sure he would, but that would not be convenient.'

'And why is that, pray?'

'Because I do not intend remaining in London for very much longer, Lord Dunstan. That is why.'

'You are not leaving before I have had the pleasure of receiving you at Dunstan House on Thursday evening, I hope?'

In answer she took the book he was still holding and placed it back on the shelf, conscious as she did so that their fingers touched. She moved away from him quickly, disturbed by his close proximity but refusing to show it—although she strongly suspected he was aware of it and found it amusing. Assuming a calm, almost blasé expression, she smiled.

'That all depends on Mr Fraser, Lord Dunstan.'

'And you wish to visit the pleasure gardens that evening, as I remember. Ranelagh or Vauxhall?'

'Why, I—we, that is—have not yet decided,' she stammered.

'Good. Then you should not be disappointed if you have to put off going.' His expression suddenly changed and the lightness disappeared from his tone. He looked at her hard, moving closer. 'Come, now, Miss Divine, let us cut the preliminaries, shall we? You strike me as being a sensible young woman—and a beautiful one—although from my experience the two do not always keep good company.

'I find you extremely attractive and it is obvious we were made to know each other better—that our paths were destined to cross. Should Mr Fraser find he has another engagement tomorrow night, you could accompany Mr Hacket to Dunstan House or come by yourself. You will be well received and find it extremely rewarding.'

Even though Louisa had spent all her life buried in the country, away from the sleaze and corruption of London, she would have had to be a simple, naive fool not to have known the implication of his words. Insulted, hot, angry colour flooded her cheeks again and she took a step back abruptly, gazing at him with pure loathing.

'I think you are mistaken, Lord Dunstan. I am not for sale.'

He arched his brow infuriatingly. 'Oh! I thought all the ladies who attended Lady Bricknell's parties were?'

'I can assure you that this one isn't. Goodbye, Lord Dunstan.'

Louisa turned and marched out of the shop with all the dignity she could muster, never having been so insulted in her entire life. But what did she expect, she rebuked herself furiously, after brazenly showing herself at a party thrown by a notorious socialite of Lady Bricknell's ilk? Lord Dunstan, along with every other man present, could not be blamed for believing her to be a whore.

Alistair watched Louisa go with a brooding attentiveness in his eyes and not without a good deal of interest, extremely puzzled by her behaviour. Hostility from the likes of her was not something he had encountered before. Most young ladies were more than eager to be amiable to him.

But in Miss Divine's voice there had been something sincere which troubled him. She was not of a common kind, and there was also about her a mysterious, almost sweet and gentle allure. Could it be that she was different from the others? But no, he told himself harshly, striding out of the shop, angry that she had been capable of rousing in him a moment of weakness.

He knew from harsh experience that a woman's face could be deceptive. Why should Miss Divine be any different? If that was her real name, which he very much doubted, which gave him all the evidence he needed of how good an actress she was and how well practised in the arts of deception. But as he strode along Fleet Street towards the Mitre tavern he was unable to cast her from his thoughts, for every time he saw her—in surroundings so very different from the ones before—she succeeded in getting under his skin.

She had the poise of a woman fully conscious of her beautiful face and figure, and his instinct detected untapped depths of passion in her that sent silent signals instantly recognisable to a lusty,

full-blooded male like himself. The impact of these signals caused
an ache to start deep inside him and brought a smouldering glow
to his eyes as he imagined what it would be like to possess such
a glorious creature—and that was the moment when he marked
Miss Divine as his own.

Somehow Louisa managed to turn in the direction of Henrietta
Street, trying to still the angry trembling inside, her cheeks still
burning with shame. Lord Dunstan was despicable, even more
despicable than she recalled, and she detested him thoroughly—
for what he was, what he thought she was, and for what he had
done to James. But with every step that took her further away
from Mr Brewster's bookshop a plan was forming in her mind, a
plan so shocking she hardly dared enlarge on it. It caused her heart
to pound so hard she could scarcely breathe, for it was a plan no
gently bred young lady would dare think of, let alone consider.

Yet as she walked with her head down, completely unaware of
the people around her, she fixed her mind on the plan, and, with
a cold logic, let it grow until she could think of nothing else. At
one stroke Lord Dunstan had presented her with an answer to her
problem. He was obviously attracted by her, assessing her for the
possibility of an amorous affair. He had told her that he wanted
her and would reward her well. By giving herself to him, it could
wipe out James's debt entirely.

The thought of giving herself to Lord Dunstan sent a chill down
her spine, but it did not shock her, the events of the past twenty-
four hours having drained her of all feeling so there was hardly
any emotion left in her. If her capacity to feel had been intact,
everything inside her would have protested and rebelled against
the plan forming in her mind, for she hated Lord Dunstan. But
with her feelings and emotions deadened by the anxiety of the
situation James had created her thoughts were entirely practical.

Nevertheless, there was a battle taking place within her soul, a
battle between right and wrong, as taught her by her mother and
the religious teachings of the church in which she had been raised.
What she was considering would have been wholly abhorrent to
the gentle woman who had raised her, who had stressed time and

again that fornication before marriage was a mortal sin which would result in hell fire and damnation.

But, driven on by desperation, Louisa pushed these thoughts away. She and James had been impoverished for a long time, but had always managed to keep their heads above water. She was determined they would not become beggars. If there was a way of holding onto everything that was precious, of saving herself and James from homelessness and starvation, then she would do everything in her power to do so, and, if there was any understanding in heaven, perhaps her mother would forgive her for what she was about to do.

However, she knew James would never agree to her plan, and told herself that he need know nothing about it until such a day when she might have to tell him. And as for Lord Dunstan, he would continue to think of her as Miss Divine, and, afterwards, when the retrieval of James's IOU had been accomplished, she would disappear from his life as though she had never been in it and return to Bierlow Hall. There she would be able to pick up the normal threads of her life with no slur attached to her name. The shame would be something she alone would have to bear.

Chapter Three

By the time Louisa reached the house there was a curious lightness to her step and a freedom in her heart. She knew that what she was planning would place her in unfamiliar territory, but she could not bear to contemplate the alternative. The more she thought about it, the more she became convinced it was the answer to all their problems.

She was surprised to find Timothy there alone, and disappointed to find that James, despite his circumstances, had left for the Somerset coffee-house in the Strand to meet up with some of his acquaintances, who usually gathered there in the mornings for breakfast and to converse.

'I've been waiting for you, Louisa,' Timothy said on a serious note. 'When I arrived Alice told me both you and James were out, but that you would not be long. I've nothing doing today so I thought you and James might care to take a stroll in St James's Park with me this afternoon. It's a pleasant day and we could watch the soldiers on parade at Horse Guards. Afterwards we could take tea somewhere pleasant and later you and James can be my guests for supper. Come, what do you say? It might be just the thing you need to help cheer you after the unfortunate events of last night.'

Louisa gave him a grateful smile. 'Thank you, Timothy. That's extremely thoughtful of you. I must say it sounds like just what I need right now. However, I'm glad you waited. There is something I wish to discuss with you,' she said brusquely, handing her cloak to Alice and going into the sitting room, closing the door after Timothy had followed her inside. She stood before the fireplace, her hands folded quietly in front of her and her face set in lines of resolve. 'Tell me more about Lord Dunstan, Timothy. Is he married?'

Her question came as some surprise to Timothy. 'No—not any more. He was once, I believe, but something happened and he and his wife parted. I don't know the details exactly—in fact, I think there are few who do for certain. It all took place at his home— Huntswood, in Sussex. Bit of a mystery, if you ask me—it was all so secretive—but from what I remember of the gossip at the time, I think she ran off with someone else.'

'I see. What else do you know about him?'

'Alistair Dunstan is a very private man, Louisa, who is a regular attender at Westminster, taking his seat in the House of Lords. Apart from attending White's—where he is often to be found playing cards well into the night, he is not often seen in fashionable society—and when he is it is always at the theatre or some event of Lady Bricknell's. As you know, he is extremely wealthy— owning a large estate in Sussex and having inherited certain properties here in London from his wife—and by all accounts he is a shrewd man when it comes to investments. He has a finger in several industrial developments, both in England and abroad. He is always reticent about his personal, private affairs.'

'And I can understand why, if his wife preferred being with another man.'

'So tell me, why the curiosity?'

'Because I think I know a way of clearing James's debt, and it is important to me to know whether or not Lord Dunstan has a wife. It will make all the difference to what I am about to do.'

'May I ask why?'

Louisa faced him steadily, looking so young, so fixed and determined. 'I have decided to become Lord Dunstan's mistress.'

Appalled and alarmed, Timothy stared at her. 'What?' he gasped. 'Louisa! Have you taken leave of your senses? You cannot be serious about this?'

'I am deadly serious, Timothy,' she replied firmly. 'It is not a matter I would jest about.'

'But you can't. You cannot sell yourself to pay off James's debts. It—it's diabolical. It—it's obscene,' Timothy protested forcefully. 'I cannot believe you are saying this—that I am hearing this. You! You and Lord Dunstan!'

Louisa swallowed hard. 'Yes. I have to. Timothy, Bierlow is not just my place of birth, it is my life,' she explained. 'I have nothing else, don't you see that? Do you think I have not anguished over this...what I have to do...on the chance I am taking? If James and I are to retain what little we have, then I have no choice—unless you can think of some other way.'

'You know I can't, Louisa. But if I had the money I would give it to you—you know that.'

Louisa smiled, knowing he spoke the truth. As the younger son of a lord with a modest estate in Oxfordshire, Timothy had inherited neither title nor fortune. His position was not unlike James's, except that unlike James, with his intemperate desire for pleasure, and who seemed to be hell-bent on self-destruction, Timothy knew how to control both his spending and his gambling.

'I know, and thank you, Timothy,' she said. 'You're a good friend—none better—to both James and me. But this is something I am going to have to sort out myself. It's just a pity James doesn't feel the same way, instead of drowning himself in liquor and waiting for something to turn up. He's always been like that. Ever since the death of our parents he has had so many misconceptions about life. The estate—such as it is now that most of the land has been sold and we are left with just the house and the tenant farms—makes demands on us that should, in all fairness, have been seen to before James allowed himself the luxury of pleasure.'

There was sympathy in Timothy's eyes which told Louisa he understood exactly.

'I have to agree with you there,' he said.

'For a long time now I have lived a spartan existence at Bierlow, making do with just the bare necessities. The estate has never meant as much to James as it does to me,' she said with a trace of sadness. 'I know that, and he's always hated the country. When he did spare the time to visit he would cheer me and promise that everything would soon be all right again—and like a fool I wanted to believe him—but it never was. I love Bierlow, Timothy. It holds so many memories. It's my home. I can't see it go. You do understand, don't you?'

Timothy smiled with understanding. 'Of course. But you'll have to leave one day—when you marry,' he stated gently.

'I know. I understand it can never be mine—not in the way it will be James's—and I accept that, but I must keep it in the family. James may not appreciate it now, but I am sure he will in time—when he finds the right woman and marries and settles down to have children.'

'James doesn't realise how lucky he is to have you for a sister. But I cannot let you go ahead with this. I am on your side, first and foremost,' he said soothingly, 'and you shouldn't be worrying about this sort of thing. It is for James to get himself out of this mess. Believe me, Louisa, it's for your sake I say this. If you go ahead with this crazy idea your reputation will be in shreds in no time at all. You know that, don't you?'

'Of course, but I do not place my virtue above retaining all that is important and dear to me—to me and to James, even though he doesn't yet know it. The shame is something I shall have to live with, but what I am about to do countless women have done before,' she said quietly. 'No one will know who I am. Lord Dunstan will think of me as Miss Divine. He need never know I am James's sister. I shall disappear from his life just as soon as I have what I want.'

Timothy frowned, his eyes piercing right through her. 'You have seen Lord Dunstan since last night, haven't you, Louisa?'

'Yes, I have,' she admitted. 'At Mr Brewster's bookshop in Fleet Street when I was there earlier to purchase a book I wanted. We met quite by chance.'

'And he approached you—propositioned you?'

'Yes.'

Timothy's expression became violent. 'Good God! Has the man no scruples?'

'Why should he?' she replied with slight irony. 'I was at Lady Bricknell's party, don't forget. That alone condemns me in his eyes. It is only natural he would assume I am James's mistress.'

'Louisa, please don't do this,' Timothy pleaded. 'You don't know the kind of man Alistair Dunstan is—what you are letting yourself in for. You have no knowledge or experience of men like him and you could very soon find yourself out of your depth. The man is cold and ruthless and as hard as steel. He attracts women effortlessly, leaving a trail of devastation in his wake. If he wants you, he may refuse to let you go—and you may not want to—but if he tires of you he will discard you like a broken toy. Better James is sent to the debtors' gaol than that.'

Louisa paled. 'That I could not bear, Timothy. James would never survive it.'

'In my opinion a gentleman is better off dead or humbled than alive and proud at the expense of his sister's virtue,' he scorned.

'Nevertheless, I have to do this—my mind is made up,' Louisa said in a curiously flat and unemotional voice. 'I will be a quiet bedfellow for Lord Dunstan—not a willing one. I think he will soon be more than happy to be rid of me.'

As to that, Timothy very much doubted. Living in isolation, Louisa had no concept of men of Lord Dunstan's calibre. If she did but know it, her face and figure were her fortune, and he couldn't think of any man who would willingly part with her having once possessed her—including the formidable Lord Dunstan. His face took on a judicial look.

'And what will you tell James? You will have to tell him, you know. Do you think that for one minute he will agree to this madcap idea?'

'I have no intention of telling him. He mustn't find out, Timothy. Please—please promise me you will not tell him,' she pleaded.

Timothy's face was grim. 'It seems you leave me with little choice, but I don't like it, Louisa. James is my friend and there have never been secrets between us. If he should find out about this—and that I was a party to it—it could very well mean the end of our friendship.'

Louisa sighed, looking at his kind face and seeing it was full of concern for her. 'I know. I am sorry to place this burden upon you, Timothy. But I do not believe it would come to that. Your friendship means a great deal to James.'

'Have you arranged a meeting with Lord Dunstan?'

'No, but James insists on accepting Lord Dunstan's invitation and going to Dunstan House on Thursday evening. I shall accompany him, and I would like you to come too, Timothy, to keep an eye on him, just in case he is tempted to play cards and we find another stack of IOUs at the end of the evening.' She sighed deeply. 'It will be difficult enough persuading one gentleman to return his IOU—any more would be quite impossible.'

'Yes, I'll come, but do you think that once you have been with Lord Dunstan, and you have what you want that you will remain untouched, that it will be easy to forget and carry on as if nothing has happened? Because it won't. You will not be able to leave your demons behind, Louisa, and the harder you run, the harder they will chase you. You are heading straight for your downfall. Not even the craziest gambler would risk this.'

'Then let us be thankful that, for James's sake and my own, I am not a gambler,' she said, 'otherwise nothing would be done.'

She frowned, suddenly thoughtful, thinking of all the painted and gaudily dressed ladies she had seen at Lady Bricknell's house. 'My biggest problem is what to wear. I do not possess any fashionable gowns, and heaven forbid I should be seen wearing the cream one I travelled up from Surrey in—the one I was wearing when I went in search of James last night—which is plain and deplorably out of fashion. All my other dresses are at Bierlow, most of them faded and mended anyway, so they would not do either, and I cannot possibly afford a new one. It is imperative that I make an impression.'

'Perhaps I can help there. My sister Amelia is about your size, I should think, and has more gowns than she knows what to do with. I'll see what I can do.'

Louisa smiled gratefully. 'Oh, Timothy, would she mind?'

He grinned. 'No. If I know my woolly-headed sister she'd not even notice their disappearance if I took them without her knowing.'

'Oh, no,' Louisa said quickly, shocked that Timothy might do just that. 'You mustn't do that. You must ask her properly, even though she might refuse.'

In the midst of this grave situation a twinkle came into his eyes. 'I think I can answer for my sister. I promise she will be only too pleased to lend you anything you might need. In fact, because of her fondness for James, which never ceases to amaze me considering his unappealing habits,' he said, not unkindly, 'she'll look on it as a pleasure.'

'Thank you,' Louisa said, her expression serious, her eyes troubled as she realised that Timothy had now become her ally as well as her friend. 'I want to shine, Timothy. I have to dazzle Lord Dunstan. He has to want me enough to pay me four thousand guineas.'

Louisa's face was heartbreaking in its hope, causing Timothy to marvel at her spirit. How he wished he could make her change her mind about going ahead with this madcap plan, but he knew her well, knew how stubborn she could be, and how difficult to dissuade once her mind was made up. It seemed to him that she was as blinkered as any carthorse, refusing to see, or even contemplate, anything but a satisfactory outcome to her forthcoming visit to Dunstan House.

'If you insist on going ahead with this ludicrous plan of yours, then we shall see to it that Lord Dunstan is unable to resist you.'

It was with immense relief to Louisa that James returned in sober mood and had no objection to their all going to St James's Park for the afternoon. In fact, he welcomed the opportunity to get away from the confines of the house, where brooding on his situation would only make it a thousand times worse.

The park was lovely and full of people, some strolling whilst others gathered in clusters to gossip. There were swarms of rosy-cheeked, excited children playing all manner of games, and pretty young girls flirting with young bloods and off-duty soldiers. An abundance of multicoloured flowers in beds and borders added a vivid splash of colour to the park, and the grass, where people lolled about, was like soft green velvet. Fallow deer roamed free and were a constant delight to the children, in particular, who loved to feed them. They were so tame that they took bits of food gently out of their hands.

The three of them watched the soldiers, resplendent in their colourful red and blue uniforms, parading at Horse Guards, which was one of the main attractions of the park during the afternoons. Afterwards Timothy bought some oranges from a hawker, which they ate as they strolled towards the northern boundary of the Mall, where they purchased mugs of fresh warm milk, drawn from the cows tethered in a line to posts.

James continued to be in a morose mood, and, while Timothy tried to coax him out of it, Louisa wandered down to the edge of the lake to watch the ducks swimming and diving on the sparkling surface. Startled when she heard someone call out her name, she looked up and saw Sir Charles Meredith advancing towards her.

Always in the forefront of fashion, and with a high sense of style, he was sporting an extraordinary scarlet three-piece suit, the buttonholes of his coat heavy with gold embroidery. His jabot was frothy and elaborate, his cuffs beautiful, and his white silk hose, rising from diamond-buckled shoes, fitted tightly over well-muscled calves to his knees. He carried a small beaver hat, and, with his bobbed wig, he looked like an exotic tropical bird.

Although they had met only briefly at Bricknell House the evening before, it had been long enough for her to make an assessment and form her own opinion of him, despite Lord Dunstan and James, which was one of dislike; she detected a good deal of craft and guile about the man which she found off-putting.

His eyes roved in arrogant appreciation from her hair to her face, to the slender column of her neck, her shoulders and her breasts. The look she found insolent, causing her indignation to rise, but when he favoured her with such a charming, engaging smile, his teeth flashing white as they caught the sun, she suddenly found it impossible to be rude to him and melted a little, returning his smile. His very look made it plain to her that he desired her unashamedly, and, in her present confused state, she was ready to find comfort in any kind of positive feeling.

'Good Lord! Miss Divine! So it is you,' he enthused as he joined her, bowing with an elaborate flourish and a smile. 'What a surprise. You can't believe what a pleasure it is for me to see you again, and so soon. Who would have thought it?'

'Who indeed!' smiled Louisa.

'My luck's certainly in. It is fortunate for me that I find you all alone,' he said in a lazy drawl.

'Not quite, Sir Charles,' she said, looking to where James and Timothy stood. They were so heavily engrossed in conversation that, as yet, they were not aware that Sir Charles had approached her.

Sir Charles followed her gaze and scowled, but he quickly ignored them and fixed his gaze on Louisa's face once more, his countenance restored to good humour. 'You look ravishing. Damn me if I can remember when I last saw a prettier face than yours.'

'Oh, I'm sure you can if you try,' Louisa said, her wonderful amber eyes filled with wry amusement, noting that his voice lacked sincerity, and that he spoke with well-regulated practice.

'It is the kind of face that is capable of driving a man to distraction. Ever since I saw you last night, I confess I've been thinking about you—a great deal, in fact—and now here you are.'

'I'm sure you'll soon get over it.' There was no doubt about it, she thought with cynicism, not deceived or beguiled by his easy chatter. He was dazzling, with a lying, flattering tongue in his head.

He raised one languid eyebrow. 'You're having a pleasant stroll, I hope?'

'Yes, thank you. Very pleasant.'

He glanced towards James. 'Fraser looks down in the mouth, I see, although the poor chap has a right to be after his rotten luck last night. He lost heavily to Lord Dunstan, I believe.' His gaze settled on her once more, his face lustful, with a certain excitement in his eyes and an air of lecherous anticipation emanating from them. 'If it prevents him entertaining you in the manner to which you are accustomed, might I offer my services—? When you can escape his watchful eye, of course. Nothing would please me more.'

'Thank you. I'm flattered. But that won't be necessary, Sir Charles,' she said, more reluctant than ever to divulge that James was her brother and not her lover, beginning to think the subterfuge accorded her some protection against men like Sir Charles Meredith. 'I have not yet grown so tired of him that I would willingly leave him for another. You do understand, I hope?'

'Then he is fortunate. Such devotion is a rarity indeed in our society. But he neglects you, I see. Any man who can neglect such a beautiful creature is a fool.'

'Most men are fools, are they not, Sir Charles?' Louisa countered.

Sir Charles's eyes focused narrowly on hers. 'Ah! You have wit too, I see. I would steal you myself if you were not already spoken for,' he said softly, with a sly smile and a lowering of one heavy eyelid that constituted a wink. 'So take care that you do not drive me to distraction, otherwise you will learn how far my desires can carry me—Mr Fraser or no.'

Louisa gave a delicate lift to her brows. 'Are you always so persistent, Sir Charles?'

'Always,' he said as he began to accompany her back to where James and Timothy were still deep in conversation. 'You think I'm insufferable, don't you?'

'Yes,' she admitted, unable to prevent a little smile playing at the corners of her mouth. 'Quite.'

He was not at all disturbed or offended by her honest reply. 'Well, I can be quite a charming and delightful chap when you get to know me. I have an appalling reputation, I know, but I would ask you not to listen to gossip, Miss Divine. You shouldn't believe everything. I'm not ignorant of what's said about me, and I'm afraid I have been dreadfully maligned.'

She laughed lightly. 'Then I'm sorry to put a dampener on your ego, Sir Charles, but until last night, when we met in the doorway at Bricknell House, I had never heard of you before in my life.'

He sighed regretfully. 'That's what comes of spending too much time in the country. It stultifies one's mind and leads to boredom.'

'Possibly. But you can set your mind at rest,' she said, looking up at him sideways, meaningfully. 'I have never been one to listen to gossip—only facts.'

Neither of them saw a group of four people coming towards them: a man, two women, and a young boy. Having just replied to something amusing Sir Charles had said, which had brought a smile to her lips and a sparkle to her eyes, Louisa suddenly noticed their approach, and her smile froze as her gaze became fixed on them.

One of the women, whom she thought to be in her mid-thirties, was handsome and quite tall, her gloved hand placed lightly on the gentleman's arm. The other woman Louisa saw was much younger, still a girl, in fact, perhaps sixteen or seventeen years old. Her hair was dark and arranged in ringlets which bounced delightfully when she moved her head, and she was extremely pretty, with a vivacity and freshness to her manner. The young boy, who she surmised must be the older woman's son, sported a shock of dark brown curls and was happily skipping along beside them. But it was the gentleman who caught Louisa's eyes and held them, for it was Lord Dunstan.

Both parties stopped abruptly, leaving several paces between them, Lord Dunstan's gaze barely resting on Louisa before sliding to her companion, his eyes so cold she thought they could annihilate a man.

Louisa noticed how the older woman paled and drew in her breath quickly, her hand rising to her throat as her eyes were drawn towards Sir Charles, as if seeing a ghost. Lord Dunstan's features froze, and taking the woman's arm, after throwing Louisa a glance which was like a poison dart, he abruptly stepped off the path and began walking away, calling sharply to the boy and the young lady to follow, but not before Louisa had seen his eyes darken with anger and contempt.

She watched them go, noticing how the young woman paused and looked at Sir Charles with surprise, staring at him openly and with all the innocence of her tender years, clearly dazzled for the first time in her life by a supremely handsome man, allowing the corners of her inviting mouth to twitch slightly, and looking curiously exposed as she caught her breath and flushed a bright pink. Her eyes were as big as saucers and held far too much eloquence as she gazed at him wondrously, until she responded to Lord Dunstan's sharp order and reluctantly tore her eyes from his.

She had looked so startled that Louisa was convinced she could not have uttered a word if her life had depended on it. Casting a sideways glance at Sir Charles, she saw his full pink mouth turn up in one corner in a grin, and beneath his heavy, drooping lids his eyes were filled with amusement and idle speculation as he watched her hurry away.

Filled with confusion by Lord Dunstan's show of rudeness, Louisa was puzzled by his behaviour and that of the older woman, but recalling the intense dislike Lord Dunstan so clearly felt for

Sir Charles, which he had made evident on both occasions she had met him, she thought he must have good reason to cut him in public so deliberately. However, she thought, with some regret, considering what she had in mind where Lord Dunstan was concerned, it was unfortunate that he had seen her with Sir Charles Meredith; no doubt it would not help her cause and he would draw his own conclusions and be reluctant to have anything to do with her, despite what he had said to her at Mr Brewster's bookshop.

In an attempt to dispel the coldness that the brief encounter with Lord Dunstan had caused her, Louisa smiled up at Sir Charles, beginning to walk on. He fell into step beside her.

'I saw the way the young lady looked at you, Sir Charles, which you must have observed for yourself. It would seem you have an admirer, and I suspect it amuses you to have a flirtatious exchange with such an innocent young girl.' She spoke lightly, an innocent herself, unprepared for Sir Charles's reply, which her untutored mind regarded as obscene.

'I agree she is extremely pretty—and ripe for more than a mere glance. The crux of the matter is, though, that she is Dunstan's sister, and, as you will have observed for yourself, he and I are not the best of friends. However, it is such a waste to keep that appealing little virgin tucked away at his home in Sussex.'

Louisa stared at him, shocked that he should exhibit such an unrestrained interest in such a young girl. 'If she is to remain in that condition, then in my opinion I think it best that she remains there, Sir Charles,' she chided, 'under her brother's watchful eye and away from the rakes and debauchees of London—away from such destructive, immoral influences as yourself, for it is clear to me that her innocence and naivety only adds to her attraction in your eyes.'

He laughed lightly, a lewd, lascivious gleam in his eyes. 'You are right, I admit it. The sight of so much innocence excites me—makes me imagine those pleasures and sensations, such as Miss Dunstan can never have experienced, being aroused by me. I find the aura of pure virginity combined with youth and beauty irresistible. And the seemingly unobtainable is always the most desirable to me, my dear Miss Divine—as is the case with yourself,' he said huskily as his eyes devoured her soft lips.

'But if I wanted to sample the innocent delights of the adorable Miss Dunstan I would not be put off by her brother,' he went on. 'No, indeed I would not,' he said without preamble, quietly, firmly and convincingly, his eyes following the retreating figure of the alluring young woman, who turned her head briefly to look back once more.

There was a hard gleam in his eyes, his gaze speculative and predatory as he watched her disappear amongst a group of trees, along with the other members of her group. His words caused Louisa to swallow down a sudden rush of revulsion. She observed the way his eyes followed the young woman, and it troubled her and created a feeling of unease. It was an incident she was to recall at a later date, but for now she put it out of her mind. Quickening her stride, for she was suddenly eager to be done with his company, she drew a shaky breath.

'What on earth have you done, Sir Charles, that makes Lord Dunstan scowl at you so whenever the two of you meet?'

Louisa noted that suddenly he was no longer his usual, smiling, convivial self, that a seriousness had descended on him as he fixed his unreadable gaze straight ahead.

'He bears me a personal grudge—and it is I who should be doing the scowling, Miss Divine. I am guilty of nothing where that gentleman is concerned. Any wrongdoing was done by him, not by me.'

'Why? What on earth has he done that is so dreadful?'

His face became grim, his eyes hard, and there was something so terrible in their fixed, unnatural brightness that Louisa felt her throat tighten. He spoke slowly, quietly and deliberately, each word enunciated.

'He cheated me out of the woman I was to have married.'

'Oh! Then should it not be you who bears the grudge, Sir Charles?'

He grimaced, seeming not to hear her as he became immersed in some unpleasant thought. His lips compressed and his gloved fingers closed on the brim of his hat, crushing the edge, leaving Louisa in no doubt as to the depth of hatred that existed between himself and Lord Dunstan.

'I-In what way did he cheat you?' Louisa asked nervously, for

Sir Charles Meredith no longer resembled the man of a few moments before, all trace of the charming rake he portrayed to the world having vanished. The expression in his eyes had become ugly, his features contorted almost beyond recognition. The expression was fleeting and soon passed, but it left Louisa with a sinking feeling and a sense of regret that she had unwittingly prodded a wound that was still raw, seeping and extremely painful for both men.

'He married her himself when my back was turned—when I was unable to do anything about it. But it backfired on him miserably, which was no more than he deserved,' he uttered fiercely. 'However, it is all a long time ago and in the past.'

'But not forgotten by either of you, it would seem?'

'No, indeed. He did me a grave injustice and the day will come when I shall pay the almighty Alistair Dunstan back in full for what he did to me, Miss Divine. Some day,' he whispered, with an undertone of such savage force that Louisa fought a shiver of fear. 'You'll see.'

Louisa's curiosity was sharpened and she wanted to know more—there was so much he had not told her, but she was not to learn anything further about what had occurred between Sir Charles and Lord Dunstan, for at that moment James and Timothy, displeased to see her talking to Sir Charles, came to reclaim her.

Trembling but managing a smile, shaken by the brief insight Sir Charles had given her into the feud that existed between himself and Lord Dunstan, an insight that left her feeling decidedly uneasy, she watched as he politely and abruptly excused himself to Timothy and James. Her brother was coldly contemptuous of the man's frank admiration of her. 'I do not like that man, Louisa,' James muttered, scowling at Sir Charles's receding figure as he swaggered away. 'You will do well to steer clear of him in the future.'

'Yes, I intend to,' she replied absently, a memory of the cold, savage look of vengeance she had seen in Sir Charles's eyes flickering in her mind. Their conversation had left her with a feeling of oppression and horror, and she experienced a certain surprise at his severe accusation against Lord Dunstan. Was it true? she asked herself. Had Lord Dunstan married the woman Sir Charles would have married himself? If this was the case, then surely the lady concerned would not have married Lord Dunstan had she not preferred him to Sir Charles?

But Sir Charles had revealed that the marriage had gone miserably wrong for Lord Dunstan, and with that she could only conclude—as Timothy had suggested—that it had broken down and his wife had left him for someone else. She tried to envisage what both Lord Dunstan and Sir Charles must have suffered, and yet she had a distinct feeling that Lord Dunstan's suffering had been the greatest. She did not know enough of what had transpired between them, nor did she know either of them well enough to defend one's conduct against the other, but having just had an insight into Sir Charles's character, which seemed to have a tendency to evil, she had no wish to know more.

His manner, his way of speaking and his countenance she found repugnant in every degree. It had been enough to tell her that he did not possess any of the virtues that constituted a gentleman, and that he had many years of idleness and vice to atone for.

James moped about the house in a state of deep depression as Louisa began preparing herself for the unpleasant occasion of dining at Dunstan House. She managed to persuade him to put off fetching the deeds to his estate from Surrey and presenting them to Lord Dunstan to pay off his debt until the following week, in order to give her time to retrieve his IOU.

She reminded herself that if what Timothy had said was true— that Lord Dunstan attracted women like a magnet—then after her sharp rebuff at Mr Brewster's bookshop, and seeing her with Sir Charles Meredith in St James's Park, he might be angry and no longer interested in her.

For her plan to succeed she must make him want her—want her to such an extent that he would be prepared to agree to her terms to possess her. And as the time drew near for her to ready herself for the evening in front of her—perhaps the most important evening of her life—apprehension began to give way to panic.

She was undecided about which gown to wear, for Timothy had presented her with three to choose from, as well as several items of undergarment, telling her that his sister had been only too delighted to be of help.

He had told Amelia that Louisa had arrived in London having absent-mindedly left her finest dresses behind in Surrey, and was mortified, on finding herself invited to an important event, to discover she had nothing to wear and unwilling to go to the expense of buying something new. Amelia had been only too happy to loan her some gowns.

Louisa finally settled for one of deep crimson satin, by far the most alluring of the three. Its vivid colour and low-cut *décolletage* would be more in keeping with the occasion and the people she would be mixing with than the other two, which were in pastel shades and rather modest in design. She declined the wearing of even the smallest hoop to lift the dress, preferring instead to let the skirt fall softly from the waist.

At first she had balked at the thought of accepting the clothes, but realising she had no choice, if she wished to succeed with Lord Dunstan, and that she was in no position to turn charity away, she began to dress, feeling as she did so her last remnants of pride melt like the morning mist beneath the sun.

To add to the part, but without too much artifice, she applied just a little powder to her cheeks and a little salve to her lips, and, with skilful fingers, Alice helped her arrange her newly washed hair in an elaborate creation of glossy waves and curls, with three heavy ringlets dangling at the back, one of them resting on her bare shoulder.

When she was ready she surveyed her appearance in the full-length mirror and saw her radiance reflected. She barely recognised herself, feeling transformed by the gown's magnificence, and experiencing a sensuous pleasure in its satin softness. She flushed at her image. The gown, with its elbow-length sleeves, was bold and quite dramatic and extremely daring, its firm-fitting bodice cut low, and the fullness of the skirt emphasising her tiny waist and falling in luxurious shining folds to her slippered feet. She suspected it had not belonged to Timothy's quiet, sheltered sister at all but to another, more worldly lady of his acquaintance, of whom she would prefer to remain in ignorance. However, she would for ever hold the lady in her debt if she managed to succeed in seducing Lord Dunstan.

It was certainly not the type of gown she would normally have chosen to wear, she thought, sighing as she turned from the full-length mirror, but if she was to play a harlot she might as well look the part.

They were to travel to Dunstan House in Timothy's carriage and on being told by Alice of its arrival she took a deep breath and left her room, her skirts sweeping the stairs as she went down. She saw both her brother and Timothy waiting for her in the hall and was fully aware of the impact her appearance would have on them. With Alice's help she had been transformed from the pretty little country girl her brother had never troubled to look at into a striking young woman it would be difficult for anyone to keep their eyes off.

When James and Timothy saw her their eyes opened wide in sheer amazement—Timothy's with undisguised appraisal and James's with shocked disapproval. He was unable to believe that the beautiful, sophisticated creature descending the stairs—showing enough of her bosom as to be positively indecent, and smiling only as one of London's social butterflies knew how to—was his sister.

'Dear Lord, Louisa!' he objected crossly. 'That is hardly a suitable gown for you to wear—and I dare hardly ask where you acquired it.'

'Then I wouldn't, if I were you—in fact,' she quipped, throwing Timothy a knowing smile of gratitude from beneath her lowered lashes, 'I'm not entirely sure where it came from either, nor do I wish to know. However, if an evening at Dunstan House is to be anything like an evening at Lady Bricknell's, then I would say it is perfect for the occasion.' She faced Timothy, making him a sweeping curtsy. 'What do you think, Timothy? Will I do?'

Timothy's brown eyes were twinkling. 'You'll do all right, Louisa. You look ravishing,' he assured her emphatically.

'Well, if you insist on accompanying Timothy and I,' said James sullenly, 'you must be introduced as my sister. I cannot permit you to go on calling yourself Miss Divine. It's quite ridiculous.'

Louisa gave him a cross look, in no mood to be bullied tonight of all nights. 'Ridiculous or not, that is who I am to be if I am to enter the sort of company you keep. We will look foolish if you suddenly announce me as your sister, when only two nights ago I was someone else. And, anyway, I am not accompanying you by choice, James. I am merely coming along to make quite sure you do not dig us deeper into debt than we are already. If I see you so much as look at a card or dice table, I shall personally intervene and embarrass you to such a degree that you will not dare set foot in polite society ever again. Now, are we ready?' she said, pulling on her long gloves with a brusqueness that brooked no argument. 'We don't want to be late.'

With a few quiet grumbles James followed Timothy and his sister out to the waiting carriage. Louisa climbed inside, about to embark on a mission as dramatic and fateful as any she had undertaken before or would ever do again.

Seated across from Louisa, Timothy glanced at her, seeing that she appeared cool and collected and well schooled for what lay ahead of her, but behind her composed mask of elegance he sensed the fissures that lay deep.

Ever since Louisa had left Lord Dunstan at Mr Brewster's bookshop, and after seeing him again in St James's Park, she had tried not to focus her mind on him, but now she was within minutes of facing him once more her panic increased and she could hardly believe what she was about to do. His name spun through her mind with a combination of loathing and dread, and she told herself she would rather sleep with the devil than Lord Dunstan.

And yet the feelings she had experienced on the three occasions when they had met on her coming to London this time took some understanding; she had felt herself being drawn to him against her will by the compelling magnetism he seemed to radiate, and the memory of his smile and how he had looked at her, how his incredibly blue eyes had hardly left hers for a moment and the intimacy of his lazy gaze, made her tremble and heat course through her body.

She was experiencing a great deal of nervousness at the disagreeable prospect of meeting him again, and as the carriage arrived at Dunstan House nothing could calm her mounting tension. Dunstan House was one of several fine mansions in Piccadilly. Backing onto Green Park, it was set in formal flower gardens, the high walls keeping the rumble of wheels and street cries at bay.

With James in front of them Timothy took Louisa's hand, feeling her fingers tremble. Passing through the doorway, they made their entry into the gilded interior. He bent close to her ear. 'You look lovely,' he whispered reassuringly. 'Are you still determined to go through with this—even though James is bound to find out? And don't forget that anything connected with Lord Dunstan becomes instant gossip and spreads like wildfire. If you succeed, and when it's discovered you are James's sister, you will become the focus of a scandal. Can you cope with that?'

'I have had four years of learning to cope, Timothy,' she replied with bitter irony. 'Having to deal with relentless adversity has made me strong and taught me to hold my head high. I shall not let a scandal worry me unduly if I can hold onto Bierlow Hall.'

She cast an eye over the assembled groups, knowing Lord Dunstan was present but unable to see him just then—and the prospect of seeing him, extremely conscious of the purpose of her being there, set her treacherous pulses racing. With a natural grace and a serene smile on her lips, she felt an odd sensation of unreality.

As they entered further into the large, extremely grand and impressive marble hallway, with huge polished doors opening into sumptuously furnished rooms beyond, the sheer magnitude and beauty of the house seemed overwhelming and utterly breathtaking. It shone with the brilliance of hundreds of candles. Mirrors glowed with refracted light from the crystal and diamonds strewn around the bare throats of women. An army of exquisitely attired footmen in scarlet and gold moved among the guests, bearing silver trays balancing sparkling glasses of champagne.

Breathing deeply and glancing at the assembled guests, Louisa suddenly found herself the object of dozens of pairs of eyes. It was as though she stood in a blazing light as everyone seemed to turn towards her. Every male and female, young and old, seemed to focus on her, some staring frankly while others looked at her with unconcealed curiosity. Many of the gentlemen looked with open admiration, and several of the ladies with barely concealed hostility, having already seen her at Lady Bricknell's house two evenings earlier and perceiving her as the first really serious competition in months.

To Louisa the company appeared to be very much the same as

it had been at Bricknell House. There was a sense of glamour
about the gathering, yet it seemed more subdued somehow, rather
than a rout. But no doubt at some time later in the evening, when
the liquor reached their heads and loosened any inhibitions they
might possess, the guests would sit down to cards, by which time
Louisa hoped she would have accomplished her purpose and they
could leave.

Suddenly her smile froze on her lips and she became oblivious
to all else as her gaze became locked on a pair of exceptionally
vivid blue eyes across the hall. Lord Dunstan was just emerging
from a room with Lady Bricknell by his side. Without taking his
eyes off Louisa, he murmured something to his companion, who
followed his gaze and seemed to smile knowingly and with a good
deal of satisfaction, before drifting from his side to speak to someone else—and Louisa would have been astonished to learn that
Lady Bricknell's invitations to James and Timothy to attend her
supper and card parties, in the hope that eventually Louisa would
appear, had borne fruit at last.

With a growing sense of alarm and a general feeling of unease,
Louisa watched Lord Dunstan start towards them with long, pur-
poseful strides, seeming to grow larger as he neared, his eyes compelling. His black suit was immaculate and without a crease in the
fabric stretched across his strong shoulders, his cravat and white
silk stockings dazzling white. His presence was inescapable. He
overshadowed the room and his guests parted to let him pass, his
eyes searching Louisa's face, his expression one of slight amusement and something which, to Louisa's indignation, looked very
much like triumph.

Her flesh grew hot and a tremor passed through her now she
was face to face with him once more. A smile of frank admiration
gleamed in his eyes when he looked at her, his sternly handsome
face stamped with nobility and pride, his powerful, muscular body
emanating raw power and sensuality. At any other time, had any
other man looked at her in the manner Lord Dunstan looked at
her, she would have been extremely insulted and been tempted to
slap his face. But, remembering the farce she was to play out to
the bitter end, she swallowed her pride and gave him a ravishing
smile, lighting her eyes with intelligence.

'I'm so glad you could come, Mr Fraser—Mr Hacket,' Alistair said, and when he spoke the sheer, concentrated power of his presence was vividly apparent. His greeting embraced all three, but his gaze rested on Louisa. 'And you, too, Miss Divine,' he murmured, fascinated by her, noticing how her face captured and absorbed the soft glow of the candles.

There was a serenity of expression and stillness that hung about her like an aura, and seeing her again was an experience he had not sufficiently prepared himself for. She was beautiful, far more beautiful than any woman present, and she intrigued him, troubled him, and his instinct told him that hidden desires were at play beneath the thin layer of respectability. She was still yet watchful amidst the hive of gossip, her face settled in cool, unblinking remoteness, which distinctly whispered 'Don't touch'.

'Is it your intention to exact revenge later, Fraser—to recoup what you lost to me two nights ago?'

Unhappy and pale, James managed to smile, but there was no disguising his anxiety as he cast a swift glance at his sister, licking his lips nervously and saying, as if prompted, which did not go unnoticed by Alistair, 'No, not this evening, Lord Dunstan. Tonight I intend to refrain from any form of gambling. I shall be a passive observer, nothing more.'

Lord Dunstan nodded slightly, not really surprised. If the man was as impoverished as he suspected then he could ill afford to run up any more debts. He had met a lot of men like James Fraser—reckless young fools, prepared to risk everything over a game of cards or the throw of a dice. 'Very wise, sir. Very wise.'

'You—you have a beautiful house, Lord Dunstan,' remarked Louisa in an attempt to draw the conversation away from gambling.

He shifted his gaze back to her. She had the look of a girl, but he felt she was a woman in every sense of that meaningful word, and yet she seemed incredibly unsoiled. She possessed a poise and dignity that was absent in most of the women present, and she was sexually elegant and extremely desirable in her crimson dress, bearing no resemblance to the rather prim young woman he had encountered in St Paul's Church two months earlier and more recently at Mr Brewster's bookshop.

The moment he had looked into her eyes she had assaulted his senses and he had become determined to possess her. But who was she, he wondered, and why hadn't he seen her before if she was Fraser's mistress? And was she as unfamiliar to Charles Meredith as she would have him believe? After seeing them together in St James's Park, he was beginning to doubt it.

'Thank you. It would give me great pleasure to show you around later—if you like.'

'Why—yes. I'd love to,' she replied.

He left to greet more of his guests who continued to arrive, but Louisa had the impression that his attention never left her.

Chapter Four

Louisa watched Alistair move among his guests, thinking they were like mere shadows in his orbit. Handsome and distinguished, he seemed to dominate the company, and the ladies around him gazed at him provocatively from under fluttering eyelashes and pouted their crimson lips, every one of them alluringly seductive. But his manner towards them was curiously cold, despite his smile, which puzzled Louisa. When dinner was announced he came back to them, and with a courtly gesture offered her his arm, the pull she exerted on his gaze so strong it was as if she had called his name.

'You don't mind if I escort Miss Divine into dinner, do you, Fraser?'

'No—no,' spluttered James, unable to object even if he wanted to, experiencing the first stirrings of unease at the attentions their illustrious host was paying towards his sister. 'Of course not.'

The moment Louisa placed her hand on Alistair's arm he was surprised by the leaping, wolf-like passion of his response. Eyebrows went up and lips twisted, and sly, secret smiles were exchanged behind fluttering fans as they passed by on their way to the dining room.

'I am pleased to see you have lowered your sword, Miss Divine, and honoured Dunstan House with your presence this evening,' Alistair said, bestowing smiles to right and left as they moved towards the dining room, while keeping his voice low so as not to be overheard.

'Thank you for inviting me,' she answered, smiling softly. 'However,' she said, looking obliquely up at him from beneath her thick fringe of dark eyelashes, 'my rapier may be sheathed, Lord Dunstan, but I will have you know that it is every bit as sharp and lethal as it was the other day.'

With slightly raised eyebrows he glanced down at her, his gaze and his crooked smile drenching Louisa in its sexuality and bringing an attractive flush to her cheeks.

'I do not doubt that for one moment. It will make the play between us all the more exciting. I would like to apologise for my rudeness when we met in Mr Brewster's bookshop. Clearly you are a stranger to Lady Bricknell's parties and may not have known the type of ladies who attend them.'

'It very soon became evident to me, and you were quick to assume I was one of them. But I must tell you that you have the wrong opinion of me, Lord Dunstan,' she said with a slight haughtiness. 'I may have been at Lady Bricknell's party, but I am no harlot.'

Alistair's blue eyes seemed to burn down into hers. 'You say that and yet you flaunt yourself in public in the company of the most notorious rake in London—a man who boasts his conquests and who is not ashamed to tell the world that no woman has ever denied him.'

'And how was I to know that?' she said, springing quickly to her own defence. 'I told you that we had not met before the evening at Bricknell House. Before that night I had never heard of Sir Charles Meredith, let alone of his dubious reputation. And when you saw us together in the park it was not as it seemed. We met quite by chance—and he can be extremely persistent. If you had taken the trouble to look before so rudely walking away, you would have seen I was with Mr Fraser.'

'I have my reasons for not acknowledging Charles Meredith, Miss Divine. It was unfortunate that you were with him at the time and bore some of the brunt of my rudeness. Had you been alone it would have given me great pleasure to introduce you to my sisters, but my older sister's abhorrence is almost as great as my own where that gentleman is concerned.'

'I see,' said Louisa, feeling curiously relieved on being told that the woman was not romantically involved with him but was his older sister, and absently surmised that the little boy she had seen belonged to her.

'But how was I to know you are cast in a different mould to the rest of the women who were at Bricknell House that night?' Lord Dunstan went on. 'I went too fast in my conclusions and I apologise, but knowing nothing about you I had no reason to think otherwise, and you cannot blame me for making you an offer— even if you are apparently attached to someone else. You are an extremely attractive and desirable young woman.'

'Come, now, Lord Dunstan,' Louisa said, her voice under control—almost thoughtfully calm as she slipped into the part she had set herself. 'Isn't that what every gentleman says to a lady he's propositioned?'

He gave a lift of one eyebrow and smiled down at her. 'Wit as well as beauty,' he said softly. 'I like that. Fraser's a lucky man. No wonder he wants to keep you all to himself. My offer was turned down, as I remember—unless—you've reconsidered it?'

'Yes, I have,' she replied as he held her intent gaze, his own as uncompromising as she could have wished for.

'It still stands, you know,' he said, 'You will want for nothing. I can be generous—as you will discover.'

'I see. Then, knowing that, I shall think about it a little more over dinner,' she said, her dimples appearing as she tilted her head to one side, smiling demurely, with eyes as warm and bright as a brightly plumaged bird, astonished at how easy it was to play the coquette.

There was no time to say more as they walked towards the table. The large dining room was lavishly decorated and adorned with huge baskets and vases of flowers. The long table, which was a delight to the eye, sparkled and shone and was laid out like a fabulous work of art. Spread with lace, it almost bowed beneath the weight of china and crystal and ornate silver. A myriad of candles flattered the complexions of the ladies—especially the older ones who were finding it increasingly difficult to camouflage the tell-tale lines of age with powder and paint. But the warm light made Louisa's creamy skin glow, emphasising her youthful skin and giving an added warmth to her amber eyes.

The soft music of fiddles drifted in from a room beyond. Halfway down the table, Louisa was seated next to James and across from Timothy, whose attention was occupied throughout the meal by two pretty young women on either side who flirted with him outrageously, one of whom he found fascinating, with ravishing blue eyes and a mass of raven-black hair. The food was exquisite and there seemed to be gallons of wine and champagne, of which the guests imbibed far too freely, Louisa observed with distaste, their behaviour becoming louder and more uninhibited as the meal progressed.

Observing the man at the head of the table, she saw that his expression was one of cynicism and disdain as his eyes moved over the gathering, as if all present were beneath his condescension, which puzzled Louisa. These people did not seem his type. They hung around him, eager to incur his favour and influence, the sort of acquaintances she would have imagined a man of his stamp would have gone out of his way to avoid.

As the general mood began to lighten only he seemed unchanged. He surveyed the undignified scene with a mocking and cynical air of amusement. A glass of claret was beside him and Louisa strongly suspected that not a single drop had touched his lips. Not for one moment did he relinquish his dignity. His eyes were as hard as iron but, when they collided with hers, hidden beneath she saw a sudden spark and could read a leashed sensuality. She experienced a quiver of alarm about the powerful feelings that passed between them like an invisible current.

Louisa ate little, having no appetite and having to force the delicious food between her lips, too nervous to be hungry, and yet those watching her would not have guessed what was going on behind her serene exterior.

Little did she know that Alistair was giving her the same scrutiny that she was giving him, noticing that like himself she wasn't drinking, that her glass remained half-full and untouched, and when the footman offered to fill it she placed her hand over the rim. She had lovely hands, he noticed absently, with long fingers, and he tried to imagine what they would feel like in caressing mode.

He sat transfixed, equally puzzled by her as she was by him.

From beneath hooded lids he observed how she conducted herself with dignity, speaking little to those around her, content to observe the scene with what he thought to be a critical eye, seeming to despise the company and the meaningless chit-chat it engaged in. She remained unmoved, as if none of it had anything to do with her.

But when she turned her warm amber eyes on him they trailed over him provocatively, languorously, conveying a message, and yet there was innocence in every look and line of her perfect body, which, he thought with cynicism, was all part of the act. Yet it was the first time in years that a woman had invaded his imagination—not since... But as he was about to let his thoughts wander and resurrect the past angrily he thrust them back into the dark, secret corners of his mind, unwilling to allow them to intrude into the present.

Later, when people began drifting into the card room, where tables had been set up and the clack of rolling dice could already be heard, Louisa was relieved to see James, under the watchful eye of Timothy, in conversation with a group who preferred to converse and imbibe of more liquor, for the present abiding by his promise to her not to be drawn into the card room.

Feeling anxious and impatient for the evening to be over so they could return home, she looked to where Lord Dunstan was standing with a group of gentlemen, regarding her from across the room, his handsome face hard and predatory. Taking a deep breath, and with a docility that astounded her, for in a situation such as this she should have been trembling all over, never having purposely sought a gentleman's attention before, she moved towards him, feeling that now was the time to confront him.

Alistair watched her come closer. She was a breathtaking vision in crimson satin, and looking as dangerous as a suppressed tropical storm. He noticed that when she walked her steps were light, and she had an unconscious swing to her body, a natural grace, the material of her dress fluid and glowing with darting shafts of light and moving with her, making one imagine her rounded hips and her long slender legs beneath the flowing skirts. She was too exquisite to be flesh and blood. Feeling the blood pounding through his veins, he drew a long, quivering breath as he watched her.

'Good Lord!' said one of his companions softly. 'She cannot be real. Where in God's name did Fraser find her? Where has he been hiding her? Every male here tonight is dreaming of an alliance with her. Do you suppose she might be looking about for someone more exciting than Fraser to warm her bed? What an exquisite creature.'

'My thoughts exactly,' said Alistair softly, without taking his eyes off her. 'And I, gentlemen, intend getting to know her better. Excuse me.'

Quickly he moved across the room to meet Louisa. His warm, embracing gaze fell on her and she felt ravished by it. She felt her heart tilt, as if it was more than prepared to be lost to him.

'You promised to show me your house, Lord Dunstan,' Louisa murmured. 'Would now be convenient?'

'I haven't forgotten, and I think now would be as good a time as any.'

With a look towards Timothy, who had been watching her closely since the end of supper—a look that told him she was leaving the company for a while and he was to keep a close eye on James—she allowed Lord Dunstan to escort her from the room. Without speaking, they crossed the hall and entered another room, passing through it onto a wide terrace.

It was the middle of August and an ocean of stars dappled the sky, the glow of the moon drenching them in a warm light. Roses clambered profusely over the stone balustrade, giving off a heady, intoxicating perfume, and causing Louisa to breathe in their fragrance. Alistair paused beside her, and in the sombre light examined the lines of her face as she looked out over the darkened garden, startled once more by her beauty, which was almost a physical sensation. He marvelled at the fine-boned modelling of her face, the creamy hue of her skin and the fluidity of her gestures. With her hair arranged to allow soft tendrils to play around the clear lines of her face, she looked at once ravishing and vulnerable.

Louisa turned and met his eyes questioningly, the sheer, concentrated power of his presence disturbing her, making it more difficult for her to regard him as an enemy. 'I thought you were going to show me the house, Lord Dunstan?'

'The house was not what I—nor you, for that matter—had in mind. Am I right?' he said, now that he was alone with her finding her even more compelling as they examined each other carefully.

His voice was incredible, of a depth and timbre that caressed Louisa's flesh and brought a quiver to her limbs. She knew she would have to tread carefully, otherwise every preconceived plan would go out of the window. Never had she met a man like Alistair Dunstan, and—Timothy was right—she was in danger of getting out of her depth and forgetting the real purpose of her visit to Dunstan House.

'Yes,' she admitted, fighting to calm her rioting nerves and maintain her equilibrium—to ignore the seductive tug of his eyes and voice.

'Forgive me, Miss Divine, but I could not help noticing how quiet you were throughout dinner. I have the distinct impression that you do not find the company to your liking.'

'You are observant, Lord Dunstan. Yet if I seemed quiet perhaps it is because I am a stranger among your guests. But what of you?'

'Oh?'

'I observed that you seemed critical of the company and I wondered why you bother to hold such lavish parties when you clearly hold every one of your guests in contempt—or is it that because of your contempt you can speak your mind if they annoy you?'

Alistair looked at her hard for a moment, relieved to find she was not in the least intimidated or impressed by who he was, or the overpowering evidence of his great wealth. He saw how much her own person she was, her expression wiser than her years, a trace of wariness around her wide amber eyes. His smile was soft when he spoke.

'You are very perceptive, Miss Divine, but I must tell you that I do not entertain often—especially not the sort of company present this evening. It just so happens that Lady Bricknell is an extremely good friend of mine—as was her late husband—and I have been promising her for some considerable time to return her hospitality and invite her and some of her friends—a few of them my own, I confess—to Dunstan House. But tell me, in your opinion, what sort of company ought I to keep?'

'The sort whose conduct and behaviour is proper and conventional.'

'But not nearly as much fun,' Alistair teased with a lazy, devastating smile.

'Forgive me, Lord Dunstan, but you did not look as though you were enjoying yourself to me. You do not strike me as being the kind of man who would allow convention to dictate your every move, but such company does not enhance your dignity or your good name.'

'And you would know all about that, wouldn't you, Miss Divine?' he said quietly, meaningfully.

Louisa had the grace to flush and drop her gaze, for it was a brutal reminder of what she was doing. She hated it. She was about to transgress from all her principles, and she was sick with horror and self-disgust. It was ugly and she was beginning to regret ever coming to Dunstan House, but thinking of Bierlow Hall, and her fear of her much beloved brother being sent to Fleet Gaol, gave her courage and re-established in her own mind her determination to succeed. Lord Dunstan might take away her innocence and make love to her unresisting body, but these things would not reach her thoughts. So long as she remained mistress of these she could still hope to return to her life as she had known it.

She raised her eyes, aware of the searching intensity of his gaze as she favoured him with a melting smile, which made Alistair's blood run warm in his veins and the heat of it move to his belly.

'If I were to find myself among such company no doubt I would be treated with contempt and condemnation, but at all costs I would try very hard to hold onto my dignity.'

Alistair smiled, his eyes glinting with wry amusement. 'I do not think my own dignity is at stake, and, even if it was, I fail to see how the company I keep would redeem it. And where my good name is concerned it, too, has been questioned on more than one occasion.' He moved closer. 'So, Miss Divine, shall we get back to the matter uppermost in both our minds? Having had time to consider my offer a little more over dinner, do you accept?'

'That depends on how generous your offer happens to be, Lord Dunstan.'

'What have you in mind?'

'Four thousand guineas.'

Their eyes met and held, irresistible force colliding with immovable object. Alistair nodded slightly, his expression hard.

'You set a high price for yourself. But four thousand guineas?'

'Yes. No less.'

Ah, thought Alistair as light suddenly dawned on him. Very clever. Realisation of what she was doing hit him like a hammer blow. His eyes narrowed and he looked at her with scarcely concealed anger. 'Forgive me, but to my reckoning that is exactly the sum of Mr Fraser's debt to me.'

'Yes.'

He nodded slowly, watching her intently, his expression coolly impassive. 'So—you value yourself so little that you are prepared to sell yourself to pay off your lover's debt?'

Louisa smiled up at him mischievously, the eloquence of her eyes conveying their own subtle and unmistakable message. She was surprised at the facility with which the conversation tripped off her tongue. 'Not sell, Lord Dunstan. I prefer to think of it as a trade—a barter for James's IOU. You have something I want— and I have something you want. Don't you agree?'

'The balance is wrong.'

'It sounds good to me.'

'It is hardly on equivalent terms,' Alistair growled, beginning to feel that things weren't going the way he wanted.

'No. But as no currency exists it will be a satisfactory trade. Besides, the definition of a mistress, Lord Dunstan, is a kept woman. And as James is on his uppers, so to speak, he can no longer afford me. I cannot be a kept woman if he has nothing with which to keep me now, can I?'

'And what kind of man is it that allows his mistress to prostitute herself in this manner?' he said harshly.

Louisa shrugged. 'James doesn't know—and he would be outraged if he did,' she admitted. 'But that night at Lady Bricknell's he lost everything to you, Lord Dunstan. Unless he can raise the four thousand guineas to settle his IOU, he will have to sell his estate, and if that is not sufficient to cover the debt then he will find himself in the debtors' prison.'

Alistair's lips twisted with irony. 'Should that be the case, then considering the Fleet is full of men in similar situations to himself he will find himself in company conducive to his own.'

Alistair leaned against the balustrade and continued to study Louisa intently. 'You bewitch me, Miss Divine,' he confessed after a moment, in a rather blunt manner. 'Absolutely. I've never met a woman quite like you.'

'No two people are the same, Lord Dunstan.'

'From the moment I saw you I have not been able to get you out of my mind. No woman has had this effect on me in a long time—and I've known a lot of women.'

Louisa became quite still, all her instincts telling her to turn away, that he was capable of inflicting on her the kind of emotional damage that she'd suffered the moment she'd realised James had brought them to ruin.

'You flatter me, Lord Dunstan.'

'Do you have many gentlemen friends?'

'No. I'm usually too busy to do much socialising. And you? Do you have many lady friends?'

'Plenty. That way one doesn't become involved.'

'That can lead to you becoming lonely.'

'And so can being too busy, which is why I think we should get to know each other better. I'm not usually so nonchalant about such things. Usually I take a woman and enjoy her company, but all too soon I become bored with her. I have a distinct feeling you will never bore me, Miss Divine, which is why I am prepared to spend a fortune to have you. I would set you up in your own house in a respectable district. You would have your own horses and carriage and servants. I promise you you would find me more than generous and want for nothing.'

'I do not care for those kind of presents, Lord Dunstan. I am not an innocent to be carried away by your charms and wealth—and nor am I like the other ladies whose company you keep, who hang around eager to incur your influence, impressed by your wealth and magnificent house. Those things mean nothing to me.'

'And what about their owner? Are you not tempted to know me better?'

'It—it is true, I hardly know you,' she faltered.

'We could soon remedy that. I think you would find it interest-ing to discover more.'

'I am sure you are right, Lord Dunstan,' she replied, trying to still the rapid beating of her heart.

'Perhaps you are afraid, is that it?'

'No, not at all,' she answered coolly.

'I am glad to hear it. But I should tell you that I am not like James Fraser.'

'That I do know. The two of you are worlds apart. However, despite wanting to help James, Lord Dunstan, I am no easy con-quest. You know my terms.'

'And are they not open to negotiation?'

'No. For four thousand guineas I will spend one night with you. No more.'

His eyes narrowed with disapproval. 'Oh, I think I would want more than that if I am to pay such a vast sum of money.'

'Take it or leave it, Lord Dunstan,' Louisa said, her voice low and direct, her lovely eyes challenging.

Alistair frowned. He had to give her credit, he thought to him-self, fighting down a rush of disgust. At least she was honest about what she wanted. She couldn't have been plainer. And, in retro-spect, he had to respect her honesty and courage if not her stan-dards.

Unable to resist her challenge, his eyes became hard and he smiled slightly with self-assurance. If she believed that after one night spent in his arms she would be able to walk away and forget him she was mistaken. As his body as well as his brain began to respond to what was being offered, he was aware of the pleasure to be obtained, of what her mouth would feel like, the silk of her firm yet supple body in his arms, moulded to his, and he was even more aware of the danger he would be courting: making Miss Divine his mistress would, unlike all the other faceless women who had gone before—except one—be no five-minute affair. She was not a woman to be tumbled, enjoyed and forgotten.

But his desire to possess her was so strong he could not resist her. He was determined to have her, whatever the price, his instinct telling him she would be well worth it.

'I must say, you drive a very shrewd bargain.'

'Perhaps that is because I know my own worth, Lord Dunstan.'

'Spoken like a true professional,' Alistair said coolly, the implications making Louisa squirm. 'But what if I don't like your terms? What if I consider you too expensive?'

'That would be regrettable. In this instance money is my object,' she replied softly.

'Of course. In your profession what you do and money are inseparable partners.'

There was a sardonic emphasis to his words and he saw two high spots of colour form on her cheeks. A series of emotions passed over her face, darkening her eyes which settled themselves into icy politeness.

'That is often the case,' she answered, her anger warring with her pride. 'But I have told you that I am no whore,' she said, her resentment at his preconceived notions firming her voice which was on the verge of shaking.

'You mean you don't make a habit of selling yourself?'

'No—and it may surprise you to know that this is the first time.'

'Then I can only conclude that you must care a great deal for Mr Fraser to be prepared to make such a sacrifice,' said Alistair, jealousy searing through him with the force of a butcher's knife, wondering why it should matter so much.

'Yes, a great deal, as it happens.'

Alistair nodded, moving closer, determined that by the time he had finished with her all thoughts of James Fraser would have been wiped clean from her mind.

The closer Lord Dunstan came, and struggling desperately to ignore the sensual pull he was exerting on her and his sexual magnetism, which was overwhelming, despite the panic that was welling up inside her Louisa forced her mind to remain in control. She sensed he was becoming irritated by her refusal to be swayed from her firm stance and that pleased her.

With his incredible good looks and potent male allure, and wealth beyond her imagination, he thought he only had to snap his fingers and any woman he took a fancy to would fall willingly into his bed. Well, he would see she was different from the others and would not so easily succumb to his charms. Men like Alistair Dunstan weren't used to being bested by a woman. It did not sit well with him and she hoped it would strengthen his desire to possess her. But she was perplexed by the strength of the emotions he evoked in her, and, try as she might, she could not shake off the effect he was having on her.

'Then what can I say?' Alistair said, his eyes compelling as they looked down into hers of velvety softness. 'If I am to spend four thousand guineas on one night of love, at least give me a sample of what I am to expect—so I can be assured I shall receive value for my money.'

Alistair's eyes captured Louisa's, a lazy, seductive smile passing across his handsome face, curling his lips, and against her will she felt herself being drawn towards him, knowing she should step back and walk away, but she was too inexperienced and affected by him to do that. Belated warning bells screamed through her head and her eyes became fixed on his finely sculptured mouth as he came closer still, and to her helpless horror she knew he was going to kiss her.

She was trapped and she knew it. She was mesmerised by him, like a moth to a flame, and she felt her heart suddenly start pounding in a quite unpredictable manner. He was looking into her eyes, holding her spellbound, weaving some magic web around her from which there was no escape.

'Come here,' Alistair said huskily, 'and show me.'

The darkening of his eyes, the naked passion she saw in their depths, seemed to work a strange spell on her, but it was his tone and not his words that conquered her, and, without knowing what she was doing, obediently she found herself moving into his arms, her entire body beginning to tremble with desire and fear. There was nothing she could do to still the quiver of anticipation as he lowered his head and covered her mouth with his own.

The shock of his lips on hers was one of wild, indescribable sweetness and sensuality as he claimed a kiss of violent tenderness, evoking feelings she had never felt before. Imprisoned by his protective embrace and seduced by his mouth and strong, caressing hands, which slid down the curve of her spine to the swell of her buttocks and back to her arms, her neck, burning wherever they touched, Louisa clung to him, her body responding eagerly, melting with the primitive sensations that went soaring through her,

her lips beginning to move against his with increasing abandon as she fed his hunger, unwittingly increasing it.

Feeling all her resistance, all her will begin to crumble and disintegrate, the moment was one of madness, and she said good-bye to any last-minute doubts she might have had about giving herself to him to pay James's debt. The sweetness of the kiss, of yielding to it, of willingly parting her soft lips for his searching tongue, made her confused with longing. Unconsciously, and too naive to know how to hide her feelings, her arm rose and slid over his wide, masculine shoulders and she slipped her hand behind his neck, a movement which, in her inexperience, was an act of pure instinct to Louisa, unaware that to Alistair it convinced him further that she was no different from any of the other women under his roof.

When he finally drew his mouth from hers an eternity later, Louisa reluctantly surfaced from the glorious Eden where he had sent her, her face suffused with languor and passion, her eyes luminous.

'Now you know how much I want you,' he murmured, his lips close to hers, his breath warm and caressing, well satisfied with her response, knowing it would be no great effort persuading her to become his mistress despite the devotion she felt for James Fraser. 'And you want me. Admit it.'

Too naive to hide her feelings, Louisa stared up at him, her face like an open book for him to read. She had discovered in being with him, in being kissed by him, what it was like to be violently attracted to a man without loving him, and that came in her category of wantonness. Heat scorched through her body when she met his dark, smouldering eyes which studied her, feature by feature, as though he could not gaze enough.

He finally released her, breaking the slender, fragile thread that had held them together a moment before—fragile yet invisibly binding, for Louisa would never be able to forget. The combination of perplexing emotions that engulfed her left her paralysed. Hot, embarrassed colour covered her cheeks as they faced each other, their breathing ragged.

'Come,' he said, taking her hand. 'We must go back. You say you are to leave London very soon. How soon?'

'Next week.'

'Then you will come to me here on Saturday. Is that agreed?'

Louisa looked at him with a level gaze, unable to believe she had been victorious, that she had captured her enemy, but when she looked into his mesmerising, vivid blue eyes she had a peculiar feeling that she was the victim, that because of the emotions he had succeeded in awakening inside her, emotions and desires which had left her wanting more, she was like a poor, helpless rabbit caught in a snare. His words went through her like a flame and her face flushed immediately. Her purpose was still strong, and yet she doubted.

Swallowing hard, she nodded. 'Yes.'

'Then it is settled. I am not by nature a man cut out for waiting and the two nights between will be an agony, but,' he said, starting to walk back inside the house, 'I will manage to survive, knowing I will have you at the end of it. And I will have you,' he said, pausing in his stride and looking down at her, raising her hand to his lips. 'That I promise. But come,' he said. 'There is something I want you to have before we return to the others, something I know you will appreciate.'

Puzzled, Louisa followed him into a room lined with books, a huge desk covered with neatly stacked papers and folders in the centre. Going to it, he opened a drawer and took out a small package which he handed to her. Louisa looked at him questioningly, wondering what it could be.

'Open it,' he said softly. 'It's a gift—and, I would like to think, the first of many. Perhaps it will atone for any offence I might have caused you when we met at Mr Brewster's.'

Louisa removed the paper to discover a small book, a brand-new volume of poetry by William Collins, the very same book she had been hoping to purchase at Mr Brewster's bookshop when she had encountered Lord Dunstan.

'Oh,' she gasped, fingering the beautiful leather binding, flattered to know he had been thinking of her when they had parted—and she with such anger. 'What can I say? It's beautiful—thank you. I shall treasure it always.'

Alistair smiled when he saw her delight. 'Perhaps you will think of me whenever you read one of Mr Collins's poems. But don't thank me now. Save your appreciation for Saturday night,' he said softly, meaningfully, his smile widening when he saw her cheeks flush rose-pink and confusion leap into her glorious eyes. Lowering his head, he again captured her lips, feeling them open and yield their sweetness. Cupping her breast, he felt the hardening of her nipple, despite the covering fabric of her gown, and he could tell that, for all the unusual circumstances, he would have a responsive lover in this woman he so desired.

'Come,' he said, lifting his mouth from hers. 'I am sure our absence has been noticed and commented upon, so I think we should be getting back.'

Together they returned to the others, Louisa engulfed with so many conflicting emotions, she had never been so confused in her life. Holding the volume of poetry in her hand, she felt a curious warmth for the man who had given it to her—the man she had every reason to despise.

Something had happened to her that she had not bargained for. She had never for one moment imagined a kiss could be like that, and she could not deny that she was attracted to Alistair Dunstan in a way that astounded her. If she was not careful she would be in danger of falling into a trap of her own making and becoming sidetracked from the real purpose of her visit here tonight, making her doubt that once she had accomplished her goal on Saturday night she would be able to walk away with her emotions intact.

Every eye in the room turned towards them when they entered, and as Louisa's gaze swept over them she saw that every face was secretly smiling, sneering. Knowing perfectly well what they were all thinking, she was suddenly sick with shame and disgust, feeling that she was trapped in a bad dream and wishing passionately that she was elsewhere, that she was back home at Bierlow and had never come to London. Alistair turned to speak to one of his guests, unaware of Louisa's torment, of how she was frantically trying to think of a way of extricating herself from the room. Thankfully Timothy, who had been anxiously watching for her return, came to her rescue.

'Ah, here you are, Louisa,' he said, causing Lord Dunstan to turn back to them when he heard Timothy speak her name, not having known she was called Louisa until that moment. 'Come, let me get you some refreshment. Please excuse us, Lord Dunstan.'

'Of course.' Courteously he bowed his head to Louisa, his eyes narrowing with displeasure when he saw Timothy put his arm around her waist and draw her away, jealousy and anger searing through him like a knife at the familiarity of that possessive gesture. But his face gave no indication as to the violence of his feelings. It was the face which had won him many a game of chance, for it showed not a flicker of emotion nor an inkling of his thoughts, and Louisa would have been both surprised and shocked to learn that, at that moment, he would have settled any sum she cared to name to ensure no man other than himself ever touched her again.

So far she had given nothing away, and Alistair strongly suspected she guarded her privacy fiercely, but he could not rid himself of the feeling that behind the exquisitely beautiful façade there lurked another woman—one quite different.

'Thank you for rescuing me,' Louisa said to Timothy as he led her to where James was lounging with a merry group across the room, her insides still quaking over what had just taken place between herself and Lord Dunstan.

'My pleasure,' he replied in a low, urgent voice. 'But stop looking like a frightened rabbit and smile at me. Everyone's watching you. You must know what they're thinking—what they're saying. You and Lord Dunstan have been gone so long the gossip has started already. Don't look so humble, otherwise these people will eat you alive. James is not at all pleased at the attention you've drawn to yourself, and to him.'

Beneath half-lowered lashes Louisa glanced once more at the company around her, wretchedly wanting to lash out at those leering, smirking, painted faces. Instead, she clenched her teeth and shut her ears to the speculative conversation and pulled herself together, composing her features into a serene mask and favouring Timothy with her most ravishing smile.

'What happened?' he asked. 'Did you succeed in propositioning our host?'

'Yes,' she whispered. 'He agreed to my terms.'

'And?'

'I am to return here on Saturday,' she answered, her expression bland as she looked straight ahead, seeing James leave the group he was with and come towards her, fixing her with a hard, reproving glare.

'Where have you been?' he muttered angrily, careful not to draw further attention to themselves by openly displaying his displeasure as everyone began to turn away. 'How dare you make such a ridiculous display of yourself? Have you any idea what people are saying? It's not like you to act so brazenly. Your behaviour is highly reprehensible, Louisa, and I insist we leave this very minute,' he said. Her conduct had sobered him up and he sounded unaccustomedly assertive, having been humiliated and made to look a fool by his sister, who everyone took to be his mistress—and one who had shamelessly deserted him for a man of more handsome looks and means.

'Lord Dunstan has just been showing me his house, James.' Louisa smiled, speaking lightly in an attempt to humour him. 'That is all—and nothing to get so worked up about.'

'I think you should wait a while before you leave, James,' said Timothy. 'If you leave now you will only give credence to what people are saying.'

Wishing to avoid further gossip, reluctantly James agreed to do just that. 'Very well. If you say so then I suppose we must. But half an hour. No more. Besides,' he said sullenly, taking a large gulp of brandy, 'there's little pleasure to be had when the tables are barred to me.'

Chapter Five

With a sigh, Louisa excused herself and went to find the room which had been set aside for the ladies, eager to relax for a few moments away from inquisitive eyes. It wasn't until then that she realised she was still holding the book Lord Dunstan had given her, and, finding the room empty, without even a maid on duty, with a little smile she seated herself in a chair and began to flick through the pages, eager for the time when she would be able to read it properly.

At that moment the door opened and someone came in. Looking up, Louisa saw it was Lady Bricknell, and she had a peculiar feeling that she had followed her into the room. Over the years Lady Bricknell had acquired a formidable presence, tall and statuesque, her strong, handsome features bearing down on any challenge with icy authority, and she was clearly a force to be reckoned with. She was, Louisa thought, dressed in the most garish taste, but her presence was undeniable.

Louisa rose, closing her book and smoothing her skirts, intending to leave, but Lady Bricknell put out a bejewelled hand and stopped her, her shrewd eyes assessing her from a tranquil face.

'Don't go, my dear. I've been waiting for the opportunity to be introduced to you all evening. As you've no doubt gathered by now, I am Lady Bricknell—and you are Miss Divine, I believe?' she said, without reservation.

'That is correct,' said Louisa, glancing at her uncertainly, having already wondered about the nature of Lady Bricknell's connection with Lord Dunstan, suspecting they were frequently in each other's presence.

'How curious. Forgive me for asking, but is that your real name?'

'Why would it not be?'

Lady Bricknell's eyes twinkled with mischief. 'Oh, no reason. It just strikes me as being a little theatrical, that is all. And you need not tell me your real name if you prefer to keep it a secret.' She smiled, lowering her tone in happy complicity. 'I would rather remain in ignorance than be fobbed off with a falsehood. You are here with Mr Fraser?'

'Yes,' said Louisa, beginning to relax, finding Lady Bricknell not at all as she had expected. Her tone was warm and when she smiled it was quite entrancing. In her mid-thirties, she was still at the height of her beauty, in a certain style, and it was not difficult to see why she was such a popular figure.

'Then it is monstrously unfair of him to have deprived us of your company for so long. However, I have to confess that I've been watching you and I can tell this isn't to your taste. You cast your eye over us as if we are a crowd of vacuous idiots, and, speaking for at least half the company here tonight—' she chuckled, patting her vivid red hair into place as she glanced quickly at her reflection in the mirror, the jewels on her fingers catching the light and casting dancing patterns on the walls '—I have to say you are not wrong. You must have seen for yourself that most of the guests are vapid, full of endless, empty twitterings.'

'I apologise if I give that impression. It is not my intention to appear rude or to give offence.'

'I'm sure it isn't, my dear,' Lady Bricknell said kindly. 'You are extremely lovely, and I find it strange that we have not seen you at any of the functions before now.'

'That is because I have only recently arrived from Surrey.'

'Then that explains it. It is easy to see why Alistair is so taken with you—despite the fact that you are not free.'

Louisa paled and stared at her. 'I—I beg your pardon?'

'I know Alistair too well, my dear. He is always appreciative of a beautiful woman. The way he looks at you with particular interest tells me he has singled you out. In fact, you are the first woman he has shown a serious interest in since that unfortunate affair with his wife. He is susceptible and you are attractive.' She looked at Louisa searchingly. 'And you are attracted to him, otherwise you would not have left us all to be alone with him for such a long time. Is that not so?'

Louisa stared at her mutely, and Lady Bricknell could read, by the sudden colour that sprang to her cheeks and the confusion in her eyes, that she had hit upon the truth.

'You must think me frightfully inquisitive and outspoken,' she went on, a faint glint of anxiety showing behind the bland smile, 'and you must forgive me, but do not be mistaken by all this. Unlike many men of Alistair's background, he is a private man and stays away from frivolous intrigues, even though several ladies have made their availability known to him. Let's face it, he's got the kind of mesmerising looks and charm that would make him a lady-killer if he wished. Women find him irresistible. Oh, he is a man of consummate experience and has not been without his amorous affairs, but the reality is somewhat different.'

'Why are you telling me this, Lady Bricknell?' Louisa asked, her features impassive.

'Because you are not like the rest. You're different. I can see that, and I should hate to see you get burned. My instinct tells me you do not altogether understand the way of the world or society as we do—and, as someone who knows it only too well, take my advice and return to the country.'

'I understand things much better than you think, Lady Bricknell,' Louisa said quietly, looking at her steadily. 'Are you sure it is not because you want Lord Dunstan for yourself?' she dared to venture.

Instead of being angry, Lady Bricknell smiled broadly and chuckled, her eyes twinkling with merriment, dispelling any notion Louisa had that she and Lord Dunstan's relationship was anything other than platonic.

'Oh, my dear—you really are quite naïve, aren't you?' she said, not unkindly. 'Anyone who knows me will tell you that any passion that was between Alistair and myself burned itself out many years ago, long before it even started, in fact—and I am much too old for him.'

'You do yourself an injustice, Lady Bricknell. Looking as beautiful as you do,' smiled Louisa, 'I do not believe that for a moment.'

Appreciative of the compliment, Lady Bricknell's eyes danced. 'You are extremely generous and a flatterer, my dear. Thank you. However,' she said, on a more serious note, looking at Louisa intently, 'Alistair and I remain friends—good friends—which cannot be said of most women of his acquaintance. You're flattered by his attentions, I know. Every woman is whom Alistair deems to cast his eye over. He is marked with a proud arrogance and an indomitable will, and I advise you to think very carefully before becoming involved with him. I am saying this for your sake as well as his.'

'You—you mentioned his wife?' Louisa asked tentatively.

'Yes. She hurt him desperately. It is a subject he always avoids talking about, but since that time he has held virtually every woman he has come into contact with in contempt, regarding them as being irrelevant—both dispensable and replaceable. If you are drawn into an affair with him, and find yourself wanting to remain with him, take care—because when a woman becomes possessive he quickly becomes unobtainable. His liberty is too important to him at present. I would not wish to see you get hurt.'

'Thank you, Lady Bricknell. I appreciate your concern—but, being a stranger to you, I am somewhat puzzled by it.'

For a moment Lady Bricknell was silent as she regarded Louisa a little sadly, and then she said, 'Yes, I am sure you are. It's just that you seem so young and innocent. I wanted to warn you before it is too late.'

'Thank you, but I am no woolly-headed milksop come to town for a few days, so dazzled and blinded by the excitement of society and its ways that I do not see the sordid disillusionment. I am not nearly so naive as you imagine me to be, Lady Bricknell. I am experienced enough to recognise a gentleman's intentions, and to know when to step back.'

Smiling graciously, Lady Bricknell turned and walked towards the door, but then she turned and looked back with a strangely reflective, cynical smile. 'I thought so too at your age. Unfortunately, with one husband and a string of lovers behind me, I was easily tempted by a handsome face—and more so when a fortune was dangled in front of me like a carrot to a donkey. I had a dreadful habit of stepping forward instead of back, and jumping in with both feet. It would seem that I have been incapable of learning by experience to conduct my life in less turbulent waters. Goodbye, my dear.'

Louisa watched her go, strangely touched by Lady Bricknell's obvious concern for her well-being. How she would like to take her advice and return to Surrey immediately, but unfortunately it was already too late.

Louisa was quiet in the carriage taking them away from Dunstan House. The whole evening and what had transpired had left her numb. It didn't help either that her thoughts kept returning to Lord Dunstan's embrace and devastating kiss, making her aware of her own femininity, and making him appear so very desirable. How he would be as a lover was beyond her experience to imagine, but she did not believe she would be disappointed. He could not have been unaffected by their embrace either, otherwise he would not have agreed to pay the high price she had placed on herself to warm his bed.

But she was puzzled by him. He held many mysteries, mysteries she was not too eager to solve, having many qualms about the solution. He fascinated her and she could not even begin to understand the convolutions of his character.

No human being had ever made her feel like this, so at first she did not recognise the feeling. If he could render her defenceless after one kiss, causing a weakness to spread through her body like liquid fire that left her wanting more, what would she be like after sharing his bed? The memory of his burning touch, and his kiss, and the dark, hidden pleasure it had stirred within her, roused her to fresh paroxysms of desire.

He had kissed her as though he owned her—which, she thought with bitter irony, in a way he did, until after Saturday night. But could she blame him? He thought she was easy, because at their very first encounter at Bricknell House she had given him good reason to think so, and her behaviour tonight had confirmed his opinion. And had she not set out to encourage his advances yet hold him at a distance until he became mad with desire for her?

But how she would like to show him how wrong he was, that she was serious-minded and correct in every way, and that when he begged for her to go to him she would coldly turn away.

Back in Henrietta Street she said goodnight to James and entered her room, cold with memory, and with secret tears of helplessness gathering in her eyes.

When Timothy called the following morning, in the hope that Louisa would have had second thoughts about going to Dunstan House the next day, he found her alone. She was pale and the shadows around her eyes told of her sleepless night. His heart was wrung with concern and pity at her plight.

'Louisa, you must see that what you are doing is sheer madness,' he said, determined to have one last try at making her see sense. 'You're far too respectable to sully yourself in this manner. You're so young—an innocent. Lord Dunstan will eat you alive.'

She shook her head in a helpless gesture. 'I have to go through with it, Timothy. What choice have I? I am desperate.'

'Have you any idea what will happen to you—what he will expect of you?'

Louisa flushed to the roots of her hair, wanting to ask him for guidance but too embarrassed. 'I am not ignorant as to what happens between men and women—but I do admit that I have no idea how to go about being a seductress.'

Timothy looked grim. 'I don't think you'll have to seduce Lord Dunstan, Louisa. Just be your usual lovely self. I can assure you that he will do the rest,' he told her bluntly.

'At least it will be for just the one night.'

Timothy was unconvinced. 'If he is prepared to waive James's IOU for one night of love, then I very much doubt he intends for it to be a momentary diversion. I do not believe you are as resilient as you would like me to think. Will you be quite calm and able to deal with it when the time comes?'

Louisa sighed, asking herself as she had countless times throughout the night if she would be able to detach her body and mind from what was going on, what he was doing to her. Would she want to?

'I think so. I feel like an actress on the eve of a new performance, all my senses concentrated on making it a success—for on that success my own and James's survival depends. I have to make it the performance of my life, Timothy, and my instinct tells me that if I keep a level head I can do it—and survival is a question of instinct. Dear Lord, let it serve me well tomorrow night. But how am I going to escape James?'

'That is already taken care of. My parents share Amelia's fondness for James and have invited him to Kettering, our family home in Oxfordshire, for the weekend. You too, as it happens, but no doubt you can come up with some excuse to get out of it.'

Which she did, pleading a headache and telling James that with the present unhappy state of their affairs she was in no mood for socialising. James accepted this, but to her alarm she saw he was touched by a feeling of guilt that he should be prepared to embark on a jolly weekend when she was so obviously suffering from his actions.

In the end Louisa managed to persuade him to go to Oxfordshire, telling him that a short break in the country air would do him good, saying that nothing could be achieved by his remaining at home in London. So Timothy arranged to collect him first thing on Saturday morning, leaving the carriage free for her own use.

Filled with trepidation and an unfamiliar tingling of excitement due to the clandestine nature of her secret assignment, Louisa woke on Saturday morning with a clear sense of purpose, strangely relieved that the moment of her confrontation with Lord Dunstan had arrived.

Later in the day, as she prepared to go to Dunstan House, she had reason to be grateful to Timothy for procuring the two dresses that had belonged to his sister. They might not be the height of fashion, but they were not so outmoded as to appear ridiculous. In fact, they were extremely elegant and quite pretty.

She dressed with extraordinary care, and the dress she chose to wear was a violet taffeta. It had a modestly low bodice, trimmed with lace, with a waistband of deeper violet. The sleeves, also trimmed with lace, were elbow-length and the full skirt belled out over several white frilly undergarments.

Her arrival at Dunstan House was expected and she was shown inside by a servant where she was met in the hall by Alistair, who did not attempt to hide his glow of appreciation as his eyes rested on her. He was dressed in a dark green coat and grey breeches, the snowy whiteness of his elegant cravat emphasising the blueness of his eyes, and Louisa was conscious only of his magnificence and became transfixed. With his dark brown hair brushed back, his face stamped with nobility and pride and his muscular body emanating raw power, he seemed extraordinarily tall and broad-shouldered as he came towards her.

Although she was trembling inside, Louisa faced him with outward calm. He held her hand when she would have withdrawn it a moment longer, and when he looked at her she felt his eyes slide into her, turning her bones to water. Now she was faced with the situation she had a peculiar sense of inadequacy, a fear that no matter what she did or said it would seem foolish to him. Any idea she'd had of casting a spell over him, of behaving in a manner which was so very alien to her, had disintegrated the moment she stepped inside Dunstan House and saw him again.

Sensing her unease, Alistair smiled into the soft, anxious amber eyes. Never had he met a woman who had such a stranglehold on his emotions. Initially he'd believed it might be because he hadn't been amorously involved with a woman in a while, but the more he thought about it, the more he realised that it was she, herself, whom he wanted. Not only did he want her, he wanted her to want him, to banish all thoughts of James Fraser from her mind.

This worried him, because he did not intend becoming trapped in the kind of relationship he'd had with Marianne, his beautiful, unscrupulous wife, eight years ago, the kind of relationship he had thought was perfect, only to have his love and desire used against him like a treacherous weapon in her hands. Her betrayal and desertion when it came had almost destroyed him and he could not forget. Not since that time had any woman succeeded in coming close. He used them to satisfy his needs and then forgot them, casting them aside in the same callous manner as his wife had cast him aside.

But from his first encounter with Louisa Divine his instinct had told him she was not like the rest. She had become the supreme object of his desire, and her sensuality somehow seemed more potent in the demureness of her violet gown.

'Am I early or late, Lord Dunstan?' Louisa asked, finding the house strangely quiet after the laughter and frivolity of her previous visit. She tried not to let apprehension mark her features, with those disturbing eyes of his levelled on hers—eyes that were difficult to meet, their expression unforgettable. 'I was not certain what time I should come.'

'As long as you are here the time hardly matters,' he said, his voice deep, the warm, intimate look in his eyes vibrant and alarmingly alive.

'Did you think I might not?' she asked innocently, the full import of the risk she was taking by coming here making her quake inside, thinking that he was looking at her in a way that was already much too personal, too possessive.

'Oh, I knew you would,' he replied assuredly as he put his hands on her shoulders and, lowering his head, kissed her mouth, his lips soft against hers.

The kiss was so unexpected that it took Louisa completely unawares and all she could do was catch her breath quickly and stare at him. He stepped back, watching her with a kind of lazy amusement.

'How lovely you look,' he commented, his eyes travelling over her in open admiration. 'And where is Mr Fraser? I hope he is not likely to come hammering on my door to drag you away.'

'No—he won't do that. He—he is away—staying at Mr Hacket's home in Oxfordshire for the weekend.'

'I see. How very convenient. Would you care for some refreshment—some wine, perhaps?' he asked, taking her hand and leading her inside a small drawing room just off the hall.

For a moment, as their fingers touched, Louisa felt as if the warm grasp of his hand reassured and strengthened her, but what she had not expected was the sudden leap of her heart or the upsurge of eagerness that brought a sparkle to her eyes which had been absent before. She glanced up at him and saw that he was smiling at her, reading her thoughts.

'I'm not hungry—and, no, I would not like a glass of wine. Though some tea would be welcome,' she said, neither hungry nor thirsty, but thinking it would help pass the time.

'Of course. Tea it is. And please try to relax. You really have nothing to worry about.'

Louisa insisted on pouring the tea herself, finding that keeping her hands busy helped cover her confusion beneath his disquieting gaze. She handed him a cup ceremoniously and they sat quietly together while they sipped their tea, until the brightness of the late afternoon outside drew them onto the terrace, where they sat looking out over the beautiful walled garden, the everyday sounds of London only just heard from beyond.

Louisa glanced towards Alistair and saw him sitting perfectly still, watching her intently, and she felt as if in some extraordinary way time stood still. Something in his expression held her attention and she experienced a strange feeling in her innermost self that something was happening which was almost beyond her control. It was urgent and primitive, and in that moment she found it impossible to be afraid of him or even to fear what he might do. It seemed to her that in the confines of the beautiful garden, where the sun was sinking in a crimson blaze in a sky the colour of indigo, they were alone in a world that had no substance or reality.

'Have you known Mr Fraser long?' Alistair asked at length, his voice pulling Louisa from the strange spell that had seemed to enclose them.

'Some considerable time,' she replied softly. 'And you?'

'I confess we are not well acquainted. In fact I know very little about his background. He is from Surrey, I believe, with a modest estate.'

'That is correct. His parents' death several years ago left him impoverished, and the only way poor James could raise some money was to resort to gaming—which, as you well know,' she said truthfully, with a reluctant smile flickering round the corners of her mouth, trying to sound light-hearted while her heart ached for her brother, 'he does not do at all well. Unfortunately it has become a compulsion. Not all who gamble are blessed with your genius, Lord Dunstan.'

'I am not invincible. I don't always win.'

'No, I don't suppose you do. But then, you can afford to lose, whereas four thousand guineas is astronomical to James.'

'Then all the more important that it is returned to him. But there are other kinds of gambling,' he said quietly.

'Oh? Such as?'

'Right now I am gambling on you. Are you worth four thousand guineas for one night of love?'

Louisa met his gaze. 'I'm afraid that is something I cannot answer, Lord Dunstan. Only you can decide that.'

'Then I shall let you know tomorrow,' Alistair said, rising. Taking her hand, he pulled her to her feet. 'Come, let me show you the garden before the light fades. And my name is Alistair. If we are to spend the night together I find it absurd that I have to go on calling you Miss Divine. I think we can dispense with the formalities, don't you? Your name is Louisa, is that not so?'

There was a caressing note in his voice and Louisa's face scorched crimson at his reference to the night to come, realising that not for one moment would he allow her to lose sight of what would come later—what he expected of her. 'Yes,' she replied, glad of the opportunity to change the subject. She didn't want to talk about James.

Walking beside Alistair, Louisa was becoming increasingly aware of him. There was a slow, sensuous laziness to his movements that was contradicted by the dangerously hard lines of his handsome face and the flashing blueness of his eyes, which, no matter how covertly she looked at him, seemed always to be studying her. He was like a beautiful large cat, poised and ready to pounce. She was rapt by his sheer animal magnetism. It made her feel uneasy, yet strangely excited and vulnerable.

'You spend some considerable time at Westminster, I believe?' said Louisa.

'Yes—more than usual with the war against France dominating every debate. It is the main reason why I keep this house on. I would much rather spend my time at Huntswood—my home in Sussex—but it is important that I take my seat in the Lords, especially at this time.'

'Tell me about Lady Bricknell?' Louisa asked. 'I have never met anyone quite like her.'

'And you are not likely to again. She is a remarkable woman. Despite her appearance and the fact that she is indubitably a hedonist, being a lover of pleasure in all its aspects and dimensions, she will not enjoy them if there is not some spark of intelligence or spirit to intrigue her—which is why writers such as Johnson and Garrick and painters like Gainsborough and Reynolds are numbered among her wide circle of friends.'

'And in that are you two of a kind?'

Alistair smiled, his blue eyes alight with irony. 'I suppose you could say that.'

'And have you been acquainted long?'

'Yes. There is a camaraderie between us that springs from long acquaintance. We first became acquainted through her late husband, who was a very close friend of mine, and more so when I was at a time in my life when I needed a friend,' he said softly, a distant look entering his eyes as his memory took him back to a time Louisa knew nothing about. 'She is always fun to be with,' he went on quickly, 'pleasure-loving, confident, spirited—and with a tolerance for understanding and compassion when dealing with others.'

'She certainly seems to be a popular figure,' Louisa remarked.

'She is indeed. I think you will find that the reason people love her is because she's so irreverent and brutally honest.'

'And, I shouldn't wonder, because she throws the most exotic parties.' Louisa smiled impishly.

'That, too,' Alistair grinned.

The ease with which Alistair talked, and his manner, relieved Louisa from restraint and she began to relax, her nervousness and apprehension forgotten as they strolled along the paths. A short while in his company was already beginning to have an effect on her, making her feel that they had known each other a long time. He had a subtle way of drawing her out of herself, encouraging her to talk, and as the evening progressed and unfolded they became excited by each other's company, by their experience of coming together.

They discussed topics of interest to them both—politics, art, books and their creators—which Louisa soon realised were a major force in his life. He was the most open-minded man she had ever

met, making her see books and paintings she thought she knew in
a completely different light.

'You are extremely knowledgeable on these matters,' Louisa
commented when they were seated opposite each other at a table
impeccably set for two in the dining room, the atmosphere warm
and intimate.

Alistair smiled as the servant set the delicious food before them,
before discreetly leaving them alone.

'Initiated by the Grand Tour of Europe my father insisted I
experience when I was a young man,' he explained. 'He considered it an important, if not an essential part of my education when
I left Oxford, lecturing me at length before I left about how I had
to spend my time mastering foreign languages and gaining knowledge in the customs and cultures of our continental neighbours,
rather than enjoying myself in idleness, as so often happens.' He
smiled. 'For myself, I would much rather have remained at home
in Sussex learning how to run the estate.'

'But your travels around Europe must have broadened your
mind and developed and influenced your taste for foreign culture?'

'Yes, they did, but as it turned out my father died when I was
in Germany, and I had to return home early and get on with the
everyday running of the house and the estate. Having the farming
and forestry to see to, and other ancillary work, as well as three
villages to oversee, proved to be a colossal task.'

'And yet you still manage to spend a considerable amount of
your time in London, otherwise—as you say—you would not have
need of this very fine house,' Louisa commented.

'Westminster does take up a considerable amount of my time—
and I do have several other business commitments that cannot be
attended to in Sussex. However, I do have two extremely capable
bailiffs and agents to take care of the estate when I'm absent.'

The meal went quickly as Louisa asked him about the countries
he had visited, fascinated by the ease of their conversation and the
strangeness of having it. He talked with relish and held her rapt
with sparkling tales of his travels so that she could almost smell
the scented breezes of the Mediterranean. She listened in fascination to stories of his adventures and experiences in France and
the states of Italy, marvelling when he told her of the splendour

and treasures of Florence and Rome, and trying to imagine the beauty of the Swiss mountains and German states, of the individuality of the many people he had met. She drank in his words, glowing with wonder and a little light-headed from the few sips of unaccustomed wine she allowed herself to drink.

His tastes were many and varied and he was extremely knowledgeable about most things, answering her questions and listening to her comments with interest, speaking to her as an equal and enjoying the debate when her opinion differed from his own, laughing when the discussion was in danger of becoming heated.

'I am truly amazed at the people you know,' Louisa sighed enviously, 'from peers of the realm to poets, artists and writers, members of an avant-garde, people who explore the territory I find so interesting. I am beginning to see them and their society in a new way that distinguishes what they do from my own endeavours. You live an interesting life, Alistair.'

'I try my best,' he murmured, a smile moving across his lean features. 'You must feel free to borrow as many books as you like from my library. I have a considerable range for you to choose from—although it is not as extensive as the library at Huntswood. But I am sure there will be something to suit your taste.'

'Thank you. You are very kind. But I must decline your generous offer.'

'Might I ask why?' His eyes were gently enquiring.

'Because after tomorrow we shall never see each other again.'

'And you are sure of that, are you?'

'Yes. Quite sure.'

Alistair's face became set in lines which were quite unreadable, but his blue eyes danced as much as to say he didn't believe her for one moment. However, he did not pursue the subject.

After the meal they drifted back into the drawing room, sitting across from each other on either side of the fireplace. A fire glowed in the hearth, the evening having turned cool, and the soft glow of candlelight cast a little pool of intimacy around them.

'You are fortunate in being born male,' said Louisa, continuing the conversation, putting his offer to borrow books from his library and her blunt refusal from her mind. 'With no questions asked you are able to travel, to meet people of different races—generally to do as you please. It seems monstrously unfair to me that the same privileges cannot be accorded to both sexes.'

'I have to agree, that does appear to be the way of things—and, as you say, it is grossly unfair. And what is your definition of a woman's role in life, Louisa?' Alistair asked with a lazy smile.

'Oh, to marry and have children,' she said in a matter-of-fact way. 'To take care of the home and live her life in unwholesome, repressed domesticity—and to be a modest, silent, obedient help-mate to her husband.'

Alistair threw back his head and laughed aloud, and Louisa realised that when he did that he seemed much younger than when his face was in repose.

'Modest, silent, obedient helpmate,' he repeated with consider-able amusement. 'Somehow I feel you are ill suited to the part. You may look fragile and weak—yet, if the truth be told, I believe you are as strong and determined as the most obstinate mule.'

'Now you are teasing me.' Louisa reprimanded him gently, find-ing herself quite intrigued by this confounding man as her mouth trembled into a smile to match his own, and she realised how her antipathy towards him seemed to have melted away in the most curious way. Listening to him, enjoying his company, she had come completely under his spell, hopelessly vulnerable to him. 'But I do think that marriage should be a partnership, where all things are shared equally between husband and wife.'

The amusement vanished from Alistair's eyes and they became serious, probing and questioning. 'And what is your lot in life, Louisa?' he asked quietly.

A look of regret entered her eyes. 'Oh, I would have it better,' she murmured softly, with more feeling put into those few words than she realised and which Alistair detected, making him curious as to her background, realising that he still knew nothing about her whatsoever.

'But what better guardian of that abode than a gentle woman who is in love with her husband?' he said softly.

Louisa's expression became wistful. 'I have never been in love.'

'Not even with Mr Fraser?'

'No—at least—not in the sense you mean. But you have,' she dared to say with frank curiosity, smiling—the kind of smile that warmed and lit up her lovely eyes, the kind of smile that elicited confidence and drew a response.

Instead of closing up, of guarding his privacy, as Louisa had expected on recalling her conversation with Lady Bricknell, when she had told her how hurt he had been by his wife's desertion and how he never spoke of her, Alistair settled his steady gaze on her thoughtfully, feeling gregarious and communicative in a way he had not felt in a long time. If he was surprised by her comment he did not show it.

'Oh? Who told you?'

'Lady Bricknell. You were married. You must have been in love with your wife.'

His expression became grim and pain passed across his features. From his expression Louisa sensed that it had been a turbulent relationship, but the pain she'd seen vanished and his features were already perfectly composed when he looked at her.

'I was in love, I admit it.' He hesitated, and for a moment Louisa thought he wasn't going to say any more. When he did, his voice was quiet, hesitant, almost as if he was testing his ability to talk about it, making her already regret having mentioned his wife. 'But love makes fools of us all. It blinds one to someone's shortcomings and warps one's judgement. I was young and naive, taken in by the first beautiful face I saw. I was twenty-one at the time we met—Marianne, my wife, a little older. Unfortunately things did not turn out as I hoped. I admit I saw the warning lights before we married.'

'Then why did you not heed them?'

He looked across at her. 'I never could resist a challenge—especially when the gauntlet has been thrown down by a woman as beautiful as Marianne.'

'Even though you might get burnt? As you evidently were.'

'And why do you say that, pray?'

'Lady Bricknell told me how much your wife hurt you and that since that time you have regarded every woman with contempt—considering them both dispensable and replaceable.'

'Good Lord! You make it sound as though I am motivated by desire and nothing else. You must have had quite a conversation with Lady Bricknell,' Alistair remarked with considerable amusement.

'Yes, I did.'

'At least one good thing came out of my marriage to Marianne.'

'And do you mind if I ask what that was?'

'My son.'

Chapter Six

Louisa stared at Alistair in astonishment, remembering the little boy she had seen him with in St James's Park.

'Your son! Was that the little boy who was with you in St James's Park?'

'Yes. His name is Mark. The young lady was my sister, Sophie, and, as you know, the other lady was my older sister, Julia. She is married to Sir Joshua Gresham and lives at Richmond. Mark is staying with them at this time and I had just taken him to see the parade at Horse Guards.'

'I see. But, if we can return to Marianne, just because one woman did you wrong there is no need to punish the rest.'

'I don't.'

'That's not the way I see it.'

'Oh! And how do you see it, may I ask?'

'That perhaps your retreat from marriage—from happiness—is your defence against reality.'

'And how can you assume that happiness automatically comes with marriage?'

Louisa sighed. 'I can't, I suppose. But Lady Bricknell made it plain that you regard women through a chink in your invisible armour. In fact, if you did not enjoy having fun so much I would advise you to become a monk,' she chided gently. 'When something like that happens to a person it's a bit like falling off a horse. Whereas you have lost your nerve and would no doubt have it shot, others climb right back into the saddle and get on with it.'

'Like you?' he said softly, referring to the way she had rallied to James Fraser's rescue the minute James had found himself on the brink of penury.

'Yes,' she replied calmly, meeting his steady, all-too-knowing gaze. 'Like me. Did you love your wife very much?'

'I thought I did—in fact, for a time she was the centre of my existence. Yet she did not reach my mind or touch me spiritually. I made a mistake—but I had to experience living with her to realise it. I well remember my ecstasy, the wonder of it. I also remember the doubt, the bewilderment that came after, followed by the pain and torment the knowledge of the truth brought me when she was disloyal—and the brutality and the struggle for self-preservation that came when she went.'

He fell silent, and his eyes fastened on a sudden spark that flamed and danced out of the glowing embers of the fire, but Louisa, glancing sideways at him, thought he did not see it. As she watched him a faint frown seemed to slide over his face like a dark shadow, and again she was made to regret having mentioned his wife.

'I'm sorry. I—I hope you didn't mind me mentioning your wife. I always talk too much when I'm excited.'

He looked at her and met her eyes, staring at her for a moment, and then he shrugged and smiled, the moment of melancholy having passed. He settled his gaze on her face, noticing the way her hair glowed like the dancing flame in the hearth, how it shone with an inner light, making his hands ache to gather it up and feel it slip through his fingers.

'No. It all happened a long time ago. I have no reason to hide anything. It is better to speak of such things than keep them hidden,' he said, but Louisa saw his eyes held more seriousness than his voice, which told her it still affected him more than he would have her or anyone else know. There was a host of questions she wanted to ask him about his wife—about her relationship with Sir Charles Meredith—but his expression forbade it. She was curious to know what had happened to her and the nature of her betrayal. However, not wishing to probe further into what was obviously an extremely sensitive matter, she declined to ask.

'But I shall never marry again,' he went on, his words and his eyes conveying a message. 'I am not looking for a wife.'

The message received, Louisa smiled, her eyes teasing when she looked at him, trying to dispel the constraint that was in danger of tainting the atmosphere between them.

'Especially not when you have already been provided with an heir to leave your ancestral pile in Sussex to?'

'Precisely,' he smiled, picking up the bait and beginning to relax once more, finding her company both stimulating and charming. 'I have an heir in Mark. So perhaps you can understand why I am content to remain as I am, to go my own way and to enjoy being pursued by those who desire the title of Lady Dunstan and the prestige that goes with it.'

'And always careful to elude capture,' said Louisa softly.

'Always. You are beginning to know me a little too well, Louisa,' he said, sitting back in his chair and regarding her closely. 'However, I have talked a great deal about myself and as yet I know absolutely nothing about you. Who are you, Miss Divine?' he asked softly. 'And why do I have this peculiar feeling that you are the one who is being evasive?'

'Because I am. It's best this way,' she answered, averting her eyes, beginning to feel uncomfortable beneath his much too penetrating, enquiring gaze, feeling the atmosphere changing between them to one of warm, vibrant intimacy.

'You are a strange young woman, Louisa. I find your company both pleasurable and enlightening.'

'Thank you, although I suspect you prefer the company of an intelligent woman—a woman who is a conversationalist rather than one who has nothing to say except yes and no.'

'Aye,' he laughed, his eyes twinkling. 'But there are those whose belief it is that a man is better pleased when a good dinner is placed before him than when his wife spouts Italian or Greek—as my good friend Samuel Johnson has often said.'

'And who will agree with Milton's view that woman was created for man,' said Louisa drily.

Alistair shook his head with a rueful smile. 'You are more intelligent than most women of my acquaintance, and if you are not careful you will have me falling in love with a woman's mind—

but her physical attributes cannot be ignored,' he murmured, his gaze languidly sweeping over her, his eyes settling on the gentle mounds of her breasts straining beneath the violet dress, measuring, lingering, a slow smile curving his lips.

The soft sincerity in his voice, the tone of it, rippled over Louisa's skin and took her breath away; behind the words she detected an intractable force, coercing, seducing, and she was drawn to it, remembering her purpose for being there. She frantically tried to think of something to say, something light that would restore the easy camaraderie and repartee of a moment before, but it was beyond her wit to do that and so she could only stare at him and draw a long, shaking breath.

Alistair smiled. 'You are not only beautiful and clever but mysterious also. Allow me to give you a word of advice. Be careful what you express with your eyes, Louisa. They are far too eloquent. Being a man of the world, I am quick to interpret their language. I may know nothing concerning your background but, in the short time we have known each other, I have come to know a great deal about you as a person—and by tomorrow morning I hope to know a good deal more.

'In your eagerness to relieve Mr Fraser of his desperate plight you have elected to sell yourself to set the matter right. My instinct tells me that such behaviour is not your forte, and, if I were the gentleman I am reputed to be, I would bow before your admirable sacrifice and send you away unsullied, clutching Mr Fraser's IOU. Yet it puzzles me to know you are willing to forfeit something of such high value, merely to save Mr Fraser's hide, so I ask myself, why should I not avail myself of your offer and sample for one night the sweet pleasures to be gained from it? No doubt I will degenerate still more from what I am already, but I think I can live with that.'

Slowly he rose from his chair and came to stand in front of her, looking down at her. 'If I were to return Mr Fraser's IOU to you without condition, would you still wish to leave?'

His voice was low, with a husky rasp, and his eyes held Louisa's captive, gleaming in the dim light. The effect of his warmly intimate expression made her heart turn over. She knew she should say yes, that she didn't want to stay, but his potent virility was acting like a drug to her senses, the tug of his voice, his eyes too strong for her to resist. Sensations of unexpected pleasure washed over her, making her want to stay, making it impossible for her to leave. She realised it was no longer possible to put a stop to what she had so dangerously begun—and did she want to? she asked herself. The answer was clear—no, she didn't, and what she felt had nothing to do with James or anyone else.

What was happening to her? She had never felt like this, but she recognised the feeling. It was happiness, a feeling she had not felt in a long time, and never with such warmth, such intensity. Alistair took her hand and pressed it gently, seeing the answer in her eyes.

'I think we should continue this conversation in more comfortable surroundings, don't you, Louisa?' he said. 'Come. Let us retire to the bedroom, where neither conscience, Mr Fraser, nor Marianne will intrude tonight.'

Louisa took little notice of the magnificence of the bedroom, with its many exquisite objects and works of art, of the tasteful furniture, and thick carpets into which her feet sank. The only thing she was conscious of was the huge bed holding centre stage—waiting—and the man she was to share it with in so little time.

Slowly Alistair moved towards her, towering over her, his physical presence rendering her weak. In the soft glow of the candlelight her amber eyes were huge, like those of a wide-eyed kitten, luminous and infinitely lovely. She ran her tongue over her lip, unconsciously teasing.

'This,' he said, glorying in the tender passion in her eyes, feeling the heat flame in his belly as he drew aside the curtain of her hair and placed a kiss in the warm, sweet-scented nape of her neck, 'is the moment I've been thinking of ever since I first saw you.'

As his lips trailed over her flesh, with a gasp of exquisite pleasure she threw her head back and closed her eyes. 'I cannot believe this is happening,' she breathed softly. 'I am heading for something I cannot possibly know how to handle.'

'Then I think it's about time you learnt,' he replied softly, seductively.

The feel of Alistair's lips was strange, and the hot, melting unfamiliarity of it made Louisa gasp again, causing a natural hunger to stir deep within her young and healthy body. Nothing existed but this man and the husky timbre of his voice and his hot, dark eyes upon her. The next moment she was in his arms, the pressure increasing as they tightened around her and he bent his head, his sensual mouth claiming hers in a kiss of violent tenderness.

Louisa felt all her resistance disintegrate as she returned his kiss with all her innocent, unselfish ardour, feeling his hands moulding her close. Slowly his hands rose and caressed the nape of her neck, his splayed fingers running through her glorious mane of golden hair.

Lost in the stormy kiss, Louisa was not at first aware when his fingers began to pull at the tiny buttons up the back of her dress, but when she realised what he was doing a wave of panic swept over her. Pulling away slightly, she opened her eyes, warmth flaring in the pit of her stomach at his scorching look.

'Wait,' she whispered. 'What are you doing?'

Seeing the apprehension in her eyes, her uncertainty, Alistair felt a moment of puzzlement, but then he smiled slowly. 'What do you think I'm doing? Someone has to remove your clothes and—when the need arises—I make a perfect lady's maid.'

Realising he must not suspect her innocence, Louisa's lips trembled into a smile. 'I usually disrobe myself, but if you insist...'

'I do,' he murmured.

Louisa had so little knowledge or experience of the intimacies that took place between men and women. She was a complete novice. In her isolation at Bierlow there had been no stolen kisses or embraces for her, and now, suddenly, knowing she was on the brink of the unknown, for the first time in her life, her pulses began to race dangerously.

She watched with fascination as Alistair unfastened her dress, letting it slide down over her hips, and in a moment he had removed her undergarments with an ease which told her it was not the first time he had undressed a woman. She heard his quick intake of breath as her body was slowly revealed to him, his eyes fastening hungrily on her naked beauty. Her skin was white and cream and gloriously lovely, and he was bewitched, helpless to resist temptation.

Louisa drew in a rapid breath, enthralled by what was happening to her—by her own nakedness, and his, after he had removed his clothes unselfconsciously, to reveal the muscled, well-honed body of an athlete. She flushed and tried to avoid looking at his manhood, and Alistair smiled, charmed, and bent his head, his lips tracing the line of her face, her long, graceful neck, like a flutter of wings, causing the blood to pound through her veins with the heat of desire, causing sensations to ripple through her from somewhere unknown, and she sighed in infinite pleasure.

Immediately passion flared between them and suddenly they were on the bed, although she could not remember how they came to be there, with his mouth moving lingeringly over hers, unable to stifle a gasp when his lips left hers and took possession of her breast. Never would she have suspected that the feel of a man's lips on such a secret part of her body could create such incredible pleasure.

By degrees she pressed closer to him and quivers coursed through her. She looked into the smouldering darkness of his eyes above her as he continued to kiss her, his desire growing stronger. She smiled enticingly, arching her neck while he kissed the white, soft flesh of her throat, feeling like an escaped bird which had been caged too long as she allowed herself the freedom of abandonment. Hungrily he caressed the slender outline of her body, cupping her breasts, touching her here, caressing and kissing her there, so that no part of her escaped, her sighs and moans feeding his ardour, fuelling his passion.

She moved sensuously among the sheets, as if to evade him. Desire flared in Alistair, and, reaching out, he caught her in his arms and kissed her fiercely, his hands moving through the sheets to embrace her slim form, feeling her breasts, taut and pressed against him. He thrilled to her, his hands sliding lower to search and caress her womanhood. Louisa's instinct at such an intimate invasion was to object, to thrust him away, but he filled her with such exquisite promise as he continued to stroke, to arouse her, that she moved her hips instinctively against him, pressing, arching herself closer, as if an unknown force was compelling her.

Alistair's breath quickened against her throat as he began to surrender to a primitive and powerful, desperate need that became a torment inside, the restraint he had shown so far vanishing in his desire to possess the woman writhing beneath him, her hands soft as they moved feverishly over the muscles of his shoulders, down his long, hard back, lingering on his narrow waist and taut hips.

Spurred on by the hot, demanding feel of his lips, vibrantly aware of his raging desire, Louisa's response was unrestrained. She was engulfed by a burning need, an exploding mass of feeling, everything but the present obliterated from her mind as her body became a stranger to her and developed a life of its own. She moaned, her hands tangled in his hair, her back arching in helpless surrender. Aware of his arousal, she moved of her own accord beneath him, urging him. They came together almost instantly and with a violence so unexpected that Alistair did not see the tears that sprang to her eyes or the pain that crossed her face as she turned her head away—but the few seconds of pain were lost in what came after.

As Alistair moved inside her, Louisa felt something wild and primitive growing, something so wonderful that her consciousness receded as she unwittingly drove him to unparalleled agonies of desire, and just as she thought she must cry out, ask him to stop, the sheer pleasure at being with him took her over. Their need for each other overwhelmed them, and Louisa's body, released at last from its long-held virginity, became insatiable for his love. Her mind and all her anxieties seemed to dissolve so that she was aware of him and only him as he controlled all her senses. She seemed to be hurtling through space where there was no past, no future, no responsibilities, only this moment.

Her passion devastated Alistair, and when they lay spent, their bodies entwined in moisture, the hot climactic world that had held them in its grip began to subside. Louisa's hair spilled over them both like a silken sheet, and he lifted it off her face, seeing that her expression was one of peace and perfect tranquillity.

When she opened her eyes she seemed to be awaking from a deep sleep, and her eyes were huge and warm with passion. Alistair was lying on his side, looking at her in wonder, his face strangely calm and his dark head supported on one fist, the waving locks of his hair drooping over his moist brow. He kissed her lightly, lovingly, and she stretched languidly like a kitten, moving her body into the curve of his and closing her eyes.

'Don't imagine you're going to sleep,' Alistair breathed huskily, nuzzling her ear. 'I have not done with you yet.'

Her lips curving in a soft smile, Louisa looked up at him. He noticed that her eyes had taken on a peculiar deep lustre and that her skin, like his own, was damp and glowed with an inner fire. She sighed, feeling neither shame nor guilt. Raising her hand and combing her fingers through his hair, she grasped a handful and pulled his head down to hers, reaching for his mouth with her own, and he responded, feeling the softness of her lips, her body beginning to move against his with an inviting confusion of invitation and denial.

Again they made love, but now slowly, intently, and with a tenderness which was beyond anything either of them had ever known. Alistair, somewhat surprised to find Louisa naive and unskilled in the arts of making love, introduced her to new fields of pleasure, teaching her how to give him pleasure, how to reach fulfilment, teaching her, too, some of the games lovers played, watching as he awakened her into a tantalising creature who breathed sensuality, whose body pulsated with fire.

Amazed by her own sensuality, Louisa allowed him to guide her, becoming lulled into a sense of inertia, his lovemaking sending her to another place. Her body arched against the man who held her, moved with her, firmly, gently, carrying her to unexpected delights, until, in a state of complete exhaustion, they slept.

When Louisa awoke she stretched and raised her sleepy eyelids, disappointed not to find Alistair still beside her. She flushed with embarrassment when she remembered what had occurred between them during the night, finding it curious that she should feel no sense of shame or regret at what she had done. She sighed, stretching languorously, feeling sexually awakened, and free of ignorance and anxiety.

She wanted to shout her bliss to the world. Instead, because she had only allowed herself this one night, she would have to cultivate her secrecy, but she would be haunted by the sense that she would never again know such passion, such ecstasy.

At that moment the door opened and Alistair walked in, fully dressed. Louisa raised herself onto one elbow, her hair tumbling about her shoulders and her lips breaking into a soft smile of welcome. She looked lovely, with her cheeks flushed and her eyes warm and softly seductive and inviting, all of which Alistair failed to notice, being in the grip of an ice-cold, venomous rage.

The smile froze on Louisa's lips when she saw his expression as he came to stand over her, causing her to shrink before his towering, masculine presence and lofty demeanour. His face as he stood looking down at her was frightening, fixedly calm, and yet alight with a cold flame of rage and filled with a dark contempt. Instinctively, like a small child she drew a loose sheet over her nakedness, feeling something inside her curl up and die when she met his eyes, unable to see anything of her lover of the night. Her gaze went to his hand, seeing that he was holding a piece of paper in his fingers, which she recognised as James's IOU. With a savage gesture he thrust it at her.

'Here. I believe this is what you require—what this charade has been about. Take it and get out. You've certainly worked for it. Let us say I have been paid in full.'

He had a way of speaking that was chilling in its effectiveness. He turned to go, but, utterly bewildered and unable to understand what had happened to turn him into this cold, dispassionate stranger, Louisa swung her legs over the edge of the bed and stood up, clutching the sheet to her throat with shaking fingers. 'Alistair—wait. Please tell me what is wrong? What have I done?'

Alistair turned back to her and his gaze passed over her with cold contempt before travelling to the bed. He did not reply at once.

Louisa followed the direction of his gaze, her stomach sinking when she saw the tell-tale bloodied sheet, hidden until then by their bodies and the night. Mutely she stared at him—a figure made of porcelain, still and white—her eyes glazed. His blue eyes pierced hers, and she realised that nothing she could say would counteract the truth that she had been discovered. Too late, she saw the reason why she had roused his temper to a pitch she could never have imagined. There was something close to murder in his blazing eyes.

'I had not expected to be the first with you. Why did you not tell me you were a virgin?' he demanded harshly, his handsome features as hard and forbidding as a granite sculpture, his eyes as brittle as glass, anger uncoiling from his stomach and surging through him with all the savagery of a man betrayed—deceived— which was something Alistair's implacable will would never allow him to forgive.

Louisa's cheeks flamed at the scathing tone of his voice, failing to understand why her being a virgin should have created so much wrath in him, unable to see, as yet, that in her ignorance and innocence she had blundered into an irretrievable, appalling error.

'I—I—'

'Had I known, I would not have touched you.'

'But why?' she cried, her voice a mixture of pain and despair. 'Why does it matter to you so much?'

'I have my reasons. I do not know what game you think you're playing, lady, but I am not in the habit of deflowering virgins. Your cover is broken, Miss Divine—or is it something else? I really have no idea who you are.'

'Perhaps it would be better if we kept it that way,' Louisa whispered, her voice trembling with emotion. 'I feel you would be none too pleased with my identity.'

'You are right. Under the circumstances it is best I know nothing about you,' he said, his face hardening into an expressionless mask, his eyes probing hers like dagger thrusts. 'You are a schemer and a liar. Because of who I am, I have become accustomed to being pursued by socialites, and it would not be the first time a woman has insinuated herself into my bed with marriage as her object—and if you think I feel flattered that you gave me that which you have clearly denied Mr Fraser, then you are mistaken.'

His eyes glittered with a fire that burned her raw, his words flicking over her like a whiplash. Louisa's eyes filled with helpless tears of misery. She wanted to shout that James was her brother, but, reluctant to reveal her identity in case her shameless conduct became known and ruined her reputation beyond redemption, she felt unable to discuss her present circumstances with Alistair. After all, he was still a stranger to her—and she to him—despite their previous intimacy.

'I realise what you must think, but it is not as it seems. You are right. I have not told you the truth,' she said, her voice pitched very low.

'That is something I have worked out for myself.'

'Whilst I have not exactly lied to you, I have been less than honest,' she said, moving towards him.

'Stay where you are,' he ordered harshly. 'I have no wish to listen to more of your lies. Last night you told me you were not a whore—but I have to say you gave a fair imitation of one. I find it hard to believe the alluring temptress who offered herself to me so willingly was a virgin. If it is true that you came to me solely to procure Mr Fraser's IOU, then you must think a great deal of him to throw away your virtue with a total stranger to retrieve it.

'No doubt you can justify your reasons to yourself, but your conduct tells me all I need to know about your moral standards, Miss Divine. However, I feel I must congratulate you,' he said, his eyes flicking over her with cynical contempt. 'With your face and body—not forgetting your other irresistible charms—you have an extremely promising career as a whore ahead of you.'

Louisa gasped, her cheeks burning as she felt anger flare up inside her caused by his insult, his injustice. How could he be so cruel? How could he say these things to her? Her anger gave way to uncontrollable wrath.

'How dare you?' she flared. 'How dare you hand down judgements on me when your own behaviour is highly reprehensible? You are hardly a person of irreproachable character, Lord Dunstan,' she accused, reverting to her former address.

'Oh, I do dare,' he replied, his voice scathing, mocking, his face white with fury, his cold eyes impaling hers. 'A man may do and say anything he pleases with goods he has purchased. You gave me no indication that you were a proper young lady who expected the highest standards of gentlemanly behaviour from me. Any decent, well-bred young woman would have endured hell-fire and damnation rather than do what you have just done. I dare say that, unless you can persuade Fraser to marry you and make an honest woman of you, you will go down the same sordid road as countless women before you.'

'The kind of women whose company you enjoy so much,' retorted Louisa with heavy sarcasm.

'If you like,' he replied coldly, 'but I do not feel I have to justify what I do to you. Now I have initiated you in the skills of lovemaking, you should be well qualified to follow that age-old profession—and I am certain you will do very well by it. Now get dressed while I order the carriage to take you home. I want you out of my house and out of my life.'

Drowning in an agony of shame and humiliation, Louisa watched him go. The desolation of his sudden departure, and the manner of it, overwhelmed her. A sob rose from the pit of her stomach to her throat and she threw herself onto the bed, burying her face in the pillows as she wept in silent misery, feeling the full force—the reality—of what she had done. She felt cheap and soiled, and Alistair had been right. She deserved his condemnation. She had behaved no better than a whore.

In the silent, helpless misery of despair, she got up from the bed, reproaching herself, hating herself, wondering what could have possessed her, what she could have been thinking of to allow herself to submit to this mindless, wicked weakness. Why, oh, why, had she not listened to Timothy? He had warned her how she would feel afterwards—of the terrible guilt and shame that would be like demons in her life and never leave her—and that it would be impossible to carry on as though nothing had happened. After what she had done, to escape her terrible shame, she wanted to wither away and die.

Hot tears of physical and emotional suffering coursed their way down her cheeks as she dressed hurriedly and, clutching the object of her misery, James's IOU in her hand, blindly she ran from the room and the house, glad that Lord Dunstan was nowhere to be seen, for at that moment she had no wish to see him ever again.

From a window in the upper part of the house Alistair watched Louisa, pale and stricken, climb into the carriage and drive away. Only then did he turn and stare at the empty room, in the house which had been alive with her presence until he had ordered her to leave.

When he'd woken and seen her lying in the crook of his arm, her body glowing and warm from their lovemaking, he had looked at her, watching as she slept, thinking how heartbreakingly lovely she was—a picture of alluring innocence and intoxicating sensuality. Her slender body had lain stretched across the bed like a beautiful white snow leopard, and he had wanted her with a fierceness that took his breath away. She was beautiful, dignified and ladylike in her demeanour, but beneath the façade of serenity and gentleness she was sensual and provocative. When he had made love to her they had been sexually attuned to each other and she had satisfied him completely, in a way no other woman had before—not even Marianne.

But on seeing the tell-tale stain—stark evidence of her youth, her innocence—instinctively, with his senses reeling, he'd known she was not what she seemed and that she spelled trouble to his well-ordered life. He would have none of that. After his turbulent marriage to Marianne he had reconciled himself to a life of transient affairs, which satisfied and relieved his body and left his emotions intact, but he suspected that this one occasion would prove unforgettable.

All manner of thoughts raced through his mind—suspicions and questions which would have to remain unanswered. Had retrieving Fraser's IOU been the sole purpose of her agreeing to spend one night of love with him? Or was she some shallow little rich girl looking for excitement? No well-bred young lady, who would normally be seen exclusively among the company of the social élite, would have been seen dead attending one of Lady Bricknell's parties, and nor would she have risked her reputation by indulging in such wanton behaviour that would damage any chance she might have of making a decent marriage.

Was she an impoverished but well-bred young woman out to make a decent marriage? And would her outraged father come hammering on his door, demanding he make amends for compromising his daughter? To be damned, he thought angrily, summoning one of the servants to have the carriage brought to take him to his club. He'd have none of it.

Yet try as he might, he could not banish Louisa from his mind so easily. She had a way of getting under his skin and insinuating herself into his mind that troubled him. She was physically appealing, with a face and body that drugged his mind, but she was also appealing in other ways, with an intelligent sharpness of mind and a clever wit that he admired, making her pleasant company and interesting to be with. It puzzled him that it should make him angry that she could be bought so cheaply, and his anger was exacerbated by a kind of rage that she should demean herself, and by an inexplicable disappointment.

With his experience, he should have known as soon as he'd begun making love to her that she was a virgin. But it had been a long time since he had made love to a woman, and when she had writhed beneath him like a full-blown temptress, driving him on with an uncontrollable force, he had failed to notice any pain and discomfort she might have been feeling.

He recalled the dignity with which she had borne his insults, his rage. It had touched him deeply, almost weakening his resolve not to become involved with a woman in the way he had been with Marianne in the early days of their marriage—and why, he asked himself, did the feelings Louisa had evoked echo his feelings about his wife, feelings which had been buried deep for so long? There had also been a moment when the compulsion to comfort and protect, to hold her, had been so strong that he'd had to keep his hands rigidly in control lest they stray of their own accord.

When she had come to him he had wanted nothing more than to make her his mistress and to keep her in style, until he had discovered that she was unsullied, untouched by any other man, and that had suddenly posed a threat, a danger to his peace of mind. She was dangerous because never having belonged to another man made her different, gave her added appeal, and he could so easily fall in love with her—and become completely undone into the bargain.

Alistair had no wish to sacrifice his freedom, to become shackled in that way to a woman ever again. He'd been there once and had no mind to travel down the same road twice. Disgust replaced his anger. He told himself that, no matter who she was, she had the makings of a skilful harlot and he'd be well rid of her. If he made her his mistress, she would make his life a living hell.

How long would it be before he found himself wanting to share his life with her in every way? How long before she betrayed him with another, as Marianne had done? After all, if she thought her virtue of such little importance that she could sacrifice it without a qualm—and with a virtual stranger at that—for such a small matter as an IOU, then who was to say she would not do so again when she had the desire to look elsewhere for sexual fulfilment?

Alistair coldly consigned Louisa Divine to the past. She was already dead to him, and any feelings he might have had for her were wiped clean from his heart. But memory was the worst thing of all, and that he could not erase from his mind.

Somehow Louisa could never remember the journey from Dunstan House to Henrietta Street. It was a blur, something she preferred not to dwell upon. After all that had transpired Bierlow Hall and its problems seemed so far away, and the emptiness in her heart without Alistair was so piercing that she seemed unable to keep the relative importance of them in proper proportion. She didn't wait for James to return from Oxfordshire but, full of guilt and confusion, like a whipped dog seeking shelter to lick its wounds in private, she decided to return to Bierlow where she belonged, where she could indulge herself in anonymity and solitude.

If James discovered what she had done he would never forgive her. Never. Humiliation and shame pounded through her. She would never be able to look him in the eyes, knowing what she was guilty of. He would despise her and she could not blame him. But why was she so upset? she asked herself. Why did she feel so wretched? Hadn't she got what she wanted? With the return of James's IOU everything would go back to how it had been before—except that it wouldn't be the same. Nothing would ever be the same again because she wasn't the same any more.

And so she returned to Surrey, leaving James the retrieved IOU and a short note explaining that she had returned to Bierlow. With any luck at all he would not enquire too deeply into Lord Dunstan's reasons for returning it, but she had a distinct feeling that it would not be too long before James arrived at Bierlow, demanding to know what she knew about the matter. It was a situation she would have to deal with when, and if, it arose.

On her return she threw herself into her work, trying to pick up the threads of her life, devoting herself to the well-being of the few people who worked at Bierlow and depended on her for their subsistence, trying to blot what had happened to her in London from her mind—to blot out Alistair Dunstan—but the whole night she had spent in his arms stood out with such agonising clarity that it made her weep.

Swamped with self-retribution and tortured by memories, she told herself that she was a shameless wanton, soiled and used and unfit for any gullible male who might come along in the future and want to marry her. She had broken all the rules that had been made to protect young ladies from experienced men like Lord Dunstan, rules that governed the moral code of a young lady of her class.

Isolated in her private misery, adamantly she refused to think of him, but despite herself a tremor of remembered passion and bitter-sweet memories sometimes coursed through her. The continuation of that desire he had awoken in her confounded her. She was still reeling from the impact of him, shattered by the power of the physical attraction she felt for him. She had never realised she had been capable of such intense passion. Nothing in her experience had prepared her for what he had done to her, or the emotions he had aroused, triggering off an explosion of sensuality, the like of which she could never have imagined, prompting her to respond in a way that had astounded her. They had been lost to everything but each other, their lovemaking having a frenzy that made everything pale beside it—and every other man she might meet in the future.

A letter arrived from James who, having returned from Oxfordshire, was cock-a-hoop to find that Lord Dunstan had returned his IOU, although why he should have done so remained a complete mystery to him. He wrote informing Louisa that he was to give up the house in Henrietta Street and return to live at Bierlow and would explain his reasons for doing so when he arrived. Louisa was astounded, unable to believe that James would give up his wayward life and return to Bierlow to live the quiet life of a country gentleman.

But at this time Louisa had a growing anxiety that all was not as it should be with herself, and there was a nagging fear in her that could not be dismissed. She often felt unwell, especially early in the morning when she became plagued by bouts of nausea and dizziness, which gave her reason to suspect the worst—that she might be with child.

Disbelieving and shocked, she would not accept that this could be the reason why she felt so ill. She was unprepared for this sudden explosion in the quiet landscape of her life. It was a nightmare, one she would wake up from soon, but it soon dawned on her that it was no nightmare. It was tenacious, terrifying reality, and when her suspicions were duly confirmed she was devastated.

Her face became pale and drawn, her mouth tense, and there were dark circles under her eyes. She could not sleep, her predicament and her future causing her to lie awake night after night worrying, pondering over what she should do—and how she was going to tell James.

Chapter Seven

Bierlow Hall was a magnificent stone mansion built in perfect proportions. At the end of an avenue of oaks, it was set in the heart of the gently undulating Surrey countryside, and, despite its sad air of neglect and lonely isolation, standing a mile away from the ancient and picturesque village of Bierlow, no one could fail to be impressed by it.

Determined to make good his brotherly shortcomings, James arrived at Bierlow Hall, in surprisingly high spirits and with an enthusiastic air of purpose, six weeks after his letter to Louisa. He was immediately concerned when he saw her pallor.

'Truly you do not look well, Louisa. Have you seen the doctor?'

'No—no. I am fine, really, James.' She managed to smile. 'Do not concern yourself. Perhaps I've been doing too much of late—that is all.'

'Well, from now on everything is going to be different. I've always left everything for you to shoulder in the past, but no more. I was scared, I don't mind admitting,' he confided to her seriously, 'when I thought we were on the verge of losing everything and that I might be thrown into the debtors' gaol. There is nothing like a shock of those proportions to make one sit up and take stock of one's life, I can tell you. It forced me to ask myself where it was leading, living as I was. It's made me realise that, if I want to hold onto what I have, I am going to have to work at it, which is exactly what I intend doing. From now on I am going to make a virtuous attempt to reform my way of life.'

Louisa listened to him in astonished silence, unable to believe this was her brother speaking. She realised from the intensity of his voice that he was not speaking idly, and she wondered what could have brought about this startling change in him. Was it his relief at being reprieved by Lord Dunstan, or something else?

'I'm going to devote all my time to this place from now on,' he continued on an enthusiastic note, looking out of the long windows which opened onto the tangled, neglected gardens. 'It's time I did something useful—and besides, if I mean to marry, I cannot possibly bring my bride here with the house as it is. I have not been trained for anything except to be a gentleman of leisure,' he said with a regretful sigh, 'with very little money, unfortunately.'

At last Louisa was beginning to understand his reasons for returning to Bierlow. 'Have you someone in mind, James?' she asked in a very small voice, hope stirring inside her that this might be so.

'Why—yes,' he answered with a little tremulous smile. 'There is someone—Amelia Hacket. Timothy's sister. Her parents, I think, will have no objections to the match, providing I start to take life more seriously and change my ways. It is important that I prove to them that I can take care of Amelia in the style in which she has been raised.'

Louisa was truly delighted for him, having already gathered that Timothy's sister was somewhat enamoured of James, despite his profligate ways. 'Oh, James, that's wonderful.'

'You've never met her, have you?'

'No. As yet I have not had that pleasure, but Timothy always speaks fondly of her.'

'She's adorable, Louisa.'

'Yes, I'm sure she is.'

'You'll like her, I know you will. If she marries me I shall be the happiest, the luckiest man in the world.'

That he loved her Louisa knew to be the truth by the look in his eyes, the sudden quiver of his mouth and the softness in his expression and his eyes. She was happy to see this change in him, and at any other time she would have been overwhelmed by it, but much of the joy she would have felt was overshadowed by her own unhappy predicament.

James looked around the large salon they were in with a critical eye, glancing with distaste at the faded and unfashionable decor, at the threadbare carpets and curtains. Thankfully the furniture was fine and of good taste, chosen by their mother after her marriage.

He sighed. 'The old place is a credit to you, Louisa, although it is sorely in need of attention, and from what I saw of the gardens they resemble nothing short of a jungle. I am sure that when we begin hacking away we'll discover a veritable zoo living in there.'

'I know that, James, but I do my best,' Louisa replied harshly, in no mood after all she had been through for his criticism.

Hearing the hurt in her voice, James reproached himself for the insensitivity of his words. 'I know you do, and I am not criticising. Truly. However, with a good gardener, and a lick of paint here and there—and if we purchase some new curtains and have the chairs re-covered, and such like—we'll soon have it looking better.'

Louisa listened to him in silence, wondering where the money was going to come from to achieve all this. However, she was happy to hear him sounding so positive, and hoped he was in earnest about what he intended doing at Bierlow and would not hotfoot it back to London the minute he became tired of it, as he had in the past.

Seeing the enthusiasm lighting up his face, she saw something of their father in him, who had worked hard to keep the estate intact, struggling against bankruptcy caused by bad harvests, whilst serving as a magistrate and county alderman, gaining respect from all who knew him. She prayed that James had truly seen the error of his ways and would grow to be like their father.

Over the years since their father's death, James had sold land off piecemeal to neighbouring landowners in order to finance the running of the house—the cost of which Louisa was careful to keep to a minimum—and to support his own more lavish lifestyle in London.

'Tomorrow I shall ride around the estate and see what has to be done. I shall also call on Mr Fenchurch and Mr Bramwell,' James went on, referring to two of his tenant farmers. 'With so little money in our coffers we might have to review their rents—and others who rent property on the estate. I am only thankful that

I don't have to hand it all over to Lord Dunstan, after all.' His expression suddenly became serious and thoughtful, as it often had of late, when he pondered over Lord Dunstan's reason for returning his IOU. 'I just wish I knew what it was that prompted him to return my IOU. Such a thing is not normally done.'

Although she was quaking inside, Louisa knew the moment had come when she must tell James everything, for the longer she concealed the truth from him,the harder it would be to confront him with it later. She swallowed hard, knowing she somehow had to get through these next unpleasant moments with her brother—and the thousands of others over the next few days, months and years when, because of the unfortunate predicament she found herself in, she would have to suffer the severe censure and ridicule of friends and neighbours alike.

Noticing his sister's sudden pallor and frozen stare, James looked at her with a sudden suspicion and he frowned and came to stand close to her.

'Do you know anything about it, Louisa? Were you there when it was returned? Did Lord Dunstan return it in person?'

For a moment all Louisa could do was stare at James, unable to find the words to tell him about the hideous, sinful thing she had done. Her mouth trembled and she averted her eyes. Her distress instantly communicated itself to him and he became alarmed, seeing tears brimming in her eyes when she raised them to his.

'Louisa! What is it? What's the matter?' he asked with tender concern, wondering what it could be that seemed to upset her so much. 'You know more about this than you are letting on, don't you?'

Biting her trembling lip, she nodded, appeal filling her eyes as they begged his understanding. 'Oh, James,' she whispered. 'I have done something so terrible that I do not know how to tell you. I—I am so ashamed.'

'Louisa,' James said, his voice quivering, unable to stand the suspense a moment longer. 'For God's sake tell me what it is. What have you done that causes you such distress?' he demanded, his tone climbing an octave higher and sounding urgent as he reached out and gripped her arms with a savagery unusual in him.

Louisa swallowed hard, fixing her eyes on her brother's. 'I—I went to Lord Dunstan—and—and I slept with him, James,' she stammered, 'in—in return for your IOU.'

James stared at her mutely, the tenderness in his eyes turning to bewilderment and disbelief, before becoming hard and accusing, and she had to bear the brunt of his anger, his disgust. That sense of dread which she had tried to press to the back of her mind rose up to materialise at last as James continued to look at her, disbelieving, appalled and aghast at what she had told him. Finally his temper became explosive, the depth of his anger reducing Louisa to feeling as helpless as a child.

'You were Lord Dunstan's whore? You let him tumble you between the sheets like a harlot? Is that what you are saying?'

She nodded dumbly, unable to speak.

'Louisa, you must have taken leave of your senses. You are too young and inexperienced to take on a man of Lord Dunstan's ilk. He eats women like you for breakfast.'

'Oh, James. How can you of all people be so cruel as to say that to me?' Louisa cried despairingly, tears she could no longer hold back spilling from her eyes in rivulets down her cheeks. 'I could see no other way. I did it for us. I had to. You know how much Bierlow means to me. I could not bear to let it go, nor could I endure seeing you dragged off to the Fleet.'

James was unmoved. 'You idiot,' he said fiercely. 'How could you be so stupid? You should have let me worry about that. How could you—my sister—take it into your head to do something so cheap—so deplorable? And with Lord Dunstan of all people. The minute my back was turned you went creeping to him, to beg that he return my IOU by the only means you knew how.'

Louisa closed her eyes. This was something she could not argue against, for she knew it to be the truth.

'I should have known on the night we went to Dunstan House that you were up to something—plotting something,' James went on relentlessly. 'That dress, which was so shocking in both colour and design—and the time you and he were absent from us all. Dear Lord, have you any idea how humiliating it is for me to discover you went grovelling to him on my behalf? How do you think that makes me look in his eyes?'

James was extremely angry. In fact Louisa could not remember having seen him so angry. 'Lord Dunstan thought I was your mistress,' she said, in an attempt to explain, braving his wrath.

'A whore, Louisa, and open to offers,' he accused cruelly, 'and you let him go on believing that. How could you?'

'If I had told him I was your sister he would have had nothing to do with me and we would still be in the mess which was of your making, James. He cannot be blamed.'

'Oh, yes he can,' he said through gritted teeth. 'A man of his reputation and experience cannot be absolved from blame. I could kill him for this,' he said with a savagery that shocked Louisa.

'No, James. It was my fault. I made a mistake.'

'Then you will have to live with your mistake,' he snapped. 'What is done cannot be undone.' He fell silent and drew a long, shuddering breath as he paced to and fro, striving to gain control of his temper as he raked his shaking fingers through his hair.

'Thank God he was ignorant as to your true identity and you will never have to meet again. That way there is every chance that none of this will come out. It's the sort of gossip which could damage any chance you might have of making a decent marriage in the future, the sort of gossip that would prove titillating to those who would listen.'

Louisa's limbs were trembling so violently that, unable to stand any longer, she sank onto the sofa, clasping her hands in front of her, crushed by the full weight of what she had done, her stupidity, her gullibility—wondering how he would take the rest of what she had to disclose.

'I'm sorry, James. I am so, so sorry,' she whispered helplessly. 'But it is not as easy as that. There is something else I have to tell you.'

He spun round on her, anticipating her words. 'What? What could possibly be worse than what you have told me already?'

'I—I am to have Lord Dunstan's child.'

She spoke the words so softly that had James been further away he would not have heard them. As it was, they were of such tangible magnitude that they hung in the air—in the silence—between them. He became rooted to the spot and stared at her in abject horror at her disclosure, rendered speechless, seeing the truth written all over her guilt-stricken face.

'I—I do not understand,' he stammered.

'It—it's quite simple, James.'

The colour drained from James's face. He swallowed hard. 'This isn't true. It can't be,' he said, total disbelief written on his face, a maelstrom of conflicting emotions whirling through his head. 'Good God,' he gasped at length, shattering the silence. 'Are you certain?'

Louisa nodded, unprepared for the pain, the fear, the confusion she read in her brother's face.

Suddenly James's whole body began quivering with rage and his eyes blazed in his face which had gone from white to livid. He had seen what happened to other men's sisters who had disgraced themselves. They were pilloried and humiliated, their whole family becoming objects of derision. But Louisa! Louisa was decent and had been raised by God-fearing parents. How could she have done this?

In earnest meditation he began pacing up and down the room once more, wondering how best to deal with a situation such as she had just presented him with, whilst saving them both from humiliation and ruin. Timothy's father would not consider him a suitable contender for Amelia's hand when it became known that his sister was to bear an illegitimate child.

'Then this alters matters,' he said, desperation in his every move, in his every look. 'I know Lord Dunstan is in London at this time. I shall return there immediately. As your brother and your guardian it is my duty to confront him with this and insist that something is done by way of reparation.'

'No,' Louisa cried in despair.

'Yes, Louisa,' he said, looking at her hard. 'The damage is done, but I intend to see that he supplies the means whereby you don't suffer by his actions for the rest of your life. He has a duty to face up to his responsibilities and I shall make damned sure that he does.'

Louisa stood up in alarm. 'Don't go, James. Please don't go,' she pleaded. 'It will serve no purpose. After what I did he will feel nothing for me but loathing and contempt. He will never marry me—and nor would I wish him to under such circumstances—and I could not bear the humiliation of receiving any money from him. I—I neither want to see nor have anything to do with him again for as long as I live, and I am certain he feels the same about me. I am so sorry, James. I'll go away. No one need know. I'll manage on my own somehow. I will do anything to protect you from the humiliation and disgrace which will fall on you should it become public knowledge.'

'Don't be stupid, Louisa. Where would you go? No, this has to be faced.'

James towered over the trembling, distraught girl who was making every effort to stem the tide of tears flowing wretchedly down her pale cheeks, who had so daringly and bravely tried to hold onto all they had and to keep him out of gaol. She had succeeded in doing so at the cost of her virtue and to find her world falling apart around her. Her strategy to put everything right had backfired with a terrible vengeance. Despite his anger, his disappointment and hurt pride, and the fact that she had humiliated him to the very depths of his being, there was room in his heart for pity.

Not in his worst fears had he imagined that his lovely, untouched sister might give herself to a man in the cheap and shoddy manner which was reserved for the women who inhabited the bagnios in the seedier areas of London. The realisation of her self-sacrifice came home to him with full force. This tender-hearted, self-effacing young woman had surrendered her virtue, which was what she had least wanted to do, because at the moment of decision she had been unable to see any other way out of their predicament.

Their father had made them promise to keep Bierlow secure, and Louisa had fulfilled it on his behalf. He should be thankful and appreciative, not reproachful—and he was deeply ashamed that he had been the one to drive her into Lord Dunstan's bed. It was his recklessness at the gaming tables that had brought them to this, and because he had been incapable of finding a way out of the predicament himself.

But that Lord Dunstan had dared, had had the temerity, the sheer effrontery, to use her so abominably was deplorable, and he would not allow him to walk away without so much as a blemish to his character. His anger returned hot and strong.

'I cannot simply ignore this. The matter is extremely serious. If you are to retain any dignity at all, and either of us are to show our faces in public again, I have no alternative but to confront him with this. He has compromised you and he must answer for it. I shall leave for London first thing in the morning.'

This he did, leaving Louisa awaiting his return with dread. Not for one moment did she believe Lord Dunstan would want to marry her, and she could not see him accepting James's outrageous suggestion that he should do so. And why should he? she asked herself bitterly. Why should he rescue her from a predicament that was entirely of her own making?

By the time James reached London and Dunstan House, having had time to assess the situation more clearly and sensibly, his anger had abated somewhat. He was wise enough to know that if anything at all was to be salvaged from the mess, and he could reach an understanding with Lord Dunstan, anger and recriminations would serve no purpose. Besides, looking at the situation from Lord Dunstan's position, Louisa was right. When he had embarked on his seduction of her, he'd had no idea she was James's sister, hell-bent on saving his neck and their home. He'd have done much the same under the circumstances. But he could not overlook the fact that his sister's reputation had been ruined beyond recall.

When James was admitted to Dunstan House it was to find Lord Dunstan on his way out.

Alistair stiffened when he saw James Fraser in the hall, his eyes narrowing, clearly not at all pleased to see him, his presence at once reminding him of Louisa, whose exceptional beauty and intellectual turn of mind still haunted him—and whose deceit still had the power to raise him to scorching anger. He received James coldly.

'As you see, Fraser, I am just on my way out,' he said, his tone curt and dismissive.

For a moment James shrank from confronting the older man, unable to believe this man of steel was responsible for ruining the reputation of his lovely, innocent sister, but conscious of the purpose of his visit he braced himself, his face taking on a youthful dignity as he moved forward to meet the proud and powerful Alistair Dunstan. He was prepared to defend his sister's good name by challenging him to a duel, if required, despite the gentleman's reputation as an expert with both sword and pistol, and he himself not trained in either.

'I apologise if I have chosen an inopportune time to call, Lord Dunstan, but what I have to say is of the utmost importance and cannot be put off. I shall not take up too much of your time.'

'I see,' Alistair said icily. 'Then perhaps you had better step this way where we can speak in privacy.'

James followed him inside the room where, unbeknownst to him, Alistair had presented Louisa with a book of poetry by William Collins on the night of his party.

'Can I offer you some refreshment?' asked Alistair with steely politeness.

'No—thank you. This is not a social call. We both know why I am here.'

'When I returned your IOU, Fraser—' Alistair's voice rang out in crisp, precise tones '—I hoped that would be the end of the matter.'

'So did I,' James replied, making a monumental effort to keep his temper under control. 'Indeed I hoped so, until I was made aware of your reason for returning it, Lord Dunstan.'

'I see. Miss Divine has decided to enlighten you, I take it?'

James bristled on hearing him speak the name he never wanted to hear spoken again as long as he lived. 'Miss Divine,' he rasped, with considerable emphasis, enunciating each word carefully, 'which was a ridiculous name invented by Louisa for reasons which I shall make clear to you given time, is my sister, Lord Dunstan. She is not, as she led you to believe, my mistress.'

With grim satisfaction James observed the muscle that was beginning to twitch in Lord Dunstan's rigid jaw, and saw his eyes becoming hard with grinding anger. Alistair stared at him, James's revelation pounding through his brain like a million hammers. Burning rage at his own stupidity and blindness poured through him. At last everything fell into place—why she had behaved as she had, and why she had tried so desperately to save this man, so boldly confronting him, from ruin.

'Your sister! I see,' he said coldly, his voice indicating no surprise at the revelation. 'That explains certain things about her be-

haviour which have puzzled me. Although I have to say the resemblance between you is only slight. You must believe me when
I say that, if I had known this, I swear I would not have laid a
finger on her.'

'How noble of you, sir. You took improper advantage of Louisa
and her reputation has been irrefutably damaged, whereas to you
I believe it was nothing more than a meaningless dalliance.'

'I confess that it did start out as a simple diversion, but you
have to give her credit,' Alistair said, fighting down a surge of
disgust when he recalled how expertly she had managed to dupe
him, and how easily she had lost her virtue to him. 'Your sister
certainly knows how to set about capturing the attentions of the
opposite sex.'

'That is not how it was and you know it,' James replied, striving
to keep his anger in check as he considered what Lord Dunstan
said about Louisa highly offensive. 'Louisa is an exceptional girl,
warm and outgoing. She is also extremely intelligent and has always had an understanding about most things way beyond her
years. She is sensitive in many ways, but she can also be infuriatingly headstrong and as stubborn as hell.'

'Don't feel that you have to sell your sister to me, Mr Fraser,'
Alistair said scathingly, with a mocking curl to his lips. 'She did
that herself most admirably. I do know her, don't forget. To my
cost, I have had first-hand experience of falling prey to her winning ways. At the time I had no reason in the world to believe
she was anything other than what she seemed. Come now, with
your experience of such affairs, you must know they are not to be
taken seriously.'

'It is quite a different matter when they happen to concern my
sister. As Louisa's brother and guardian you must see that it is my
duty to defend her reputation and good name.'

'Of course. I would do much the same if it were my own sister.
But your own behaviour in all this puzzles me somewhat,' Alistair
said, his eyes narrowing as he fixed James with an icy stare, 'for
it is clear that you were prepared to go along with this charade.
As I recall, you made no effort to rectify matters, either at Lady
Bricknell's, when you lost so devastatingly to me at cards, or when
I invited you here. Why did you not make it plain at the time that

she was your sister? Am I really to believe you had no part in this whatsoever?'

'I most certainly did not, sir,' James replied with indignation and angry force. Although, having had time to contemplate the situation on his journey back to London, and remembering the dress Louisa had suddenly appeared in for her visit to Dunstan House, having wondered at the time where she could have acquired it, he strongly suspected that Timothy must have been a party to it. He would have a few choice words to say to his friend when next they met.

The indignation that sprang to James's lips, and the force of his words, left Alistair in no doubt that he was ignorant of his sister's actions. James Fraser could be accused of many things, but lying was not one of them.

'Nothing I can say can excuse my own part in all this,' James went on, 'and I have reproached myself many times for going along with it. Louisa's appearance at Bricknell House that night was as much a surprise to me as it was to everyone else, and I truly believed she wanted to accompany me to supper here merely to keep an eye on me—to make sure I did not fall further into debt than I was already. Her fabrication was to save me from ridicule and embarrassment, which would have been the case had she appeared by my side as an over-protective sister in such company. I had no idea of her intentions where you were concerned, otherwise I would never have allowed it.

'She has given me a full account of her disgraceful actions and the lengths to which she went to retrieve my IOU—and I have to say that I was both shocked and horrified. No matter what your opinion is of me, Lord Dunstan, I am a gentleman by birth and, as a gentleman, fully intended honouring my debt to you. Because of my sister's stupid, irresponsible act, which I must tell you was totally out of character, she has brought shame and dishonour to our family name and ruined whatever chance she had of making a decent, respectable marriage in the future.'

'That is unfortunate,' Alistair replied with amazing calm.

'Can't you see that, being naive and inexperienced, she acted on pure instinct? I understand Huntswood means a great deal to you, so perhaps you can understand how much Bierlow Hall means to Louisa. It means so much to her that she was prepared to run any risk to hold onto it—and, if I had settled my debt to you, I would have been forced to sell.'

'And you were prepared to do that?'

'Of course.'

'I see. Then I can only assume that your family home means less to you than it does to your sister, otherwise, with nothing else to stake, you would not have run the risk of gambling it away at the card tables. Has it not occurred to you, Mr Fraser, that your own conduct is to blame for your sister's actions?'

'Yes, of course. I am deeply ashamed of my past conduct— especially where Louisa is concerned—and have nothing to say in my defence. But it is not myself I came here to discuss, Lord Dunstan. It is you, and what is to be done to repair the damage done to Louisa's reputation.'

Alistair's eyes snapped sharply onto James's face. Surely he did not have the temerity to demand that he marry her? 'Naturally you are outraged and wounded, because in your eyes I took advantage of her and you have come seeking reparation. But let me tell you here and now, Mr Fraser, that I have no intention of making the ritualistic proposal. The mistake was hers entirely. She offered herself to me, and believing she was no different from all the other women who attend Lady Bricknell's parties, I had no qualms about accepting her offer. She is an extremely beautiful young woman. What man in his right mind would refuse her?

'You are right. She is intelligent and a delight to converse with, and she has no illusions where my views on marriage are concerned. I made them quite plain to her. So—what would you have me do? What is your purpose in coming here? I can well understand your anger. Indeed, were it my own sister I would have done much the same. But the situation was of her making. Not mine. I will not marry her. That is out of the question.'

'Not even when I tell you she is with child? Your child, Lord Dunstan—for it cannot be anyone else's.'

Alistair was struck dumb. His entire body stiffened and he stared at James with incredulity, before his face hardened into a mask of freezing rage. Suddenly it was as if the sun had gone out and everything around him began to close in, suffocating him. He stood still, taut, fierce tension marking his mouth. He didn't believe it. He couldn't believe it. The sense of anger built to agony, and, with a sharp, terrible clarity, he began to realise that he'd made a fatal blunder. He'd been deceived—neatly, wholly, properly deceived.

'And I am to believe this?' he finally rasped into the reverberant silence, which to him seemed almost a lifetime later.

'What I have just told you is the truth,' James snapped bitterly, Lord Dunstan's lack of interest or concern for Louisa's well-being, apparent from the moment he had stepped inside the house, at last causing his own anger to snap and his frustration to explode. He stepped towards Alistair, his face livid and his hands clenched into fists by his side.

'My sister—who has rarely been away from her home—had never been with a man in her life before she encountered you. She lacks the advantage of your years and experience and—being an experienced man of the world as you are, Lord Dunstan—you must have known that. Did it not occur to you that you might get her with child? Did it not enter your head that such a thing might happen?'

Alistair glared at him. Not a muscle of the handsome, authoritative face moved. He had recovered himself quickly. 'No. At the time I confess it did not.'

'Why not? Because you wanted to sever it from your mind while you took your pleasure of her—as you would do with anything else unpleasant you don't want to know about? How dare you speak as if it were all her fault?' James fumed, his voice vibrating with fury, too enraged to notice that Alistair's hard face was wiped clean of all expression.

'You have compromised my sister in the most dastardly way imaginable, and I had hoped that you, above all people, with a reputation for honour and for fair dealing with others, would answer for it. It appears I was mistaken. I see that you are arrogant and cold beneath all your trappings and fine looks, Lord Dunstan. How many other hearts have you trampled on? How many other women have you loved and then cast aside? How many other fatherless children have you begotten, who are running around with your stamp on them?' Angrily he spun round and strode towards the door, where he turned and looked back. 'I can see that nothing has been achieved by my coming here today so I will bid you good day. I only hope your conscience lets you sleep at night.'

'Wait,' Alistair said curtly. Having no intention of becoming involved in what promised to be a bitter quarrel, he let James's harsh accusations pass over him. Normally he would be outraged at being confronted and spoken to in such a manner in his own house, but he knew the words were spoken in anger and frustration, and he could well understand James's concern for his sister. 'Where is she now?'

'Where do you think? At Bierlow Hall feeling absolutely wretched—and completely overwhelmed by what has happened to her. I am afraid that to cover her shame, and to prevent total disgrace falling on me—for I hope to marry myself in the near future—she is thinking of going away until the child is born. After that—only she can decide.'

'I see. You hope to marry, you say?'

'Yes.'

'And this situation with your sister might prove awkward for you, an embarrassment, should it come out; is that what you're saying?'

'Of course.'

Alistair nodded, his eyes sweeping over him with condescension as he began to realise that James Fraser's sword was double-edged, that the purpose of his visit and his anger was not only for his sister's well-being but also for his own self-interest.

'You must realise that this has come as a tremendous shock to me. However, contrary to your harsh opinion of me, let me assure you that I intend giving the matter serious consideration,' he said, in an implacable voice that warned James not to argue further. 'If, as you say, the child is mine, you may rest assured that I shall make suitable provisions to provide for its future.'

'And Louisa?'

'My consideration will be for the child,' he said with cold indifference, unable to focus on Louisa at present.

'Then I suppose I shall have to be thankful for that,' James replied. 'I shall be at Bierlow Hall when you have decided what is to be done. Good day to you, Lord Dunstan.'

James stalked from the room, leaving Alistair to stare after him with a clenched jaw.

After James's departure Alistair stood staring out of the window for a long time, ordering a footman to cancel his carriage that was to have taken him to his club, no longer in any mood for socialising.

Self-disgust and burning fury coursed through him, reality crushing down on him as he suddenly found his life infuriating and complicated. Everything was out of his control and in a state of utter confusion—and all because he had been unable to keep his hands off Louisa Fraser.

He had spent years of evasion, trying to avoid a situation such as this, ignoring the whispers and sighs of women eager to shackle him once more with matrimony. And he had succeeded, believing himself immune, but it had only taken one look at Louisa, one curve of her lovely lips, for him to fall into a trap of his own making. He cursed himself for a fool.

Deep inside, what Marianne had done to him—her betrayal and the tragedy that had come afterwards—still haunted him. He had deliberately put the memory away, not wanting to look too carefully, but now he found it rising to the fore like some terrible spectre, so that he became caught up in its grip once more. To become deeply involved with a woman again was a situation he had always diligently avoided, but when he thought of Louisa, and her unhappy situation, he felt an uneasy pang of guilt.

He remembered how she had been, how she had looked—at Vauxhall, at Bricknell House, and that other time in the church and at Mr Brewster's bookshop—when she had acted every inch a gentlewoman, and he should have known that that was precisely what she was. He recalled her incredible passion when she had lain in his arms, her sweetness, how she had driven him mad with desire, and how he had been unable to put her from his mind.

That night spent with her had been like a drug to his senses that he could not name but could not get enough of. She had fed his hunger, and ever since she had left a dull listlessness had trailed after him. He had hoped the memory of her would dim, but since their parting his passion for her had not grown less—and neither had the pain.

He hadn't realised she had gained quite so much power over him. How could he have imagined for one minute that she was promiscuous? Yet, with a little encouragement from her, he had convinced himself that she was and treated her as such—and she had been too proud and desperate to retain her precious home to allow him to think anything else.

But, when he recalled the cold-blooded manner in which she had given herself to him to retain her family home, what pained him most of all was the fact that he could have been anyone. Her weak moral standards left her wanting in his eyes. His experience with Marianne had given him a contempt for ambitious, self-indulgent young women, who thought nothing of breaking their marriage vows. It was an experience he had sworn never to repeat.

He was unwilling to become involved yet again with another such as Marianne—and Louisa was no better. Yes! In essence she was just like her. Marianne, too, would have used the same kind of tactics to get what she wanted, having learned that there was no reason to tell the truth if it was to one's advantage to tell a lie.

And as to marriage! No. Not when he had his life perfectly under control. Never. Never again would he be shackled to a woman in wedlock. He did not want another woman at Huntswood, either at his table or in his bed. His physical needs were satisfied well enough by women seeking diversion for a few night hours, women who wanted from him what he wanted from them. But what was to be done?

Common sense battled with his conscience. Could he cast away his child as well as its mother in so callous a manner as to cause them to suffer for the rest of their lives?

Chapter Eight

Travelling from the village of Bierlow towards Bierlow Hall, the landlord of a local inn where he had stopped for refreshment having given him directions, Alistair's carriage moved at a steady pace, passing farms and thatched cottages, the road winding through a chequered patchwork of fields and long stretches of woodland. As he drove up the impressive avenue of oaks, with sunlight piercing the branches and dappling the lane with shadowy, dancing speckles, gradually the high ivy-clad wall that enclosed Bierlow Hall and its gardens came into view, the gables and tall chimneys of the large mansion projecting above.

Alistair was surprisingly impressed by what he saw, although it was obviously run-down and in dire need of attention. The Frasers' lack of money was reflected in the house itself, with its peeling paintwork and wild tangle of garden, but, when he first saw the house, he was unprepared. It had for him an aura of a time gone by, and there was a quiet grace and beauty in its neglect, and one had the feeling that its family was not extinct. He found himself drawn to it. He liked it—liked its warmth, its suggestion of an inner peace.

Through his own enquiries he knew the Frasers were an old and distinguished family in the county, but the extravagance of James Fraser and his weakness for the gaming tables had frittered away most of his inheritance, leaving his sister to live on a virtual pittance at Bierlow Hall. His thoughts went back to the time he had observed Louisa in church the morning after seeing her at Vauxhall, when he had witnessed her misery for himself, strongly suspecting her brother's reckless and utterly selfish behaviour to have been the cause.

As he stepped down from the carriage, Mrs Marsh, the elderly housekeeper, in a large white apron and white mob-cap, her hair hidden beneath the pouched crown, opened the door to see who was calling, becoming flustered and bobbing awkwardly on seeing the magnificent carriage and being confronted by such a formidable-looking gentleman. She was unused to opening the door to such distinguished visitors.

Alistair stepped inside the house, which was spotlessly clean and had a warm and welcoming aspect. It exuded the scent of beeswax and freshly hung herbs.

'Is Mr Fraser at home?'

'No, sir. I am afraid he is about some business on the estate.'

'And his sister?'

'In the garden, I believe. I shall go and fetch her this instant if you will be so good as to wait in the drawing room.'

'No,' he said, as she was about to show him the way into a room leading off from the hall, noticing through the half-open door that it was tastefully furnished, the hangings somewhat faded. 'Thank you, but do not trouble yourself. I shall find her myself.'

Before Mrs Marsh could direct him he had stepped briskly outside and was walking along the overgrown paths, drawn towards the sound of something creaking among a group of trees way beyond the house. He moved through the shrubbery, following the winding narrow path until he eventually came to a clearing. There seemed to be a golden mist about him, heightening the hues of a beautiful copper beech, resplendent in all its autumnal glory, its branches spread out like a gigantic parasol. Hanging from one of them was a swing, and sitting on its board was Louisa, gently swooping to and fro, careful not to let her feet touch the ground, her wonderful mane of strawberry-blonde hair flowing behind her.

Alistair paused, transfixed on seeing her like this. He had forgotten what a wonderful rich colour her hair was—like sunlight on gold—and seeing her again made every one of his senses clamour for her. There was that same fierce tug to his senses on being near her as there had been that first time he had seen her at the Spring Pleasure Gardens at Vauxhall.

He'd forgotten what a remarkably beautiful woman she was, with her rounded limbs, the way her head moved with a swaying grace, and a soft, inviting, lilting expression to her lips. He watched as her skirts and petticoats lifted when she stretched out her legs to gather momentum on the swing, revealing her shapely stockinged calves and fancy blue garters, calves he remembered as being white and like silk to touch.

Brusquely, he recollected himself and what it was that had brought him to Bierlow Hall, drawing himself up sharply, thinking disparagingly, as his inner turmoil turned to self-scorn, that he was a fool to think like this, a fool to be taken in by her. Inside she was every bit as deceitful and conniving as Marianne had been before her. She evidently had the ability to belong in whatever setting she happened to be in, and he found that realisation quite unsettling.

But one thing stood out bold and clear above everything else in his mind, something that was more important to him just then than his feelings for Louisa, and that was his unborn child. After his common sense had done battle with his conscience, his feelings had become possessive—and he knew he could not, would not, disown a child of his blood.

When he'd finally left London for Bierlow, he had decided that he had no alternative but to marry Louisa if he wanted to save his child from the taint of illegitimacy. But, because he could feel neither trust nor respect where she was concerned, she would have to agree to a marriage on his terms: it would be one of convenience, with nothing between them except the duty they each had towards the child.

Absorbed in her thoughts, Louisa did not realise Alistair was there until he stepped in front of the swing a short distance away. Shocked out of her reverie, immediately she scraped her feet on the ground and stopped, the violence of their parting springing instantly to the fore. Lightning seemed to scorch across the space between them, burning, eliminating everything in its path. Everything was obliterated but that invisible physical force searing through her body, so that she felt her flesh throb in agony as every nerve sprang to a trembling awareness of him—and instinctively she knew it was the same for him.

An unbidden flare of excitement rose up in the pit of her stomach, followed quickly by dread when she thought of the reason that had brought him to Bierlow Hall. Warily she watched him, looking at him nervously, wishing she could cool the waves of heat that mounted her cheeks—wishing she could run away, for she had not expected that he would come.

Everything about Alistair Dunstan spoke of control and command and she felt unable to confront him. She didn't want to. She wasn't ready. When James had returned from London in an angry mood after his confrontation with Lord Dunstan, he had left her in no doubt as to what Alistair's feelings were on being told that she was James's sister and with child due to her own foolishness.

She left the swing and stood utterly still, and with her translucent skin and her vast eyes, which were as wide and solemn as a baby owl's, she had an ethereal quality. Like a free spirit she confronted him, her head poised at a questioning angle, her hair spread over her shoulders like a ray of golden light, watching him approach as if she were some forest creature. But there was a shadowed hollowness to her cheekbones and she was pale, which told Alistair that the first weeks of her pregnancy were not going well.

But apart from this he thought she was different, somehow, and his heart took a savage and painful leap at the sight of her. She seemed like someone he had never seen before, looking more at home here than in the salons of London. She was like a child, making it hard for him to believe he had been taken in by a mere slip of a girl—and yet it was a woman who looked at him, with a woman's eyes.

He was aloof, his own eyes icy, metallic. His gaze swept over her, narrow and assessing, as if expecting to see her waistline already thickening with child, before snapping on her face. Trembling beneath the blast of his gaze, Louisa waited for him to move closer, her hands folded quietly in front of her, thinking how handsome he looked. He wore shiny black knee-boots, snug-fitting grey breeches and a dark green frock coat, unbuttoned to reveal a pale grey satin waistcoat.

Her heart beat madly as she gazed on his face, having thought she would never set eyes on him again. Until that moment she had thought she remembered exactly what he looked like, his well-chiselled features stamped indelibly on her mind, but what she saw now did not resemble what she remembered of him. Everything about him exuded brute strength and his eyes bore down into hers with cynicism, his jaw set and ruthless.

As she waited for him to speak to her, her eyes searching his granite features, she saw no sign of the passionate, sensual side to his nature, of the man who had held and kissed her with such tender passion. The expression on his face caused her an involuntary shiver, which was not one of pleasure. He moved closer, his penetrating stare relentless.

'So—this is where you live,' he said without preliminaries, abruptly breaking the silence between them at last.

'As you see,' Louisa replied with cool civility, prepared to be on the defensive, recognising that the stern set of his face and the thin line of his lips did not suggest much tolerance or forgiveness. 'But I do not think you have come to talk about the house.'

Alistair began pacing up and down in front of her in a slightly agitated manner, clearly angry at this unfortunate disturbance she had brought to his life.

'I have to say this is an unfortunate turn-out,' he said sharply, with slight accusation. 'Had I known this would happen I would never have got involved with you. It was bad enough finding out you are James Fraser's sister, but to be told that you are to bear a child—my child, it would seem—is insupportable.'

'It is a terrible thing that has happened—but it has and there it is. I—I behaved badly, I know. I was stupid, a naive fool, and I make no excuses for what I did. I was so desperate to retrieve my brother's IOU from you to save us from ruin that it never entered my head that this would happen. I should have known there would be repercussions for my behaviour—but I expected nothing on this scale.'

Alistair veered round, his eyes fierce, no longer able to control his anger. 'You're right. I should have sent you away the moment you arrived at my house. You came intent on deception and I cannot forgive you for that. I was deceived. *You* deceived me—

and I was a fool to be taken in by you. I will never be able to understand how you could stoop to lies and subterfuge to accomplish what you considered to be a worthy goal—how you could put practicality before ethics.'

'What can I say? I'm sorry,' she said quietly, wondering how she could begin to defuse his wrath, her remembrance of the night they had spent in each other's arms being how he'd had the ability to render her defenceless, causing her to fling caution and reason to the four winds. 'I realise that you must despise me for what I've done, and I cannot say that I blame you.'

'What you did no respectable woman would have dreamed of doing—which is a category from which you chose to eliminate yourself,' he said derisively.

Louisa's cheeks burned from the casual cruelty of the remark.

'No matter what my feelings are regarding you, Miss Fraser,' Alistair went on coldly, fixing her with a piercing stare, 'they must be cast aside for the time being. I am here to settle this unpleasant affair as quickly as possible and with the minimum of fuss. Before we go any further and I agree to a marriage taking place between us, I want to be absolutely certain that the child is mine.'

Two high spots of indignation highlighted the flush on Louisa's cheeks and a spark of anger flared in her eyes, while feeling astonishment at his words. Not for one moment had she thought she would receive an offer of marriage from him.

'Of course the child is yours,' she said fiercely. 'You are the only man I have ever been with. You saw the evidence with your own eyes—which you so brutally and coldly pointed out to me. I apologise for not being who and what you thought I was—a woman who had already dragged herself through the beds of half the gentlemen in the kingdom—but I cannot see why my being a virgin put you in such a state.'

He gave her a hard look, his mouth tightening as he stared at her. 'No, I don't believe you would. Of course, you know that your brother came to see me?'

'Yes, and if you must know I tried to prevent him—but in his outrage he wouldn't listen. He feels responsible for my welfare, which is only natural, I suppose.'

'He made that perfectly clear.'

'The child need not concern you—and, indeed, I must say I am surprised that you have come here. You know very well that I never expected to see you again—especially after you condemned me in so cruel and harsh a manner.'

'I said nothing you did not deserve,' he said, unrepentant. 'But did you think I would abandon you—knowing this?'

'Please do not feel you have a duty towards me. Whatever I want, it is not that—to hold you through some obligation that would make a mockery of what we shared that night, however brief it was.'

There was no trace of gentleness on his handsome face, no softening when she reminded him of that night. His blue eyes were like chips of ice. 'Don't confuse physical desire with love. Just because you shared my bed—because I made love to you—does not mean you touched my heart. However, this changes things between us.'

'It needn't. You can go back to London and forget you ever came here—forget about me and the child. I promise you that I shall not come looking for you in the future.'

Alistair threw her a look of angry exasperation. 'You can be very stupid.'

'Can I? I realise that the last thing you want is to marry me—and I do understand. If you will cast your mind back, it was never part of our agreement to go beyond that one night. What happened was entirely my fault. I accept that, but do not forget that it takes two to make a child, Lord Dunstan, and such a development is sometimes inevitable when a man and woman share the same bed—or so I was led to believe,' she said with heavy sarcasm.

'I did not do it alone. I realise this complicates matters for you, and to avoid any embarrassment—either for you or for James—I intend going away until after the child is born. Contrary to what James said to you,' she said, with a proud lift to her chin, 'I want nothing from you. Do not feel under any obligation.'

He looked at her hard, distant and unresponsive. 'I don't. My obligation is towards the child. Since your brother left after imparting this information to me I have given the matter a great deal of careful thought, and I confess in the beginning nothing would have made me even contemplate marriage to you. I planned to make some money over to the child and put some in trust until a later date—but I would despise myself if I did not try to do better than that. You say the child is mine—which, because I already have a son, will not make him my heir should it be a boy—but he must be spared the stain of illegitimacy.'

'And if it is a girl?'

He looked at her coldly. 'She will still be my daughter and Mark's sister, and deserves better than what you intend for her.'

'And how do you know what I intend, Lord Dunstan?'

'I assume it is your intention to have the child adopted.'

Louisa stared at him as if he had struck her. Alistair saw the pupils of her eyes dilate until the amber had almost disappeared, and all the blood drained from her face until even her lips were pale.

'Then you do not know me,' she said, with so much anger in her voice that every word was clipped. 'That is precisely the kind of arrogant assumption I would expect you to make. But you have never been more wrong. No matter what my circumstances are, if I were the poorest and meanest creature on God's earth, nothing and no one will ever persuade me to part with my child. I've told you. I expect nothing, I want nothing from you. You are not required to marry me.'

Alistair's jaw tightened, his eyes burning furiously down into hers, while feeling a surge of relief and thankfulness that she had spoken as she had. 'In all conscience it would appear I have no alternative, but it is certainly not to save your reputation that I do so. Get it through that pretty head of yours that I do not want to marry you—not you or anyone else. I have lived through one disastrous marriage, which taught me that it is an unpleasant experience I have no desire to repeat.'

'I would have imagined you would have too much common sense to attribute to all women what you have experienced in one,' she said cuttingly.

'You would say that. You, who showed me so much vulnerability, so much generous passion—a woman who in her loving was so like Marianne—putting me on the defensive. In my own fear of repetition I aim to make damned sure that I keep you at arm's length. We will go through a ceremony—but a ceremony does not make a marriage. It will be no more than a formality. All you will get from me is my name and rank. It will be what the French call a *marriage blanc*. Pragmatically, it will be a marriage of convenience—in the best interests of the child—with nothing between us but the child, and what I am offering you is also a way of maintaining your honour and dignity. Of course, I would have preferred none of this to have happened, but my child is paramount to all else.'

Louisa looked at him coldly. 'Our child, Lord Dunstan,' she countered. 'Still, I am glad to see you are not entirely without self-interest,' she said scathingly.

'What else? It will hardly be a matter of love. In fact, I no longer know what the word means. Marianne burned almost every emotion out of me. Poets may write about it. Balladeers may sing about it. It exists for others—but not for me. So, despite the feelings and emotions we aroused in each other on that night we came together, the depths of passion we reached, do not fool yourself into believing ours will be a love match. I might even go so far as to say that, under the circumstances, it will be a forced marriage—and, for myself, a source of bitter regret,' he rasped, his voice low and harsh within the silence of the trees.

Louisa glared at him, wondering what Marianne had done to cause so much hatred—or what he was guilty of as far as Marianne was concerned that had made her turn from him to someone else.

'Spare me your sentiments on love, Lord Dunstan,' she scoffed furiously, feeling the need to give back hurt for hurt. 'I comprehend perfectly how you feel. But what makes you imagine I want to be your wife when you insult and degrade me at every turn—when you make me an offer of marriage so unwillingly? You have certainly said nothing that can tempt me into accepting to live in such a miserable state for the rest of my life with a man who despises me. How dare you assume that marriage to you is a solution to all my troubles,' she cried, 'when you're the cause of them? I am certain that marriage to you would make them a thousand times worse. I would rather live in wretchedness than submit to that.'

Alistair's eyes blazed suddenly, with the incredible blueness of a sapphire, as he felt the savagery of her words goad him to further anger. 'You brought this on yourself. You chose your own fate,' he snarled, his voice so strong and vibrant that Louisa recoiled from it. 'You offered yourself to me for the sake of your home. You wanted to retain it so badly that you were prepared to run any risk for it. I can understand that in a way, but there are some risks that nothing can justify. If you play with fire you must be able to take the consequences.'

Rage rose up like flames licking inside Louisa. 'Ever since my parents died I have never been accountable to anyone for my actions—not even to James, who, regardless of the fact that he was my guardian, was never here anyway. As far as he was concerned, Bierlow Hall was only an asset—something he could sell—to whittle away slowly to feed his gambling. And the way I see it you are no better. I cannot forget that his ruin was inflicted by you.'

Alistair's eyes narrowed, flashing dangerously with anger. 'And in that you are mistaken.'

'I don't think so,' she went on recklessly, the colour heightening on her cheeks as she glared at him with bitter accusation, heedless of his mounting rage. 'You knew his situation and yet you continued to raise the stakes of the game higher and higher until he had nothing left. It was clear to me that night, Lord Dunstan, that for some selfish, malicious reason of your own—which no motive in the world can excuse and which I have no wish to know about— you derive immense pleasure from riding roughshod over everyone, especially those whose situation in life is not equal to your own. Anyone in situations such as these should be treated with compassion, not derision and scorn. Where James was concerned you succeeded admirably, and I can only pity anyone else who has the misfortune to stumble into your path. All this is largely of your doing.'

'My doing!' Alistair exploded, showing incredulity at her outburst and no sign of remorse. 'I would not have expected you to deceive yourself on that score. Your brother had no one to blame for what happened but himself.'

'Nevertheless, you can see why the terms of your offer are detestable to me. It is far better for a child to be happy with one parent than wretched with two.'

It was exactly the reaction Alistair had expected from the proud beauty who had let him believe in London that her life was one long, frivolous social whirl. This he now knew to have been nothing but a charade, and that, living in the country for most of her life, she'd had little contact with the social complexities of London. She stood quivering beside the swing, her hands clenched by her sides, visibly struggling to regain her composure as she tried to decide what was best to be done. He felt his own anger begin to melt and he looked at her thoughtfully for a moment, touched, despite himself, by her obvious distress, and perhaps also by some private scruples.

'Louisa, you must be sensible,' he said on a more gentle note, his expression grave as he combed impatient fingers of frustration through his hair. 'You cannot bring up a child on your own. You will never endure the disgrace and humiliation when it becomes public knowledge. People can be extremely cruel in such situations. The scandal will be intolerable. You will never withstand it alone.'

'Better to be pilloried than married to a monster.'

Her stubbornness provoked Alistair's eyes to blaze with renewed fury. 'And you will find out what kind of monster I can be if you carry on in this vein, lady,' he growled. 'The child you are carrying is mine, don't forget. I *will* have a say in how it is reared and I refuse to have it brought up a bastard just because its mother—in her abominable pride—refuses my offer of marriage. It is not an offer I make lightly, as well you know, having already had one obligation in the past. Lord knows, I don't want to sacrifice my freedom—but if you did not find it difficult sacrificing your virtue to a total stranger, then I suppose I shall have to take a lesson from you and grin and bear it.'

'And with sentiments such as these you expect me to agree to become your wife?' Louisa flared incredulously. 'What a sad and sorry pair we would make. When I set about retrieving my brother's IOU—when I allowed myself to transgress against all my principles, breaking every rule that I had been taught with regard to my virtue—it may surprise you to learn that that night I sacrificed something else, Lord Dunstan, something which was just as precious to me as my virtue. My self-respect.'

'And was it worth it? Was it worth all this?'

'If you mean was it worth retaining my home then yes, it was worth it. My only regret is that I could not think of a way of keeping Bierlow Hall without using you to do so. As for the child—only time will tell. I only hope that *you* got *your* money's worth, Lord Dunstan.'

A thin smile drew his stern lips apart. 'As things have turned out, it would seem I've got a good deal more. So is it agreed that we will be married?' he asked, choosing to ignore her angry outburst of a moment before, his instinct telling him she would come to see the sense of his offer, despite her aversion to him. When he saw her hesitate, with defiance and resentment continuing to glare out of her eyes, he moved closer, his angry face only inches from her own. He caught her arm as she was about to move away, his fingers gentle, but they seemed to drive into her, sapping her strength, her resistance, and any hope she had of escape.

'Marrying me is the only possible solution to your problems, you know,' he went on. 'If you refuse, then consider your brother. He will have to partake of your disgrace—and any hope he has of marrying well will be dashed. Can you live with that on your conscience, as well as depriving a child of its father?'

Still Louisa hesitated, abruptly turning her back on him when he relinquished his hold on her arm, struggling against the insidious feeling of surrender which was steadily crushing her, her immediate sensation being one of drowning. How could she endure living with a man who laid down such harsh conditions as he had? Then came the realisation that she had no option. What did it matter whom she married as long as her child was spared the stigma of illegitimacy?

Suddenly nothing seemed important any more. Everything paled beside this. He was right, she thought, with all the bitterness that came with defeat. She really had no choice. But, when she considered what her feelings were for Alistair Dunstan, she could not deny that he drew her like a magnet. In fact, where he was concerned her mind was all confusion, for she wanted to be his wife, to belong to him, as much as she wanted to be free of him.

As if all her energy had drained out of her, her shoulders drooped and she turned to face him, her throat constricting painfully, and suddenly she wanted to cry. Endeavouring to keep her voice steady, she spoke quietly, her eyes tear-bright.

'Very well,' she conceded. 'You are right. I have no choice. But with so much bitterness and so many differences between us our marriage will be a sham. I don't know you. How am I to judge what kind of husband you will make?'

Reading panic overlying her inner torture, Alistair's expression softened a little. 'Few couples know each other really well before they marry. You will have to take me on trust.'

'It seems I shall have to.'

'We neither of us know what the future holds, but if we are to have any kind of life together we must strive for an amicable partnership. For the sake of the child we must be united. My mother died when I was a boy, and, despite the love of my father and my elder sister, Julia, who became like a mother to me, it is a dreadful lack for a child when one parent isn't there.'

'You will allow me to return to Bierlow Hall, won't you? It will always be an integral part of my life.'

'I would not wish it otherwise. But Huntswood will be your home.'

'Thank you.'

'Then, if that is settled, for obvious reasons there must be no delay. The wedding will take place very soon. You do wish to be married in Bierlow, I take it—not in London?'

She nodded. 'Yes.'

'Then I shall call and see the minister when I pass through the village on my way back to London. The first of the banns can be read this coming Sunday.'

Louisa stared at him in astonishment. 'So soon?'

'Yes. It is best. You will leave the arrangements to me, but there will be no pomp at the ceremony. That must be understood.'

'That will suit me perfectly.'

'I would like you to come to London to meet my sister, Julia. I would also like you to be fitted out with a new wardrobe before the wedding, which she has very kindly offered to take charge of.'

Louisa's heart sank at the thought that he had discussed her with his sister, and she wondered just how much he had disclosed to her. 'You—you have told her about me?'

'Naturally. Julia and I have few secrets from each other,' he replied brusquely. 'Do you have any friends or relatives who you can stay with in London?'

'No. No one—and James has given up his house in Henrietta Street.'

'Then have the goodness to present yourself at Dunstan House in town tomorrow. My plans for immediately after the wedding are to take you to Huntswood. Fortunately it is a convenient time for me to leave London anyway, my business being concluded, and I am sure you will like it there. It is very peaceful—not unlike Bierlow. The countryside should remind you of it.'

At that moment James appeared, coming hurriedly along the path towards them, having been told by Mrs Marsh that they had a distinguished visitor who had gone into the garden to find Louisa.

Abruptly Alistair turned from her. 'I will discuss the terms of the marriage with your brother before I leave.'

'Wait,' Louisa said, halting him as he was about to turn away. 'What is it?'

'I—I have to ask about your wife—Marianne? Where is she? What happened to her?'

'Never fear,' he said, his handsome lips curling with light irony. 'I am not about to commit bigamy if that's what's worrying you. Marianne is dead. She was killed in unfortunate circumstances on the night she left me.'

An icy thrill ran through Louisa as she watched Alistair walk away from her, an awful sense of shock invading her entire being, although why she should feel this way puzzled her, for she had never really given much thought as to what had become of his former wife. But, with a certain conviction in her heart, it flashed through her mind that there had been something mysterious and sinister about her death. Then she shuddered, casting the awful thought to the back of her mind, refusing to fill her head with such nonsense and telling herself not to be silly.

As she began making her way slowly back to the house, she had to admit that she was curious as to the manner of Marianne's death, and why she had not heard that she was dead before now. Neither Timothy nor James seemed to be aware of it either, for she was certain they would have told her. And when she had spoken to Alistair and Lady Bricknell about her they had failed to mention it, leaving her with the impression that she had left him for someone else and that as a consequence he had divorced her.

Whatever lay behind the mystery, all thoughts of Marianne were obliterated when she realised, with a pang of almost unbearable anguish, how little time she had left at Bierlow Hall before she must leave for London.

The following day it was a subdued Louisa who left Bierlow Hall to travel to London. She would not return until the wedding. A listlessness settled over her as she sat across from James, who was immensely relieved and pleased with the developments. It was all turning out far better than he'd dared to hope. Louisa was confused by all that had happened, by the changes that had suddenly turned her life upside down. In a moment of anger, confusion and despair she had committed herself to this course. She was sick in mind, bewildered, and weary in body, made worse because her pregnancy often made her feel quite ill.

When she entered Dunstan House she could not help remembering the last time she had been there—or the moment she had left in such dreadful circumstances. She could not have foreseen that she would enter it again as the future Lady Dunstan. Alistair wasn't there, but had left instructions with the servants—who received her with welcoming smiles—that she was to be shown to the bedchamber that had been assigned to her. It was situated at the back of the house because it was quieter, overlooking the gardens and Green Park.

It was with tears in her eyes that she said goodbye to James, who was to stay with Timothy at his family's town house in Long Acre until they returned to Bierlow for the wedding, and he promised to return to Dunstan House the following morning to see her and Lord Dunstan. She watched him go, her mind crying out for him not to leave her, wishing she could be with him. However, apart from Timothy, she had never met any other member of the family, and it would have been most inappropriate of her or James to have suggested such a thing.

Already she was feeling homesick and so very lonely, wishing she were back at Bierlow Hall. Her determination not to let it slip out of her family was the reason for the sorry plight she was in now, but at least that particular anguish would be lifted if James was sincere and abided by his decision to remain there, and she was content that he firmly intended marrying Amelia—something her parents would not have considered had she, Louisa, refused to marry Alistair and her condition had become public knowledge.

Alone in her bedchamber, she moved to stand by the window, aware that an uncertain future loomed ahead. She tried to quell the nervous fears that were mounting inside her as the time drew near when she must face Alistair. Dusk was fast approaching and lengthening shadows stretched across the park, of which she had a splendid view over the high garden wall. In the silence that shrouded the vast house, with a sigh she let her thoughts wander.

Was it so short a time since she had been in this very house— in another room, Alistair's room, in his bed, when her body had quivered with fear and anticipation? How happy she had been that night, despite her reason for being there, when she had loved Alistair with all her youthful being, and when he had made love to her with a passionate intensity, initiating her in the overwhelming joys of love. But tonight no man would come to her in this house. No desire would come to claim her body in which life was growing.

She moved towards the bed in the centre of the room and tiredness overcame her. Lying down on the quilt, she closed her eyes, drifting off into a deep slumber, knowing nothing else until she was woken by a maid, who had come to tell her that Lord Dunstan had arrived home and was asking for her. With a pounding headache she rose, feeling quite ill and wishing she could stay in her room and not face anyone that night. In an attempt to revive her flagging spirits and cool the heat inside her head, she swilled her face with cold water. Tidying her hair, she smoothed her skirts with trembling fingers before following the maid downstairs, who showed her into the room where she had taken tea with Alistair on her previous visit to the house.

The room was empty and her mind was in a strange, feverish state as she waited for Alistair, but then she heard his brisk step on the tiled floor of the hall outside. The door opened and he came in, closing it behind him, and she was unprepared for the way her heart began to pound, becoming loud in her ears so she thought she might pass out at any moment.

He regarded her coolly, like a stranger, distant and completely different from the man she had spent the night with in his bed, who had made love to her with such intimate tenderness. Fear stirred inside her, fear and consternation at the gulf that had opened between them. He stood looking at her, and there was a sudden quickening in the depths of his eyes when they rested on her face, but there was no welcoming smile to soften his stern and masterful features.

They were not the same two people who had come together before. Then, Alistair had seen Louisa as a potential mistress, and they would have claimed nothing from each other but the pleasures to be enjoyed in each other's arms. Men did not marry the women they chose as their mistresses, and as his future wife he saw Louisa as someone completely different.

Crossing the room, he seated himself, motioning her to a chair opposite, not wanting to get too close, but close enough to look at her, near enough to smell the delicate perfume of her skin. He was sternly formal, bearing no trace of a happy bridegroom, seeming awesome and remote.

'Please sit down.'

He had no difficulty in sustaining an air of cold detachment, which had become second nature to him over the years. It was his most useful weapon when dealing with the attentions of the opposite sex. Lord knew, he'd had enough practice.

Her head pounding with an ache that was like nothing she had experienced before, compounded of misery, built-up tension and her condition, Louisa mechanically obeyed, sitting quite still, her hands folded on her lap as she waited for him to speak. What she had seen, that sudden spark in his eyes on seeing her, had been extinguished like a flame. The man who had loved her so ardently had withdrawn from her completely, which she would have to accept as just punishment for what she had done.

'I apologise for not being here when you arrived. I've been to Richmond to fetch Julia, who has only recently returned from Huntswood, where she has been spending a short time with Mark and Sophie. When I returned I was told you were sound asleep, so I instructed the maid not to wake you until it was almost time for dinner.'

'Thank you. I was more tired than I thought,' said Louisa quietly, trying to ignore the dizzy nausea spinning round inside her, 'and sleep is the best way of shortening a period of waiting.'

'How are you?' he asked suddenly, the question abrupt, although he was concerned to see that the lustre had gone from her eyes. Her face was like a delicate piece of carved ivory, so pale, but he thought it only served to emphasise the purity of its lines. Clearly she was not finding the early weeks of her pregnancy easy, and he was surprised by the concern and sympathy that washed over him.

She gave him a faltering little smile, knowing he was referring to her pregnancy, which caused her some embarrassment, and she felt her cheeks flush. It was surprising, for modesty was not a word that would normally apply between two people who knew each other's bodies as intimately as they did.

'I have felt better, I cannot deny,' she confessed, although she gave him no indication of how dreadful she was feeling at that moment. 'But it does improve, I am told. Pregnancy is supposed to be a natural process for women, so I shall have to endure it as best I can.'

'Have you seen a doctor?'

'No,' she said softly, looking down at her hands. 'I was both ashamed and afraid to face the doctor who has attended me all my life with this.'

He nodded, understanding this perfectly well. 'Then I shall arrange for you to see one here in London before we leave for Sussex.'

'Thank you. Your—your sister is here, is she?' she asked in an effort to divert the conversation away from the child.

'Yes. She has expressed a wish to meet you.'

'Then I look forward to meeting her. Am I to meet your son— and your other sister?'

'No. Both Mark and Sophie are at Huntswood. I shall introduce you when we go down there after the wedding.'

'And your sister's husband? Am I to meet him also?'

'I'm afraid not. Being a politician, Joshua is immersed in his work at Westminster, but you will meet very soon. Julia and her husband often travel down to Huntswood. You will like him. He's a quiet, gentle man. Julia has kindly offered to stay here to act as your chaperon until we leave for Bierlow for the wedding, in order to protect your reputation—which we both know has been ruined through both our faults,' he said drily, 'and which I have no intention of blackening still further.

'Normally Julia would not consider it seemly for a bride and groom to sleep under the same roof until they are wed and would have taken you to her home at Richmond to stay, but Dunstan House is closer to the shops and, as things stand between us, it hardly matters anyway. Tomorrow it is her intention to take you shopping for a new wardrobe. She knows the most fashionable shops to visit and all the best dressmakers, who will measure and fit you for an extensive trousseau.'

'That is extremely generous of you.'

'Generosity doesn't come into it. As Lady Dunstan it is important that you dress accordingly. I shall also expect you to behave as befits your new status. In short, there will be no scandals—nothing to bring shame and disgrace to the name you will bear. Is that understood?'

'Yes, of course.' She felt colour flood her cheeks. 'What have you told your sister?' she asked, fully prepared to be met with abject disapproval and hostility when she came face to face with Julia. 'She—she knows about the child?'

'Naturally. It is hardly the kind of thing that can be concealed.'

'What was her reaction? Was—was she terribly shocked?' Louisa asked tentatively.

'At first—which was to be expected. But her relief on being told I was to marry again outweighed the shock and any objections she felt on learning of your condition. Ever since my first wife died she has been forever telling me it is high time I looked for someone else.'

'Then I can only hope that she approves of me,' whispered Louisa.

Instinctively Alistair knew there would be instant rapport between them when they met, and he was to be proved right.

'If it makes you feel any easier—despite what I told you yesterday when I visited your home about there being no secrets between Julia and myself—I did not tell her of the circumstances that brought us together, which are known only to ourselves, your brother and his friend Timothy Hacket. I would like to keep it that way. I am sure you will agree that it is a matter that needs delicate handling.'

'Of course.'

'I doubt Julia would approve of such conduct in the future Lady Dunstan. I also dread to imagine what effect it would have on Sophie should she come to learn of it. It is hardly the kind of example a brother should set for a sister of such tender years. I am not proud of the way I behaved, and I have no wish for my indiscretion to be exposed to either of my sisters.'

The bitterness in his tone was unmistakable and Louisa saw mockery in his eyes when she glanced at him and was wounded by it—more so because of her own guilt in the affair. Until that moment she wouldn't have believed she could feel more ashamed than she already did.

'I understand,' she replied quietly.

Alistair watched the tension and emotion play across her lovely, expressive face, and for the life of him he could not think why he was being so hard on her, why he was finding it so difficult to put her at her ease, but then, remembering all their previous encounters, she always had robbed him of the ability to think rationally.

'I have told Julia that we met at the Spring Gardens at Vauxhall some time ago—which is no lie even though we were not introduced at the time—and that we became better acquainted after that.'

'I see. At least I shall know what to say to her should she ask me—and I must thank you for sparing further damage being done to my already lacerated pride. Had you told her the sordid details, then my humiliation would have been complete.' Drawing a long, shaky breath, Louisa clasped her hands in front of her and met Alistair's hard gaze, determined to call for a truce.

'Must you make everything so difficult, Alistair? Must there be enmity between us?' she asked quietly, cautiously. Encouraged by his lack of argument, she continued. 'I realise how difficult—how inconvenient—marrying me is for you, but surely nothing that has happened should make us treat each other badly. There is one thing I will ask of you. Can we not at least be cordial towards each other? There is no reason why not, is there?'

Alistair wavered, unable to resist the soft appeal in those huge amber eyes of hers. He sighed, his expression becoming more relaxed as he capitulated a little. 'No. None that I can see. And you are right. We must both try to make the best of things.'

Louisa had to suppress the urge to utter a deep sigh of relief, for at that moment the door opened to admit a tall, attractive woman, whom she already knew to be Alistair's sister, recognising her after seeing her in St James's Park—that unfortunate day when she had been with Sir Charles Meredith, whose presence had prevented introductions being made between them at that time.

Chapter Nine

Julia was dressed in her favourite shade of willow-green, her dark hair dressed neatly and shining softly in the candles' glow. Having recovered from the shock Alistair's news of his forthcoming marriage had caused her, and despite the fact that the lady he had chosen to be his wife had no dowry—although he had guaranteed her suitability, her deceased father having been a gentleman of some repute, if somewhat impoverished—and that she was in an extremely delicate condition, she was prepared to overlook these unfortunate facts in her delight that her brother had decided to settle down at last.

It would be a mistake to say that at first she had not had her doubts, feeling that a marriage based on such a beginning was a prelude to disaster, a disaster Alistair could well do without after his turbulent marriage to Marianne. She had even questioned him about the paternity of the child, asking him if he was absolutely certain that he was the father. He had assured that her he was and that he would take full responsibility. But he was not happy. She could see that. However, the situation was of his own making, and if the child was indeed his then he was under an obligation to marry Louisa Fraser. Whatever the circumstances were that had brought Alistair and Louisa together were between themselves. She would not interfere.

But secretly her hopes, which had become subdued since his unhappy marriage to Marianne had ended so tragically, had soared when he had told her. Since that time he had showed no genuine fascination for any one woman, and she had begun to despair that he ever would.

A spark of interest showed in Julia's eyes as they immediately rested on Louisa, who stood watching her, pale with apprehension. She smiled, in an effort to put her at her ease, moving across the room with poise and a slow grace, her eyes tender, for she was determined to befriend this beautiful young woman who had brought her brother once again to the brink of matrimony.

Alistair introduced them, thankful that Julia had been so over-come with shock on being confronted by Charles Meredith in St James's Park all those weeks ago, that she had failed to notice that Louisa had been his companion, which might have created an un-easy beginning to their friendship.

Julia took Louisa's hand and pulled her down onto the sofa, her serene blue gaze resting on her softly. All her doubts about Louisa making Alistair a suitable wife dissolved when she saw her. She felt an instant liking for this rather quiet, unhappy young woman and drawn to her in a way that surprised her.

She was more lovely than Alistair had described, despite the fact that her classically beautiful face was taut with anxiety and uncertainty. She had a lost, almost desperate appeal in her eyes, and was no doubt feeling demoralised by her condition, but as their gazes met she felt a surge of confidence, suddenly conscious that beneath the pleasant exterior of this woman, with her soft feminine elegance, was a will every bit as strong and stubborn as Alistair's.

'I am delighted to welcome you into the family, Louisa, and look forward to getting to know you better.'

'Thank you,' Louisa replied, a little shyly, seeing she need not have worried about meeting Julia, and finding her kindness com-forting after Alistair's coldness. She was so gently solicitous that she found herself warming towards her. Fighting desperately to ignore her throbbing headache, which simply refused to go away, she managed a pale smile. 'You are very kind.'

'And you are extremely lovely, my dear.' Julia's eyes twinkled. 'Now I begin to understand how impossible it was for Alistair to resist you.'

Louisa flushed, embarrassed by her words, and a dark scowl of disapproval appeared on Alistair's face at his sister's outspokenness, but Julia laughed lightly, well used to her brother's occasional dark moods and disapproving looks and knowing how to temper them. She was not in the least sorry that her words might have caused either of them to feel a sense of awkwardness.

'Alistair has told me the reason why you have to marry with such haste, Louisa,' she said on a more serious, gentle note, with just a trace of reproof in her tone, 'which is unfortunate—and I have to say that I cannot countenance such behaviour. Time presses, however, and it is not for me to sit in judgement or to interfere in something which is entirely between your two selves. That is your affair. I am just very relieved that you have both seen the error of what you have done and decided to do the honourable thing. You have an obligation to the child to marry—but I do hope you also feel deeply enough about each other to marry in these circumstances.'

Alistair's gaze met Louisa's, but she could read nothing in it. Julia's quiet, imperious tone would have been enough to daunt even the strongest heart—and Alistair was no exception, although not the type of man to be easily intimidated by a woman, and had it been said by anyone else he would have launched a bitter attack. But this was his older sister, whom he loved and respected, and he took her gentle reproach lightly, prepared to be tolerant, and Louisa suspected that Julia would not overstep the mark by antagonising her brother.

'Is the sermon over, Julia?' Alistair asked tersely.

A smile lit up her whole face and she laughed easily. 'Yes. No questions, I promise. It only leaves me to wish you both every happiness. Alistair tells me he is to take you to Huntswood immediately after the wedding, Louisa. Is that not so, Alistair?' she said, looking once more at her brother, her seriousness of a moment before having disappeared.

'That is my intention. When news of the marriage gets out it is bound to create a stir. It is my wish to avoid the inevitable curiosity and questions. Besides, I am anxious to introduce Louisa to Mark and Sophie. The sooner they become acquainted the better.'

'I agree. You will like Huntswood, Louisa,' Julia said. 'It's a lovely old house and Mark, who is six years old, is adorable. As for Sophie,' she said on a deep sigh, her brow creasing in a slight frown, 'she is a high-spirited sixteen-year-old girl, who is becoming increasingly wilful the older she gets. Unfortunately I cannot spend as much time with her as I would like to, and Alistair cannot see why I worry about her—which is so typical of a man when he has other matters he considers are far more important to worry about than a headstrong younger sister.'

Her lips broke into a sudden smile as she looked at Louisa. 'But who knows, being more her age you might understand her better than I do, Louisa—and it will do her good to have another woman in the house she can converse with. Now come along. Let's go and eat. It's been a long day—and I don't know about you but I am ravenous.'

How Louisa wished she could feel the same. Throughout the meal Alistair was silent, with an ironic set to his mouth, prepared to let his sister do most of the talking, which she did with relish, regaling Louisa on all she could expect to find at Huntswood. Louisa tried to concentrate, to listen with politeness and enthusiasm, but it was no good. She was so very tired and her head still ached abominably. All through the meal the struggle went on within her. She ate half-heartedly, nibbling at her food, not in the least hungry, and wanting more than anything for the meal to end so that she could escape to her room.

Seated across from her, Alistair was studying her pale and strained features, noticing the absent way she toyed with her food. He regarded her anxiously, concerned by the quietness of her tone when she spoke.

Louisa shifted in her chair, becoming uncomfortable under his scrutiny, casting her eyes down at her plate, until she promptly demonstrated all her pent-up misery and tension by putting a hand to her head as a wave of dizziness swept over her and she broke out in a cold sweat. Letting the spoon fall from her fingers, it clattered loudly onto her plate. Immediately Julia's eyes were full of concern and she placed her napkin on the table and rose, but before she could reach her Louisa gasped and asked them to excuse her, quickly springing from her chair and running from the room.

Feeling her heart labouring in her breast, in a sick muddle of distress, Louisa could see the stairs ahead of her through a fuzzy arc across her vision. They suddenly seemed a long way off and she stared at them in the dimness, nausea overwhelming her as her vision wavered. She knew she ought to try to cross to them, but her body had lost the ability, and her mind could not summon the will. Her legs were suddenly heavy, so heavy she could not move them, and she sank down to her knees before falling forwards onto the cold tiles of the hall.

Although Julia, who had anxiously followed her, was quick to spring towards her, Alistair was there first, scooping her up into his arms.

'Poor child. This is all too much for her. What must she be going through?' said Julia, in alarm, coming to stand beside him.

'Have one of the servants fetch Dr Sheridan,' Alistair ordered. 'I'll carry her to her room.'

Surfacing out of the swirling darkness that had briefly claimed her senses, Louisa half opened her eyes when she found herself being placed on something soft. In the gathering darkness she saw a shadowy figure above her, recognising Alistair, his features harshly etched, and she stared up at him desperately. She could hardly see him for the dizzy blackness that swam before her eyes. She struggled to rise but an awful feeling of sickness and Alistair's hands placed firmly on her shoulders made her sink back, breathing deeply, onto the bed.

Alistair looked down at her, taking a deep breath, relief and emotion spinning around him when she opened her eyes, but he saw in them an expression of silent pain. Her face was like wax, her eyes enormous, and the look in them was so touching that he felt a surge of deep compassion. Suddenly tears welled behind her eyes, treacherously threatening to burst and pour down her cheeks. He saw them shining, and sighed.

'That bad, eh?'

Biting her trembling lip, she nodded and turned her face away.

'It's all right,' he murmured softly. 'Everything is all right. Don't try to talk.'

He spoke more easily than he'd spoken to her in a long time, causing instant warmth to spring up inside her. 'I'm so sorry,' she whispered. 'I feel so dreadfully ill. I can't think what is the matter with me.'

Gently touching her chin with his fingers, Alistair turned her face towards him. 'Can't you?' he murmured, with a lazy, tender smile that surprised her and made her senses leap, and made her think he was behaving like a concerned and devoted husband. But a bitter pain twisted her heart and she reproached herself for being a fool, telling herself that she should know better, that his tenderness was feigned.

'I think we both know it is a small matter of the child. You told me you weren't feeling well earlier.'

'That's true. But today I feel far worse than I have before.'

'I believe that can be put down to nerves and the stress of the journey to London. You've been through a lot recently. You need rest,' he said softly, smiling, kindly and concerned. 'Just lie there. The doctor will not be long in coming.'

Having sent one of the servants for the doctor, Julia entered, busying herself with bathing Louisa's face with eau-de-Cologne. Louisa smiled up at her gratefully.

'Thank you.'

The doctor when he came, after an examination at which only Julia was present, confirmed her pregnancy and that her sickness was due to it, reassuring her that it was not serious and that it would pass. After making her drink some kind of cordial, a short while later the sickness left her and colour began returning to her cheeks.

Julia left to show the doctor out and Alistair returned to the room. His eyes were drawn to Louisa as if by a magnet. His heart beat faster. He could see the fluent shape of her body beneath the bedclothes in relaxed perfection, one leg drawn up a little higher than the other. He suddenly found himself wishing he could pull the covers back and climb in with her, for the memories of their night together lingered—a remembrance of sensations.

In silence Louisa watched him approach the bed. His presence sparked a pleasure inside her so sharp she felt bruised by it. She tried not to dwell on the memory of being in this house with him before, where she was still able to hear his whispers of endearment, to feel the surge of pleasure when he had touched her, made love to her, the remembrance of it making her want to weep. She hoped he would never realise that the hunger she still felt was so intense it continued to haunt her and make her think of it every time she looked at him.

That was when she realised she could not live without him and that she was glad she was marrying him, even though he did not want her to be his wife in the true sense. From the very first he had laid a spell on her and nothing would ever be the same again. Unconsciously she had come to love him on the night they had spent together, and above all else she wanted him to know that the child inside her had grown from that love.

Alistair stood looking down at her with an odd, contemplative look, feeling a strange urge to protect. She seemed so childlike, and pure as Sophie. A forelock of blonde hair had fallen to her eyebrows, and, still holding her eyes, instinctively he reached out and slowly swept it back, gently tucking it behind her ear.

'How are you feeling now?'

'Better, thank you. Just tired, that's all,' she said listlessly.

'Then I'll disturb you no longer and leave you in my sister's capable hands,' he said softly. 'Goodnight, Louisa.'

She watched him go as Julia entered, and she swallowed against the tightness in her chest. Once again her eyes clouded over with tears she found impossible to repress.

'I'm so sorry. I did not mean this to happen,' she mumbled miserably as Julia approached the bed. 'What must you think of me? I'm not usually so weak or so emotional.'

'The doctor said it's to be expected in your condition,' Julia said gently.

Louisa nodded, gulping down her tears. 'I know.'

'Sadly, Joshua and I were never blessed with children so I am hardly the person to give advice,' Julia told her, sighing deeply, and Louisa detected a note of regret in that sigh. 'I hope you don't mind Alistair telling me about the child, Louisa. He had to tell someone and he and I have always been close. We've always been open and honest with each other.'

Louisa lowered her eyes, not wanting Julia to see the agony in their depths, as all the painful moments since James had almost ruined them swept over her. 'No, I don't mind—but you must have been shocked.'

'No. I wasn't shocked. Surprised is the word I would use—and pleased. You see, Alistair decided that after his marriage to Marianne, which was tempestuous, to say the least, and far from happy, he would never give another woman the chance to hurt him again. I've been telling him for years to forget about her and what she did to him, and marry again—if not for his own sake then for Mark's. I do my best and do adore the child, but he does need a mother. It will be hard for Alistair to give up his independence, I know, but it's high time he settled down and distanced himself from some of the people he is sometimes seen with.'

Louisa glanced at Julia sharply, detecting a note of censure in her tone. 'Oh! What do you mean?'

'I would not dream of advising Alistair on his choice of friends—indeed, he would not stand for it—but I am not ignorant of the fact that he often keeps the company of Lady Bricknell and her associates when he's in town. Oh, their relationship is purely platonic, not of an intimate nature, you understand, Louisa,' she said hurriedly, when she caught Louisa's sharp, enquiring glance. 'Her husband and Alistair were close friends for many years before his tragic death in a riding accident.'

'Alistair has told me this,' Louisa said, in an attempt to make it easier for her.

'And you have met her?'

'Only very briefly.'

'She is high up the social scale, I grant you, which makes her desirable in consequence, but there is nothing genteel about her behaviour. It is well known that she keeps open house and her soirées can be described as ostentatious routs, and I consider the people who attend them to be a sad set of beings.'

Louisa listened with quiet amusement, wondering what Julia would say if she were to tell her that she had paid an uninvited yet brief visit to one of Lady Bricknell's soirées herself, and that, recalling the conversation between them at Dunstan House, she had found her to be a woman blessed with complacency and kindness, being at ease and affable, and she could well understand why she was such a popular lady.

'Her husband left her immensely rich, I believe, and a woman with such a colourful character is bound to be popular, I suppose. But, Julia—how can you say you were pleased when Alistair told you about the child? You must see that he doesn't want to marry me,' Louisa said in a low voice, meeting Julia's eyes directly.

'Now that I cannot believe, Louisa. Alistair took improper advantage of you and has a duty to stand by you. Besides, he must feel something for you, otherwise you would not be in the condition you are now. I can see you care for him a great deal,' she said softly.

Louisa swallowed hard. 'Yes,' she whispered, realising with stark reality that she did care for him, deeply. 'I do. Very much.'

'Well, then—try not to worry about anything else. It is not good for the baby. And I wouldn't worry too much about Alistair, either. I know my brother. Oh, he is the most stubborn man I have ever known. His mind is so strong, so powerful, that it can completely override all his emotions. After Marianne's death he stored them all away—both his emotions and his memories—separating himself from anything whose loss could cause him further anguish. When wronged he is unyielding—refusing to forgive or forget.'

Louisa sighed sadly. 'Then, knowing this, I have little hope of softening his attitude towards myself.'

Julia smiled softly and, reaching out, gave her hand a reassuring, comforting squeeze. 'You are being too hard on yourself. Alistair has a wilful heart and will stand his ground, but he'll come round. He wouldn't allow himself to be forced into anything he objected to—which goes to show that under his male arrogance and indomitable pride he cares for you too.'

Louisa gave a wry smile. 'I think it's the child he is thinking about.'

Julia frowned in disagreement. 'Be patient with him, I beg you, and do not underestimate yourself, Louisa. You are an extremely beautiful young woman. Any man would be proud to have you as his wife. And Alistair will not be able to resist you once you are married. You'll see. He isn't made of stone, you know. I want nothing more than for the two of you to fulfil each other's lives— as mine is with Joshua.'

'With everything that is between us it will be no easy matter,' Louisa sighed, with a far-away look in her eye.

Julia glanced at her curiously, strongly suspecting that there was more to Alistair's relationship with Louisa than he had told her, and she sincerely hoped that whatever it was would be resolved once they were married.

'There is nothing that cannot be defeated, Louisa—not even my brother's indomitable will and stubborn refusal to see beyond his own situation. And when the child is born it is bound to draw you closer together. It will be a bridge between you. You'll see.'

'Julia—what was she like—Marianne?' Louisa asked tentatively as she rose from the bed and was about to turn away, her feminine curiosity about her predecessor getting the better of her. 'Was— was she very beautiful?'

Julia's smile faded and her face became grim as she averted her eyes, her voice strained. 'Yes, she was. I would be lying if I said otherwise. But she was also completely selfish, having learned from an early age how to twist men round her finger—and Alistair was no exception.'

'Then perhaps he fell so much in love with her that she cast a spell over him, so that he can never love another woman again,' Louisa sighed.

'No,' Julia laughed. 'It wasn't like that. Alistair can be a passionate man, but he can be remarkably disciplined when he so wishes. Marianne scarred him deeply, and after her women became a bitter fruit for him.'

Louisa listened, amazed, for her remembrance of Alistair's love-making did not bring to mind an embittered man. Quite the opposite, in fact.

'But—forgive me, Louisa. I think you should ask Alistair about Marianne. I make no secret of the fact that I never got on with her and could never forgive her for treating him so abominably, so my opinion of her is extremely biased.'

She smiled suddenly, clearly not wishing to embark on further discussion about her brother's first wife. 'Now, I can see that you're tired so I'm going to leave you. I'll have one of the maids assigned to you until we can find one to attend you on a more permanent basis. Providing you are well enough, we have a heavy schedule tomorrow, if we are to fit you out with a new wardrobe, so I hope you manage to get some rest.'

'I will—and thank you, Julia. You have been very kind—more than I deserve.'

Feeling much better the following afternoon, Louisa went shopping with Julia, who happily transported her into a world of high fashion. They went to the most fashionable milliners, hosiers and glove makers to be found near the Exchange, then to the smartest drapers, where they purchased the finest linen petticoats and nightdresses, going on to the silk mercers on Ludgate Hill before finishing in New Bond Street, Julia advising and superintending the choice of colours and materials for her new gowns. Alistair had insisted on only the finest, and very soon Louisa's head was in a whirl as she was measured for a wide range of sumptuous gowns, some designed for the future to accommodate her expanding waistline.

Having finished the shopping for one day, and feeling pleasantly exhausted, Louisa emerged into the afternoon sunshine to the waiting carriage, leaving Julia inside the shop to make arrangements for further fittings for the gowns she had been measured for, and to instruct the proprietor to have items they had purchased that day delivered to Dunstan House.

At that moment Louisa saw Sir Charles Meredith sauntering down the street, dressed as magnificently as if he were going to a Court ball. His expression was one of hauteur and pleasant civility, and his eyes glowed when he saw her, complimenting her appearance, a smile parting his sensual lips.

'Why, Miss Divine! It's been an absolute age since I last saw you in St James's Park. Too long, in fact,' he said, smiling down at her with good humour.

Concealing the rush of dislike and repugnance that washed over her on seeing him again, for she had no reason to be uncivil to him, Louisa gave him her usual courteous attention, but there was no welcoming smile on her lips.

'I've been at home in Surrey since then and only returned to London yesterday.'

'I see. I've been away myself until recently.'

'To your home, Sir Charles?'

'Yes. In Sussex.'

Suddenly he had all Louisa's attention. She'd had no idea that he lived in the same county as Alistair. 'Really! Whereabouts in Sussex?'

'A village close to Huntswood, the home of Lord Dunstan, as it happens,' he told her quietly, watching her reaction and smiling faintly.

Louisa gave him a level stare, all her senses suddenly vibrating and alert, her instinct telling her that there was some underlying, devious reason for him telling her this. 'And was the country not to your taste, Sir Charles?'

His eyes slipped her a stealthy glance. 'On the contrary. It has its charming, feminine diversions—one young lady in particular has claimed my attention—and I intend returning there very soon. But country ways are monotonous and too confined for my taste, and I do not care to be away from London for long.'

'Then perhaps the lady you pursue could be persuaded to come to London, too?'

'Unfortunately not. She is rather young, you see,' he said quietly and with a conspiratorial lowering of an eyelid, scarcely troubling to conceal his glee, 'and, if it is not the servants or her dragon of an elder sister on sentry duty twenty-four hours a day who restrict her movements, she is often under the watchful eye of her dominant brother. But in time—with a little gentle coaxing and planning—I am sure I shall succeed in prising her away.'

Louisa stiffened and found herself staring at him, finding it odd that she should think of Sophie, Alistair's sister, at that moment, and that she should recall the conversation she'd had with Sir Charles in St James's Park, and his crude remarks after Alistair and his sisters had moved on that day. The encounter had been brief, but it had shaken her, because the bold message in his eyes had told her that he had marked Alistair's young sister down as a victim. She remembered all too clearly how he had looked at her—and what he had said about the unobtainable being the most desirable.

If she was concerned by her thoughts she concealed it, for if matters were so hostile between Alistair and Sir Charles, then Sir

Charles was hardly likely to pay court to his sister. And Sophie was so young, only sixteen, in fact, and no match for an experienced man of Sir Charles's unprincipled reputation, a man almost twice her age.

But he had told her himself that he would make Alistair pay for what he had done to him, for stealing Marianne away from him. Would he dare compromise or harm Sophie in his desire to exact revenge? No, she thought, reproaching herself severely for thinking such fanciful, ridiculous thoughts. She must dismiss such imaginings from her mind. However, her every instinct was alert and made her wary of him.

'For the time being,' he went on, breaking into her thoughts, his gaze moving from her mouth to her breasts with rakish leisure and then to her eyes, 'there is someone equally desirable standing not so far away from me at this very moment.' Initially his interest had been bestowed on Louisa half in jest, wanting to prolong and enjoy the chase—his eager pursuit being for the sheer novelty of the experience—but now he desired more from the delectable Miss Divine. 'Let us arrange a meeting.'

Astonishment arched Louisa's brows and she felt her cordiality slipping, no longer able to hide the distaste she felt for Sir Charles Meredith—especially in light of her suspicions where Sophie was concerned.

'What? You are impertinent, sir. That is not possible—and nor do I wish to have anything to do with you on those lines.'

He chuckled, undeterred by her sudden show of anger. 'I cannot believe that. Fraser is not always so attentive towards you. Come, now, charm is hardly his stock-in-trade, is it?'

'I am allergic to your kind of charm, Sir Charles. It does not seduce me,' she said curtly, meeting his gaze directly, knowing the moment of truth had arrived. 'It is time I confessed who I really am. Contrary to what you may believe, James Fraser is my brother, not—as you surmised and for reasons of my own I let you believe—my lover.'

Sir Charles stared at her, both startled and pleasantly surprised, believing that nothing now stood in his way. 'Good Lord! Who would have thought it? You mean you are not Miss Divine after all? That it was all a charade?'

'That is correct. My name is Louisa Fraser.'

He chuckled softly, his eyes gleaming. 'You're a plucky little gamester, aren't you, my dear? This alters things considerably. If it was a game you were playing then I like games too. In fact, some of them I happen to be very good at. We could meet—spend an evening together.' He was adamant.

'No, sir. I think not.'

'But you must. I find you an immense challenge.'

'Do you?'

'Indeed. I must tell you that I am an obstinate man, Miss Fraser, and noted for my persistence.'

'Then you will be disappointed. You see, I am not free to spend an evening with you, and nor do I wish to,' she said sharply.

'I will not take no for an answer.'

His tenacity was beginning to anger and irritate her, which made Louisa's tone lightly contemptuous when she spoke. 'It is quite out of the question, Sir Charles. I am betrothed.'

Sir Charles's brows rose slightly in frank astonishment. 'Betrothed? May I enquire to whom?'

'Yes, you may. It is no secret. It is Lord Dunstan I am to marry, Sir Charles. Your neighbour, I believe?'

Sir Charles's reaction was one of absolute shock. He drew back and his smooth, amiable manner vanished immediately, his countenance taking on a look of anger. 'My, my,' he jeered wrathfully, looking at her as if she were a traitor. 'Things have moved on apace in my absence. I must say I find it strange that Dunstan should choose to marry a woman whose brother he damn near ruined. Is his desire for you so great that he has rescinded that debt?'

'Whatever the reason, Sir Charles, it is none of your affair,' Louisa replied coldly.

'And you believe his intentions towards you are honourable?'

'If you are implying that he is playing fast and loose with me then you are mistaken,' she said, with a calm that belied her rioting feelings. 'Everything is arranged. We are to be married before the month is out at Bierlow, my home in Surrey.'

Sir Charles's jaw tightened and his lips twisted in a malicious sneer. 'Then so much the worse for you,' he said grimly. 'You are a fool if you imagine you are to be the next Lady Dunstan. He thinks no more of you than all the other faceless wonders who have tried to capture his eye in the past—since he killed Marianne.'

Louisa felt her heart freeze and she went very pale, his words searing through her like the hot blade of a knife. For a moment she thought she was going to faint. She stepped back from him, all the people milling about in the street becoming grey formless shadows as she stared at him, disbelieving, thinking she was going mad. Unless it was this cool, insolent creature, who seemed determined to ruin everything for her, who was the madman.

'What did you say?'

'That he killed Marianne—the woman who was to have married me—as surely as if it had been his hands that held her head under the water in which she drowned.'

A sound of hysteria and denial rose in Louisa's throat, which did not pass her lips, followed close by a wave of sick disgust sweeping over her. At this moment in her life, when she was already battered inside, survival for herself and her unborn child was all-important to her, and nothing Sir Charles Meredith could say would convince her that Alistair was guilty of committing such a horrendous crime. She favoured Sir Charles with a glance of biting contempt.

'You are lying,' she flung at him with shaking fury, recovering her self-possession as she hastened to defend the man she was to marry. 'I do not believe you. Alistair may be accused of many things, but I do not believe he would commit anything as culpable as murder.'

'He may not have struck the blow—in a manner of speaking, you understand—but the result was the same.'

'I find your accusations both vile and rash and I have no wish to hear more,' Louisa fumed. 'Whatever is between you and Lord Dunstan has nothing to do with me.'

The savagery in her tone startled Sir Charles. 'You are wrong, my dear. It has everything to do with you if you are to become his wife. Perhaps you will think twice before you consider shackling yourself to a murderer,' he hissed, his voice low and quivering. 'He destroyed my life. He will destroy yours in the same rotten manner if you let him. If you marry him you are a fool.'

He ended on that note, for at that moment he caught sight of Julia approaching and his face turned puce. He scowled angrily, bowing briskly. 'Excuse me. Your servant, madam.'

'Wait,' Louisa said quickly, halting him as he was about to turn away, alarmed at the hatred that festered inside him, hate that had clearly increased a thousandfold over the five years since Marianne's death. 'Whatever it was that happened between you and Alistair was a long time ago. Can you not let the matter rest? Please, Sir Charles, do not make mischief,' she begged.

'Mischief! God forbid I should do that,' he responded in an acid drawl, the cords of his neck above his jabot standing out, quivering and tense, his eyes becoming the eyes of the devil as his gaze, steady as a rock, held Louisa's. 'But when you see Miss Sophie Dunstan—please give her my warmest regards.'

So, Louisa thought in alarm, she had been right in her assumptions after all. 'You are organising an infidelity with Sophie to avenge her brother, aren't you?' she blurted out.

His eyes became narrow and cold. 'Alistair Dunstan cut the ground from beneath my feet the day he stole the woman I was to marry. As you said, it was a long time ago—but I do not forget the wrong he did me and I intend to make him suffer for it. I'm a patient man, Miss Fraser, and I am also a determined one. I hate and I wait—for the opportunity to strike back. Good day.'

He left Louisa's question unanswered, but she knew, without any doubt, that he would strike at Alistair through Sophie.

Julia, whose face was drawn and tense as she watched Sir Charles's figure retreat down the street, came to stand beside Louisa. In shock on seeing the man who had caused Alistair so much untold misery in the past, she failed to notice that Louisa's face was white, like alabaster, as were her lips, and her eyes dark, for the threatening quality of Sir Charles's words had left her in the grip of an ice-cold fear.

'Forgive me, Louisa. I don't mean to pry—and I do so merely out of concern for Alistair. But how well are you associated with that gentleman?' It was an enquiry phrased tactfully, but still a request for an answer.

Trying to compose herself, Louisa took a deep, shuddering breath, deciding to keep Sir Charles's vile accusations to herself, not wishing to upset Julia.

'Not very well. In fact I hardly know him at all. We have met before briefly on only two occasions—one of them in the park that day when you came upon us.'

'I see. Forgive me, I was so upset at seeing Sir Charles that I do not remember seeing you. But my advice is not to have anything to do with him. Would that be too much to ask?'

'Why, not at all. The gentleman is persistent and I do not like him in the slightest. Forgive me, Julia, but perhaps if I knew what he was guilty of where Alistair is concerned it might help me to understand.'

Julia lowered her eyes, but not before Louisa had seen a cloud pass over them.

'Alistair cannot forget or forgive Sir Charles Meredith's offences against him. He did him a great wrong in the past, Louisa. There is a tendency to evil in Sir Charles. He is a greedy, nasty, black-hearted man, who survives on his charm and wit and the enormous fortune his father left him. So do not be deceived by his flattering, frivolous temperament. He can be truly dangerous if it suits him—if he has reason to be.'

Louisa looked at her, wondering if Julia should be saying this as a warning to Sophie instead of to her. Suddenly she was impatient to go to Huntswood, to reassure herself that her suspicions and fears where Alistair's younger sister was concerned were groundless. And as she thought over the accusations Sir Charles had made against Alistair she found it more and more difficult to disregard them as the jealous ravings of a man spurned by the woman whom he would have married, had Alistair not come along.

At least she now knew how Marianne had met her death—that she had drowned—and no doubt she would learn of the circumstances leading up to her death, given time. But one thing she would not believe was that Alistair had killed her.

Chapter Ten

The sun was setting in a ball of flame when Alistair and Louisa finally reached Huntswood after their wedding at Bierlow Church. It had been a quiet affair, the quietest the people of Bierlow had seen in a long time, which had raised eyebrows and questions, for, considering the identities and importance of the couple involved, they had expected a lavish affair in which they could all partake, to say the least.

Because it was Alistair's second marriage, and owing to the circumstances, there had been a subdued note to the whole proceedings, and apart from James and Julia and her husband, Joshua, there were no other guests.

In a gown of champagne-coloured silk gauze Louisa had stood beside Alistair at the altar, a stranger, and yet not a stranger—so dark, so handsome. At the time she'd been aware of nothing but his close proximity and his firm hands when they'd slipped the ring on her finger, and for the first time since entering the church she'd met his eyes, darkly serious and intent, and had had to quell the ache that rose inside her when she remembered her dreams of how her wedding day would be. There had been nothing romantic as she had always imagined—nothing but a seal on a promise that must be kept.

When Alistair had placed his hand over hers she had felt herself possessed, and at the same time had known a rush of happiness that he was the possessor. To this man she had committed her life and that of her child, and from that moment she'd known how it must be between them. Also, in that moment, she'd recognised the emotion that had struck her when she had walked into his arms the first time he had kissed her at Dunstan House. She no longer had any doubts that she was deeply and irresistibly in love, and this revelation sealed the bond between them, but she dared not let him know it yet. She must nurse and cherish her secret, and hope that in time he would come to feel the same about her.

Alistair had insisted on leaving Bierlow immediately after the ceremony, fully intending to be at Huntswood, some twenty-five miles away, before nightfall, but it was obvious to him how much Louisa loved Bierlow, how much she would miss it, and he'd tried to make her leaving as painless as possible. When he'd asked if she was ready to go, emotion had caught in her throat and her lips had twitched in a tremulous smile, her lovely eyes misting with tears, making him suddenly realise how devastating this situation must be for her, having to leave the place she loved, the people she loved, in order to face life in a place completely alien to her, with a man who didn't want her...

And yet that wasn't entirely true. He did want her. Every time he looked at her sweet face he wanted her, and, he thought with a twinge of regret, if she had not deceived him and behaved so shamefully, resurrecting so many bitter memories of his life with Marianne and her ultimate betrayal, then he would have been willing to give their marriage a chance. Perhaps when the child was born, when they had both had time to adjust to the situation and each other, there might be a better understanding between them.

After wishing them well, Julia and Joshua had returned to London, but how Louisa wished that Julia could have accompanied them to Huntswood. How much easier it would be for her to settle in to her new home if she were there.

Ever since Louisa's first evening at Dunstan House, when she had collapsed and Alistair had carried her to her room, there had been a softening in his attitude towards her, his manner becoming friendly and solicitous, and she'd been thankful he continued to be so on their journey to Huntswood. He'd pointed out famous landmarks and places of interest on the way, and made sure the coach stopped for brief periods at the wayside coaching-inns so that she might refresh herself. Some of the time, with the swaying of the coach and the warmth, she'd slept, finding it impossible to ward off her tiredness.

Alistair had allowed his gaze to linger on her features, unable to put his feelings into words, at these times. He'd observed how young she was, how pale and exquisite her face was, resting against the upholstery, making him realise that, despite his vow not to touch her, it would be virtually impossible to keep his hands off her now she was his wife.

The journey had seemed long and tedious to Louisa, so when Alistair pointed Huntswood out to her across a wide, fast-flowing river she was heartened, pleased that it was so near at last, and yet her nervousness and apprehension at entering her new home and meeting Sophie and Alistair's son increased.

She gazed out of the window of the coach, enthralled. The size of the house, with its Dutch gabling and ramparts, half hidden among the trees, was impressive, and yet it looked comparatively modest in its superior setting. Huntswood stood on high ground, close to the Sussex Weald, a high area of broken country suspended between the hills of the North and South Downs. It was a place of charming villages on green hillsides once cloaked by the vast, prehistoric Forest of Anderida. With a great bowl of heather to the west and vistas of grassy vales where sheep, deer and cattle roved, the setting was superb.

Louisa sighed, entranced, not having known what to expect and pleasantly surprised. It was sheer perfection.

'You like it?' Alistair asked softly, watching her closely and pleased by her reaction.

'Who would not?' she breathed, without taking her eyes off it, warm in her admiration. 'I never expected anything like this. It's beautiful.'

'I have always thought so. Standing as it does on rising ground, with trees, as you see, stretching for a wide extent all around, it allows for wonderful views of the surrounding country, which at all times of the year is startlingly beautiful.'

'How long has your family lived here?'

'More than two hundred years—since Tudor times, in fact. The first notable member of my family to come here—when Huntswood was no more than a fortified manor house—was Sir Thomas

Dunstan, whose company was much sought by Henry VIII. History has it that the King visited frequently to hunt in the vast deer park, which was enclosed at that time. But—' he smiled, his eyes twinkling with humour '—I believe he also had an eye for Katherine Dunstan—one of Thomas's pretty daughters—whose portrait you will see hanging in the Great Hall.'

Louisa listened, all interest, having learned all about the six wives of Henry VIII—but the fact that he had had so many had done little to appease his appetite for the pursuit of further sexual conquests outside the bonds of matrimony.

'What happened to her?'

'When Thomas saw the way the wind blew, he had her dispatched post-haste to stay with a relative in the north of England until Henry's ardour had cooled.'

'And did it? Was it far enough away? For if history is to be believed—and if his ruthless pursuit of Anne Boleyn is anything to go by—when Henry set his sights on a woman it was more than her life was worth to dare to refuse him.'

'Fortunately the pretty Katherine escaped his royal clutches, and not long afterwards she married a young lord from over the border in Scotland.'

Louisa smiled, relaxed and warmed by the story—a small insight into his family's history which somehow made its members seem less like strangers to her. 'Then I'm relieved to hear it.' She paused a moment before she asked him a question, one which had been uppermost in her mind since leaving Bierlow. 'Alistair, what will you tell Sophie and Mark? Will you tell them about the child?'

He looked across at her sharply. Her eyes were focused steadily on his face. 'No—not yet. I would prefer to wait. Sophie is young and impressionable so the matter will take delicate handling. I have no intention of exposing my indiscretions to her, or to Mark, for that matter, although he is too young to understand at present. It is also my intention to shield your reputation as well.'

'Thank you,' Louisa murmured, grateful for that. Her humiliation and shame would exist, but at least no one would know about it but themselves.

'As yet the child isn't noticeable, so we will leave it a while until we find an opportune time to tell Sophie. However, we cannot pretend we were married some weeks ago—and nor would I wish to, for I find any form of deception abhorrent.'

Louisa blanched, for this was just one more painful reminder that he would never forgive her own deception where he was concerned.

'Our wedding this morning cannot be concealed,' he continued, seemingly unaware of the discomfort his words had caused Louisa, 'especially not from Sophie—and it will no doubt cause some raised eyebrows among the servants when the child arrives early. I have not been to Huntswood for some weeks—matters of state and business having kept me in London, you understand—but I sent word on ahead so we are expected. Naturally the staff will be curious to meet you and want to know all about you.'

Louisa was daunted by this and wondered what would be required of her as mistress of Huntswood. No doubt she would be expected to take charge of the running of the house—something she was no stranger to—but Huntswood would be on a much grander scale from what she was used to at Bierlow Hall.

As if reading her thoughts, Alistair smiled. 'Don't worry. You'll soon get used to the running of the house. Huntswood has a large staff of servants, but Sophie and our extremely competent housekeeper, Mrs Mullings, will familiarise you with everything. We entertain quite often—local dignitaries and suchlike—especially when Julia and her husband are down from London. But you can rest assured that I have no plans to entertain anyone for the present, and nothing too strenuous will be required of you—at least not until after the child is born.'

They passed through Wyndham, a large, pretty market town with a square in the centre and a triangular green sloping down to the river. It also had several fine, half-timbered houses clustered around an ancient Norman church, with a huge yew tree in the graveyard. On the outskirts they passed several exceptionally large houses and one in particular, which stood well away from the rest, built behind high stone walls, an impressive, stately mansion, caught Louisa's eye.

'You must have some wealthy neighbours if they are able to afford such fine houses, Alistair. Who lives there?' she asked casually. 'In that beautiful house behind the high walls?'

Alistair didn't look, he didn't have to, knowing perfectly well to which one she referred. His expression became grim, his eyes glinting like steel flints as his gaze became fixed on her face.

'An acquaintance of yours. Sir Charles Meredith,' he said, with a coldness that chilled Louisa to the marrow.

'Oh,' she breathed, the sound scarcely discernible above the rumbling of the wheels, feeling as if all the wind had been knocked out of her.

'I have made my feelings plain where that gentleman is concerned, Louisa,' Alistair said sternly. 'Needless to say we have nothing to do with that family. Mercifully he spends the majority of his time in London so we are spared his presence at Wyndham. His mother still lives there—at Furstam Manor—with his younger brother and two of his three sisters, the other having married and gone to live in America. His father died several years ago, having made his fortune in the East India Trading Company and owning considerable properties in London, and he left Sir Charles an extremely wealthy man.

'However, because he has expensive tastes and is inclined to gamble recklessly, some of the property has been sold off to meet his debts. But he continues to go on spending as if there is no end to his money. It's a pity he isn't more like his brother, who is more conscientious and takes care of the business.'

'I see,' Louisa murmured quietly, having no wish to discuss the offending gentleman when she recalled her last unpleasant encounter with him—his dreadful accusations against Alistair and his unsavoury, threatening remarks directed at Sophie, which she hoped and prayed were empty and would come to nothing.

She had been unable to think of little else these past two weeks, and the hatred that existed between the two men horrified her. She knew she should tell Alistair about her encounter with Sir Charles, but because of his reticence to speak to her of the past—of his marriage to Marianne, which she understood was too painful for him to discuss—she considered it best to let sleeping dogs lie, not wishing to stir up trouble when there might be none. Besides, she reprimanded herself sternly, she was a sensible, rational human being who should know better than to let her imagination run away with her and speculate about things she did not understand.

But the mystery about Marianne and the circumstances surrounding her death remained, and her curiosity would not diminish until she knew all the facts.

'Why are we heading away from the river and Huntswood?' she asked suddenly as they began to leave Wyndham behind.

'Unfortunately there is no bridge at this point so we have to travel further to cross the river and double back on the other side. It's a nuisance, not only for visitors to Huntswood, but also for farmers and tradespeople wanting to cross either way. Plans for the construction of a new bridge are currently being drawn up.'

On the other side of the river it was sheer perfection. The trees, having shed their shiny green leaves of summer over the ground in a carpet of yellow, bronze and burnt copper, daubed the countryside in autumn. Oaks and beeches and long avenues of chestnuts, as old as the Tudors, stretched up to the house, which was even more impressive up close, the surrounding gardens and ancient trees giving it an air of quiet dignity as the sun set in a blaze of glory over its rooftops.

Louisa was overwhelmed by the magnificence and antiquity of Huntswood. Stepping inside the great timbered hall, where the staff had gathered to welcome them home, she had a strange feeling of passing into another world and that her life would never be the same again. She could feel the past closing in on her, wrapping itself around her, but it was in no way unpleasant or threatening—in fact, it was quite the opposite, for it gave her a warm, welcoming glow deep inside. The house was distinctly mediaeval, with a great fireplace, and with weaponry hanging from the walls, along with ancient ancestral portraits, which stared down with sombre expressions at this newcomer in their midst.

All her worries about meeting Sophie and Mark were dissolved the moment Alistair introduced her to them. Sophie was slender and extremely pretty, with a rose complexion and soft blue eyes shaded by long lashes. Her every movement was smooth and graceful, and there was an artlessness in her manner, which suggested promise of her developing into an extremely lovely young woman. She welcomed Louisa with unaffected pleasure and sincerity, and clearly did not remember seeing her in St James's Park

when her attention had been captured by Sir Charles Meredith—
and Louisa had no wish to cause Alistair embarrassment by drawing attention to the incident. Behind Sophie, Louisa caught a
glimpse of a bright-eyed, happy face beneath a shock of dark
curls—her six-year-old stepson.

At first the little boy only had eyes for his adored father, who
swept him into his arms and gave him a fierce hug, before setting
him on his feet once more. Alistair's pride as he looked down at
his son could not have been more evident. Taking Louisa's hand,
he drew her forward.

'There is someone I want you to meet,' he said gently to the
little boy. 'This is Louisa, my wife—your stepmother, Mark.'

Mark came towards her a little hesitantly at first. He couldn't
remember his real mother and was unsure what a stepmother was.
A little bemused, he gave Louisa a direct look, regarding her seriously, and she noticed that he bore a remarkable resemblance to
his father, but, unlike his father, Mark's eyes, which were wide
and as darkly grey as a winter's sea, were from a different strain.

Louisa prayed silently for acceptance, hoping he would not reject her. On impulse she reached out and took his small hand in
her own, and bending down, so that her face was on a level with
his, she smiled warmly into his eyes. 'I know this must be as
difficult for you as it is for me, Mark—and as much of a surprise—
but I've looked forward to meeting you so much. Your father's
told me all about you—and you too, Sophie,' she said, smiling up
at the young woman standing beside Alistair, who was looking
with wonder and admiration at her beautiful new sister-in-law. 'I
do hope we can be friends,' she said to Mark, 'and that you will
help me find my way around this lovely house of yours. It looks
so huge I shall be sure to lose my way without guidance.'

Mark made no attempt to pull away and a little smile began to
tug at the corners of his mouth. He seemed to be assessing her,
and when his eyes ceased to regard her so seriously and his smile
gradually broadened, which was a delight to see, everyone present
began to relax and look at one another, certain that he approved
of his new stepmother and that a good start had been made. It also
brought a relieved smile to Alistair's features and he seemed to

relax, which told Louisa how apprehensive he had been about this meeting between herself and his son.

'I'll make sure you don't get lost,' Mark said, with a bright, eager light shining in his wide eyes, his face taking on a look of enthusiasm, no longer seeing this beautiful lady as a stranger. 'Huntswood is very old, you know, and I can show you the room where Papa says King Henry VIII slept a long time ago. The bed is huge—but then so was the King,' he told her with a considerable amount of childish gravity.

'Then I shall look forward to seeing it, Mark. I'm so glad you and I are going to be friends.'

'So am I. What shall I call you?'

'Louisa will do fine for now.' She smiled gently.

'And do you fish? We have a large pond in the park well stocked with carp and pike. I love to fish when someone will take me.'

'I like to fish, too,' Louisa replied truthfully, having spent many a happy hour when her father had been alive fishing in the river close to Bierlow Hall. She laughed. 'Although I must confess that I'm not very good at it and have never caught anything very big.'

'We could go tomorrow—can we, Papa?' he asked, his eyes bubbling with excitement as he tugged at his father's hand.

Alistair laughed lightly, ruffling his curls. 'I think we had better give Louisa time to settle into her new home before dragging her off to the fish pond, Mark. There will be plenty of time for fishing later. Now, come and let me introduce you to the staff,' he said, putting an arm gently around Louisa's waist and drawing her towards the line of waiting servants, sensing her tension and wanting to get the formal introductions over with so she could retire to her room, 'and then I'm sure you would like to be shown to your room so that you can rest a while before dinner. You must be very tired.'

'Thank you,' she murmured gratefully, feeling more tired than she cared to admit, and deeply conscious that he kept his arm about her waist as the introductions commenced.

'Let me show Louisa to her room,' Sophie offered eagerly afterwards, hoping for a chance to become better acquainted with her new sister-in-law. 'I'd like to. You stay with Mark, Alistair,' she said, throwing her young nephew a cross look. 'He's talked of nothing else but your coming home all day so that my head positively aches.'

'Thank you, Sophie. I'd like that,' smiled Louisa.

'I can't tell you how happy we are to have you here, Louisa. Your room has been prepared for you—next to Alistair's, of course. I hope it will be to your liking. Facing south, it gets plenty of sun, and it overlooks Wyndham and the valley. I have also taken the liberty of appointing a maid to attend you—and I'm glad I did for I see you did not bring one with you. In his letter informing us of your imminent arrival, Alistair said you might not. Her name is Edith. She is extremely competent and I'm sure you will like her, but if not you can employ someone more to your liking.'

'Why—thank you, Sophie. I'm extremely grateful. I'm sure she will be perfect,' Louisa said, wondering what Sophie would say if she were to tell her she had never had a maid to attend her in her life, that such a luxury was beyond her means. 'You have been extremely busy on my behalf.'

'I hope your journey to Sussex wasn't too difficult,' said Sophie as they climbed the stairs. 'Whenever I go to London to stay with either Alistair or Julia I can't say I look forward to the journey.'

'It was tedious, but not uncomfortable. Do you visit London very often, Sophie?'

'Yes. I love the excitement. Unlike Huntswood there's always something to do. I do so love the theatre and strolling in the parks. Sometimes I stay at Dunstan House with Alistair, but more often than not I stay at Richmond with my sister, Julia, and her husband. Have you met Julia?'

'Yes. She was present at our wedding this morning with her husband.'

Sophie's expression became subdued. 'I would like to have been there too. When I was in London several weeks ago, had I known Alistair intended marrying, I would never have returned to Huntswood.'

'It—it was rather sudden, Sophie,' Louisa explained, 'and the ceremony was over very quickly. Alistair was eager to reach Huntswood before dark, you see.'

'Was Julia well?'

'Yes, she was. We've become good friends over the weeks of our acquaintance—as I know we will, Sophie,' Louisa said, linking her arm through hers in an attempt to dispel her disappointment over not being at the wedding. She already felt a closeness with her lovely young sister-in-law, who was on the brink of womanhood.

'Yes, I'm sure we will,' Sophie replied, smiling brightly once more. 'Oh, it's going to be so nice having someone in the house I can talk to. Huntswood can be very lonely at times—especially when Alistair is away. I visit friends in Wyndham and the surrounding neighbourhood, but it can hardly be compared with London.'

Sophie's shy awkwardness touched a hidden chord in Louisa. She reminded her so much of herself at that age, having to come to terms with spending most of her time alone at Bierlow Hall without her brother.

Louisa's bedchamber was one of gracious elegance, sumptuous in both design and colour. The ceiling was white and gold, the walls decorated in a delicate shade of pink and hung with mirrors and pictures. Louisa was overwhelmed at the extravagance and unaccustomed luxury, looking with longing at the large comfortable bed, hung with rich, deep pink brocade, which matched the curtains framing large windows. They opened onto a balcony overlooking the gardens below. There was a door connecting Alistair's room to hers, a door she was certain he would keep locked, yet through which he could come to her at any time he chose—but would he? she asked herself. With a desperate longing, she hoped he would.

Like a shadow Edith flitted about the room, industriously unpacking Louisa's trunks and hanging the beautiful gowns that Alistair had bought her in her dressing room. She was very young and smiled with shy nervousness when Sophie introduced her to her new mistress, but Louisa soon discovered that despite her youth she was an extremely capable and competent young woman and would suit her very well.

Dinner was a quiet affair, the conversation dominated by Sophie and Mark, who normally ate upstairs with his tutor, but as a special treat was permitted by his father to join them in the dining room. Louisa, though quiet, listened with interest. However, she was extremely tired and had little appetite for the delicious, excellently cooked food in front of her, and was impatient for the moment when she would be able to retire to her room without appearing rude.

She was acutely conscious that this was her wedding night and her stomach was tense, her nerves unnaturally sensitive, as she awaited the night to come with a feverish anticipation. The softening in Alistair's attitude towards her over the days before their wedding, and during the long journey to Huntswood, when she had been touched by his thoughtful solicitude, encouraged her to think that he might cast aside the harsh terms of their marriage agreement, laid down so firmly when he had visited her at Bierlow Hall. Secretly, she desperately cherished a desire that he would do so, having to quell a wild surge of hope every time she met his gaze across from her at the table.

Alistair was the perfect host and companion. He complimented her on her gown of dark blue silk, cut low to reveal the softness of her white shoulders. All through dinner, although he listened and responded politely to his sister's lively conversation, as she eagerly brought him up to date on everything that had been happening in the neighbourhood during his absence, there was a keen, watchful glint in his eyes when they rested on Louisa. He was not unaware of how weary she must be feeling after the long journey from Bierlow, and how she was struggling not to show it, but her face was pinched and drawn into a pale cameo.

After the meal Alistair escorted her out into the hall, turning to her after he had said a fond goodnight to Sophie and his son. She looked up at him nervously, not knowing what to expect now they were alone. Slowly his eyes slid over her face, the moment one of intimacy, without tension, and felt by them both. Neither of them spoke. Alistair took her hand and pressed it gently, looking into her eyes.

'Are you feeling unwell, Louisa? I noticed you ate very little at dinner.'

'No,' she whispered, the touch of his hand resurrecting the same wild, fateful quivering she had felt before, in which nothing mattered but the warmth that spread inside her. 'I am quite well. I was just not very hungry, that is all.'

'I hope you will be happy at Huntswood, and not miss Bierlow too much.'

Louisa smiled softly. 'Bierlow was my home for too long for me not to miss it,' she told him, 'but Huntswood is my home now. I'm sure I shall be very happy here. Indeed, who would not be? It is a beautiful house.'

'And tomorrow you will see more of it. The park and gardens are sure to impress you.' He smiled softly. 'I congratulate you. You have made a conquest. Mark has taken to you better than I dared to hope. He has just told me how much he likes you.'

'And I like him. It would be difficult not to. He's a delightful boy.'

'Yes, he is. He is a great joy to me.'

'I can understand how you feel.'

He looked at her intently. 'I know it will be no easy matter to feel affection for a child who is not your own, Louisa—but I would be pleased if you would try to find some pleasure in his company.'

'I will—I promise. Each day I shall set aside some time to spend with him.'

'I would like that. Mark's best interests have been paramount to all else since his mother died—and still are,' he murmured, releasing her hand, his look becoming one of preoccupation and complete absorption as he glanced up the stairs, where his son had disappeared with his tutor, suggesting that the brief moment of intimacy which had just now passed between them was, for him, already past.

It grieved Louisa to think how little it had meant to him, how little she meant to him.

He looked down at her once more. 'Today has not been too taxing for you, I hope?'

'No, not at all—but I am rather tired. I—I shall feel better after I have rested,' she said softly, palpably aware of him, of his closeness, but seeing nothing in his expression to suggest that he might have changed his decision and would come to her room later. But

the fluttering under her heart would not be stilled, and her lungs
were so empty of breath that all she could do was look at him, all
thought suspended.

Placing his hands on her shoulders, he looked deep into her
eyes, seeming to read her thoughts, feeling her need—as well as
his own. A softening crossed his face, but only for an instant,
before his expression became unreadable, as he took perfect command of himself.

'The terms of our marriage haven't changed, Louisa. They are
still the same,' he told her. 'We both understand that ours is no
ordinary marriage. There are too many similarities to my first for
it to be that, and I am determined that this time I will get it right—
that there will be no repetition of what I went through with Marianne. Our relationship has had strange beginnings. There has been
no courtship for us to get to know one another as other couples
do, no preliminaries of gentle wooing. Had things been different,
I would have sought your brother's permission and there would
have been acceptance followed by a long betrothal and finally
marriage, but because of the circumstances there was no time for
that, which is why I want to take things slowly at first. Do you
understand?'

Louisa nodded, too disappointed to reply.

It didn't occur to Alistair that perhaps he was being unfair to
Louisa, but he wondered how long he could hold out before he
succumbed to her irresistible beauty which he had secretly come
to love. Dropping his arms, he stood back, which was one of the
hardest things he had ever done. He turned his head to escape the
soft bewitchment of those lovely, imploring eyes. Dear Lord, he
thought wretchedly. What would it take to break down the barriers
he had erected against her?

But his hurt went too deep. However difficult his life had been
since the death of Marianne, he had not deviated from his determination never to fall into the same trap again. Yet as he looked
at Louisa, a pale vision of loveliness, he wanted her, wanted to
make love to her as was his right, while the cruel shadow of his
resolve struggled with the emotional shambles of love and hate,
his stupid pride and the abominable physical desire that possessed
him.

'Goodnight, Louisa.'

Louisa wanted to complain, to tell him it wasn't right, that his rejection of her was cruel and shocking, and that it wasn't fair to treat her like this now that she was his wife. But, for her pride's sake, with a smile and her eyes downcast, she said goodnight, she too wondering what it would take to break down the barriers he had erected against her.

Alistair did not see the strain on her face as she climbed the stairs when she knew he was no longer watching her. Any hope that he might disregard what he had said to her before making their marriage vows was shattered. Nothing had changed and she had been a silly, conceited fool to think it had. It was foolish, she thought angrily, to be so consumingly in love, when he felt nothing for her at all. Her pride and her love were both suffering, but she would not let him see her feelings. Her emotions had to be held in check, and he would never know how much the effort cost her.

That night she dreamt of Marianne, realising the following morning that she had probably slept in the same bed. She opened her eyes and stared about the room—Marianne's room—but there was nothing to suggest she had been there. There were no pictures, nothing. Yet this had been her room. She knew it instinctively. The shadow of her predecessor was everywhere. Everywhere she felt Marianne's ghostly presence.

It would be no easy matter to assert her own character and personality at Huntswood, a house her husband had shared with another woman, but she was fiercely determined to try. She also intended to fulfil the role of Alistair's wife in all its aspects—except one—and she fully intended that, by whatever means it took, that aspect would come later, after their child was born.

With a painful effort Louisa managed to overcome her bitter disappointment and accept the blow that fate had dealt her as she became totally immersed in her new life. Her days followed the same pattern. Outwardly everything was seen to be as it should be between herself and Alistair, and everything due to a wife Alistair gave to her—everything but himself. They lived in the same house, and yet existed in separate areas.

Much of the time Alistair spent with Mark, when the child

wasn't at his lessons, and the rest of the time he was so busy with estate affairs that Louisa seldom saw him. In fact, most days he did not set foot in the house during the daylight hours. He would ride off early in the morning with his bailiff or someone else and she would watch him go, wishing she could accompany him—but from the beginning he had refused to allow her into the saddle until after the child was born. She was touched by his solicitude, but she did not fool herself, feeling that he was concerned less about her welfare than about the welfare of the child.

Yet he had seemed much happier in recent weeks, the brooding, sombre look that had been there in the early days of their marriage having lifted, although where she was concerned there was a wall around him a hundred feet thick.

Because of the state of the nation he was forced to return to London—to Westminster—to sit through long debates in the House of Lords, not only about the continuing war against France in Europe, but also the ongoing colonial rivalry between France and Great Britain in North America. He was gone for several weeks and Louisa missed him terribly, although she would never let him see how much.

The weeks passed into the cold, dark months of winter, and Christmas, which was cheerful enough, with Julia and Joshua down from London, came and went. It was formally announced on Christmas Day that Louisa was pregnant, and both Sophie and Mark were delighted, a delight which was shared by the whole household—even though it did cause a few eyebrows to rise in speculation as to when the child had been conceived.

As Louisa's pregnancy progressed the discomfort that had plagued her during the early months subsided. The gauntness left her face and her cheeks bloomed with health. The haunted look in her eyes was replaced by an attractive energy and also defiance, which often silently challenged her husband when they were together. Pride, and the feeling that everything would come right between them when the baby was born, made her continue to keep some semblance of normality between them. Dr Charlesworth from Wyndham called every week and at every visit reassured her that all was well, and that he had no doubt she would be delivered of a healthy baby.

Louisa missed Bierlow Hall sorely and wrote often to James, receiving the odd letter with news which was encouraging from him. She was amazed by the change in him and by the way he had taken over the running of things, without any mention of returning to his pleasurable pursuits in London.

His life had been taken over by work as he set about finding ways to increase the income of the estate, contracting better rents, which had been set some years back, without being excessive, and renting out more grazing land to the neighbouring farms to allow them to increase their herds and flocks. However, until things were seen to improve, economy had to remain a rule. Louisa was also overjoyed to learn that Amelia Hacket had accepted his proposal of marriage, and he told her he would write and let her know when the happy event was to take place.

It was Alistair who, knowing of her love of reading, proudly gave Louisa her first glimpse of the library at Huntswood. It was vast, a treasure trove of books, of precious tomes of history, religion and theology, and gems of poetry and fiction. It was a room which, to Louisa, encapsulated every culture and civilisation in the world, a room she constantly found herself in. Its bookshelves stretched from floor to ceiling, broken only by a huge marble fireplace and long windows opening onto the gardens, which had been lovingly and painstakingly created over the years by Alistair's ancestors.

When her attention was not being absorbed by the library Louisa occupied herself with household affairs, and with Sophie's and Mrs Mullings's help she began to learn everything there was to know about the running of the house. True to her word, she spent a great deal of time with Mark, which was no great chore for he was a delightful child, with an open and friendly nature, and she derived immense pleasure from his company, and was always ready to join in his games. Full of enthusiasm, he never tired of showing her some new aspect of the house and gardens.

It was inevitable that she and Sophie, who was a precocious young lady, lively and restless and full of energy, would become close. They passed many a happy hour together, walking and visiting neighbours, often taking the carriage into Wyndham to shop, and happily sewing a layette for the baby. Sophie herself had a large number of friends, who called frequently at Huntswood, and whose homes she visited in return and accompanied on outings.

But whenever Louisa was with Sophie Sir Charles Meredith was never far from her thoughts. Sophie never mentioned him—or any other young man for that matter—and much as Louisa wanted to ask her about him she thought it best to leave well alone. If Sir Charles had made Sophie's acquaintance at some function or other when he had last visited his home in Wyndham—and Louisa had every reason to believe he had, following her last conversation with him when she had been shopping with Julia—hopefully Sophie had not been favourably impressed by him to think the matter worth mentioning.

Yet, when Louisa recollected the time she had been strolling in St James's Park with Sir Charles, and the mesmeric look of complete adoration that Sophie had been too young and inexperienced to conceal when she had come face to face with her handsome neighbour for the first time, she very much doubted it, suspecting that Sir Charles Meredith was a secret Sophie kept locked in her heart.

Her suspicions about Sophie's association with Sir Charles were confirmed one cold, overcast day in March when they took the carriage into Wyndham to purchase some white ribbons and lace, to sew onto some dresses for the baby, from the haberdashers in the high street.

They had just stepped out of the shop into the street when Louisa caught sight of Sir Charles riding slowly in their direction on a beautiful bay horse. She observed him with a sickening jolt, although she was not really surprised to see him. Unfortunately, Sophie had seen him also, causing her eyes to fill with rapture and a gasp of pleasure to escape from between her softly parted lips. She stared at him, transfixed, and it was then that Louisa realised the reason for her high spirits—somehow she had suspected he might be in Wyndham today.

On recollection, Sophie had been acting rather strangely lately, and today she had spent too much time dressing and having her maid arrange her hair in a slightly different, more sophisticated, adult style. She should have been suspicious then that Sophie had hoped—or, worse, had arranged—to meet Sir Charles Meredith.

'Sophie! Please do not stare so at Sir Charles Meredith. It is most unbecoming,' Louisa reproached her with unusual harshness, but Sophie had become so carried away that she appeared not to notice.

'Why?' she breathed dreamily. 'There's nothing wrong with letting my eyes dwell on him, is there?'

'Dwell? Feast, more like! You're looking at him as if you've never seen a gentleman in your life before.'

'I haven't. At least—not one who looks like Sir Charles. Do you know Sir Charles, Louisa?'

'Yes. We have met,' she replied drily.

Wanting to avoid quarrelling with her, Louisa tried to keep calm, for, to her dismay, Sir Charles had spotted them and was riding purposefully in their direction, looking impeccable and extremely dashing in purple, an infuriating smile curling his handsome lips.

Louisa acknowledged him with a faint nod and the merest flicker of a smile, drawing her cloak around her in an attempt to conceal her heavily pregnant, cumbersome figure. But not quick enough, for Sir Charles's sharp eyes had already studied her attentively and observed her condition, and his smile became a knowing sneer. Louisa felt her skin crawl just to be near him, and, in that first moment of meeting, everything that had been said on their previous encounter, almost six months ago, was uppermost in both their minds.

'Why, Lady Dunstan,' he drawled with slight emphasis on her name, 'how wonderful it is to see you again. And how do you like living at Huntswood?'

'I like it very well, thank you, Sir Charles,' she replied coolly, with all the composure she could muster.

'I'm happy to see Dunstan is of an understanding nature and leaves you to your own devices—allowing you to wander about Wyndham at will.'

'And why wouldn't he? I am hardly likely to come to harm now, am I?'

'I hope not.' He cast his eyes in a superior way over her but it was on Sophie that they settled as he dismounted. He executed a courtly bow, and the lascivious look he gave Sophie as he took her hand and placed it to his mouth, his lips lingering too long on her slender fingers, going way beyond that of ordinary interest, aggravated Louisa's anger.

'And Miss Dunstan,' he said with a soft seductiveness, exaggerated, Louisa suspected, for her benefit.

When she had told him she was to marry Alistair he had become another person from the charming philanderer she had first known. It was clear that he hadn't forgiven her.

'I am always delighted to find myself in your company,' Sir Charles continued, which brought a jolt to Louisa's senses, confirming her suspicions that the two of them were already acquainted. 'There isn't a woman in Wyndham who can match your loveliness, my dear—with the exception of your sister-in-law, of course,' he said, almost by way of an afterthought.

'I am surprised to see you in Wyndham,' said Louisa. 'It is a long way from London and there can be very little in the way of entertainment to suit a gentleman of your exuberant tastes. I remember you once saying that you found the country monotonous and confining, Sir Charles.'

His eyes again switched to Sophie, who was blushing prettily with pleasure, and he resembled for all the world, Louisa thought angrily, a wolf about to pounce on a defenceless lamb. Sir Charles was too devious and too clever by far—and Sophie too young and easily beguiled.

'Oh, it has its compensations and diversions to make it more pleasurable.'

The attention he was paying Sophie, who was lapping it up as a kitten lapped up cream, made Louisa's cheeks flame with anger, and the meaning behind his words was all too clear. Sophie and Sir Charles exchanged a glance—almost conspiratorial, Louisa thought, noticing how Sir Charles responded quickly to Sophie's over-bright smile, how his eyes flashed back at her, all the familiar charm and vitality he had used on herself not so very long ago back in full force. She also noticed that, however hard she tried to hide it, Sophie waited breathlessly for his attention.

Louisa was deeply worried and could feel dread settling all around her, cold and threatening. She had not forgotten the savagery of the words she had exchanged with Sir Charles when they had parted in London, which had left her feeling afraid that he might use Sophie to avenge himself on Alistair for marrying Marianne. She tried to still the wild beating of her heart, knowing nothing would be achieved by showing her anger.

'And are you here for long?' she asked, her voice sounding surprisingly calm.

'Several weeks—at least until the roads are no longer axle-deep in mud and I can return to London. No doubt we will find ourselves bumping into each other now and then.'

'No doubt,' said Louisa coolly, placing her parcel of ribbons and lace on the seat inside the carriage just as it began to rain. 'Please excuse us, Sir Charles. As you can see, it is beginning to rain. We must be getting back to Huntswood. We have already been gone longer than we intended.'

'Of course. Do not let me detain you. Good day.'

His gaze swept over Sophie once more, but his bow included them both and then he was gone, riding jauntily down the high street.

Chapter Eleven

On the journey back to Huntswood, as the rain fell heavily out of a sky the colour of slate, Louisa forced herself to speak calmly to Sophie, who was staring silently out of the window, the play of tender expressions on her face perfectly easy for Louisa to read.

'Sophie—forgive me. I do not wish to pry, but how well do you know Sir Charles Meredith?' She saw Sophie go tense and flush softly, turning her head away.

'I don't—not really.'

'Did you know he was to be in Wyndham today?'

'No. My maid—who is friendly with one of Lady Meredith's maids—told me Sir Charles was home from London for a few weeks, but that is all.'

Louisa sighed. 'And you naturally thought you might see him in town?'

Sophie turned back and looked at her steadily. 'Yes. Is that so very wrong of me, Louisa?'

'No, not really,' she smiled. 'But when did you become acquainted with him? Have you met recently?'

'Oh, no. We did meet on one occasion last September—at a friend's house. He just so happened to call on her parents that day. We were introduced, but I have not seen him since.'

Louisa believed her. 'I'm glad to hear it, Sophie, because Alistair does not like Sir Charles at all, and would not take kindly to you forming a friendship with him. You do know there is enmity between them, don't you?'

'Yes, I do,' she admitted, 'but I have no idea as to the reason. I cannot understand what he has against him. Sir Charles is so charming—his manners impeccable. When I first saw him it was in London—in St James's Park one day. Alistair refused to acknowledge him—in fact, he and Julia seemed to go out of their way to avoid speaking to him, and, much as I pleaded with them to tell me what it was they disliked about him, all they would tell me was his name and that he was a gentleman of ill repute.'

Louisa blanched, remembering the day only too well, and thankful that Sophie had been too taken with Sir Charles to notice that she had been his companion. 'Then you must heed their words, Sophie, and have nothing to do with him.'

'I will try, Louisa, but I simply cannot get him out of my mind,' she said, her expression one of animated rapture. She did not tell Louisa that in that first moment of seeing him in St James's Park she had fallen hopelessly in love with him. Her innocent young heart had found a new way of beating, and he had filled her head with such new and exciting dreams that she could not sleep at night. She was completely bewitched.

'Never have I seen a man so handsome,' she went on breathlessly, her eyes aflame, 'and imagine my delight on finding out that he was Sir Charles Meredith and lived in Wyndham. Don't you think it astonishing that we have never met him before—or any of his family?' Suddenly she looked at Louisa, alarm springing to her eyes. 'Oh, Louisa, you won't tell Alistair we've seen him, will you?' she said, reaching out and grasping her hand. 'He'll be sure to question me about him, and, if he dislikes him so much, he'll stop me visiting my friends if he thinks there is any chance of our meeting.'

Louisa was reluctant to comply, hating to keep secrets from Alistair, however small, but she had to admit that she had no desire to raise her husband's ire, and very much doubted that Sophie would become involved with a man her brother so clearly disliked. Also, since so much time had elapsed and Sir Charles had made no move to cause mischief, she could only hope he no longer had any intention of doing so.

'Only if you take that look off your face,' she smiled, observing a pretty flush that had deepened Sophie's skin to a lovely rose.

'One look at you when we return to the house and Alistair will be sure to suspect something amiss and question you anyway. You must promise me faithfully not to see Sir Charles again, Sophie, and that you will go out of your way to avoid him in the future.'

'Yes—yes, I will.'

When the birth of Louisa's baby was imminent Julia came from London to attend her. Alistair, never straying far from the house as Louisa's confinement drew near, was surprisingly tense, whereas Louisa felt more at peace and contented than she'd ever thought she could be.

Her baby was born in the last days of May, a beautiful little girl with excellent lungs. She was whole, with the natural healthiness of an infant and a fuzz of dark hair and intense blue eyes. Lying spent and exhausted after her ordeal, yet overwhelmingly happy and calm, Louisa turned her head on the pillow, watching in a dreamy haze as Alistair gazed adoringly down at his daughter—their daughter—in her crib, his expression softer than she had seen it for a long time.

Picking her up with the confidence and expertise of one who had done it before, and holding her possessively in the crook of his arm for a moment while he studied her sleeping face with all the arrogance of a proud father, he brought her to the bed, placing her between them as he perched on the edge. Louisa placed her arm about her daughter, nuzzling her head with her lips.

'Well, Alistair,' she whispered, 'are you well pleased with our daughter? Is she not lovely?'

He smiled in assent. 'I am well pleased. She is as beautiful as her mother,' he said gently, raising her hand and placing it to his lips, his eyes warm and tender as they met her own. Her brow and hairline were still damp from the birth, for their daughter was no more than half an hour old. He thought that she looked defenceless, and as pale and fragile as a wind-blown flower, lying there, with a thick golden plait draped over one shoulder and her long lashes quivering over her clear and untroubled eyes.

'You see, Louisa, despite all our misgivings in the early days, it has not turned out to be such a disaster after all.'

'No, indeed,' she whispered, her eyes soft with love for her daughter. 'You don't mind that I did not give you a son?'

'I already have a son. I shall love our child irrespective of its gender,' he said, lowering his eyes to look at the tiny, wrinkled face of the baby, unable to prevent his mind going back to the time when Mark was born. How different the circumstances had been then, and how different Marianne's reaction and feelings had been towards her child, to whom she had struggled to give birth, only to reject so completely that which God had given her. He watched Louisa—who knew none of this and would be appalled by it—nestle her cheek against the baby's own. Yes, he thought, everything about Marianne had been in such stark contrast to this gentle, loving person who had given him a daughter, already so very precious to him.

'Is it your intention to nurse her yourself, Louisa?'

'Of course. There will be no wet-nurse for our daughter,' she whispered firmly.

Immersed in a drowsy warmth, Louisa's lids began to droop in sweeping shadows over her cheeks.

'I'll leave you now,' Alistair said softly. 'I can see that you want to sleep after your ordeal.'

She sighed, forcing her eyelids up once more and focusing her gaze on his. 'Yes, thank you. Although do not forget the part you played in bringing the event about,' she murmured with a teasing smile.

'No, indeed. However small the part I played, it was a truly momentous and unforgettable night,' he said with tender amusement, his eyes dancing wickedly.

He rose, lifting her hand and placing his lips on her fingers before leaving her to the ministerings of the nurse and Julia, who had witnessed part of the touching scene with a heart bursting with happiness. And as tiredness defeated Louisa and her eyes finally closed she sighed with contentment, hoping and praying that she had just witnessed a change for the better in her relationship with her husband.

As the weeks passed and the whole household seemed to revolve around the child, whom Louisa and Alistair had agreed should be called Constance, Louisa became helplessly confused. She had thought that the birth of their child would be a turning point, that Alistair would change towards her and their relationship would become more intimate—as it should be between husband and wife—but she was sadly disappointed. They were comfortable together, but he never deviated from the path he had set before her confinement. Always they were in the company of others, the only time they came into contact being at mealtimes and when they spent time with Constance, whom Alistair doted on unashamedly.

Yet Louisa often found him watching her covertly, and, on turning her head suddenly, she would see in his eyes a speculative, waiting expression, an expression of inexplicable patience that she did not understand.

When Constance was four months old, it was Sophie who suddenly brought matters to a head between them, in a way neither of them expected or welcomed. Louisa had been so preoccupied with the baby and her own personal troubles of late that she had failed to notice how changed her sister-in-law had become. On reflection, she realised that there had been moments when Sophie seemed to be distracted by some secret, intimate thought, when her attention would wander and her gaze would become fixed and unseeing on some dim and distant object, her eyes aglow and her lips soft and quivering. A cold dread settled on Louisa's heart, and she hoped and prayed that the reason for this change in Sophie wasn't that she had formed a friendship with Sir Charles Meredith, despite the promise she had made to avoid him.

Her suspicions were confirmed one day when Louisa received a friendly visit from a neighbour, Mrs Ruskin, whose daughter Cecily was a good friend of Sophie. The two girls were supposed to be spending the afternoon together at Cecily's home. Louisa mentioned this to Mrs Ruskin and asked if Sophie had arrived safely, at which Mrs Ruskin innocently revealed that Sophie had indeed called on Cecily, and that they were both attending a garden party at Furstam Manor in Wyndham, under the chaperonage of Cecily's elder, married sister, of course.

All Louisa could do was stare at Mrs Ruskin for several moments, knowing perfectly well that Furstam Manor was the home of Sir Charles Meredith. She knew from listening to the servants' gossip that he had not returned to London, and that he had been at home for several months now.

Immediately she became alarmed, all her old fears and suspicions resurrected. By the time Sophie returned home she had worked herself up to fever pitch, heightened by the thunderstorm which had broken, bringing with it torrential rain, and causing her to worry about Alistair, who had ridden over to Rotherfield several miles away, where he had gone to visit an acquaintance.

'Where have you been?' she asked Sophie sternly, the moment she walked through the door. Casting her a look of sharp suspicion, Louisa saw that there was a heightened sensitivity about her, a kind of illicit excitement, shimmering like sunlight on silk. Immediately she took her into her sitting room, where they would not be overheard by the servants, before facing her angrily. 'You told me you were going to spend the afternoon with Cecily.'

'I did,' she replied, her face carrying a look of innocence, but Louisa was not deceived.

'But not at her home.'

Sophie had the grace to look abashed, ashamed at having been caught out in an act of subterfuge. 'How do you know that?'

'Cecily's mother called to see me, and, when I asked her if you had arrived at her home, I was told that you had both gone to a garden party at Furstam Manor.' Louisa moved closer. 'Sophie, please tell me I am wrong when I say that I believe you have been with Charles Meredith. And do not tell me that you did not know he was still at home in Wyndham—that he would be present at the garden party—because I will not believe you.'

'Why—I—I don't know what you mean, Louisa.' She flushed, and not, Louisa thought, with embarrassment, but with guilt.

Louisa peered sharply into her face. 'Yes, you do. Don't look so innocent, because of late I have noticed that your behaviour has been questionable, giving rise to suspicion. Have you been seeing him?' she demanded harshly. 'Has he made any improper suggestions to you?'

Sophie's expression became prim and she drew in a scandalised breath. 'Louisa! No. Of course he hasn't. Sir Charles is a gentleman. He would not compromise a lady.'

'Sophie! You are just seventeen years old. Hardly more than a child.'

'I am not a child,' she flared suddenly, insulted as only a young woman could be who believed she was fully grown and in control of her own mind. 'I shall be eighteen in four months.'

'Eighteen still does not qualify you for a man of Sir Charles's experience. Why—he is almost twice your age. You knew he would be at Furstam Manor today, didn't you?' she demanded.

Sophie thrust her chin out in defiance. 'Yes, if you must know, I did. Cecily told me. Her sister is a good friend of Sir Charles's sister. When Lady Meredith issued her with an invitation to attend the garden party she was told it included Cecily and myself.'

Seeing the obdurate look on Sophie's face, Louisa sighed, her instinct telling her that Sir Charles had prompted his mother to invite Sophie in this roundabout way. 'Sophie, please tell me how friendly you and Sir Charles have become?' she pleaded. 'Alistair will be furious if he discovers you have been seeing him.'

Sophie tossed her head, reckless and defiant, which was uncharacteristic of her. 'But I haven't been seeing him—at least, not in the way you mean. We have met on occasion at some of my friends' houses, but that is all. And why Alistair should be angry baffles me. I cannot for the life of me understand what he has against Sir Charles. He is so charming.'

'It is not for me to say. Let it be enough when I tell you that they have had their differences in the past—differences that can never be reconciled.'

'What differences, Louisa? Why won't you tell me? And why are you so cross? I haven't done anything.'

'I am not saying that you have,' Louisa said on a gentler note. 'But Sir Charles is a man of ill repute. He is a thoroughly bad character.'

'And you know, do you, Louisa?' Sophie argued, challenging her to say more.

Louisa sighed. She wasn't very good at playing the high-handed sister-in-law. How she wished Julia were here to deal with this and had not returned to London so soon after the birth of Constance. Sophie had an expression on her face that was not just seditious but downright mutinous—so like her brother, she thought wearily—but she was determined to try to make her see sense.

'There are few who have not heard of Sir Charles's unprincipled behaviour. He is not to be trusted. Oh, he may be a man of good family and act and look like a gentleman, but he is not. He will take advantage of your youth and innocence and disgrace you and your family. You must stay away from him. There are plenty of nice young men for you to meet in—'

'How can I?' Sophie cried petulantly before Louisa could finish. 'I might just as well be locked up for all the chance I have of forming any kind of friendship with anyone. But I do not want anyone else—and Sir Charles is none of the things you say he is. His is kind and gentle, Louisa—and—and I love him.'

Looking at the passionate face before her, seeing stricken tears rising and beginning to bead her lashes, Louisa spoke more kindly, her anger draining away as a great sadness entered her heart. 'Sophie, if you can see nothing but good in Sir Charles, and if he respects you and his intentions are honourable, then why has he not called on you at Huntswood? Ask yourself that. And why have you not said anything to Alistair? By being so secretive about the affair, you must know he would not approve.'

Sophie dropped her eyes, for what Louisa said was true. Secretly she had been apprehensive about Alistair's reaction to her friendship with Sir Charles, which had begun several weeks before Alistair had brought Louisa to Huntswood as his wife. She had always been aware of her brother's dislike for Sir Charles, but not the reason why, which was like some dark and sinister secret. However, she had not expected such strong opposition from Louisa and was surprised by it, having hoped to win her over to her side, to help smooth the path for herself and Sir Charles.

'Yes, I do. But I cannot help myself. His manners and behaviour towards me cannot be faulted, Louisa.'

Louisa continued to reason with her, but so dazzled was Sophie by the man who had eclipsed all else in her life that she would not be persuaded that Sir Charles Meredith was anything other than what he seemed to her—a charming, handsome man, with nothing but good intentions. Because she had been no more than a child and was ignorant of all that had happened during Alistair's

troubled marriage to Marianne—as Louisa was herself, the full
story still a mystery to her, apart from being told by Sir Charles
that Alistair had married the woman he would have married himself—it would not have entered Sophie's head that Sir Charles had
more than likely set out to meet her by design.

Silly, foolish girl, Louisa thought in frustration, wanting to
shake her, to tell her that it was not her Sir Charles wanted, and
that he was merely using her to avenge himself on Alistair for
marrying Marianne, and that he would discard her without a
thought when he had achieved this. But she couldn't tell her that.
There had to be another, less brutal way of shattering her illusions.

Louisa realised that she was in an extremely awkward position,
and wished fervently that she had told Alistair of her meeting with
Sir Charles before they'd left London—of his threatening manner
and his allusion to a friendship he was already working on between
himself and Sophie. Regardless of the anger such a disclosure
would have been certain to rouse in Alistair at the time, at least
he would have been forewarned.

Of one thing she was now certain: she could not allow a relationship to continue and develop further between Sophie and Sir
Charles without her husband's knowledge of it. She had no choice
but to tell him, knowing he would be furious, and he must be told
before Sir Charles devised some scheme to get Sophie alone and
ruin her and bring disgrace upon the whole family.

Louisa waited in a state of nervous agitation for Alistair to come
home that night. He didn't arrive for dinner so she ate alone in
her room, wondering where he could be as the hour grew later.
He had ridden to Rotherfield that morning, and she wondered if,
because of the rain that was lashing down outside, he might have
decided to stay overnight.

She allowed Edith to prepare her for bed and then dismissed
her, continuing to wait. Eventually, unable to settle, she fastened
her robe around her and left her room. She was struck by the
heavy, almost brooding silence of the great house as she soundlessly made her way down the oak staircase. On the last step she
paused and listened, her slender hand resting on the balustrade.
Everything was dark around her except for the dying glow of

the fire in the hall. Her eyes were drawn to a faint light shining from beneath a door to the sitting room, and slowly she moved towards it, pushing it open quietly and stepping inside. The room was in semi-darkness, the warm, left-over embers glowing in the hearth. She looked towards a circled radiance of golden light, where two candles burned on a small table, and she sighed with relief when she saw Alistair on the sofa, his powerful limbs sprawled out and one arm flung above his head. A stray lock of dark hair fell over his brow and his eyes were closed in sleep. He looked exhausted after his long ride from Rotherfield. He had removed his sodden coat, which lay untidily next to his muddied boots on the carpet, and there was a half-empty glass of brandy beside him.

Louisa's heart turned over when she saw him, for despite his dishevelled appearance he looked remarkably impressive lying there, with his crumpled white shirt half open to reveal the strong muscles of his neck. Slowly and soundlessly she moved towards him, without recognising the temptation that had her in its grip. She stood motionless, letting her eyes feast on him, allowing herself the luxury of studying her husband's face, feeling the same wonderful, bone-melting excitement stirring inside her that she did whenever she looked at him.

She stood gazing down at his fine-boned face in deep shadow, seeing nothing harsh about his features in repose, nothing of the familiar, authoritative sternness in the straight set of his firm, curling mouth, or the saturnine sweep of his sleek black eyebrows, slanting up from the bridge of his nose to a high arch. There was so much serenity in his face that she forgot the reason that had brought her in search of him.

Her heart ached for him, and, for a brief moment, when everything around her stood silent and still, a faint nucleus of warmth within her began to grow and spread all through her. It was like being back at Dunstan House in London again, on the night she had given herself to him in return for James's IOU—the night she would willingly have given herself to him without a thought to James's IOU.

Ever since Alistair had brought her to Huntswood she had waited for him to come to her, waited for him to change towards

her, as he must, she told herself, some time. They could not live
the rest of their lives like this—together, in the same house, and
yet strangers to one another, moving in opposite directions. Only
her memory of the one night they had shared, the night when their
child had been conceived, made her think that if it had been like
that once between them, then it could be so again. And so she
continued to wait, to want him, while humiliation and pain at his
continued rejection smouldered inside her.

Instinctively she bent slightly and reached out and brushed his
hair with feather-light fingers from his brow, uttering a faint gasp,
her heart gently leaping, when he opened his eyes and caught her
hand, looking up at her. The moment was so unexpected for both
of them that they looked at each other for the length of several
heartbeats, their faces underlit by the candles so that they were a
play of golden light and dark shadows. Alistair's features were
less guarded than she had ever seen them, and there was something
so tender in his eyes that all she could do was stare.

In the end Louisa broke the silence by saying, simply, 'I'm
sorry. I thought you were asleep.'

'No,' he murmured, reluctant to let go of her hand which he
still held. He was content to let his eyes dwell on the softness of
her lovely face, to gaze into the depths of her half-closed eyes, to
glory in the gentle sweep of her long dark lashes which dusted
her cheeks, and seeing the soft candlelight bring a gleam of gold
to the hair tumbling about her shoulders, the voluminous flounces
of lace and the soft material of her white robe concealing the
hidden delights of her body beneath.

Without being conscious of what he was doing, he moved his
head closer to hers, overcome by a strong desire to draw her mouth
down to his and taste the sweetness of her quivering lips, which
he did, succumbing to the impulse that had been tormenting him
for months, and the moment he placed his mouth on hers Louisa
parted her lips to receive his longed-for kiss, her heart soaring
with happiness. He kissed her slowly and deliberately, and Louisa
felt a melting sweetness flow through her bones and her heart pour
into his, depriving her of strength.

With a deep sigh Alistair drew back and gave her a searching
look, his gaze and his crooked smile drenching her in its sexuality.

'There are times, Louisa, when you confound me,' he murmured, placing his warm lips on her hand before he let it go and swung his long legs off the sofa, tiredly brushing his fingers through his tousled hair. 'I was just dozing. The ride from Rotherfield took longer than I intended in this rain. The road is like a quagmire.'

Her cheeks aflame, Louisa drew a long, shuddering breath, her whole being bent on recovery, on controlling her trembling legs. 'P-perhaps you should have stayed at Rotherfield and ridden back tomorrow,' she said hesitantly.

'I would have, but it wasn't raining quite so hard when I set off.'

'Have you had something to eat?' It was a commonplace question, but she could think of nothing else to say.

'Yes, I have. Come and sit down,' he said softly, taking her hand and drawing her down beside him, glad of her company and thinking how wonderful she looked. She positively glowed with health. However, he had observed how quiet she had been of late, that she was often subdued, and not at all like the young woman he had first met, and he unconsciously found himself looking for some trace of the glorious, absolutely adorable Miss Divine she had once been to him, with the inviting smile and flirtatious eyes, his unforgettable lady of pleasure—the woman he had fallen in love with, although he had not known it then.

When Marianne had died he had persuaded himself that he would never fall in love again, that he would have the strength of character to withstand such a debilitating emotion, but then he had not met Louisa. He could not remember when he had come to love her, but he could not deny that he had been unable to get her out of his mind since the moment he had set eyes on her at the Spring Gardens at Vauxhall a year last summer.

Having had time since the birth of Constance to consider their situation seriously, and because of the weeks previous to this that he had spent in London without Louisa, and the pressing matters of work on the estate, which always seemed to build up alarmingly during his absence, he regretted not having had the time to spend with her since their marriage. The situation had not given either of them the chance to get to know each other and to develop a better, closer relationship, which was essential if they were to live together as man and wife in the true sense.

He was impressed by the way she had settled down, and amazed how quickly she had learned to manage Huntswood and its huge contingent of staff, and Mark adored her, which was the biggest blessing of all. But he now considered that enough time had been wasted and he was about to rectify matters without any further delay. Night after night he had fought the desire to go to her and now he could no longer help himself. He wanted her in his life and in his bed, and, if her passionate response to his kiss was an indication of how she felt, she was of the same mind.

'Tell me what it is that keeps you from your bed at this late hour? Can't you sleep—is that it?' He looked at her with a questioning lift to his brows, his head cocked to one side, a faint smile hovering at the corners of his mouth. 'You weren't worried about me, were you, Louisa? Did you think something might have happened to me when I was so late?'

Louisa's breath caught in her throat and a warmth crept through her veins and stole up her cheeks, when she heard the husky timbre of his voice and saw the unexpected desire in his eyes, which glowed almost black in the dim light.

'I—no, of course not,' she murmured, which was not quite the truth, for, despite the anxiety that had plagued her throughout the evening about Sophie's friendship with Sir Charles Meredith, the thought that something awful might have befallen Alistair on the long and lonely ride from Rotherfield had begun to worry her. 'Or—maybe—just a little,' she admitted hesitantly.

Alistair smiled. 'Then I am pleased to discover that my wife does not forget about me altogether when I am away from home,' he teased gently, and Louisa became riveted by his sparkling gaze that contemplated her for a moment seriously.

The warmth and privacy of the room, enhanced by the presence of the dying fire, invited silence, wrapping itself around them, which was as well, for there were so many things each wanted to say but could not—not now when a slender thread of something deep was beginning to grow between them. Louisa was sorry she would have to spoil the moment by telling him about Sophie, knowing exactly what his response was going to be when she did, and she wanted to hold back for as long as possible, to maintain and savour this wonderful sense of closeness between them for just a little while longer. But it was not to be.

Alistair turned and fixed her with a level gaze, his instinct telling him it must be a matter of some importance to have kept her from her bed.

'What is it that is so urgent you have to come seeking me? Is there something you want to tell me?'

'Yes,' she replied, meeting his eyes. 'Alistair, I have to speak to you. I have no wish to intervene in matters of which I am ignorant, but I am extremely worried about Sophie.'

His jaw tightened and he frowned, standing up and going to rake the embers in the hearth. 'Is it so important that it cannot wait until morning?' he asked, with his back to her, a trace of exasperation in his voice.

'Yes, it is.' Louisa rose and went to stand beside him. Unable to find any way of softening the blow, she came straight out with it. 'It—it not only concerns Sophie, Alistair, but Sir Charles Meredith, also.'

Alistair stiffened and rose to his full height. His eyes were hard as they fastened on Louisa's, giving her all his attention, and the sweet, unexpected drift of happiness she had felt only moments before was already melting into the shadows. 'What are you saying?' he demanded. 'What has Charles Meredith got to do with Sophie?'

'A friendship has developed between them—a close one, if what Sophie has told me is true.'

'Sophie always speaks the truth.'

'I know. That is why I am so concerned.'

'How close?'

'As yet, I do not believe it has gone beyond the bounds of propriety.'

Quickly Louisa told Alistair all that had occurred that day, and everything Sophie had disclosed about the depth of her feelings for Sir Charles. Alistair listened in a stony silence, cold and disbelieving, aware of nothing except the quiet voice of his wife and the implacable hatred he felt for Charles Meredith. He had expected Louisa to tell him something unpleasant, but not this—not that Charles Meredith had deliberately wormed his way into his sister's affections in order to avenge himself on him. He began pacing the room, his anger tight-leashed, but Louisa could sense it emanating from him in waves and see that his mind was working furiously.

When she fell silent his face darkened and rage struck him as her words brought home the inevitability of the truth. He felt as if someone had bludgeoned him. Raking a hand through his hair, finally he erupted.

'My God! I should have foreseen something like this. How long has it been since he first approached her?'

'Since before we were married. He came to Wyndham in September for a while, and they met at the home of one of Sophie's friends, whose family also happen to be friends of Lady Meredith, Sir Charles's mother,' Louisa explained. 'Whether their meeting was by chance or design, only you will be able to decide that, Alistair.'

'Charles Meredith is not a man of sense and honour. I knew he wanted to avenge himself on me—but I did not believe he would stoop so low as to use my seventeen-year-old sister to do it. The man is as cold, crafty and calculating as a snake,' Alistair said through clenched teeth.

'I'm so sorry, Alistair,' Louisa whispered.

'And what did you say to her?' he asked, swinging round to face her. 'I hope you made it plain what my feelings would be when I found out about this, and that I will not tolerate her friendship with this man—a man who is my most bitter enemy and almost twice her age.'

'Of course I did, but how could I make her understand why when I do not know myself?' Louisa cried indignantly. 'Sophie is a high-spirited girl and refused to listen to anything I had to say. As far as she is concerned Charles Meredith is Mr Perfect—whose intentions are entirely honourable. She became angry and resentful of my interference. After our confrontation she flounced up to her room, locked herself in and has refused to come out since. You have told me nothing about what occurred between you and your first wife, or Sir Charles's part in it, Alistair, so how could I be expected to tell Sophie anything when I am almost as ignorant of the facts as she is?'

'I'm sorry, Louisa. It's not your fault. But please believe me when I say that Charles Meredith's enmity was not of my seeking. I had no idea when I married Marianne that she had already promised herself to him. Had I known this and the terrible repercussions, I would never have proposed to her in the first place. No doubt it gave him immense satisfaction knowing that she made my life a living hell.'

'And did Sophie not know of this—living here with you both? I do not know how it could have been concealed from her.'

Alistair shook his head dejectedly. 'No. She was away staying with Julia at Richmond for most of the time—and was too young to understand anyway. After that—after Marianne died—I had no reason to tell her anything.'

'Until now,' Louisa said quietly. 'Don't you think you should?'

'Yes—I see that I shall have to. I'm sorry if she gave you a difficult time, Louisa, and I shall speak to her in the morning. But if she thinks she can flout my wishes and my authority then she is mistaken. I shall keep her locked in her room twenty-four hours a day if necessary—in order to make damned sure she does not see Meredith again. He is a worthless libertine who has seduced half the women in London and has the morals of a sewer rat. If he makes any further attempt to contact Sophie—or so much as looks her way—I swear I shall run him through.'

Louisa blanched at the ferocity of his words, believing he meant it. 'Do you intend confronting him, Alistair?'

'Eventually I shall—but first of all I intend speaking to Sophie. When she has told me everything that has passed between them, then I shall decide. But how in God's name has it managed to go on for so long without my knowing about it before now? Had you no notion of this?'

Louisa stared at him bleakly. It was as if the sun had suddenly gone out and her heart began to pound. It was the moment she had dreaded, but she had to answer him honestly, having learned to her cost to be truthful in all matters where Alistair was concerned. She swallowed hard.

'Yes, I confess I did. But not from anything Sophie said—or by her behaviour.'

Alistair looked at her quizzically, speaking with an ominous quiet. 'Then how, Louisa? How?'

Nervously she turned her head away, but he leaned towards her and placed his hands firmly on either side of her face to force her to look at him.

'Answer me,' he demanded harshly. 'Do not lie to me.'

She met his eyes bearing down into hers. 'From—from Sir Charles,' she whispered, fearful of his reaction.

Inside the room there was no sound at all, the air becoming thick and suffocating. Alistair's eyes continued to stare into hers, as hard and cold as ice floes, and then, into the reverberant silence, he said, in accusing, disbelieving, angry tones, 'You've seen him? You have spoken to Charles Meredith?'

She nodded.

He took her by the shoulders, his grip so powerful it hurt. He would not spare her as he brought his face close to hers, contorted with disappointment and rage. 'When? When did you see him?'

'Before we were married—when I was shopping with Julia. I—I was waiting for her in the street when we met quite by chance.'

Alistair dropped his hands and seemed to recoil from her. 'As were all your meetings with that gentleman, I seem to remember,' he said scathingly. 'And what did he say? What did he tell you?' he demanded.

'When I told him I was going to marry you, he—he became angry—a different person, almost—and he—he told me he blamed you for Marianne's death—that he hated you and that he was patient, that eventually he would repay you for all the wrongs you had done him. He—he also implied that he had already become acquainted with Sophie,' she finished quietly.

'Did he, indeed? And did he gain your sympathy, Louisa?' Alistair asked with a savagery that made her tremble. 'Did he manage to blacken my name sufficiently so that you thought you were marrying the devil incarnate?'

'No,' she cried tearfully, raising her face imploringly to his. 'He could never do that.'

'And you thought to keep this from me? How could you let it

happen, Louisa? Don't you realise I could have put a stop to it then?'

'I know that now. Please forgive me, Alistair. I deeply regret not telling you. I—I suppose I didn't believe him, thinking that he was just trying to make mischief and that it would come to nothing. I did not want to stir up trouble when there might be none.'

'Not even your wildest imaginings could conjure up the kind of trouble Charles Meredith is capable of stirring up.'

'Please tell me what happened, Alistair—between you and Marianne?' Louisa blurted out the question before it could be halted, but it was reasonable, one she felt she had to ask.

The unexpectedness of the question caused Alistair to draw a long breath and his face to harden even more. His face took on a chalky pallor and deep lines appeared at the corners of his mouth. His manner immediately became detached and cool and he averted his gaze, and for a fragile moment before he looked away Louisa thought she saw a weariness and a terrible pain in his eyes. Without thinking, she reached out, but before her hand touched his sleeve he turned and met her look with a harsh smile, and the illusion of pain vanished.

His look, which became closed, as it always did when Marianne's name was mentioned, gave her every indication that what she had asked was not to his liking, and, with the high-pitched sensitivity of a woman in love, she knew she had come close to touching a raw nerve in him. With this latest disclosure about Sophie to worry about, she should have known that now was not the time to ask him to open his heart about Marianne.

He shook his head. 'Enough for now,' he said harshly, her simple question, innocent though it was, enough to raise him to fury, which he struggled to keep under control. 'Marianne is dead. Leave it at that for now.'

'Why won't you tell me what happened?' she persisted, knowing she was forcing an angry confrontation with him but unable to stop herself.

'Because I don't wish to discuss it at this time,' came the fierce reply. 'From the very beginning Marianne set out to make a fool of me. In fact,' he said, his lips sneering cruelly, his body as taut as a bowstring as he felt the selfish need to inflict the pain that was twisting his gut on someone else, 'she possessed the same kind of rapacious tendencies—the same deceit, the same sharp claws beneath velvet gloves—that you should recognise yourself.'

Louisa's eyes flamed and she recoiled instantly from the injustice of his unfair and uncalled-for attack, his words destroying her last shreds of self-control. The face she turned on him was white with anger, her eyes glittering, her voice when she spoke low and quivering with indignation.

'That is not fair. I am not like that, Alistair. How dare you insult me? You make me sound grasping and greedy when I am neither. You think I'm like her, don't you?' she said, growing angrier by the minute, feeling horribly humiliated. 'But if you would take the trouble to get to know me you would find we are not remotely alike—if she was all those things you have just accused her of being.'

Cold and rigid as a block of ice, Alistair watched her show of temper unmoved. 'Calm yourself, Louisa. You are overwrought,' he said coldly, picking up the glass of brandy he had poured for himself earlier and gulping it back.

'I am not,' she fumed, her eyes blazing. 'Your accusations are inaccurate and unjust. How could I possibly know anything about Marianne? How could I possibly know what she was like? All I know is that the animosity between you and Sir Charles Meredith stems from your marriage to her—because he wanted to marry her himself.'

'In that you are correct. But, as I have already told you, I was unaware of that fact when I proposed and she accepted me. Because of him, my marriage to Marianne was purgatory. Oh, at first I believed she loved me, but how quickly she changed towards me when, shortly after Mark was born, Charles Meredith came back into her life. Her sighs of contentment after making love became less frequent—dying altogether eventually. She gave herself to me with rigid submission because she was my wife and for no other reason. Her distaste for me was evident. She averted her eyes when I looked at her—became petulant. In fact, she hated me,' he admitted, his voice shaking.

'And that is what all this is about, isn't it, Alistair? You cannot forgive her for not loving you. How you must have suffered, but are you to go on allowing her to poison *our* lives together? All I ask is that there be honesty between us—honesty, trust and respect—if we are to live together as man and wife. Have you made up your mind to make me suffer for what Marianne did to you—for what I did—all your life?'

'Of course not.'

'When I came to you I was foolish beyond words,' she said, moving close to where he stood. 'What I did that night had nothing to do with James's IOU. What I gave you, I gave from the heart. Can you not remember how it was between us?'

'Of course I remember. And I would be grateful not to be reminded of how I allowed my desire for you to carry me away. I've reproached myself for it many times.'

Louisa threw back her head, her eyes meeting his proudly, a raw flame of anger springing to life in their depths. 'Why?' she taunted, smiling contemptuously. 'Was it so awful?'

'Damn you, Louisa. You know it wasn't.'

She moved closer still so that she stood directly in front of him, almost touching him, looking provocatively up into his stormy eyes. 'And what was I when I lay in your arms, Alistair? Was I wanton?'

'What else?' he growled. 'To be wanton is to show passion without love—and how could you show love when we were strangers?'

'How indeed?' she replied drily, stepping away from him, reproaching herself severely for foolishly allowing herself to think that the softening of his attitude towards her when she had first entered the room might mean that he was prepared to forget her past conduct and treat her as his wife in every respect. She now realised their minds were running along different lines, that his mind was well and truly shuttered against her. She turned from him and moved towards the door, hurt and disappointment searing through her.

'Wait,' Alistair commanded suddenly. 'I have no wish to see you leave like this, Louisa.'

She whirled round and faced him, seeing a faint smile lightening his sombre countenance, but she was tired and still angry and in no mood to be mollified. 'How generous of you, especially considering that you have absolutely no sense of my feelings. If you had, you would never have set down such stupid, unreasonable terms as to how our marriage was to be conducted.'

'Nevertheless, you entered into it with your eyes wide open. You knew what to expect, so if you feel disappointed and let down you have no one to blame but yourself. We agreed at the beginning—'

'No,' she cried, livid. 'We did not. You *told* me, and you expected me to accept it with a meek compliance. You gave me no opportunity to argue, and since then you have taken great care to avoid being alone with me. Why, Alistair? Are you afraid you might find yourself wanting me again? Is that it?'

His features tightened and his eyes became as hard as granite once more at her continued baiting, giving no indication now that he had been about to put an end to what she referred to as the 'unreasonable' state of affairs that existed between them. 'Be patient, Louisa—'

'So, I am to live in hope, am I?' she cut in with bitter irony.

'No one chooses their own destiny, Louisa, and yours is not so miserable as you would have me believe.'

She stared at him, wide-eyed, vulnerable and trembling with a mixture of rage and frustrated desire, her tantalising mouth hungry for his kisses, which were not forthcoming. And they never would be, she realised, for he was telling her that he had no intention of touching her—despite his moment of weakness earlier when he had kissed her so tenderly. He was going to abide by his original terms and make theirs a marriage in nothing but name. Bitterness rose up inside her like bile. When she had come in search of him she hadn't known what to expect, but it certainly had not been this deep-seated, emotionless resistance.

'Don't worry, Alistair,' she said, her body trembling, her fists clenched by her sides. 'I am not going to make a fool of myself by throwing myself at your feet. I know what to expect from you. You have made it plain enough. If I deceived you it was on one matter only and I am prepared to do anything to atone for it. I have never been guilty of such conduct before and never will be again—and my actions were not for my own sake but to save my brother from gaol and to save my home. I know now that in you—

with your abominable pride and self-righteousness—there is no room for human weakness—that it is beyond you—and, it would seem, none for forgiveness, either.'

Abruptly she left him, the hurt she felt on a scale too great to contemplate. It was as if everything that was wrong between them could never be put right.

That night she lay alone in her bed, yearning for the man in the next room with a desperation that frightened her. The problem seemed insurmountable and she wept bitter tears of misery and despair into her pillow, convinced she had married a man with a stone for a heart.

Chapter Twelve

The following morning the sun, shining out of a speedwell-blue sky, spilled into Louisa's room, the torrential rain which had saturated everything the day before having stopped shortly after she had gone to bed. Still angry and smarting over her confrontation with Alistair the night before, and feeling the need of some fresh air, she left the house and wandered in the direction of the stables, always happy to be with the horses.

She wondered if Sophie was still locked in her room, not having seen her since the previous day, and she sighed wearily, knowing her young sister-in-law would be none too pleased with her for telling Alistair about her association with Charles Meredith—but she had no regrets about telling him. It had to be done if Sophie was to be protected.

As she wandered into the stable yard, the sight of the horses' heads peering out over the half-stable doors and their soft whickering never failed to excite and cheer her. She breathed deeply, inhaling the familiar smell of the tack room, of warm leather and saddle soap, hearing the sounds of rubbing and scrubbing as stable boys polished the tack. She acknowledged the polite, respectful good mornings cast her way by the grooms with a smile, and stood surveying the bustling activity going on around her with casual interest, watching as fresh feed was mixed, the horse boxes cleaned out and fresh, sweet-smelling straw brought.

At that moment Alistair, returning from an early morning ride, came cantering into the yard on a powerful jet-black brute of a horse with a zigzag blaze and two white socks. She stood still and watched him as he pulled him up, envious of the spontaneous mastery he seemed to have over horses. She was a reasonably good rider, but when it came down to training them she was an absolute non-starter. How handsome he was, she thought, how striking, her heart wrenching with love as she allowed her eyes to dwell on his face, seeing the ruthless set of his jaw and his sculptured mouth. His jacket clung to his wide shoulders; in fact, everything about him exuded brute strength, making her feel quite helpless.

It was never easy to remain composed when she was with him, for his face was so intense that she was affected by the force of passion that emanated from him, that seared her flesh and melted her bones. She wanted to tell him how much she loved him, how much he had come to mean to her, but she was afraid that he would scorn her and hold it over her head all the years of her life, like the sword of Damocles.

He was to leave for London the following day, and she winced when she remembered how much she had missed him the last time he had gone, and how she had longed for his homecoming, while all the time he would not have given her a second thought. She would not be the only one to miss him this time. Mark was equally upset that he was to go and had begged and pleaded to be allowed to accompany him, but Alistair had adamantly refused to consider it, telling him firmly that he must remain at his lessons, which had upset the little boy terribly.

On seeing Louisa, Alistair slid off his horse with an effortless agility and handed the reins to a waiting groom, before striding briskly towards her, casually dressed and bare-headed, the gentle breeze ruffling his thick dark hair.

'Come along,' he said, taking her arm, his face unreadable— impassive. 'Walk with me. I want to talk to you.'

Uncertain of his mood after their angry and extremely bitter exchange of the previous night, which had opened up so many painful wounds between them, Louisa walked with him away from the stables and along an avenue of tall chestnuts. She stole a sur- reptitious look at him. The set of his jaw was rigid, his profile harsh, and she noticed the cynicism in his deep blue eyes.

'You will be pleased to know that I've spoken to Sophie,' he said without preamble. 'I have also ridden into Wyndham to confront Charles Meredith, only to be told that he left first thing this morning for London.'

'I see. I hope you were not too hard on Sophie,' Louisa said, sounding cool.

'She provoked me.'

'And you have an unfortunately savage temper when provoked. Did you upset her?'

'A bit. But anything to do with Charles Meredith brings out the worst side of my nature.'

'And?'

'And what?'

'What did Sophie say when you confronted her? That's providing she let you through the door,' Louisa murmured calmly, feeling heartily sorry for Sophie, for she knew without being told that, faced with her brother's fury, Sophie would have been like clay in his powerful hands, and would no doubt be lying on her bed at this very minute, sobbing tears of misery into her pillow. She would go to her the moment she returned to the house.

'She had no choice, and when I'd finished with her she was as meek as a lamb and agreed never to see him again,' he said, giving Louisa no indication in either his look or the tone of his voice that his victory over his sister had been hard won. 'She'll do as she's told, and that's all there is to it.'

'Sophie? As meek as a lamb?' Louisa gasped in disbelief. 'Now that I cannot believe, Alistair.'

He grinned suddenly, looking down at her, his lips curling back to reveal his strong white teeth. 'Well—not quite,' he said on a softer note, thinking how attractive she looked in her lemon dress, with her hair loosened and rippling and lifting in the wind.

'Did you tell her why you dislike Sir Charles so much?'

'I told her enough.'

'But not all of it?'

'No.'

'Then I can only hope it was sufficient.'

Alistair looked at her quizzically, seeing doubt in her eyes. 'Why? Do you believe she would defy me?'

Louisa looked at him and raised her eyebrows, her glance conveying that she did.

'She would not dare,' he growled, scowling.

'Sophie is strong-willed and her own person, Alistair, and not only that—she is in love with him.'

'She thinks she is.'

'She is seventeen and believes she is,' Louisa argued firmly, 'and when one is seventeen and in love one does not think of the consequences.'

'You sound as if you speak from experience,' he said softly.

'When I was seventeen I had no time for such frivolous diversions,' she answered tartly. 'I was too busy trying to run Bierlow Hall and to keep the wolf from the door.'

Alistair's eyes gleamed wickedly. 'And in the end you failed— or, should I say, your brother let him in?'

Louisa looked at him sharply, seeing his eyes grow more vividly blue as she followed his train of thought, knowing perfectly well that he was referring to himself. 'Yes—come to think of it, your behaviour was somewhat predatory when we first met. You even look like a wolf when you're angry, and—if you are driven to excess—I am quite sure you would bite. I only hope you did not upset Sophie unduly and that she heeds what you told her.'

'Sophie is headstrong and wilful, I grant you—and is prone to argue and demand her own way, but she is not stupid.'

Louisa sighed deeply, finding it difficult to repress a smile. 'She is like someone else I know,' she said meaningfully. 'The very image of her brother. She resembles you a good deal, Alistair— in more than looks.'

He raised his eyebrows in wry amusement and a smile pulled at the corners of his lips. 'Yes, I fear she does,' he agreed.

They walked on a little way in silence, coming to the end of the avenue of lofty chestnuts on the brow of a hill, from which they could look down over the green treetops to Wyndham and the river winding and rushing its way through the valley bottom, seeing the new bridge that was now under construction at the heart of the small town, which would make life a good deal easier for residents and travellers alike.

'How long will you be in London, Alistair?'

'Not too long, I hope. I'd prefer not to be going at all, but with the country engaged in this crucial struggle with France, I feel that I must. I have decided to take Sophie with me. A few weeks in Richmond with Julia to keep an eye on her will not do her any harm—and she will be safe from the kind of temptation which Charles Meredith seems to represent.'

'But you have just told me that Sir Charles has gone to London. Are you not afraid that they might meet?'

'I doubt that. Meredith will be unaware that she has left Huntswood—and Julia will see to it that she remains at Richmond.'

'I see,' Louisa said. She would miss Sophie but Alistair was right. A short time spent under Julia's watchful eye would do her good, and take the worry off herself for a while. 'Take Mark with you,' she said suddenly, knowing how much the child wanted to be with his father.

One of Alistair's black brows went up and he took a long, cool look at her, irritated by her request, for he had already told Mark that he must remain at Huntswood and the subject was closed to discussion.

'No, Louisa. I thought I had made it plain that Mark is to stay here with you. I will ask you not to take issue over this because I will have my own way in this, as in everything else where Mark is concerned—however painful you might find it.'

'But can't you see that he wants to be with you?' she persisted, remembering how upset Mark had been when he'd discovered his father was going away—the sight of his tear-filled eyes and mournful face when Alistair had refused to let his son accompany him driving her on. 'Long before Constance was born he was the most important person in your life, and, much as he adores his new sister, he is a little jealous of all the attention you give her.'

'I'm sure you'll be able to deal with it when I've gone,' he replied, trying to stifle his impatience. 'Mothers do, don't they?'

Louisa stopped walking and stared at him. 'But he is not my child.'

Alistair's face was expressionless when he paused and looked down at her, but in his eyes a spark flashed, grim and formidable. 'The moment you became my wife you also became the mother of my child.'

'Oh, for heaven's sake,' she cried, springing rapidly to the attack. 'I am his stepmother and I am devoted to him, you know that, but you are his father and he wants to be with you. He has felt a little left out of late—neglected, if you like. This is a sensitive time for him, Alistair. Mark is still a child.'

Alistair's eyes narrowed dangerously. 'How dare you reproach me? Are you accusing me of neglecting my own son?'

'No, of course not. That is not the issue and you know it. All I am suggesting is that a little time away from here—alone with you—would do him the world of good.'

Alistair remained unmoved as his mouth settled in a firm, hard line. 'As you say, Louisa, Mark is still a child and I do not want to take him away from his lessons.'

'That can be easily remedied. Take Mark and his tutor with you to London.'

'No.'

'Then I suppose it is too much to expect you to put off going to London for a while?'

'It is. I have to go. Mark will be perfectly all right here with you. He has been before. I do not see why this time should be any different.'

'Then we did not have Constance,' Louisa cried, having to summon all her patience to stop herself bursting out in fury. Alistair's aggressive manner angered her beyond belief. 'You are too fond of your work, Alistair,' she accused bitterly. 'Does your family always have to take second place? You are either away in London applying yourself to the weighty matters of state, or immersed in your work here. I cannot for the life of me see why you go to the expense of employing bailiffs if you insist on doing everything yourself.'

With her cheeks flaming, she turned and began walking briskly back up the avenue of chestnuts, uncaring whether he followed her or not. But he was soon beside her, matching her stride for angry stride, having listened to her harsh accusations and choosing to misconstrue their meaning, which only succeeded in increasing her fury further when he next spoke.

'And is that what this is all about? Do you miss my company,

Louisa—my absence from your bed? Are you complaining?' he asked, with a mocking smile, his eyes gleaming cruelly.

'How can I miss what I've never had?' she retorted, glaring sideways at him. 'Besides, I have got to like things perfectly well the way they are. It is no hardship for me. You have made it plain by your absence from my bed that it holds no charms for you. So go to London, Alistair. No doubt you will find it full of beds with women who will be more than willing to satisfy your needs— which, I have often thought, might be your true reason for going there.'

'Then think that, if it pleases you to do so. That is your affair. But let me remind you that fidelity was never one of your virtues either, Louisa,' he taunted mockingly.

His jibe was cutting and unjust. Stung, Louisa seethed with rage and pain. How could he insult her so? Ever since she had married him she had kept the wilder side to her nature under restraint by self-discipline, which was now about to crack. She stopped abruptly, feeling that the pain in her throat would strangle her.

'How dare you? From the very beginning you have gone out of your way to hurt and humiliate me. I asked for none of this. I have not forgotten what I did, Alistair, but I will thank you to refrain from mentioning something that I have since had cause to regret bitterly. Marriage is supposed to be a partnership,' she said, her eyes snapping, 'and as a partnership it has certain obligations. But this is no partnership, is it, Alistair? And so any obligations we should feel for each other have gone by the way. This marriage—apart from producing Constance—has fulfilled none of our expectations.'

Alistair's face became grim and impassive, and his eyes were cold, with a compelling arrogance, when they looked at her, each word she uttered bringing him to the crumbling edge of violence. 'Then I should tell you that I have decided to improve matters between us. Now Constance is over four months old I am ready to put the past behind us. If we are to have more children, then we can hardly do so occupying separate beds.'

With a pounding heart, Louisa stared at him in astonishment, unable to believe he was saying what she had despaired of ever hearing from him, but then her soft lips tightened and her eyes blazed her defiance, flashing scorn.

'*You* are ready? *That* is exactly the kind of arrogant assumption I would expect from you. And what makes you think that *I* am? I am not someone to be used when the fancy takes you and cast aside when your desire has been slaked. What has all this been, Alistair—some kind of test you have put me through and which I have now passed? Do you consider I will make you a suitable wife after all?'

'I had to know what kind of woman you are. Remember that we did not know each other. You could have been a clever adventuress or any number of things.'

'Then think yourself lucky that I was not a courtesan,' she scorned, feeling too insulted to be comforted.

'So! You refuse to share my bed?'

'Yes, I refuse.'

His eyes narrowed, at a point of fury where reason was in danger of leaving him. He drew himself up to his full height. His jaw was rigidly set, his lips white. 'Think very carefully, Louisa.'

'I have.' She threw the words at him. 'I have had almost twelve whole months to think. Your treatment of me has been abominable.'

'You are my wife,' he ground out, 'and a man may treat his wife in any way he sees fit—within reason, of course.'

'But of course,' she scoffed, tossing her head in defiance, knowing that she was placing her whole marriage in jeopardy. 'Like a possession, you mean!'

Alistair seethed inwardly. An anger so intense seized him that he trembled with the force of it. 'If you like. But I will not endure your viperish tongue, your hostility or your defiance. Try my patience too far, Louisa, and you will find out what I can and cannot do.'

'Then do your worst, Alistair, which is what you are good at,' she flared, ignoring the danger signals in his blazing eyes. She was too angry to stop now. 'To the devil with you, I say. I care nothing for your anger, or your bullying. But if, after all these months of passive neglect, you think you can just crook your finger and I will fall into your bed you are mistaken.'

'Then, as you so delicately put it earlier, there are plenty of beds with willing occupants in London. I shall not fail to avail myself of one of them if I so wish.'

'Then do so and see if I care. I cannot for the life of me imagine what they see in you to attract them.'

Alistair stared at her for a long moment, and then the line of his mouth became cruel. 'Can you not, my dear wife?' He thrust his face closer to hers, thinking how adorable she looked with her cheeks flushed and her eyes spitting fire. 'Then perhaps I will show you.'

Louisa became frozen as Alistair's eyes travelled from her face to her angrily heaving bosom, her delicious curves riper than they had been before the birth of Constance. When his eyes rested on her lips she found her voice, unnerved by the unleashed sensuality she saw in his expression.

'Don't you dare touch me—' But almost before the words were uttered his hands were twined cruelly in her hair and he ground his mouth savagely against hers, his lips punishing and bruising. She struggled against him, the pain as he held her head almost beyond endurance. She had dreamed of this moment when he would kiss her, but this was not the kind of kiss she had wanted. This kiss was forced on her in anger and contempt, and his desire to humiliate her, and it roused her to red-hot fury.

As abruptly as he had seized her, so did he release her, so that she stumbled back from him. He glared at her, at her hair lying in tangled confusion over her shoulders, her cheeks a vivid scarlet, and her mouth tender and bruised.

Louisa was beside herself with rage, and, far from compliant, she flew at him with a storm of anger. He stared at the savagery in her eyes as he took hold of her arms to hold her away from him, while she pummelled his chest with her fists, wanting to strike out at him and hurt him with all the fury inside her heart. Calming herself, she shook herself free of him and stood back, her body trembling.

'I shall be glad to have you gone from here. I would rather die than have to endure the company of a husband who treats me so despicably—who sees me as nothing more than a machine to produce his children.'

Alistair's expression was grim. 'You were wrong when you said your bed held no charms for me, Louisa,' he said through clenched teeth. 'It is because it does that I avoided it—because it held too many similarities to your predecessor.'

'Oh, shut up,' she fumed, walking on. 'I do not want to listen. I do not wish to hear the name of your first wife ever again. All I can say is that the more I hear of her, and the more I know of you, the more I pity her and find myself feeling extremely sorry for her, having been in the impossible situation of being married to you—a bully and a lout. I do not blame her for leaving you— in fact, I am amazed she stayed with you so long. You are a monster, Alistair Dunstan, and I wish I'd never set eyes on you.'

Walking briskly beside her, Alistair endured her outburst, his face an impassive mask. He saw how pale she was under the heavy mass of hair, and that her amber eyes were bright with bravely held, angry tears. She looked lovely, and he had only to make one single, very simple movement to stop her and take her in his arms, to wipe the anger and pain from her eyes, but her words, her rage, had driven him into a tyrannical mood and no power on earth could have made him yield to that desire.

His eyes were merciless as he reached out and grasped her arm, bringing her to a standstill once more. She lifted her head and stared at him haughtily, jutting out her chin, and Alistair felt the anger pounding in his temples for she looked wonderful, defiantly, agonisingly so.

'Do not deny me, Louisa. I warn you I will not allow it.'

Her eyes flamed. 'Like a fool I gave myself to you once before. I shall not do so again until *I* am ready. Go to London, Alistair. It cannot be too soon for me. And do not feel that you have to hurry back.'

She snatched her arm from his grasp and marched away from him, uncaring whether he followed or not.

His face grim, his hands clenched by his sides, Alistair watched her disappear in the direction of the house. He was too angry and afraid of what his actions would be if he followed her and caught up with her.

From the beginning of their marriage he had resigned himself to endless fascinating torture because there was no other rational choice if he wanted to retain his sanity—always holding himself in restraint, curbing his emotions, knowing all the while that Louisa was fighting her own demons. He'd had to keep the barrier in place, at least until after their child was born and he could see the way the wind blew. And just when he'd decided to tell her how much she had come to mean to him, how much he loved her, and that he had decided to make their marriage complete, she had denied him with such violence that she might just as well have laughed in his face, turning on him like a shrew with all her claws unsheathed.

At a loss to know what to do about the unholy mess in which he found himself, he left for London with Sophie early the following morning.

For the rest of the day after he had gone Louisa was too numb and angry to feel the full pain of his leaving, but, as the shock of the angry words she had flung at him melted away, then her real suffering began in all its agonising sharpness and cruelty. All she had ever wanted was Alistair's love, and she had sent him away. He would never forgive her.

Yet when she thought of the manner of his leaving, how cold and unemotional his farewell had been, how hard and implacable his eyes as he had calmly told her he expected to be gone for several weeks, Louisa's blood boiled afresh. Oh, damn him, she thought fiercely. How could he go away and leave her like this? Did he think that she, his wife, would consent to be buried alive in the heart of Sussex while he went off to enjoy the pleasures of London? She'd go after him. She'd make him care for her. Without more ado, she ordered Edith to pack her clothes and those of the baby and Mark, and the following morning, accompanied by Edith and a nursemaid, she followed him to London.

It was very late when the tired party arrived at Dunstan House. The house immediately became chaotic as rooms were hastily prepared for them all, and a fire lit in the nursery for the baby and the nursemaid. Louisa was told by the butler, who had been thrown into a state of utter confusion by her unexpected arrival, that Lord Dunstan was not at home and that he was staying with his sister at Richmond. Tomorrow, after spending the day at Westminster, he had a theatre engagement in the evening at Covent Garden and was expected at Dunstan House afterwards.

Louisa didn't know whether to feel relieved by the absence of her husband or disappointed, and when the butler asked if she would like a message sent to Richmond, to inform him of her arrival, she decided against it. She was tired after the long journey, and after settling the children down for the night she would be in no mood for another angry confrontation with him.

She was surprised the following afternoon when Lady Bricknell called at Dunstan House, sweeping in like a ship under full sail and greeting her like an old and valued friend. With her elaborately arranged red hair and vast array of sparkling jewels, she positively dazzled, which, combined with her flamboyance, all added to her striking personality and suggested that she was a woman with many aspects to her character.

'It's so good to see you again, my dear,' she said, removing her cloak and handing it to a waiting footman, clearly intending to stay a while. 'I heard Alistair was in London so I called on the off chance.'

'He has taken Sophie to stay with Julia and her husband at Richmond, and is to go on from there to Westminster, although he is expected to return to Dunstan House later tonight, after a theatre engagement at Covent Garden, I believe,' Louisa explained, smiling, and yet feeling uncertain and slightly apprehensive. There had been so many dramatic changes to her life since her last conversation with Lady Bricknell on the evening she had come to this very house with the intention of seducing its owner. Ordering tea, she conducted her guest into the sumptuous blue and cream drawing room.

When they were settled and sat sipping the fragrant liquid from delicate china cups, Lady Bricknell set to with enthusiasm to talk of inconsequential things, gossip, mostly, about events and people she knew. But then she looked at Louisa intently, about to shift the conversation to one of a more personal nature.

'I can't tell you how delighted I was to hear about your marriage to Alistair, my dear—but I must say that it came as a tremendous surprise to many of his friends at the time.'

'I'm sure it did. We—did marry in haste,' Louisa answered, glancing surreptitiously at Lady Bricknell over the rim of her cup.

'And with good reason, I believe.' Lady Bricknell read Louisa's silence by the sudden colour in her cheeks and the confusion in her eyes, and she knew that she had hit upon the truth. 'Don't worry, my dear,' she smiled, her eyes sparkling. 'It caused quite a stir and gave people something to talk about. There was such a breath of secrecy and adventure about it all—rather like a novel, in fact, and I'm passionately fond of novels. Everyone found it fascinating that Alistair—a self-proclaimed single man after his turbulent marriage to Marianne—should suddenly up and marry a woman no one knew. You must tell me more about it.'

'There is little to tell,' Louisa said in a low voice, fixing her with a level gaze. 'But you are a good friend of Alistair's, Lady Bricknell, so you must know he was under an obligation to marry me.'

She nodded, unsmiling, observing a deep sadness and forlorn look in Louisa's wide eyes, and her instinct told her she was looking at an extremely unhappy young woman. 'Alistair never feels obligated to do anything he doesn't wish to, my dear. However, I think that your marrying is a good thing. You will be good for him. You are just what he needs, and I hear he is devoted to little Constance.'

'He is indeed. Unashamedly so. Indeed, there are times when I envy our daughter his attention,' she said quietly.

Lady Bricknell must have followed the thread of thoughts on her face, for she smiled knowingly. 'If it is any consolation to you, I know that Alistair was very much attracted by you the minute he laid eyes on you at the Spring Gardens the summer before last. Believe me, my dear, I recognised something in his expression when he looked at you that I hadn't seen in a long time.'

'Not since his marriage to Marianne,' stated Louisa quietly and with a hint of bitterness.

Lady Bricknell nodded gravely. 'That's right. I know little of what went on between them—he was always so reticent to speak about it—but I do know that she made his life a misery. He deserved better. But what about you, Louisa? Would you like to tell me what is worrying you—what it is that causes your eyes to fill with so much sadness? It's plain to me that something is very wrong between you. You can rely on me not to let what you say go beyond these four walls, if that is what's worrying you.'

Yes, Louisa thought, she could trust Lady Bricknell. She liked her and felt comfortable with her, as though she had known her all her life, and she could understand how her garish clothes and forceful personality might be forgiven when she gave so generously of the warmth of her personality. It wasn't difficult to see why Alistair valued her friendship so highly. She also invited confidence, and Louisa needed badly to confide in someone. She sighed and poured them both another cup of tea, feeling she needed it, and hesitantly, tentatively, her anxious expression relaxed.

As she listened to Louisa falteringly tell her of her meeting with Alistair and how her brother had lost everything they owned to him at cards at Bricknell House, and how she had set out to entrap him to retrieve her brother's IOU, Lady Bricknell's expression changed. And when Louisa went on to tell her about the terms Alistair had laid down prior to their marriage, feeling the last remnants of her pride melting like ice when boiling water had been poured onto it, into Lady Bricknell's worldly eyes came a look of spontaneous sympathy and softness, followed by an understanding, rueful smile.

'My, my! That is quite shocking. So, Alistair has been neglecting his conjugal duties, although how he could keep his hands off you—being hot-blooded and you looking as you do—is beyond comprehension. You are not exactly the kind of woman a man can ignore.'

'He—he hasn't told you any of this?'

'Goodness, no. He doesn't tell me everything—especially not those things which are of a personal nature.'

'Then neither should I,' said Louisa softly, miserably, feeling as if she had betrayed him.

'My dear, if, by telling me, you will allow me to help put things right between you, then you will have no reason to regret anything that you have told me. I knew my instincts were correct—that your real name was not Miss Divine. But James Fraser's sister! No. I would not have thought it for a minute.'

'The trouble is, Lady Bricknell, that when Alistair told me that he was now ready to accept me as his wife in the true sense I found myself telling him that he would have to wait until I was ready.'

'Goodness! And what did he say? What was his reaction to this?'

'Naturally he was angry—as well as shocked and surprised—and immediately left for London in a terrible rage.'

Lady Bricknell chuckled. 'That is so like him. You wounded his male ego. He has always been hot-blooded, and I recall telling you he was marked with a proud arrogance and indomitable will, but if you continue in this vein you will both be dreadfully unhappy.' She gave Louisa a look of cool scepticism. 'You do want him, don't you?'

'More than anything. But what can I do? I cannot dominate him. I do not know how—and nor do I wish to.'

'Nonsense, you're a woman, Louisa—and a woman can assert an inordinate power over a man if she can find a chink in his armour and push through. When their manhood is involved, men are such weak creatures. Listen, my dear, I am old enough and experienced enough to know what I say.'

'I am prepared to expend all the patience I possess on breaking down my husband's resistance.'

'If you learn to dominate him by his senses there is no reason why you cannot obtain what your heart desires most. It is just a matter of determination and application, and of careful ministering to the embers that glow within Alistair—hidden, I grant you, but there. A beautiful woman can always work her will on a man, and her arms are a powerful weapon when they embrace him. There comes a moment when his self-defence yields to his sensual desire,' she said softly, her eyes twinkling wickedly. 'A clever and experienced woman can turn that into an advantage.'

Louisa grimaced wryly. 'Experienced I most certainly am not, Lady Bricknell, and at this moment I have my doubts about being clever,' she sighed.

'Rubbish!' she exclaimed, not unkindly. 'I do not believe that for one moment. You strike me as being an extremely clever young woman. Tonight you say Alistair is to attend the theatre at

Covent Garden—and so shall I. You, my dear, will enter society by accompanying me,' she said, her voice full of determination.

Louisa stared at her incredulously. 'But I couldn't possibly. Alistair will be furious.'

'What? More so than he is already? Yes, you can. I shall send a note to his box and invite him to join me—and I cannot wait to see his face when he sees you. It will be worth watching. You succeeded admirably in gaining all Alistair's attention once, and you can do so again. Tonight you must look your most ravishing. You must also be at your most charming and alluring. You will smile and laugh—but not too much. Make him a little jealous. Follow your instincts and you can't go wrong. You will find he will be consumed with anger, but he will be unable to resist you. You'll see.'

Louisa was not convinced. Lady Bricknell had enormous influence, and shamelessly loved forcing society to bend to her will, but Alistair—with all the iron forces of his nature gathered together against Lady Bricknell's assault—would be quite another matter.

'Lady Bricknell, what you are suggesting is that I seduce my husband.'

'And why not? When I have gone I want you to take a restorative bath and a nap so that tonight you will feel wide awake and at your best to cope with anything. Have your maid prepare your most alluring gown, for you must look beautiful—not that that will be difficult,' she smiled. 'I shall send my carriage to collect you and we will go to the theatre together.' She chuckled with pleasure. 'It will be vastly amusing to see what everyone's reaction will be when you appear—especially when it is revealed that you are Lord Dunstan's mysterious wife. You are going to be a success, I know it, and I assure you I will not have enjoyed myself so much in a long time.'

She spoke with such sincerity that Louisa could not fail to believe her. Yet, later, when she sat ensconced on the crimson-coloured cushions beside Lady Bricknell in the carriage taking them to the theatre, she was swamped with nervousness and apprehension, beginning to have grave doubts about what she was doing.

* * *

Having left a moody Sophie at Richmond with Julia, Alistair arrived at the Covent Garden theatre with Sir Edward Thornton in no mood, after a long and tedious debate in the House of Lords on foreign policy and the conduct of the war, for sitting through the next three or four hours—a mishmash of music, drama, spectacle and entertainment. But he had promised Edward, and was doing nothing else, so he sat back and waited for the performance to begin.

Several of their friends had joined them and were casually discussing the day's debate in the House. The theatre, which was not just a place of entertainment but also a place for social chit-chat, was filled with conversation, with people, observing good manners, passing between boxes paying courtesy calls to friends and acquaintances.

Since leaving Huntswood, he had been despondent and more disturbed than he realised over his angry dispute with Louisa—to such an extent that he could think of little else.

Long before he had reached London he was already missing her, the revelation of how much she had come to mean to him, how much he loved her, pounding in his brain like a hundred hammers, mingling with the torment of his cruelty towards her over the past few days. He remembered her as she had been when they had strolled along the chestnut walk together—magnificent in her anger, courageous in her defiance—and filled with an incredible sweetness and innocent, tender passion when he had kissed her on his return from Rotherfield.

He felt a surge of remorse and scolding rage at his blindness when he recalled his treatment of her over the months of her pregnancy, and the terms he had so forcefully and thoughtlessly laid down at the beginning of their marriage, uncaring whether she approved or not and giving her no chance to argue. She had been too proud to anyway. She had been quiet and subdued, enduring his coldness until three days ago when it had all become too much for her—when she had suddenly snapped and he had seen her spirit revived.

He was furious with himself and shame poured through him like boiling water. Yes, he'd been blind—blind, stupid and unfeeling. How could he possibly have likened her to Marianne—

with her viciousness and spite—who had rejected Mark so coldly, and who had laughed in his face when she had confessed her adultery? She had goaded and taunted him to the point where he could have throttled her when she had flaunted the result of her betrayal before him, telling him that she was to bear another man's child—Charles Meredith's child—a child she would love as she loved Meredith.

Louisa was none of these things. In fact, she was everything that Marianne was not. She was gentle, caring and innocent of any wrongdoing, and deep down inside he'd known from the beginning that she wasn't promiscuous, but because she had tricked him so artfully, damaging his pride, he'd insulted her by treating her as though she was. She was the most wonderful person in the world, caring and devoted to both Constance and Mark, and he had treated her abominably. She deserved better from him.

He recalled something she had said when he had returned from Rotherfield—that what she had given him that night at Dunstan House she had given from the heart. She'd been trying to tell him that she loved him, and he hadn't listened. That was unforgivable of him. Many were the times he'd wanted to go to her, knowing she was behind the closed door that connected their rooms, the image of her both powerful and tantalising. Over the months he had watched her, he had felt disquieting emotions rise to threaten his wandering equilibrium. He had wanted desperately to reach out to her, but his own stupidity over Marianne, and his pride, had held him back.

With the revelation of how deep his love was for her, it was as though his mind had become free of its burden of pain and sorrow at the same time—the kind of freedom Louisa must have felt on being relieved of the weight of the child, when their daughter was born. Unable to bear being apart from her, he would return to Huntswood to put things right between them without delay, and to hell with the state of the nation.

Distracted from his thoughts, he turned when someone knocked and entered their box, handing him a note. He smiled on opening it, recognising the familiar handwriting of Lady Bricknell. She was requesting that he might care to visit her in her box at some time during a break in the performance.

'My God!' exclaimed Edward from beside him. 'Who is that gorgeous creature with Lady Bricknell? She can't be real.'

Alistair raised his eyes and glanced across at Lady Bricknell's box, smiling his acceptance to her invitation. Absently his eyes shifted to the other occupants, two gentlemen—one he knew to be Lady Bricknell's latest swain—and a lady sitting in front of her. Recognition hit him like a thunderbolt. He became frozen, staring in stunned silence, all his tender thoughts of a moment before vanishing like a morning mist. It was as if all the breath had been knocked out of him. Anger, uncurling from his stomach, surged through him.

'That gorgeous creature, as you so aptly put it, Edward, is my wife,' he said through gritted teeth, his eyes burning across at her with a fire that scorched her raw. 'And I can confirm that she is perfectly real.'

Alistair's eyes fixed on Louisa, whose whole presence seemed to blaze across the theatre at him, eliminating all else, the pit between them becoming like a multicoloured boiling cauldron of moving bodies, but they could have been alone, facing each other across a dangerous, unbridgeable chasm.

Chapter Thirteen

Alistair kept his eyes fixed on Louisa, unable to believe she had come to London without either his knowledge or permission. How dared she defy him—force his hand in this manner? he seethed. But he could not deny that, clad in a shimmering azure gossamer-silk gown with a low scooped neckline, her neck and shoulders and the soft swell of her breasts aglow, she was like a vision from heaven. Her wealth of strawberry-blonde hair had been perfectly arranged, and one thick, glossy ringlet was draped over her shoulder. Her face and figure were flawless, and anyone looking at her would see only perfection. All through the latter months of her pregnancy she had glowed—she had been lovely then—but here among the glitter of London society she was magnificent.

With her face partly screened by her fan, she seemed to be absorbed in what was taking place around her, her attention caught by what was going on in the auditorium as she purposely avoided looking his way. He watched, growing angrier by the minute, as people entered Lady Bricknell's box, one after the other, with no other purpose than to be introduced to Louisa, bending over her hand far too long, he thought.

What the devil did she think she was up to, a smile on her lips and in her astonishing amber eyes for anyone who looked at her, fluttering her endless eyelashes flirtatiously, laughing and sighing with a demure playfulness, and inviting lingering, lascivious looks and indecent thoughts by sporting an outrageous *décolletage*? He could see that none of the raffish young men was immune to her sparkling personality, for her beauty, coupled with the mischief in her eyes, was irresistible.

Crumpling the note in his hand, Alistair rose abruptly. 'Come along, Edward. Let me introduce you to my wife. It would appear that you are the only man here tonight who hasn't made himself known to her.'

Lady Bricknell was in good spirits and full of smiles as she acknowledged several people who came to visit them, enjoying the enthusiastic reception she and Louisa received and the repartee. She had seen Alistair leave his box and knew he would be on his way. Ushering the gentleman who was bent over Louisa's hand unceremoniously out, she cast her a sharp look.

'Chin up, my dear,' she smiled, waving her fan languidly, 'and smile. Remember what I told you. Flirt just a little and be charm and graciousness personified. Mark my words—you'll have your husband eating out of your hand before the night is over. If the reception so far is anything to go by, you have already caused something of a stir.'

Louisa took a deep breath. Now that the moment had come when she must come face to face with her husband, she was afraid. Nothing in her life had prepared her for this. At that moment the door to their box opened and Alistair stepped inside, followed by Edward Thornton, and Louisa was acutely conscious that his eyes were glued to her face as he greeted Lady Bricknell, his manner cool yet polite.

'Why, how kind of you to come, Alistair,' Lady Bricknell greeted him with a cheerful heartiness. 'Louisa told me earlier when I called at Dunstan House that you would be here this evening. I had reserved a box for myself and my friends,' she said, indicating the two gentlemen sitting to one side of her, 'and took the opportunity of inviting her along. It seemed such a pity to leave her all alone when she could be here enjoying herself.'

'How considerate of you, Lady Bricknell—and how nice of Louisa to honour us with her company,' Alistair said, his voice and his eyes like ice as he looked at his wife.

The hard expression on his handsome face caused Louisa an involuntary shiver, which was not one of pleasure, but, remembering the part she was playing, she smiled sweetly. As good manners demanded, just as the theatre's orchestra began playing the overture, Alistair introduced Sir Edward Thornton.

'I am pleased to make your acquaintance, sir,' she murmured, and, stirred by some feminine impulse of coquetry—and an urge to annoy her husband—she favoured Sir Edward with her most brilliant smile.

'It's a pleasure, Lady Dunstan. I had no idea Alistair had such a beautiful wife.' He stepped back and looked at Alistair. 'You should bring your wife to London more often, Alistair. Her presence would enhance any event.'

'Yes,' he said stiffly. 'Maybe you're right, Edward.'

The performance was about to start and, after excusing himself, Sir Edward returned to his box, while Alistair sat next to his wife, determined not to leave her side for the entire evening as he watched her with brooding attentiveness. Only when everyone's attention was taken up by what was happening on the stage did he lean towards her.

'What the hell are you doing here?' he demanded, keeping his voice low so as not to be overheard by the others in the box.

Beneath his icy calm, such was the force of his fury that Louisa flinched, but, catching Lady Bricknell's sharp eyes, she took a deep breath and gave her husband a wide-eyed look of innocence.

'Why, the same as everyone else, I suppose. I am here to enjoy the play.'

'I little thought to see you engaged in such a mad escapade as this, but clearly I was mistaken. What in God's name induced you to come here? Are you out to incur my anger? Is that it?'

'What? More than I have already, you mean?'

'Don't be flippant,' he ground out, his face so close to Louisa's that she could see the ice-cold satanic glitter in his blue eyes. 'You know perfectly well I disapprove of your coming here. Had you suggested coming to London, I would have expressly forbidden you to do so.'

'Which is precisely why I didn't ask. When you left Huntswood so abruptly I suddenly felt the need to sample a little enjoyment myself. I am sorry if you are not pleased to see me, Alistair, but it's too late to do anything about it now.'

'So you might like to think, but make the most of it, for I insist you return to Huntswood tomorrow—where you should have remained.'

'With Mark?'

'Yes.'

She sighed and turned her head, looking at him, fixing her gaze calmly on his. 'Don't fret so, Alistair,' she said, with a lightness she did not feel. 'Both Mark and Constance are here with me.' With an infuriating smile, she turned away, Alistair's face having become so suffused with anger she thought he was about to have an apoplexy.

'Constance is here with you?'

'But of course. As if I would leave her behind. She depends on me for sustenance, don't forget. And if you are worried about Mark getting behind with his studies then you can set your mind at rest. His tutor will be arriving at Dunstan House tomorrow.'

Alistair's countenance became as black as thunder. 'How dare you defy me so blatantly?' his voice snarled warningly in her ear. 'You will do as I say.'

'No, Alistair,' she said firmly, quietly, her eyes unwavering as she met his gaze once more. She refused to be drawn, and holding her head up she smiled engagingly. How she would like to give his handsome, angry face a resounding slap and cut his conceit, his arrogance down to size, but instead she forced her face to remain calm. 'I am your wife and will be your equal—not your chattel to be told what I will and will not do.'

'Will you not? We shall see about that.' Alistair sat back and gave her a long, speculative look that she did not see as she focused her gaze on the stage, but after a few moments she glanced at him crossly with a sigh, wafting her face with her fan.

'If you insist on being disagreeable for the entire evening, Alistair, I suggest you return to your friends. Perhaps they will tolerate your angry mood better than I.'

Alistair didn't move and his anger did not abate as the evening drew on. It was no easy matter for Louisa to ignore his hard gaze fixed on her, but she continued to smile more vividly, and to tease and laugh with the gentlemen who kept arriving in their box with what Alistair considered to be infuriating persistence. During an interlude of music and dance she caught his eye at one point and could see that he was ready to explode. She had every confidence he would not cause a scene, and yet it was inevitable that one would come later.

But, she thought jubilantly and with immense satisfaction as she continued to play the part of an alluringly seductive woman bent on seducing her husband, at last, after some twelve months of marriage, she had the opportunity to teach Alistair Dunstan a lesson he would not forget easily. This time she would be in control, and she had no conscience about it whatsoever.

She smiled sweetly at him when she saw his dark scowl after yet another young rake had found his way to their box to be introduced to her by Lady Bricknell—a young man who left with some considerable haste on being confronted by Lord Dunstan's black look of thunder.

'Must you look so put out, Alistair?' she asked, keeping her voice low. 'It should flatter your vanity having your friends envy you your wife.'

'It gives me no satisfaction to see other men coveting my wife,' he growled. 'As soon as this damned performance is over we are leaving. Is that understood?'

'Yes. I have to leave anyway to attend Constance.'

'I am glad to see you have not forgotten where your duty lies,' he scorned.

When the final piece ended, followed by spontaneous, thunderous applause, people began pouring out of the boxes. Alistair put his arm about Louisa's waist, steady and as firm as a rock, and though it might seem to others that it was just a casual embrace to Louisa it was like a vice. He took her elbow and lost no time in steering her down the stairs to the foyer and out to his carriage, waiting in a line of others in the busy street.

'Goodnight, Louisa,' murmured Lady Bricknell, coming to stand beside her while Alistair turned to say goodnight to Sir Edward. 'You did well. Tonight I am confident that you will get your heart's desire—and tomorrow the whole of London will be talking about you.'

Lady Bricknell watched Alistair lead his wife away with a gleam in her eyes and a satisfied smile curving her lips. She had watched the changing expressions move across Alistair's fiercely handsome face all evening—from fury to the violent jealousy a man felt when the woman he loved was being coveted by others. He had clung to Louisa's side and watched her with all the substance of his being, his concentration glued to the slim and elegant figure by his side.

She had never seen him behave with a woman as he had with his wife tonight, and she was in no doubt that Alistair was deeply in love with Louisa, that his senses had known it from the moment he had first set eyes on her that night at the Spring Gardens at Vauxhall, and that his mind had only recently absorbed the knowledge. She was certain that Louisa was in for a night to remember. Suddenly, feeling very old, she sighed and turned towards her own carriage, envying Louisa more than she would ever know her youth, her beauty and, she thought with irritation, when she looked at her latest lover waiting for her beside the carriage—a rather gross, unappealing man and already showing signs of running to seed—her husband.

Louisa climbed inside the carriage and Alistair flung himself in after her. Snapping orders to the driver, he leaned back and glowered across at her in the semi-darkness, the glow from the carriage lamps making his face look demonical. Louisa sighed, settling into the corner and looking out, trying to remember Lady Bricknell's advice about remaining calm and in control of herself, and not giving way to anger. Dunstan House was quiet when they arrived, with only a footman on duty to open the door.

'Go to your room,' Alistair ground out.

'I shall—when I have seen that the children are settled for the night.'

With a whimsical smile, Louisa slowly climbed the stairs and went to check on Mark and Constance. Mark was sound asleep, his curly head peeping out above the bedclothes, but Constance was restless. As soon as her mother entered the room, as if sensing nourishment, her tiny fists began thrashing the air and her little face puckered as she let out a hungry wail. Crooning softly, Louisa lifted her out of her crib and cradled her in her arms, smiling across at the nursemaid who had come to tend her, quietly telling her to return to bed, that she would settle Constance when she had been fed.

Sitting in a comfortable chair, she opened the front of her gown and put the baby to her breast, feeling the hungry tug of the pink little mouth, which never failed to send a sensation of delight washing over her. With a sigh she watched her daughter, a tiny little being that breathed and snuggled close, until at last, replete, she fell asleep, her little head nestling in the crook of Louisa's arm. Gently placing her back in the crib, she bent and kissed her sleeping face, rosy and warm against her lips, hoping she would sleep through the night.

Arranging the front of her dress, she sighed again, and with a look of serene contentment turned to find Alistair standing perfectly still, watching her from the doorway, a curiously warm look in his eyes. He didn't speak as she walked past him onto the landing, but the scene he had witnessed of Louisa feeding their daughter had melted his anger like a summer mist when the sun came out.

He recalled the time when Mark had been born and it had been suggested to Marianne that she nurse him herself, the custom of employing wet-nurses having been abandoned by a large number of middle-class ladies, but she had shrunk with horror and disgust at the mere thought of putting a child to her breast.

Louisa walked towards her room and he followed her inside, closing the door and leaning against it. Having discarded his coat, he folded his arms and gazed at her, a half-smile curving his handsome lips. She really was the most remarkable woman he had ever met. His eyes never left her. He looked incongruous, filling the room with his presence.

Louisa's excitement was almost unendurable as, with shaking fingers, she began pulling out the combs and pins that held her hair in place, ignoring the tug of her husband's eyes as she gave it a gentle shake, conscious of the seductiveness of the gesture as she carried on with the charade, determined to play it out to the end. She knew the colour was rising in her cheeks, and that her eyes were sparkling.

Seeing the mass of her loosened hair falling in a golden cascade about her shoulders, Alistair drew a sharp breath, feeling the blood pounding in his head as he stood, watching the play of the candles' gleam on her flesh, glowing and lustrous in the golden light.

The air inside the room was sultry and warm, with tiny moths coming in through the open windows, attracted by the light, and the gentlest of breezes stirring the curtains. Louisa was the first to break the silence, looking at Alistair wide-eyed and uncertain, relieved to see his mood had lightened. Her gaze took in the sheer male beauty of him, of his darkly handsome face and the saturnine twist to his firm lips, his wide, masculine shoulders and narrow waist. In all her life she had never known a man like him, and was at a loss to understand him.

'Are you going to remain?' she asked softly.

He sauntered towards her, scrutinising her intently, his eyes drawn to her mouth. 'That is what you want, isn't it? That is what all this is about—the reason why you have followed me to London?' His eyes were beginning to glint with wicked amusement. 'I should hate to disappoint you,' he murmured, his voice low and husky.

'You won't. If you have no wish to stay then I would prefer it if you went.'

'And if I don't wish to leave?' he breathed, reaching out and very slowly tucking a thick strand of her hair behind her ear, the warmth smouldering in his eyes as he looked at her emphasising his desire to remain. 'If I want to find out if what we experienced together once before can be as good between us again, would you mind if I stayed?' he asked, with a questioning lift to his brows.

'No. I want you to, Alistair,' Louisa said, her heart beginning to pound with helpless anticipation.

Alistair placed a finger under her chin, turning her face up towards his. He searched the depths of her glowing amber eyes for a moment, seeing the pupils large and as black as jet in their centres, and then he sighed, shaking his head. 'You planned this, didn't you, Louisa? With a little collusion from Lady Bricknell, I don't doubt,' he said with mild rebuke.

'Yes, I did—and Lady Bricknell did prove helpful. But this is no game,' she told him honestly, 'and nor is it a contest. Enough is enough, Alistair. It may suit you to live the life of a monk—at least that is the impression you give me—but it does not suit me to live the life of a nun.'

He arched a sleek black brow. 'I see. Well, you were the one who talked of being equal. What would you do about it?'

Louisa stared at him, unsure how to proceed now the moment had arrived when it was within her power to win him over. He was so incredibly masculine and stood so close that she was overwhelmed by him. A faint mocking smile curved his mouth as he waited patiently for her to make a move, his heightened senses darkening his eyes and tensing his features, but she would not be afraid of him.

Following her instinct, as Lady Bricknell had advised, she rose to the challenge in an impulsive attempt to communicate with him the only way she knew how. With an enticing smile, she raised herself on tiptoe and let her hands slide slowly over his silk shirt, feeling his muscles tauten as she placed them lightly on his shoulders and began to spark the passion that had lain dormant between them for far too long.

'I would do this,' she whispered, reaching up and placing a kiss on his mouth with gentle shyness, her lips as light as a butterfly's wings, her heart hammering like a wild, captured bird's, 'and this—and even this.' And she continued to place tantalising little kisses on different features of his face, her warm breath caressing his skin, before stepping back.

Alistair responded with another questioning lift to his brows, giving no indication of the feelings her soft lips had aroused in him. No woman he had ever known had been capable of igniting such an uncontrollable rush of lust with just a few feather-light kisses. 'And is that all?'

Louisa's delicate brows drew together in confusion. 'Are you criticising me? What else would you have me do?'

'Oh, I'm sure you can think of something.'

Tentatively she put a hand over his and smiled, drawing a deep breath. With no notion of whether what she was doing was right or wrong she moved closer, love her only instinct to guide her. All along his arm his muscles were tense as he watched her, a savage, wolf-like look in his eyes. Slowly she uncurled his fingers that were clenched in a fist, raising his hand and stroking the palm with the tip of her finger, lifting it a little more and placing her lips to its warm centre, feeling the sinews tense and then relax.

She slid her fingers through his, lacing them together, feeling his eyes watching her, burning into her bowed head.

Still holding his hand, she drew him towards the bed, sitting and pulling him down beside her. They lay back and, smiling softly, she leaned over him, her breath warm as she kissed his mouth, and then held back a little, looking to see if she had reached him. His breathing had quickened and his eyes held hers like a magnet, but when she lowered her head and would have kissed him again he took hold of her and threw her back onto the bed, suspending himself above her, the sudden ferocious depth of his desire for her roaring in his ears.

'Oh, no. No more, Louisa,' he said huskily, unable to resist temptation, to withstand the glorious beauty of her. 'This is where I take over.'

Louisa gazed up into his smouldering eyes, while his hands plunged into her hair on either side of her face, holding her captive as he looked down at her. 'I know I gave you reason to think otherwise, but I am a novice at all this,' she breathed after his mouth had claimed hers in a kiss of violent tenderness.

'You seem to be doing very well to me, but I am sure you can do better. I remember I taught you well.'

'If you did, it was too long ago for me to remember,' she murmured with a trace of accusation, a gentle jibe as to his neglect of her.

'Then I shall have to teach you all over again.'

'As your wife, Alistair,' she breathed softly, 'or as Miss Divine? As Lady Dunstan you only speak to me of tedious matters—of the children's health, the state of the weather and household affairs—but with Miss Divine—' she smiled, fanning his mouth with her warm, sweet breath '—I remember the conversation being of a far more intimate and interesting nature.'

'Conversation is not what I want from you this night, Louisa,' he replied as he tried to control his hungry passion, looking down into her velvety eyes, now huge with desire. 'But tell me, my love, what is your name tonight?'

'What would you like it to be?'

'What else but Miss Divine—my adorable lady of pleasure?' he murmured, proceeding to make love to her, pausing only long enough to discard his clothes and remove hers, flinging them to the far corners of the room in his impatience to be with her.

He became lost in the exciting beauty of her, and a sharp, wonderful ache tore through him as he lay with her, with a sensual joy that he hadn't felt since that night when Constance had been conceived. His lips were warm, first on her mouth and then sliding down the long, graceful line of her neck, gentle, harmless, with the merest whisper of a caress. Then slowly, easily, where his lips had led, his hand followed and stroked, cradling her breast, soft to his touch, feeling her tremble against him, a trembling that spread over her entire body as his hand travelled downwards, over the smooth flesh of her stomach and then inward, to the gentle curve of her thighs, her skin like soft velvet.

Completely absorbed, Louisa was aflame, her body responding to Alistair's caresses like an explosion of raging thirst. He held her in a state of bemused suspension, the sensations she had experienced once before melting her inside and out. He raised his head and looked down at her, his eyes travelling in wonder and rediscovery over her body, ripe and more mature after the birth of their child, and the thought of teaching her all she ought to know again—things he had already taught her when she had discovered hidden desires in herself she hadn't known before—appealed to him.

He fastened his mouth to hers with cruel pressure, kissing her with a demanding savagery he was unable to control, feeling her lips tormenting in their intimate sweetness as he repeated over and over the compelling strokes and caresses on her naked flesh that aroused her to near madness, so starved was she for his love. She was devoid of will as she was possessed by a craving agony of desperation so great she thought she would die of it.

Pressing her back against the pillows, Alistair's breath was warm on her throat as his arms dragged her fully against his hardening body, which moved over hers, capturing her hands and pinning them together above her head as candlelight caught the hot intent on his face. Their skin touched with a burning warmth, and Louisa moaned under the aggressive power of his body as her own unfolded and opened to him, like a flower opening to the warmth of the sun.

Afterwards Alistair rolled over onto his back, pulling Louisa close so that her cheek rested on his chest. She sighed, sleepy and languid, her expression one of perfect tranquillity, her slender, silky limbs entwined with his. Lifting a hand, she brushed her fingers lightly over his chest, smiling serenely as she traced the outline of his muscular shoulders, too happy to sleep, wanting this moment to last for ever. With the sheet draped carelessly over them and his arms around her, Alistair gently kissed the top of her head, glorying in the sheer heaven of holding her.

'Well?' he murmured. 'Was it as good between us as the last time?'

'Yes. Better, I think.'

'And it will get even better.'

She sighed against him. 'Are you sorry now that I followed you to London?'

'No, not one bit. Although I think it is only fair to tell you that I fully intended returning to Huntswood myself before the week was out.'

Louisa's eyes opened wide in amazement and, raising her head, she looked up at him. 'You did?'

'Mmm. You see, my darling, when I arrived in London I was the most wretched of men. The plain and simple truth is that I missed you. I was miserable without you, and I realised just how much you have come to mean to me—how much I care for you. I love you, Louisa. Deeply. And I know you love me. I can feel it when I hold you in my arms.'

'Yes, I admit it. I do love you, Alistair. I love you as much as it is possible for a woman to love a man. I have loved you for so long, ever since the very first time you took me in your arms and kissed me at Dunstan House—the kiss that sealed our bargain.'

'Bless you, my darling,' he said, with a raw ache in his voice, bending his head and kissing her lips tenderly, all the love that had been accumulating over the years since Marianne's betrayal in that kiss. 'The magnetism between us has been there from the start—too strong for us to deny. You are a beautiful and truly wonderful woman.'

'And am I to believe you love me for my beauty alone?' she teased gently, her lips against him.

His features became solemn. 'No. I am not so stupid that I would have let your beauty alone make me love you. You have a multitude of other assets that I admire and love. You are a rare being, Louisa. You are everything I dreamed a woman, a wife and a mother could be—and more.'

Louisa tilted her head up to his and could see he was perfectly serious. 'That is a compliment indeed, Alistair. Thank you.'

'I was tortured and ashamed of my behaviour—my anger towards you the day before I left Huntswood—and I wanted to return to beg your forgiveness, to tell you how sorry I was for everything I'd done. In my arrogance and pride I have been stupid and unfeeling in my treatment of you. You have loved me all along, and in return I have scorned you, humiliated you, and driven you to weep—and still you came here to try to put things right between us. How could I have likened you to Marianne? You aren't remotely like her. You are everything she was not. She was vicious and ugly in her deceit, with no thought for anyone other than herself and Charles Meredith.'

Louisa rolled over onto her stomach and leaned on her elbows, her hair falling about them both as she looked at him lying on his back, one arm thrown casually above his head, as he spoke of his first wife.

'Tell me about her, Alistair.'

'When you asked me about her on the night I returned from Rotherfield I regret my anger—my tactlessness. I apologise most humbly, Louisa. I insulted you, which was unforgivable of me. You have every right to ask me about her, and I will tell you. It's just that I've grown out of the habit of speaking about her. In fact,' he sighed, taking a handful of her sweetly perfumed hair that tumbled over his chest in a golden cascade and kissing its waves, 'I rarely speak about her to anyone.'

'Not even to Mark?'

'No. It's wrong of me, I know, but I cannot bring myself to.' He fell silent, looking ahead, wrestling with his troubled thoughts.

'Please don't feel you have to explain anything to me, Alistair.'

'I want to. It's time I did. It's just that it's difficult to know where to begin.'

'At the beginning is as good a place as any. What was she like?' Louisa prompted gently. 'Was she fair—dark? What?'

'Her colouring was dark and she was extremely attractive. She was an only child, and hopelessly spoiled by her parents, who were wealthy landowners and lived in Kent. She was utterly selfish and I should never have married her,' he said quietly.

'Why? Why do you say that? You must have loved her.'

'At the time I suppose I did, which made me blind to her flaws. I first met her in London when I was twenty-one—young and impulsive—and we very quickly became friends. Unbeknownst to me she was already involved with Charles Meredith—a man I had heard of, living as he does in the neighbourhood. We had never met but his reputation had gone before him and I knew him to be a high-born man of pleasure. I believe it was understood from early on that he and Marianne would marry—which Marianne hoped would be sooner rather than later.

'It was unfortunate for her that Charles Meredith did not see it her way—or feel the same deep love I came to realise later that she felt for him, which became more like an obsession as time went on. He was greedy for excitement, and after bidding farewell to Marianne embarked on a tour of Europe. Secure in the knowledge that she was so besotted with him that she would wait, he promised to return after twelve months and marry her and settle down.'

'Are you saying that she married you on the rebound?'

'In a way, but there was more to it than that. I soon discovered that she used me as a pawn to get back at him. You see, Marianne had a vicious, vindictive streak, which did not become apparent to me until she became my wife, and it was not in her nature to wait. She was incensed by Meredith's lack of feeling and consideration, and on meeting me—who she could see was quite bowled over by her beauty and charm—accepted my proposal of marriage.'

'You mean—she only married you to spite Charles Meredith?'

'Yes. And knowing we were neighbours was an added attraction. It meant that she would be able to flaunt herself before him— make him suffer for choosing to enjoy the pleasures of Europe instead of marriage to her. But she quickly regretted marrying me.

She found the intimacies of marriage repugnant, and very soon began to miss the London social scene, having always enjoyed being fêted and adored by many men rather than being tied to just one—unless that one man happened to be Charles Meredith.'

'And did things get no better when Mark was born?'

His expression became grim. 'No. If anything they were as bad as they could possibly get. She made my life a complete misery. She was not maternal and did not want to conceive—wanting to preserve her figure and her beauty. When Mark was born he disgusted her. She could hardly bear to look at him. I could suffer her rebuffs, her slights and her coldness, but the lack of thought for her son was beyond endurance.'

Louisa was shocked. Thinking of her own adorable Constance, she was unable to believe a mother could not love her own child.

'When Charles Meredith finally returned from Europe after two years, he was incensed that Marianne had not waited for him. Despite her intention to make him suffer for turning from her, she could not keep away from him. Unbeknownst to me they began seeing each other. As you know I have many commitments and it is necessary for me to spend some considerable time in London. Marianne always accompanied me, always enjoying herself to the full, but suddenly she began to refuse to leave Huntswood whenever I had to go to town.

'I thought nothing of it at first, but then the rumours began—rumours connecting her to Charles Meredith. I didn't believe them—I didn't want to believe that my wife was capable of such deceit—but the rumours could not be ignored and eventually I confronted her.'

His voice became hard as the memories he was unable to forget tore through him. 'She delighted in flinging the truth in my face. She flaunted it. She was obsessed with Meredith—unable to resist him. It was a terrible time. I was unable to accept her betrayal. And then one day she told me she wanted to leave me—to divorce me. In my anger and my pride—and not wishing to besmirch my family name with something as shocking as a divorce—I refused to consider it.'

'Did you still love her?'

'No. By that time I despised her—but she was my wife and the mother of my son.' He fell silent, looking ahead, his expression bitter. At last he said, 'I blame myself for her death.'

Louisa was so surprised she stared at him. 'For what reason do you take responsibility?'

'She came to grief running away from me. If I had let her go and not gone after her, she would not have died. She drowned while trying to cross the river to go to her lover.'

'Oh, dear Lord! Alistair, forgive me, I—I had no idea—'

'How could you? There are few people who know what happened—how it was between us. That night was similar to the night I rode back from Rotherfield, with the rain pouring down in torrents, as it had been doing for days, swelling the river to such an extent that it was already overflowing its banks. When I returned from London she couldn't wait to tell me that she was carrying Charles Meredith's child. She goaded me cruelly. I was devastated. I didn't believe her, thinking she was saying it to force my hand into letting her go, and when she ran from the house I followed.'

'But why did she cross the river? Why did she not cross by the bridge?'

'Because she thought I would catch up with her and force her to return to Huntswood. When she was eventually pulled from the river and she looked at me—on the very brink of death—her face was such a mask of hatred... I shall never forget it.'

Louisa stared at him, shocked to her very soul, understanding at last why it had been so difficult for him to speak of these terrible events in his life. 'How can you conclude that Marianne's death was all your fault, Alistair? You cannot live the rest of your life as a martyr to misplaced guilt. Charles Meredith and Marianne were the guilty ones—not you. He is the one who ought to suffer. How did he react to Marianne's death? How was he affected by it?'

'I think you know the answer to that,' he replied, with a cynical curl to his lips. 'He blamed me, of course, and swore to avenge her death—no matter how long it took. But in no time at all he returned to London to all his old haunts—as arrogant as ever.'

'And—and was it ever proved whether or not Marianne was with child?'

'Yes, she was. The doctor who examined her on her death confirmed it to me—and I knew it could not possibly be mine—which no doubt made Meredith's hatred of me all the more profound.'

'He did know about the child?'

'I imagine so.'

'And would you have let her go, Alistair? When you knew for certain she was to bear Sir Charles's child, would you have consented to a divorce?'

'Yes. That's why I ran after her—to tell her. I could not have remained married to her after that. Afterwards I existed for a time in confusion and misery, despising myself and everyone else as I tried to close my mind to what had happened—to block out my bitter hatred of Charles Meredith. Mark was my only comfort.'

Louisa sighed sadly. She knew the rest. She remembered when she had been one of Alistair's guests at Dunstan House, how she had observed him, and how his behaviour had puzzled her. He had looked at the company with cynical disdain, holding everyone in contempt, as if what Marianne and Charles Meredith had done between them had turned him against the whole human race. There was little wonder he had not batted an eye when poor James had lost everything he owned to him at cards that night at Lady Bricknell's.

'You must not let what you felt for Marianne and your hatred for Charles Meredith fester and destroy in the future as it has done in the past. It is over. It is done. You must put the past behind you—along with the misery they both caused you.'

'Unfortunately, the past has a habit of catching up with one.'

'Sometimes, I know. But we are together now, Alistair—you, me and our children. Nothing can ever change that or come between us.'

Alistair studied her for a moment, seeing a face of such dazzling sweetness, understanding and love. He searched her eyes with a mixture of gentleness and gravity, a stirring of emotion swelling in his chest as he drew her closer, the intensity of the love he felt for her making him ache. It was the most profound moment of his life.

'I don't deserve you,' he murmured hoarsely.

'Yes, you do.'

He nodded slowly, beginning to understand fully the wonderful thing that had happened to him. He touched her hair and her face with his lips as though trying to convince himself that she was real, and Louisa was so happy to be with him, that everything had been resolved between them, that she could think of nothing beyond that one glorious fact.

Chapter Fourteen

In the days that followed Louisa and Alistair could not bear to be apart as they discovered things about each other that were entirely new. They both had such strong views on everything and arguments flared easily, but they both agreed that a placid partnership would not have suited them, and they soon realised that it made the making up all the more passionate and exciting.

It was an idyllic time for them and their children, a time in which they were suspended in some kind of dream, reluctant to let the outside world into their lives. But it was inevitable that it would intrude some time, which it did when James, who was in town staying with Timothy, came to call on them and to be introduced to his niece.

'Have you been in town long?' Alistair asked him when he came upon him alone in the drawing room.

'No. I came two days ago to spend a little time with Amelia.'

'And to arrange the date for the wedding—am I right?' said Alistair with a merry gleam in his eyes.

James flushed slightly and smiled, looking a little bashful. 'Yes. We are to be married at her home in Oxfordshire two months from now. I do hope you and Louisa will be able to attend.'

'We shall be delighted. I doubt you will be able to keep Louisa away. Tell me, James,' he said, pouring them both a glass of brandy, 'do you not miss the London social scene?'

'No, sir. I am quite content at Bierlow—and I shall be more so when Amelia becomes my wife. I have not been drawn into a game of cards for over a year. You were my last partner and—after that unfortunate experience—I have no desire for another.'

'I'm glad to hear it.' Alistair sat down, crossing one knee over the other as he studied Louisa's brother, glad that he had seen the error of his ways and decided to settle down to a more sedate and sensible lifestyle—which meant less for Louisa to worry about. No doubt the delightful Amelia Hacket had much to do with that. 'Have you seen your niece, James?'

'I certainly have,' James answered, with a beaming smile, having observed that marriage to Louisa and the birth of Constance had certainly made his brother-in-law less formidable and more approachable. 'I have just come from the nursery.'

'And what do you think of her? Is she not the most beautiful baby you have ever seen?' he laughed.

'She is indeed. She is quite delightful—but then, any child who is fortunate enough to have Louisa for its mother would be.'

Alistair's face became set in serious lines. 'My sentiments entirely. Your sister is a truly remarkable woman, James. She has become very dear to me. That game of cards—which was so disastrous for yourself—turned out to be a blessing in disguise for me—my salvation, you might say. Out of your misfortune came the luckiest moment of my life,' he said quietly, his expression grave, which left James in no doubt as to the strong bond of love that had grown between Alistair and his sister.

Sophie left Julia at Richmond to spend a day or two with Louisa and Alistair, her excuse being that she wanted to spend some time with Mark and Constance, but deep down she knew that Dunstan House was a lot closer than Richmond to where Sir Charles Meredith lived whilst in London. She knew he was in town and longed to see him—and fully intended to, despite her promise to Alistair that she would cease to think of him any more.

She had come to London with Alistair in subdued mood, but once out of his sight her natural resilience had begun to reassert itself. Her young heart ached for Sir Charles, whom she was certain her brother had cruelly misjudged. She loved him and he loved her—had he not told her so at the garden party at his home in Wyndham, when they had managed to be alone and he had kissed her so tenderly? Alistair could beat her and starve her, but she would not give Sir Charles up.

Unable to stand the strain of not seeing Sir Charles, whilst knowing he was only a few streets away, on impulse she wrote him a letter, pouring her love and her misery out to him. She told him that she was staying at Dunstan House for a few days and confessed her desire to see him, begging him to meet her by the garden gate that opened onto the park at three o'clock the next day. She gave the sealed letter to a young scullery maid, slipping a coin into her hand with the promise of the same when she returned and reported its safe delivery into Sir Charles's own hand, which she did an hour later. But Sir Charles sent a brief note in reply, telling her that he was unable to meet her at three o'clock and to make it seven o'clock instead.

In a fever of nervous tension and finding it difficult to conceal her excitement, Sophie waited, watching the hours of the clock tick slowly by until the appointed time—a clandestine meeting with Sir Charles a novel and exhilarating thought.

Sophie would not have been so ecstatic had she seen Sir Charles's expression when he received her letter. His lips curved in a thin smile. Perfect, he thought, with grim satisfaction. This was going to be easier than he'd thought, and, with his highly developed hunting instinct and quick grasp of opportunity, he was unable to hide his jubilation.

He held Alistair Dunstan responsible for Marianne drowning in the river that night, and since then he had embarked on a personal crusade to avenge her death, to make Dunstan pay for what he had done. He had long since decided to use his sister—an alluring little minx—to achieve this, which was why he had been so attentive towards her and why he had gone out of his way to meet her at some of the mundane functions held at Wyndham—functions he would normally have avoided, considering them beneath him to attend.

He had succeeded with no difficulty whatsoever in making little Miss Dunstan his willing slave, although perhaps if she had known the full extent and reason for the intense hatred that existed between himself and her brother she might not have been so easily duped. And now here she was in London, offering to place herself willingly in his hands. At last his patience was about to pay off. How could he refuse?

He had not consciously planned when to take action against Lord Dunstan, but this was a chance he would seize with both hands. However, Sophie's request that he meet her at three o'clock, in broad daylight when the park was at its most thronged, was quite out of the question. He had already arranged to go to the White Hart Club across the river at Southwark later the following night, which was a regular gambling haunt of his. He'd had word that it was to be a big night, and, with fresh prize money, stakes would be running high—and also hopefully his luck, which he could do with, for his debts had snowballed recently.

And so he had written to Sophie telling her to meet him at seven o'clock in the park instead, confident in the knowledge that her desire to see him was so great she would move heaven and earth to be there. After all, there was no reason why he could not enjoy both the entertainment he'd planned and the delights of the exquisite Miss Dunstan afterwards in one of the private rooms upstairs, which offered comfort and privacy for those who wished to play more intimate games.

He smiled slowly. This was just the type of vengeance he had planned, and once accomplished he would sit back and gloat over the disgrace Sophie's ruin would bring to Alistair Dunstan. His hatred and his purpose were as strong as they had ever been, stronger than his judgement if he did but know it. He did not pause to consider what judgement would be meted out on his own head by Alistair if he succeeded in ruining the innocent Sophie, thinking instead that there was something irresistibly satisfying in paying the arrogant Alistair Dunstan back in his own coin.

It was Louisa who noticed Sophie's odd behaviour, but she thought little of it at first, her mind being on the evening to come. James and Timothy were to dine with them and were due to arrive at seven o'clock. When it was almost time she went in search of Sophie. She knocked on her bedroom door and entered, only to find it empty. Seeing a strong breeze blowing the curtains, so that they were in danger of knocking an assortment of ornaments off a chest of drawers, she crossed the room to close the window, glancing absently down into the garden and pausing when she saw a figure moving hurriedly among the flowerbeds towards the gate in the wall.

She frowned in puzzlement, recognising Sophie, despite her figure being cloaked and hooded. When she saw her slip through the gate and disappear into the park beyond she had a sudden feeling of alarm, realising that Sophie had been behaving strangely ever since she had arrived at Dunstan House two days ago. An inner sense told her that something was wrong. What was she up to? she wondered. Where on earth could she be going when she knew that James and Timothy, whom she had yet to meet, were due to arrive at any minute? Suddenly she had an awful thought, too awful to contemplate; had Sophie deceived them all and somehow arranged to meet Charles Meredith?

Alistair had told her that he had given his sister a sharp talking-to about Sir Charles, and explained some of his reasons as to why he disliked him so, but Louisa suspected that he had not told his sister enough to dispel her interest in that gentleman—her instinct telling her that, where Sophie's affections were concerned, nothing had changed. Outwardly she gave everyone the impression that she had taken Alistair's words seriously and no longer harboured any romantic thoughts about Sir Charles, but inside she remained as defiant as ever. When she had left Huntswood for London both Louisa and Alistair had been so absorbed with their own troubles that they had failed to notice that anything was wrong, but anyone who knew Sophie well would have been suspicious of her meek and obedient demeanour.

Quickly Louisa went after her, hurrying down the stairs and out into the garden and through the gate. The park was quiet, the sun beginning to sink, casting long shadows across the grass. She saw Sophie ahead of her and called her name as the door of a waiting, closed carriage swung open. Sophie paused for just a moment, but then an arm appeared from the carriage and grabbed her, pulling her inside. Again Louisa frantically called her name, running forward to try and stop the carriage, but it was useless, for it immediately sped off across the park.

Louisa stopped, her heart beginning to thunder, and she had the awful sense that she was experiencing a nightmare. The terrible truth that Sophie had run off with Sir Charles Meredith dawned on her—it was the only conclusion that she could draw. And how was she to tell Alistair?

She hurried back inside the house to find Alistair at that moment receiving James and Timothy who had just arrived. They all looked at her when she came rushing into the hall. Seeing how distraught she was, Alistair immediately strode towards her.

'Louisa! What's amiss?'

Breathing hard, she reached out and gripped his arm, the words tumbling from her lips in a rush. 'It's Sophie, Alistair. She—she's gone with Charles Meredith. Somehow she must have arranged to meet him in the park. You must stop them—go after her—before it's too late.'

Every muscle in Alistair's body went rigid as he gripped her arms. 'What are you saying? She can't have.'

'She has. I saw her. She left by the garden gate. I went after her and saw her climb into a carriage. I shouted to try and stop her—but she ignored me.'

'How can you be certain it was Meredith?'

'I just am,' she cried. 'Who else could it have been?'

Alistair's handsome, aggressive face became hard in that particular way Louisa knew so well. His eyes were filled with a mixture of rage, apprehension and dread—dread that Charles Meredith's abduction of his sister had been well planned and that by the time he found her it would be too late.

'So—at last he shows his hand,' he said bitterly. 'How dare he make Sophie the instrument of his vengeance? I'll go after her,' he said, striding towards the door, realising that time was of the essence and ordering one of the footmen to go to the stables and have his horse saddled immediately—making it three when James and Timothy, who had come to Dunstan House in a carriage, insisted on accompanying him. He was in the grip of a violent rage when he turned once more to Louisa. 'I do not intend letting Meredith destroy my sister because of all the real and imagined grievances he has for myself. Where the devil can he have taken her? Which direction was the carriage travelling in, Louisa? Did you see?'

'Towards Westminster, I think.' She moved quickly towards her

husband, looking earnestly into his eyes, her face pale with anguish. 'Please find her, Alistair. I do not fear Charles Meredith,
but I am afraid of what he might do to Sophie, of the indignities
she will be forced to suffer at his hands.'

In the grip of an unnamed terror, Alistair wouldn't let himself
even imagine what Meredith might be subjecting Sophie to. He
caught Louisa up in his arms and embraced her fiercely before
twisting from her.

In a fever of apprehension Louisa watched the three of them
leave the house, praying they would find Sophie and bring her
back safely. The longer she waited for them to return, the tighter
her nerves stretched. She listened to the clock in the hall chime
the hours away, waiting, listening for the sound of their horses
returning in the street outside, dreading them returning without
Sophie.

Three hours later they returned, having scoured all the streets
around Westminster and beyond, but their efforts had come to
nothing. They had even gone so far as to visit Charles Meredith's
house and had questioned the servants, who had told them that Sir
Charles had left the house at six o'clock and was not expected to
return until tomorrow or the day after.

Louisa was in despair when she looked with pain-filled eyes at
Alistair's drawn features as he paced back and forth across the
room. She knew that what he was feeling was rage at his own
inadequacy to know where to look, and pure madness and cold
murder flared in his eyes.

'What about the watchmen and the constables?' she asked.
'Have you questioned any of them?'

'Every one we came across.' Running his fingers through his
hair, he took anxious paces to and fro. 'Where the devil is she?
How dare she go her own way—defy me in this outrageous manner? I expressly told her to stay away from Meredith.'

'Perhaps if you had told her more about why you and Sir
Charles have been at loggerheads all these years she would have
understood and not disobeyed you and continued to see him. You
know I'm right, Alistair. Won't your pride allow you to admit it?'
Louisa said, more sharply than she intended, but fear and worry
had taken away all her inhibitions.

Alistair glared at her, throwing up his hands in exasperation, but he knew she was right. He should have explained more fully to Sophie about his disastrous marriage to Marianne, and his reason for hating Charles Meredith, but it was too late for self-recriminations now.

'Point taken, Louisa,' he snapped. 'But I am not going to stand around arguing about that now.'

'Surely Sir Charles must be aware that he can be arrested for abduction?' said James, in an attempt to defuse the angry situation that was in danger of developing.

'He could, but it is clear that Sophie was not forcibly abducted. She went with him of her own volition, and, unless he harms her physically, there will be no case for him to answer—at least, not from the authorities. However, from myself is another matter. Have you checked her room, Louisa—questioned her maid as to whether or not any of her clothes are gone?'

'Yes, I thought of that. As far as she is aware nothing is missing, which indicates that she had no intention of leaving the house for long.'

'We now know that Meredith had other ideas. No doubt he had it all well planned,' growled Alistair.

Just when all seemed lost, Timothy threw just a glimmer of hope on the situation.

'Perhaps I might make a suggestion? It may come to nothing, I know, but it could be worth checking out.'

Everyone's eyes turned towards him with avid interest, willing to listen to anything that might throw some light on where Charles Meredith could have taken Sophie.

'Sir Charles is known to frequent the White Hart Club across the river at Southwark. It is one of his favourite gambling haunts and the proprietor is a close friend of his. I also know that tonight, being Friday, is the most popular night of the week—a night Sir Charles never fails to attend when in town.'

'But surely, with his mind intent on abducting Sophie, he would not pause to indulge himself in gambling?' said Louisa in disbelief.

'Who knows how Sir Charles's mind works?' said James. 'But I know the place you speak of, Timothy. It's a flash establishment as I recall, and popular. There are plenty of rooms where he could hide Sophie until he has satisfied his need at the tables.'

Louisa looked at Alistair who had remained silent as he considered Timothy's suggestion. 'What do you think, Alistair? Is it worth checking out?'

'Anything is worth it, and this we cannot ignore. We'll leave right away.'

Grabbing her cloak, which she had ready and waiting for this moment, Louisa followed them to the door. 'I'm going with you.'

Alistair turned on her sharply. 'You will do no such thing,' he thundered. 'I forbid it. You will remain here and wait until we return.'

Louisa stood her ground, facing her husband with defiance in every line of her body, her face taut and determined. 'No, Alistair. I insist on going. I have the carriage ready and waiting. We both know it isn't Sophie that Sir Charles is interested in—that he has only abducted her to strike at you. It will not be long before she realises that—and I dread to think of the effect it will have on her. She will be bewildered and terrified.'

'But what about Constance?'

'Constance is sleeping and will be perfectly all right with the nursemaid until I return. When Sophie is found there is no knowing what terrors that monster will have subjected her to. She may be in a wretched state and will need me there, Alistair.'

Seeing she was not to be deterred, and not wishing to lose any more time arguing, he nodded. 'Very well. James,' he said, turning to her brother, 'you accompany your sister in the carriage. Timothy and I will go on ahead. We'll go by way of Westminster Bridge, which is a little out of our way, I know, but we are likely to encounter delays if we try to cross London Bridge with all the renovation work being carried out just now. I just hope to God that Meredith's lust for gambling is greater than his desire to ruin my sister.'

At this time gaming houses flourished all over London, and the White Hart Club was no exception, despite being situated in an unsavoury part of Southwark where brawls were common. When Alistair and Timothy arrived, they walked past the porter who was pacing up and down outside, and an usher appeared to show and light their way up the steps from the street. Decorated in sumptuous purple and gold, the two principle rooms were ablaze with lights shining down on the green baize tables, with huge mirrors reflecting the light and many ornaments. A few small, curtained alcoves were at the side of the room, offering seclusion for those who required privacy whilst eating and drinking.

Beautiful hostesses to serve and entertain the gentlemen added to the attraction of these establishments. Patched and powdered, with crimson lips, and dressed in body-displaying gowns, they encouraged them to spend money on food and drink, but most important of all to gamble at the gaming tables, for it was often true that the more the gentlemen spent on liquor, the more recklessly they gambled. The tables used for *vingt-et-un*, loo, French hazard, dice, and several other games of chance, were run by some of the more attractive girls, who were trained as dealers, and to watch out for card-sharps.

Timothy had been right, Alistair thought as he made his way inside, shaking his head to a waiter with a proffered glass of brandy, it was a busy night, crowded with people from all walks of life. Some of the customers were rough-spoken, and when in drink became rowdy and were often thrown out into the street. But there were men in elegant frock coats, lace, and powdered wigs, who took their gambling seriously. Money flowed freely and all the tables were full, with spectators standing around watching the play, and with someone always ready to step into a chair when it was vacated.

Alistair's eyes casually yet thoroughly swept the two spacious rooms for Charles Meredith, hoping Timothy's hunch would pay off and they would find him sitting at one of the tables, but they were disappointed. They mingled easily with the crowd, pausing and pretending to watch the games in progress so as not to attract attention to themselves, whilst scrutinising every corner and passageway that led off from the rooms for their prey.

Alistair's eyes were drawn towards a staircase which led to the rooms above, rooms which offered privacy for those wishing to indulge in different, more intimate kinds of games. Couples went up and down, and with Timothy beside him Alistair slowly moved towards it, careful not to catch the eyes of two hovering strong-armed, brutish-looking men, in purple breeches and coats to match the decor, who were employed as bullies by the club's proprietor in case of trouble.

'I don't see Sir Charles,' said Timothy. 'Maybe he isn't here after all. Do you think we ought to take a look upstairs? If we can, that is,' he said quietly, eyeing the bullies warily, 'without attracting attention to ourselves.'

'Most definitely. Although it won't be easy getting up those stairs without a wench on our arms,' Alistair replied. 'But in a moment, Timothy. I think I have just seen our quarry.'

Timothy followed his gaze and gasped softly and with relief when he saw Sir Charles just emerging from a curtained alcove with a lusty-looking wench whose thrusting breasts were half ex-posed from a gaping dress, and a man whom he knew to be the proprietor, Mr Ingram. 'Good Lord! So it is.'

They watched Charles Meredith move into the other room and take a vacant chair at the French hazard table, looking as if he intended to remain for some considerable time when he placed a pile of coins and banknotes on the table before him. The proprietor disappeared into his office with a glass of brandy and closed the door.

Timothy made as if to move a little closer to Sir Charles, but Alistair placed a restraining hand on his arm, halting him, a mur-derous gleam in his eyes. 'No. Step back, Timothy. This is my affair and mine alone. I shall deal with Sir Charles Meredith in my own way and shall resent any interference. I intend to settle the score once and for all. But first we must find where he has hidden Sophie,' he said, glancing up the stairs. 'Although I have to say that I do not relish approaching one of the girls to show me around. It might prove awkward.'

'Then how do we get past them without apparently submitting to the charms of the ladies for sale?'

Using his quickness of mind, Alistair smiled. 'I believe I know a way.'

'What have you in mind?'

'Louisa and James should have arrived at the club by now. I shall recruit my own dear wife to act the part of a lady of the night. You know as well as I how adept an actress she is,' he said, with wry meaning. 'You continue to mingle, Timothy—play a game or two of chance if the fancy takes you—but keep your eye on Meredith. If he moves from the hazard table come and tell me.'

Alistair went outside and was relieved to see that the carriage carrying James and Louisa was just pulling up outside the club. Fortunately the street was crowded and the porter and ushers showing people into the club were busy. Opening the door and taking Louisa's arm, he almost pulled her out of the carriage.

'Louisa! James! Thank goodness,' he said urgently.

Louisa looked at him in alarm as James alighted to stand beside her. 'Why, what on earth is the matter, Alistair? Have you found Sophie?' she asked hopefully.

'Very likely. At least we have found Meredith. He's at one of the hazard tables—and will be for some time, I hope. And you, my darling, will serve my purpose exactly.'

Quickly he divested her of her cloak and threw it inside the carriage, looking her up and down with a critical eye. To Louisa's surprise he began removing the combs and pins that held her artfully arranged hair in place, tossing them inside the carriage also. She stared at him in dazed wonder while his hands shook her hair out so that it lay thick and full about her bare shoulders. Self-consciously she let her gaze drop to his finely moulded mouth, watching as a slow, lazy, appreciative smile moved across his face and seeing that his eyes were full of admiration.

'Now, are you going to tell me what this is all about?' she asked softly.

'I'll go inside and find Timothy,' said James.

'It's pretty congested in there, but I left him at the bottom of the stairs keeping an eye on Meredith. Mr Ingram, the proprietor, has disappeared inside his office, where, with a bit of luck, he will remain. Try not to let Meredith see you, James, otherwise—aware that you are my brother-in-law—it may make him suspect that something is afoot and bring him upstairs before we've had a chance to look for Sophie.'

'Never fear. I'll take care.'

James disappeared inside while Alistair gave his full attention to his wife. 'I recall how proficient you are at acting, Louisa.'

'Am I?'

'The best—but please don't take that as a compliment,' he teased gently.

'And what is the part you want me to play?'

'A whore.'

Louisa stared at him, unable to look affronted, for she knew he must have good reason to suggest she should play such an outrageous part. 'A whore? But I am your wife, Alistair.'

He responded with a quizzical lift to his brows. 'Spare me your maidenly protests, my dear. For the next half-hour I want you to forget that.'

'But I don't look like a whore.'

'You can if you put your mind to it. Listen to me, Louisa,' he said urgently, serious once more. 'I have a hunch that Meredith is keeping Sophie upstairs in this establishment, and I want to search without arousing suspicion. To get past the bullies guarding the stairs I have to make it look as if I am taking one of the girls who works here to the rooms above for pleasurable purposes—so don't refuse to do as I say, my love, otherwise I shall have to avail myself of one of them instead.'

'Don't you dare, Alistair Dunstan,' Louisa flared. 'But they'll know I'm not one of them.'

'I doubt it. I'd swear there's a girl to every gentleman inside this place.'

'Very well. But if I am to play a whore I might as well go the whole way.' And, so saying, she pulled her dress off her shoulders to reveal her ample bosom.

Alistair scowled, clearly disapproving of her action, and roughly jerked it back up again, almost lifting her off her feet. 'I don't want you to go that far. You can manage to look alluring without being half-naked. Remember, you can pout, pose and posture all you like—but don't overdo it. There's nothing to be worried about,' he assured her. 'You'll be by my side the whole time.'

'And if we succeed in getting up the stairs?'

'We look in the rooms. Hopefully we'll find Sophie unharmed in one of them. Whatever Meredith's intentions are where she is concerned, I think he is saving her for later.'

'I hope you're right.'

Louisa's first impression on entering the club was that it was vulgar, pretentious and tasteless, the kind of establishment she would never have entered had it not been forced on her by circumstance. With her cheeks flushed, her mouth slightly open and smiling, and her eyes sparkling with a confidence she did not feel, on Alistair's arm she sailed past a party of drunks, all of them making lewd, suggestive remarks. She laughed charmingly at an old roué in a fancy waistcoat, who was also half-drunk, slapping his hand good-humouredly when he screwed up his face to wink, and reached out to her as she passed.

'You're a fetching wench, sweetheart. Care to come upstairs with me later?'

She smiled gaily, fluttering her lashes prettily and trying hard not to look disgusted and insulted as she tossed her head. 'You'll have to wait your turn, love. You can see it's a busy night tonight.'

She caused a stir of interest, receiving more of the same before she reached the bottom of the stairs, rebuffing each offer in turn in the same feisty spirit. As she was about to place her foot on the first step and proceed to the upper floor, one of the bullies moved forward and obstructed her path, eyeing her suspiciously.

'What's this? Who're you? I haven't seen you at the White Hart before.'

Louisa's fingers tightening on Alistair's arm were the only sign of the sudden alarm that gripped her, but she managed to grin up at the bully, cocking her head cheekily on one side.

'No, you 'aven't. That's 'cause I'm new 'ere. One of the regular girls didn't show and Mr Ingram asked me to stand in. Mindst you,' she said, leaning forward to give him a full view of her ample cleavage, 'between you and me, I 'ope she misses tomorrow night as well. I could take to this place, I can tell yer. Never seen so many fine gents in one place before,' she said, looking provocatively up at Alistair, thinking how impressive he looked, so tall and striking and marvellously attractive. With his authoritative air, she could see all the other girls envying her her partner.

The bully looked Alistair up and down before standing aside to let them pass. 'Just make sure he pays you the going rate.'

'And what is the going rate?' Alistair asked him politely.

'Ten pounds.'

If the situation were not so serious Alistair would have laughed out loud. 'That, my dear, was quite a performance,' he said as they moved on up the stairs, glancing down at Louisa with admiration. He loved her like this. She was like a restless, wonderful, exciting flame fluttering in the wind.

Louisa smiled up at him. 'Thank you, Alistair. I'm doing my best.'

'I told you that you don't have to enjoy it, you little baggage,' he said between his teeth. 'When all this is over and we have my errant sister back in the fold, you and I will have some serious talking to do.'

'I shall look forward to it.'

'Have you no shame?'

'It would seem not,' she twinkled, turning and giving the bullies another smile just to defy him, while never losing sight of their purpose for being there. 'You will pay me the ten pounds when we get home, won't you, Alistair?'

He looked down at her for a long moment with his magnificent blue eyes, and then he smiled. 'We'll see about that. You'll have to earn it first.'

They were relieved to find the landing, off which there were several private rooms where the girls took their well-heeled clients, relatively quiet, with no one watching who came and went. It was obvious to Louisa and Alistair, from the sounds coming from within, which rooms were occupied. Only two remained empty and after a quick look inside the cheerless interiors, with no sign of Sophie, they moved to another landing, which, because it was dimly lit and quieter, they presumed must be the living quarters. But Alistair was determined not to leave until he had satisfied himself that Sophie was not being kept in one of these rooms.

He moved to a door at the far end of the landing, and on trying the knob found it to be locked. He was about to move on, then paused and frowned, looking at it again and knocking on it softly. When nothing happened he rattled the knob, and his demand for admittance drew a response from within. They heard a shuffling behind the door and then a voice, quiet and clearly frightened.

'Who—who is it?'

Simultaneously Louisa and Alistair uttered a deep sigh of relief.

'Sophie?' Alistair said, his head close to the door.

'Yes,' she cried, relieved to hear her brother's voice. 'I can't get out. The door's locked.'

Without more ado, Alistair put his shoulder to the door, which swung open after a few desperate thrusts, and in a flash a weeping and extremely distraught and disillusioned Sophie flung herself into her brother's arms.

'Oh, Alistair—thank goodness you've found me. I've been such a fool; I should have listened to you.'

'Yes, you should, but we'll speak of it later.' He held her at arm's length, looking at her hard. 'Has Meredith harmed you, Sophie? Has he touched you?'

She shook her head dumbly. 'No. Please forgive me, Alistair. When I met him in the park I thought it was to be for just a little while, but he refused to let me out of the carriage and drove off at such speed. I became frightened and begged him to take me back—telling him that I had been so very foolish and impulsive in sending him my letter.'

'You what?' thundered Alistair, unable to believe what he was hearing. 'You wrote to him after all I had said?'

Sophie nodded, flinching from his wrath, her cheeks awash with tears that spilled uncontrollably from her eyes.

'Did it not occur to you what his intentions were? Had it not been for Timothy Hacket we would never have found you.'

'I'm so sorry for all the trouble I've caused,' she cried.

'Alistair, please,' said Louisa. 'This is neither the time nor the place to go into this. Sophie is clearly distraught.'

'I told him you would be furious, but he laughed at me,' Sophie went on. 'He was horrid. He was so changed I could not believe it. He ignored my pleas and brought me here to this awful place and locked me in that room.'

Louisa put a comforting arm around her, knowing that when Sophie had heard Charles Meredith turn the key in the lock all her romantic dreams about him had come to a brutal and bitter end.

'We must get out of here. Which way did he bring you, Sophie? Can you remember?'

Swallowing her tears, she nodded. 'There are some stairs leading down to the street.'

Quickly they found the stairs in the kitchen of the living quarters. When they were outside Alistair handed them up into the waiting carriage.

'Wait here. I'll send Timothy out to accompany you back to Dunstan House.'

Louisa gripped his hand in alarm. 'And you, Alistair?'

He looked at her, his face grim, his eyes glittering like steel flints in the dim light. 'I have things to take care of here first. There's only one thing left for me to do and that is to settle Meredith's account.'

Chapter Fifteen

Sir Charles Meredith was having a successful night at the hazard table. The stakes had run high and heavy and fortunately the odds had been in his favour. Always a reckless gambler—believing gambling to be an effortless way of making money—he drank heavily as the night wore on, the liquor increasing his readiness to take insane risks, but his luck was in, and the money steadily piled up in front of him.

He would have liked to play on, but the club was emptying and the hostess raking in the cards. Collecting his money, Sir Charles suddenly remembered Dunstan's sister locked in the room upstairs and he smiled, realising that the evening's entertainment wasn't quite over. But, strangely, after all the years of waiting for this moment to arrive, when he could repay Dunstan in full measure, the thought of seducing his sister to do so had lost its appeal.

He was about to leave the table when he became aware of someone coming to stand behind him. He half turned, expecting it to be his good friend the proprietor, but instead he met the full cold gaze of Alistair Dunstan, who had been watching him for the past hour.

'You know why I am here, Meredith,' said Alistair in an icy voice, seeing Sir Charles's shoulders stiffen.

Sir Charles could almost feel the effort he was exerting to keep his rage under control and he smiled thinly, looking at him with cool mockery, having no intention of denying anything. He had no reason to. By being alone with him in an establishment such as this, Sophie's reputation was already ruined, which was what he had set out to do, and the letter she had written to him, which he would make public when it suited him, would damn her even further and ruin her chances in the marriage market. However, he couldn't help wishing Dunstan hadn't found her until he'd had the whole night to make certain her ruin was complete.

He sneered, having some dim consciousness of the rage that must have consumed Dunstan on finding his sister gone, becoming all the greater when he had discovered she was with him, and becoming greater still on learning she had come with him of her own free will. He was jubilant that at last he could triumph over the humiliation he had suffered over Marianne at Dunstan's hands.

'I applaud your detective work, Dunstan. I take it you have found your sister?'

Alistair's face was like granite. 'It wasn't difficult. Your habits are well known,' he said with biting scorn. 'After what you have done this night, Meredith, I have every reason in the world to kill you, but because my sister has suffered nothing more serious than a damaged heart—and a harsh lesson as to what to expect from a black-hearted villain like yourself—I will let you live.'

Sir Charles snorted with contempt. 'That's extremely generous of you, Dunstan.'

'I'm not being generous, Meredith. I haven't finished with you yet. Ever since Marianne's death, in your heated imaginings you have held me responsible—rightly or wrongly is not for either of us to judge, for only she could have done that. But when I married her I was ignorant of the fact that the two of you had an understanding. It could be said that you drove her to her death yourself when you took off for Europe and left her, and in your arrogance expected to find her waiting when you returned. Being the sort of woman she was, did it never occur to you that she would play you at your own game?'

Alistair's words were savage and taunting, causing Sir Charles's eyes to glitter with unconcealed hatred.

'Damn you, Dunstan,' he rasped. 'How dare you shift the blame for what happened to me?'

'I am not here to rake over old coals, Meredith. As far as I am concerned what happened is over and done with. But how dare you strike at me through my sister and leave her broken? To retaliate by inflicting pain and misery on such an innocent as she is a coward's way. If you insist on revenge—an eye for an eye, wound for wound—then have the guts to face me and not take it out on a vulnerable young girl who has done you no harm.'

'I may be many things, Dunstan, but I am no coward,' he seethed, his voice trembling with anger.

'Then prove it. Either we settle our differences at the card table or I shall call you out. What is it to be?' Alistair asked, with ominous coolness.

Alistair's deep loathing of Charles Meredith was profound, and after what he had done this night he would gladly kill him, but, knowing of his passion for gambling and his lack of expertise with either pistol or rapier, he knew he would choose the former. Alistair would deal Meredith a blow where it would hurt the most—his wealth. He himself was a match for any man when it came to a game of cards, and before the night was out he intended to ruin him.

Fired up by the prospect of another game, of subjecting Lord Dunstan to the same humiliation he himself had suffered at his hands, Sir Charles did choose the former. After all, his luck had been in so far—in fact, he felt as if the cards had been his to command. But when he recalled the last time he had seen Dunstan play cards at Bricknell House, ruthlessly and without batting an eye ruining the man, James Fraser, who now stood at his shoulder—whose debt Dunstan had obviously rescinded on his marriage to Fraser's sister—his sudden surge of confidence took its first knock of the night.

'I cannot think of any combination of circumstances that would make me risk my life, Dunstan, so cards it will be.'

'You will play?'

'Yes,' he hissed through his teeth, his eyes narrowed so that they gleamed like bright slits. 'I will play and make you regret ever stealing Marianne from me. Damn you, Dunstan. You may have been responsible for her death but I will not let you be responsible for my ruin. There will be just the two of us?'

'Of course. I am sure that, for a percentage of whatever either of us wins, Mr Ingram will put one of his private rooms at our disposal.'

Alistair was right. For a high percentage Mr Ingram, an odious, greedy little man, was only too delighted to let them retire to one of his private rooms, presiding over the game himself. Several people who were reluctant to go home drifted in to watch. Sir Charles put his entire winnings onto the table and Alistair put down notes almost to a similar value, having had the presence of mind to bring along some funds with such a thing as this in mind.

It was not an unusual occurrence at the club for members to stay on and play among themselves, but it was clear from the outset to the proprietor and everyone else that this was no ordinary game of cards, for the atmosphere between the two players could be cut with a knife.

The game they chose to play was piquet, and James, looking on, was forced to remember his own miserable defeat at the same game when Alistair had been his opponent over a year ago. If Alistair played with the same ruthless determination as he had then, he did not hold out much hope for Sir Charles Meredith.

As was customary the two players cut to deal—ace ranking the highest card—which fell to Alistair, giving him the choice of first deal. The cards were shuffled and dealt onto the green cloth and the game began. The flickering flames from the candles played on Alistair's chiselled features as he watched his opponent closely, quietly confident, and inside the room the air was charged with expectant excitement.

It became clear early on that Alistair's mastery of the game surpassed Sir Charles's; he had the amazing ability to reject the right cards from his original hand and an equal ability to enter into all the complicated moves which influenced the game.

The wagers were high and Sir Charles won a little and lost more, seeming oblivious to the muted murmurs of the spectators gathered around the table as he watched Alistair's long, flexible fingers shuffle again and again, flicking over card after card, producing from his hand an ace, another ace, a king, a queen. Damn the man, he seethed, feeling the luck which had been with him earlier seeping away, perspiration gathering on his brow and beginning to ooze out of every pore as Alistair prolonged his agony. Was there no stopping him?

A pulse beat at the side of Sir Charles's face, his play becoming erratic and desperate as his pile of coins and banknotes began to decrease, whilst Alistair's mounted steadily as the play went on. When Sir Charles had nothing left, he refused to cease playing, even though he knew Alistair was unbeatable, and he was reduced to signing one IOU after another.

Three hours later the game was over and the room empty of everyone but the players. Only James remained and he was waiting in the next room. Alistair rose from his chair and looked down at his defeated opponent coldly.

'I think now we are quits, Meredith. Let this be the final chapter to Marianne's life. To your life's end you will not dare to cross my path again. Is that understood?'

Despite the heat in the room and the liquor he had consumed, Sir Charles's face was waxen-white against the dark brown of his coat as he tried to absorb what had happened to him. His nostrils were pinched and he seemed to have difficulty breathing as he rose from his chair, resting his hands on the table for support.

'Aye—I understand. You may have ruined me and my family— but you deserve to live in wretchedness till your life's end for what you did to Marianne,' he said through his teeth as he glared with blood-shot eyes at Alistair, still unable to forget his torment over her loss in his moment of ruin. 'And, yes, I loved her, damn you. I'm not proud of the way I treated her, but she was the only thing in my life I have ever loved. She begged you to release her—to let her go—but you refused to consider it, choosing to live for the rest of your life with a woman who despised you rather than tarnish your noble name with a divorce.'

Alistair's mouth curled cruelly. 'Have you forgotten that on the night she left Huntswood she was running to you, Meredith? She would not have returned to me. When she plunged into the river it was almost certain death. I went after her because the conditions as they were that night were not fit to let a dog out, never mind a half-demented woman who was hell-bent on going to her lover. I also wanted to tell her that I had every intention of divorcing her. You see, nothing could have induced me to live with a woman who was to bear another man's child.'

The silence that fell on the room was so profound that if anyone had entered at that moment they would have heard their hearts beating. Sir Charles's face became filled with honest puzzlement as his mind took its time to register what Alistair was saying.

'Forgive me, Dunstan—but what the devil are you talking about?'

Alistair stared at him, his head becoming clouded. 'You mean to tell me,' he said, a sudden chill entering his bones, 'that when Marianne asked me for a divorce you were unaware that she was carrying your child?'

Horror flashed into Sir Charles's eyes. 'She was to bear my child?' he said hoarsely.

'You had no idea?'

'Of course not.' He stared ahead of him. 'My God!' he got out with an effort. 'Why did she keep it from me?'

Alistair shook his head. 'I don't know. No doubt she would have told you—in time.'

'Why didn't you tell me of this before you ruined me?'

Alistair sighed. 'Because I thought you knew.'

His shoulders sagging, as if all the life had drained out of him, Sir Charles lowered his head. 'No.' And he said nothing more. It was a quiet sound that hung between them, without anger or emotion, but it held all the cruel and bitter anguish which he felt.

Alistair turned and left the room, having reduced Charles Meredith and his family to a state of penury they could never have imagined—or deserved. He felt no satisfaction for what he had done, no sense of victory for overcoming a man he no longer considered to be his enemy, only a bitter taste of self-loathing, despising himself with a virulence that was almost unbearable for having completely annihilated someone who believed he had every justification in the world to hate him.

At Dunstan House, Sophie was recovering from her ordeal at Sir Charles's hands quite well, Louisa observed crossly and with a sense of irritation, considering the trouble she had put everyone to. Looking at her, no one would believe she had been abducted by the villainous Sir Charles Meredith just a short while ago and locked in a room above a gambling club in one of London's seediest districts. Still, she was thankful they had managed to find her before any lasting hurt had been inflicted on her. She just wished that Alistair and James had returned with them to Dunstan House, for she would be unable to cease worrying until she saw them.

Louisa realised she had Timothy to thank for Sophie's swift recovery, having been a keen-eyed observer of his attentiveness towards her since leaving the White Hart Club. As soon as Sophie had dabbed the final tears from her cheeks with Timothy's handkerchief and her eyes had fallen on him in the dim light that filtered into the carriage, they had opened wide and she had stared at him, before delight had flooded her face and she had smiled at him—a smile of promise, Louisa had thought—and Timothy had returned that smile, his expression one of wonder, disbelief and hope.

After he had said goodnight to Louisa on their arrival at Dunstan House, Sophie had watched him go, thinking what a fine-looking man he was, and as he'd gone out of the room he'd looked back over his shoulder at her, interest flaring and lingering in his eyes. No longer feeling the need to sob her broken heart out, she'd found no difficulty in returning his smile, and as Timothy had left for his family's town house in Long Acre, where he and James were staying, he had no idea of the effect he had had on her.

In her night attire Louisa sat on a cushioned window-seat in her room, refusing to go to bed until Alistair had returned, feeling weak with relief when at last, with dawn covering London in a pinkish glow, she heard his tread on the landing outside.

After parting with James he'd come directly to see Louisa, entering the room quietly so as not disturb her in case she was asleep. She rose and went towards him, her hands outstretched. He stared at her with a remote, brooding look, his gaze sliding over her face, seeing that her eyes were full of apprehension and questions.

'Tell me what happened, Alistair. What did you say to Sir Charles?'

He sighed, wearily removing his coat and throwing it onto a chair and moving to the fire, which hissed in the quiet room. 'I would like to say he got what he deserved, but between that and what eventually happens to him there is no connection whatsoever.'

'Alistair, please don't talk in riddles,' she chided with gentle impatience. 'Tell me.'

He smiled slightly, reaching out and stroking her cheek with a feather-light touch when she came to stand beside him, looking up at him, her wonderful eyes searching and questioning. 'I retaliated by doing what I do best, it would seem. I did to him what I did to James. I ruined him at the card table. I took everything he owned, and it shames me to say that, whereas I walked away without a qualm after destroying James, tonight I experienced no satisfaction in annihilating Charles Meredith.'

'Not even after what he did to Sophie?'

'No. Besides, do not forget that she wrote to him and asked him to meet her in the park. I did warn her what he was like. She should have listened to me and taken note.'

'I know. But she is so young—so inexperienced in the ways of men.'

Alistair cocked an eyebrow and smiled at her. 'Rather like yourself when you fell into my clutches, don't you think?'

'Perhaps,' she whispered.

Alistair combed his fingers wearily through his hair. 'I'm not proud of what I did tonight, Louisa. I never wanted this. To have ruined Meredith was one thing, but then to tear into him with words about Marianne and the child was another. It was quite the most despicable thing I have done in my entire life.'

He spoke with a solemnity that puzzled Louisa. 'Why—what are you saying?'

'The plain and simple truth is that he didn't know about the child. Marianne never told him. After what I had done I should have spared him that.'

Louisa looked at him mutely, unable to find words to say.

'I cannot leave things like this. I have to lay Marianne's ghost to rest.'

'What will you do?'

'I shall call on him tomorrow. I am honour-bound to put things right between us—to return all I have taken from him this night.

We wronged each other. We believed things of each other because
it suited us to believe those things, which was the worst stupidity
of all.'

'And what he did to Sophie? You know what he would have
done to her had we not arrived when we did.'

'Yes, and that I cannot forgive. I am thankful we got to her in
time and she is unscathed. But despite being a villain I believe
Meredith loved Marianne as much as he is capable of loving any
human being. That was one thing I learned tonight—something
which, in my conceit, I always doubted. He was overcome with
grief when I told him about the child.' He took Louisa's hand,
drawing her close and looking deep into her eyes. 'You do see
why I must go and see him, don't you?'

'Yes,' Louisa breathed. 'Yes, I do. And I'm glad.'

The following day Louisa waited in a state of nervous anxiety
for Alistair to return from seeing Sir Charles, clasping and un-
clasping her hands and pacing to and fro in the drawing room that
overlooked the street so that she could see him coming. Never had
she known the minutes to be as long as those she spent waiting
for him.

At last he returned. She watched nervously as he came into the
room, looking breathtakingly handsome in a coat and waistcoat of
dark green, and a shirt and neckcloth of pristine white that em-
phasised his dark colouring. A thick lock of hair fell over his face,
which was inscrutable.

'Did he see you?' she asked, moving towards him, unable to
stand the strain of not knowing what had happened. 'How was
he?'

'Yes, he saw me,' he answered, his tone frank and unemotional,
'and despite cursing the miserable lot that fate had dealt him he
was agreeable.'

'And? Has he agreed to wipe the slate clean?'

'There was no pardon or forgiveness, if that is what you mean,
but I think he is reconciled to what happened to Marianne at last.
We talked for a while.'

'But has his lust for vengeance ceased?'

'As to that, Louisa, it's no easy matter to put the unpleasantnesses that have existed between us for so long behind us—but I do believe he has no intention of carrying on the vendetta.'

'Then we can be thankful for that. Did you return everything you won from him last night?'

'Yes. He accepted my offer more for his family's sake than for his own, although he was humbled and it clearly hurt his pride to do so. He is a miserable man, Louisa. Seeing him today, it was hard to believe him to be the fine, debonair rake one sees about town, who has seduced half the women in London. When I left him he was so unlike himself in both words and looks.'

Louisa gave him a long, thoughtful look. 'Alistair, did it never occur to you that you might not have won when you challenged him at cards?'

'I was willing to take a chance.'

'And as I know to my cost you have played before,' she said, with a hint of cynicism. 'But so has Sir Charles.'

Alistair grinned, his eyes twinkling wickedly. 'I've had a little more practice, that's all.'

She gave him a reproachful frown. 'As to that, I prefer not to go into it at this moment. But what will he do now? I still cannot bring myself to like him, Alistair—especially when I think of what he would have done to Sophie. It will be no easy matter coming face to face with him again—as we must at some time or other.'

Louisa sank to her knees on the rug in front of the fire, sitting comfortably back on her feet and staring into the flames, her face rosy and warm. Seeing her troubled face, Alistair removed his coat and loosened his neckcloth and sat beside her in his shirtsleeves, one leg propped up and an arm resting lightly about her shoulders.

'You are not likely to meet him again, Louisa.'

She turned and looked at him. 'Oh?'

'Before I left he told me he is to go to America to stay with his sister. He hinted that, if it appealed to him, he might consider staying out there.'

Joy and relief sprang to her eyes. 'Then let us hope in a new country with new diversions he will let old grudges and bygones fade away. I, for one, will not miss him.'

Alistair grinned, a wicked gleam entering his eyes. 'Maybe not, my love, but I can name an army of ladies who will. The drawing rooms of fashionable London will not be the same without his colourful and vibrant presence. Not everyone is as opposed to his charms as you.'

'I'm sure you're right,' she sighed. 'When can we return to Huntswood, Alistair? London holds no attraction for me just now. Are the matters of state that are discussed so laboriously in the House of Lords so important that they must keep us apart?'

'My presence or absence will not affect the way the country is run—or the war with France. We can return to Sussex any time you like. We will stop off in London for a while when we travel to Oxfordshire for James's marriage to Amelia in two months' time. Does that make you happy?' he whispered, kissing her warm cheek softly.

'Extremely,' she said, wriggling her legs from under her to enable her to sit closer to him. 'But what about Sophie?'

He sighed. 'I admit that I am baffled by her behaviour. Despite her unpleasant ordeal at Meredith's hands, I am relieved to see she suffers no ill effects. In fact, she has recovered remarkably well and has made it plain that she has no desire to return to Huntswood for the foreseeable future. She stressed to me when I saw her earlier that she wishes to remain at Richmond with Julia indefinitely.'

'And you have no objections to this?'

'None whatsoever. I suppose we must be thankful she has come out of all this with her reputation intact. She may be only seventeen, but the sooner a suitor is found for her and she is wed, the better I shall sleep at night.'

Louisa's lips quirked in a little, knowing smile. 'I do not think you will have too long to wait for that to come about,' she said quietly.

Alistair looked at her sharply. She had her eyes lowered, as if what she had just said were the most ordinary thing in the world. 'And what, might I ask, do you mean by that, pray? Who?'

Her lips widened into a full smile. 'Timothy Hacket,' she told him, raising her eyes to watch his reaction.

At first he was stunned, finding what she had said incredible, and then his face broke into an expression of disbelief. 'Hacket?'

'Yes.'

'But they have not yet known each other twenty-four hours.'

'What does that matter?'

'But is it possible that she can feel a tug to her emotions romantically so soon after being obsessed with Meredith?'

'Why not? They are captivated by one another. Watch them together when he comes with James and Amelia tonight and you'll see what I mean. You don't object, do you, Alistair?'

He laughed lightly, drawing her close. 'Not in the slightest. After Meredith, I would find anyone else a blessing.'

Louisa turned in his arms and kissed his lips lightly. 'Thank you, Alistair. It would seem that everything has been resolved happily at last.'

'The happiest thing of all is that the situation between us has been resolved,' he answered, the scent of her perfume making his senses reel. He looked at her face, so close to his own, unable to take his gaze from her. The glow from the fire was shining on her, warming the amber light in her eyes. He had never wanted her more and he longed for the moment when they could be together in the privacy of their room and he could awaken all that was sensual in her nature.

Louisa knew exactly what was going through his mind. There was so much adoration blended with passion in his narrow eyes that she thought it was a good thing she was sitting down or her legs would have given way. Their lips met in a kiss. Unable to control his longing, Alistair devoured her mouth and she responded, as frantic as he, their passion flaring as strong as ever. Her fingers drove into his thick hair and gripped it tightly to prevent him moving away, and his arms were around her, crushing her to him as if he would never let her go.

When they paused to draw breath, they smiled in mutual happiness.

'What are you thinking?' she asked in serene contentment.

'What a delight it would be to make love to you here, on this rug, in front of the fire.'

'I wouldn't object,' she whispered, leaning over and finding his lips in a gentle kiss, 'but the servants might if they were to walk in on us.'

Hearing a sound behind them, they turned simultaneously just as the door opened. The nursemaid stood there with Constance cradled in the crook of her arm and her free hand holding Mark's. Louisa and Alistair looked at each other and smiled.

The children! The final touch to the perfection of their love.

* * * * *

MILLS & BOON

Historical Romance™

LADY JANE'S PHYSICIAN
by Anne Ashley
A Regency Delight

Lady Jane Beresford visited her cousin, but her
enjoyment was marred by meeting Dr Thomas
Carrington. Tom's blunt attitudes irritated Jane out of
her own good manners! But he knew, if she didn't, that
an Earl's daughter was far above his touch…

UNTAMED HEART
by Georgina Devon
A Regency delight! ❦ *Book 1 of 3*

Lizabeth Johnstone was shocked by her primitive
reaction to Lord Alastair St. Simon. He should be every
woman's dream, but he wasn't *hers* for Alastair was
responsible for her younger's brother's death. Her
stubborn refusal to accept help left him with only one
alternative—they'd have to get married…

On sale from 6th August 1999

2 FREE

books and a surprise gift!

We would like to take this opportunity to thank you for reading this Mills & Boon® book by offering you the chance to take TWO more specially selected titles from the Historical Romance™ series absolutely FREE! We're also making this offer to introduce you to the benefits of the Reader Service™—

* ★ FREE home delivery
* ★ FREE gifts and competitions
* ★ FREE monthly Newsletter
* ★ Exclusive Reader Service discounts
* ★ Books available before they're in the shops

Accepting these FREE books and gift places you under no obligation to buy, you may cancel at any time, even after receiving your free shipment. Simply complete your details below and return the entire page to the address below. *You don't even need a stamp!*

YES! Please send me 2 free Historical Romance books and a surprise gift. I understand that unless you hear from me, I will receive 4 superb new titles every month for just £2.99 each, postage and packing free. I am under no obligation to purchase any books and may cancel my subscription at any time. The free books and gift will be mine to keep in any case.

H9EA

Ms/Mrs/Miss/Mr ....Initials......................................
BLOCK CAPITALS PLEASE

Surname ....

Address ....

....

....Postcode.................................

Send this whole page to:
THE READER SERVICE, FREEPOST CN81, CROYDON, CR9 3WZ
(Eire readers please send coupon to: P.O. BOX 4546, DUBLIN 24.)

THE

Regency

COLLECTION

Where rogues find romance

Look out for the fourth volume in this limited
collection of Regency Romances from
Mills & Boon® in August.

Featuring:

The Outrageous Dowager
by Sarah Westleigh

and

Devil~May~Dare
by Mary Nichols

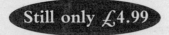

Still only £4.99

MILLS & BOON®

Makes any time special™

Available at most branches of WH Smith, Tesco, Martins,
Borders, Easons, Volume One/James Thin
and most good paperback bookshops